P9-BYS-743

BRUNNER AT HIS BEST

"A splendid, heartwarming *alien* multi-generational saga...Assured in the telling, logically and impeccably detailed and beautifully thought out...Brunner in top form."

—*Kirkus Reviews*

"When we apply the term 'epic' to SF, we give SF a whole new scale. The epic at hand spans millennia to tell of an alien race's progress from primitive superstition to the threshold of space...This is SF in the grand tradition."

—*Publishers Weekly*

"Brunner requires the grand scale to convey both the intricacies and excitements of scientific discovery ...sf at its best...a pleasure to read."

—*Locus*

FILLED WITH NEW IDEAS, QUIRKY
ALIENS, CHARMING LOVE STORIES,
AND A CONTINUING SENSE OF WONDER.
THIS IS A FASCINATING READ
AND JOHN BRUNNER'S BEST-EVER NOVEL.

Also by John Brunner
Published by Ballantine Books:

THE
CRUCIBLE
OF TIME

JOHN BRUNNER

**DEL
REY**

A Del Rey Book

BALLANTINE BOOKS • NEW YORK

A Del Rey Book
Published by Ballantine Books

Parts I and II of *The Crucible of Time* have previously appeared in *Isaac Asimov's Science Fiction Magazine*.

Library of Congress Catalog Card Number: 83-2750

ISBN 0-345-30235-4

Manufactured in the United States of America

First Hardcover Edition: September 1983
First Paperback Edition: July 1984

Cover art by Don Dixon

To Christopher Evans

In memoriam

CONTENTS

FOREWORD

It is becoming more and more widely accepted that Ice Ages coincide with the passage of the Solar System through the spiral arms of our galaxy. It therefore occurred to me to wonder what would become of a species that evolved intelligence just before their planet's transit of a gas-cloud far denser than the one in Orion which the Earth has recently—in cosmic terms—traversed.

In my attempt to invent its history I have frequently relied on the advice of Mr. Ian Ridpath, whose prompt and generous aid I gratefully acknowledge.

—JKHB

PROLOGUE

    In the center of the huge rotating artificial globe the folk assembled to await retelling of an age-old story.

    Before them swam a blur of light. Around them was a waft of pheromones. Then sound began, and images took form.

    A sun bloomed, with its retinue of planets, moons and comets. One was the budworld. Slowly—yet how much more swiftly than in the real past!—a wild planet curved out of space towards what had once been their race's home.

    "If only they had known . . . !" somebody murmured.

    "But they did not!" the instructor stressed. "Remember that, throughout the whole of what you are to watch! You are not here to pity them, but to admire!"

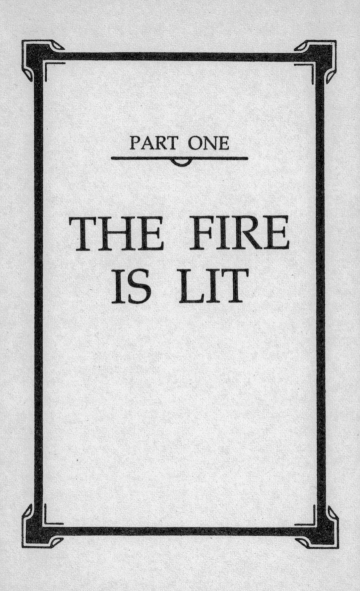

PART ONE

THE FIRE
IS LIT

I

Now the sun was down, the barq was growing tired. The current opposing her was swift, and there was a real risk she might be driven against the rocks that beset the channel and puncture her gas-bladders. After countless attempts to sting her into more vigorous activity, the steersman laid by his goad and grumpily tipped into her maw the last barrelful of the fermented fish and seaweed which served to nourish boat, crew and passengers alike. Waiting for the belch that would signal its digestion, he noticed Jing watching from her saddle of lashed planks, as anxious as though his weather-sense were predicting storms, and laughed.

"You won't be a-dream before we get where we're bound!" he promised in the coarse northern speech which the foreigner had scarcely yet attuned his hearing to.

It was hard to realize there was anywhere worth traveling to in this barren landscape. Most of the time the shore was veiled with rags of fog, because the water was so much warmer than the air. What a place to choose for studying the sky! Even though, with the sun setting so much earlier every day, it was possible to believe in the legend which had lured him hither: a night that lasted almost half a year. Not that there could ever be total darkness; here, as everywhere, the Bridge of Heaven—what these northerners called the Maker's Sling—curved in its gleaming arc across the welkin. And, near the horizon, less familiar and altogether awe-inspiring, the New Star was framed in its irregular square of utter black like a jewel on a pad of swart-fur.

But neither that celestial mystery, nor the prospect of going hungry, was what preyed most on the mind of Ayi-Huat Jing, court astrologer and envoy plenipotentiary of His Most Puissant Majesty Waw-Yint, Lord of the Five-Score Islands of Ntah. Compelled by his sworn oath, a

3

whole miserable year ago he had set forth in state, riding
the finest mount in his master's herd and accompanied
by forty prongsmen and ten banners inscribed with his
rank and status. His mission was to seek out wise folk
beyond the mountains that ringed the Lake of Ntah and
inquire of them the meaning of the New Star. His coun-
trymen had long imagined that they understood the reason
why the heavens changed—for change they definitely did.
He carried with him a fat roll of parchment sheets on
which had been copied star-maps depicting the sky on the
accession-dates of the last score rulers of Ntah, and on
the date of every eclipse during their reigns. Sixteen stars
were shown on the most recent which in olden times
had not been there, and marks recorded others which had
appeared and faded in a matter of days. But there had
never been one so brilliant, or so long-lasting, or in so
black a patch of sky. According to the philosophers of
Ntah, right action was reflected in heaven, and sufficient
of it earned a diminution of the darkness. Eventually, they
promised, the time would come when the heavens would
be as bright by night as by day.

And it had happened, and it had ceased, and everyone
was grievously disturbed, for blight and plague had followed what should have been a sign of unprecedented
good fortune...

Jing's journey had been fruitless so far, but it was not
yet doomed to failure. His store of pearlseeds from the
Lake was less than half-exhausted, for they grew stranger
and more precious as he traveled, exchangeable for more
food and longer lodging, and he had clung to his roll of
maps even though in all the lands and cities he had visited
he had met only one person who appeared to grasp their
significance. He had expected students of heaven-lore as
dedicated as himself, libraries too—albeit in alien script
on unfamiliar materials—because tradition told of merchants from Geys and Yown and Elgwim who had brought
amazing horns, hides, seeds and spices along with boastful tales about the riches of their homelands. What he had
actually found...

Half-starved mud-scrabblers incapable of distinguish-
ing dream from reality, ascribing crop-failure, blight and
murrain to supernatural beings, imagining they could protect themselves by sacrificing most of what remained to

them—whereupon, of course, weakness and fatigue allowed dreams to invade their minds ever further. Madness, madness! Why did not everybody know that the heavens bodied forth an impersonal record of the world below, neither more nor less? How could anybody, in these modern times, credit a god prepared to launch missiles at random with a view to killing people? The welkin shed messages, not murder!

His whole course since leaving Ntah had been a succession of horrid shocks. Geys, one of the first cities he had planned to visit, stood abandoned and overgrown, for—so he was told—a flaming prong from the sky had struck a nearby hill and everyone had fled in panic. Moreover, of the escorts and banners who had set out with him (any other of the court officers would have had concubines as well, but Jing was obliged by his calling to accept celibacy) most had deserted on finding how squalid was the world beyond the mountains, while not a few had succumbed, as had his mount, to bad food or foul water.

One alone had survived to accompany him into the branchways of the great city Forb, where first he had encountered learned men as he regarded learning. Yet they were parasites, Jing felt, upon their city's past, disdainful of sky-shown truths, able only to expound concerning inscriptions and petty relics which they claimed to be older than anything elsewhere. Jing was reticently doubtful, but it was impolitic to speak his mind, partly because he was unfluent in the speech of that region, partly because its masters exercised very real power which he had no wish to see turned against Ntah, and chiefly because of the nature of that power.

His tallness, and the fact that his companion was taller yet, made him remarkable. The nobility bade him to banquets and festivities as a curiosity. It was a time of dearth, as he had discovered on his way; nonetheless, the fare at such events was lavish. It followed that the lords of Forb must control vast domains—not, however, vast enough to satisfy them, as was apparent from the way they spent all their time maneuvering for advantage over one another, and instructed their interpreters to ply Jing with questions concerning weaponry. They were prepared to descend as far as spreading disease among a rival's crops, than which only the use of wildfire could be baser. Were such monsters to be let loose in the peaceful region of Ntah . . . !

Shuddering, yet determined to pursue his quest, Jing eventually discovered the secret of their dominance. It lay not in their armies, nor their treasuries. It consisted in the deliberate and systematic exploitation of the dreams of those less well-to-do than themselves, a possibility which had never occurred to him, and which the language barrier prevented him from comprehending until a lordling he had disappointed in his hope of brand-new armaments set sacerdotes upon him at his lodgings.

He had frequently seen their like bringing up the tail-end of a noble's retinue, always gaunt in a manner that contrasted greatly with the glistening plumpness of their masters, and initially he had assumed them to be nothing more than servants: scribes, perhaps, or accountants, though it was hard to conceive how such dream-prone starvelings could be relied on.

Acting, however, more like persons of authority than underlings, these visitors interrogated him concerning Ntah. Pleased to meet anyone prepared to discuss what he thought of as serious subjects, Jing answered honestly, hoping to show that the relationship between Ntah and its satrapies, being sustained by trade in information concerning what the heavens portended, was more civilized than rule by force.

Did he not—they responded in shocked tones—acknowledge the example of the Maker of All, who daily surveyed the world with His all-seeing eye, the sun, and nightly dispatched fiery bolts by way of warning that His way must be adhered to on pain of uttermost destruction? Was he not aware that the arc in the sky was the Maker's sling, that the Maker's mantle was what lighted the heavens with the glimmer of marvelous draped colors? Then he was in peril of imminent disaster, and were he still to be in Forb when it overtook him, scores-of-scores of innocent people would be caught up in the catastrophe! He must leave the city at once, or they would execute the Maker's will upon him themselves!

Jing's lifelong faith in the beneficence of the universe had been shaken, but he was not about to enter someone else's fever-dream. He did his best to scorn the warning—until the day when his sole surviving escort, Drakh, was

set on by an unknown gang and attacked with weapons
such as would never have been permitted in Ntah: prongs
steeped in the ichor from a rotting carcass, warranted to
poison the slightest cut even though it was not deep enough
to let out life.

Now Drakh lay delirious beside him, as for days past,
shivering less at the bitter air than the racking of his sickness. He would have been dead but that Jing's treelord—
a Shreeban, well accustomed to being shunned by his
Forbish neighbors and mocked by their children when he
went abroad—had called a doctor, said to breed the best
cleanlickers in the city.

And the doctor had saved not only Drakh's life (so far,
Jing amended wryly, for the licker was weakening and
the sorbers it passed repeatedly over his wound were
turning yellow) but also the mission they had been sent
on. Forgetful of his other clients, he had sat for days
greedily studying Jing's star-maps, mentioning now and
then that such-and-such a one of his forebears had claimed
to be older than this or that star: heretical information in
Forb where the Creation was supposed to have been perfect from the Beginning.

How could such dream-spawned nonsense survive the
appearance of the New Star, which for a score of nights
had outshone the Bridge of Heaven, and still after four
years loomed brighter than anything except the sun and
moon?

It might well not, explained the doctor. As people became more prosperous and better fed, so they naturally
grew more capable of telling dream from fact. This led
them to mock the sacerdotes, whose power had been
decreasing from generation to generation despite their deliberate self-privation. Now they were reduced to claiming that the New Star was a delusion due to the forces of
evil, which—they said—dwelt in that bleak zone from
which the Maker had banned all stars as a reminder of
the lightless eternity to which He could condemn trans-
gressors. But there were those who maintained that one
supremely righteous person was to be born—now: *must*
have been—who could hold up a lamp where the Maker
had decreed darkness, and lead folk out of mental en-
slavement.

Looking at the glowplants that draped the walls of his

rented home, Jing prompted him to more revelations. Were there none here in the north who studied star-lore?

The chief of them, the doctor said, had taken refuge with the Count of Thorn. Branded by the sacerdotes as victim of a divine curse, that lord had retreated to an arctic fastness where hot springs bubbled out of frozen ground—clear proof, said the sacerdotes, of his commitment to evil, for in the absence of sunlight water could be heated only by fire, the prerogative of the Maker: hence those who usurped it must be on His adversary's side. Where Thorn had gone, besides, report held that a night might last for half a year, and evil dwelt in darkness, did it not? Yet it was also rumored that those who had followed him were prosperous while everywhere else epidemics were tramping in the pad-marks of famine...

"There has been some kind of change," the doctor whispered. "My best remedies have ceased to work, and many babies bud off dead or twisted. Also there is a taint in this year's nuts, and it seems to drive folk mad. If I had more courage I too would go where Thorn has gone... Pay me nothing for the care of your man. Promise only to send news of what they have found out in that ice-bound country. It is a place of ancient wisdom which the sacerdotes interdicted, saying it was dreamstuff. I think they were in error in that also."

Now Jing, so weary he too was having trouble telling dream from fact, was come to Castle Thorn at the head of the warm channel. The fog parted. The moon was rising, gibbous in its third quarter, and as usual its dark part sparkled.

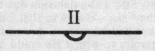

II

If Forb was old, then Castle Thorn was antique. Guarding the entrance to a bowl-shaped valley, it loomed as large as a city in its own right—not that its whole bulk could be seen from the outcrop of rock serving it as a wharf, despite the glowplants which outlined it at a distance, for its defenses were elaborate and far-reaching. On either bank bomas trembled ready to collapse their spiky branches, while masses of clingweed parted only in response to blasting on a high-pitched whistle. Prongsmen came to hitch the barq's mooring-tentacles, accompanied by enormous canifangs.

Just before docking Jing had realized that a range of hills on the horizon was gleaming pure white in the moonshine. He had said, "Snow already?"

And the steersman had grunted, "Always."

So there truly was a place where ice might defy summer. For the first time Jing felt in his inmost tubules how far he was from home.

But there was no time for reflection. A voice was calling to him in city-Forbish: "Hail to the foreigner! I'm told your prongsman is sick. As soon as he's ashore I'll see what I can do for him. I'm Scholar Twig, by the way."

Who was a person of advanced years, his tubby shortness—characteristic of these northerners—aggravated by loss of pressure in his bracing tubules, but his expression alert and manner brisk. Grateful, for Twig was the name the doctor had told him to ask for, Jing returned the greeting.

"How you know I coming?" he demanded.

"Oh, you've made news over half the continent," was the prompt reply. "Sorry we don't have anyone around who speaks Ntahish, but until you showed up most people thought your homeland was just a legend, you know? Say, is it true you have star-maps going back to the Beginning? How soon can I look at them?"

Groping his way through the rush of words, Jing recalled the protocol which attended ambassadors to Ntah.

"Not I must at once pay respect the lord?"

"He's dining in the great hall. You'll meet him in a little. First let me present my colleagues. This is Hedge, this is Bush, this is—"

It was impossible to register so many strangers when he was so fatigued. "But my man-at-arms...?" he ventured.

"Ah, what am I thinking of? Of course, we must get him and you to quarters right away!"

Detailing some junior aides to carry Drakh, Twig led the way at half a trot.

Jing could have wished to move more slowly, because nothing had prepared him for the luxury he discerned all about him. The very stones were warm underpad. The gnarled trunks of the castle were thicker than any he had ever seen, and even at this season they were garlanded with scores of useful secondary plants. Steaming ponds rippled to the presence of fish, while fruit he had not tasted the like of since leaving home dangled from overhanging boughs, and everywhere trailed luminescent vines. Through gaps between the boles, as he ascended branchways in Twig's wake, he caught glimpses of a landscape which reminded him achingly of parts of Ntah. He had thought in terms of a mere clawhold on survival, but the valley must support a considerable population. He saw three villages, each with a score of homes, surrounded by barns and clamps large enough to store food for a year—and that was only on one side of the castle. Amazing! His spirits rose.

And further still when Drakh was laid in a comfortable crotch and a maid brought warm drink. Passing him a huskful, Twig said dryly, "In case you're superstitious about fire, it's untouched by flame. We keep the bags in a hot spring."

Jing's people cared little about fire one way or the other, so he forbore to reply. Whatever its nature, the drink effectively drove away dreams. Meanwhile Twig was inspecting Drakh's licker and saying in disgust, "This should have been changed days ago! Here!"—to the maid—"take it away and bring one of my own at once. They're of the same stock," he added to Jing, "though here we have fewer outlandish poisons they can learn to cope with. Faugh! They do stink, though, don't they, at that stage?"

Now that Jing's perceptions were renewed, he had realized that the very air inside the castle stank—something to do with the hot springs, possibly. Never mind. He posed a key question.

"Drakh will live, yes?"

"I'm not a specialist in foreign sicknesses, you know! But...Yes, very probably. I'll send for juice which can be poured between his mandibles. Wouldn't care to offer him solid food in his condition."

Jing nodded sober agreement. Reflex might make him bite off his own limbs.

"Are those your maps?" Twig went on, indicating the rolled parchments. "How I want to examine them! But you must be hungry. Come on, I'll show you to the hall."

There, at its very center, the true antiquity of the castle was revealed. Despite the dense clusters of glowplants which draped the walls, Jing could discern how the ever-swelling boles of its constituent bravetrees had lifted many huge rocks to four or five times his own height. Some of them leaned dangerously inward where the trunks arched together. None of the company, however, seemed to be worrying about what might happen if they tumbled down. Perhaps there were no quakes in this frozen zone; the land might stiffen here, as water did, the year around. Yet it was so warm...

He postponed such mysteries in order to take in his surroundings.

The body of the hall was set with carefully tended trencher-stumps, many more than sufficed for the diners, who were three or at most four score in number. Not only were the stumps plumper than any Jing had seen in Forb; they were plentifully garnished with fruit and fungi and strips of meat and fish, while a channel of hollow stems ran past them full of the same liquor Twig had given him. Entrances were at east and west. At the south end a line of peasants waited for their dole: a slice of trencher-wood nipped off by a contemptuous kitchener and a clawful of what had been dismissed by diners at the north. Jing repressed a gasp. Never, even in Ntah, had he seen such lavish hospitality. It was a wonder that the Count's enemies in Forb had not already marched to deprive him of his riches.

"So many peasants isn't usual," murmured Twig.

"I believe well!" Jing exclaimed. "Plainly did I see villages with land enough and many high barns!"

"Except that on the land the trencher-plants are failing," Twig said, still softly. "Take one of these and transplant it outside, and it turns rotten-yellow. But save your questions until you've fed, or you'll spend a dream-haunted night. Come this way."

Jing complied, completing his survey of the hall. In a

space at the center, children as yet unable to raise themselves upright were playing with a litter of baby canifangs, whose claws were already sharp. Now and then that led to squalling, whereupon a nursh would run to the defense of its charge, mutely seeking a grin of approval from the fathers who sat to left and right. Each had a female companion, and if the latter were in bud made great show of providing for her, but otherwise merely allowed her to bite off a few scraps.

And at the north end sat the Count himself, flanked by two girls, both pretty in the plump northern manner, but neither budding.

The Count was as unlike what Jing had been led to expect as was his castle. He had been convinced by the doctor that he was to meet a great patron of learning, more concerned with wisdom than material wealth. What he saw was a gross figure so far gone in self-indulgence that he required a sitting-pit, whose only concession to stylish behavior was that instead of biting off his trencherwood he slashed it with a blade the like of which Jing had never seen, made from some dark but shiny and very sharp substance.

"Sit here with my compeers," Twig muttered. "Eat fast. There may not be long to go. He's in a surly mood."

Thinking to make polite conversation, Jing said, "Has two lovely shes, this lord. Is of the children many to him credit?"

The scholar's colleagues, Bush, Hedge and so on—names doubtless adopted, in accordance with local custom, when they took service with the Count—froze in unison. Twig whispered forcefully, "Never speak of that where he might overhear! No matter how many women he takes, there is no outcome and never has been, except . . . See the cripple?"

Previously overlooked, there sat a girl by herself, her expression glum. She leaned to one side as though she had been struck by an assassin's prong. Yet she bore a visible resemblance to the Count, and she was passably handsome by the standards of Ntah where the mere fact of her being a noble's daughter would have assured her of suitors. She was alone, though, as if she were an unmated or visiting male. Had he again misunderstood some local convention?

Twig was continuing between gobbles of food. "She's the reason I'm here—eat, eat for pity's sake because any moment he's going to order up the evening's entertainment which is bound to include *you* and over there"—with a nod towards a trio of emaciated persons whom Jing identified with a sinking feeling as sacerdotes—"are a bunch of charlatans who would dearly have liked to sink claws in you before I did except that I put it about I wasn't expecting you before the last boat of autumn in ten days' time. Anyway, Rainbow—who is much brighter than you'd imagine just looking at her—is his sole offspring. Naturally what he wants is a cure for infertility and an assurance that his line won't die out. So our real work keeps getting interrupted while we invent another specious promise for him."

For someone afraid of being overheard, Twig was speaking remarkably freely. But Jing was confused. "You not try read his future from stars?" he hazarded. "You not think possible?"

"Oh, it may well be! But before we can work out what the sky is telling us, we must first understand what's going on up there. My view, you see, is that fire above and fire below are alike in essence, so that until we comprehend what fire *can* do we shan't know what it *is* doing, and in consequence—Oh-oh. He's stopped eating, which means the rest of us have to do the same. If you haven't had enough to keep you dreamfree I can smuggle something to your quarters later. Right now, though, you're apt to be what's served him next!"

In fact it didn't happen quite so quickly. With a spring like a stabberclaw pouncing out of jungle overgrowth, a girl draped in glitterweed erupted from shadow. She proved to be a juggler, and to the accompaniment of a shrill pipe made full use of the hall's height by tossing little flying creatures into the air and luring them back in graceful swooping curves.

"She came in on the first spring boat," Twig muttered, "and is going away tomorrow—considerably richer! Even though she didn't cure the Count's problem, he must have had a degree of pleasure from her company..."

Certainly the performance improved the Count's humor; when it was over he joined in the clacking of applause.

"We have a foreign guest among us!" he roared at last. "Let him make himself known!"

"Do exactly as I do!" Twig instructed. "First you—"

"No!" Jing said with unexpected resolve. "I make like in *my* country to *my* lord!"

And strode forward fully upright, not letting the least hint of pressure leak from his tubules. Arriving in front of the Count, he paid him the Ntahish compliment of overtopping him yet shielding his mandibles.

"I bring greeting from Ntah," he said in his best Forbish. "Too, I bring pearlseeds, finest of sort, each to grow ten score like self. Permit to give as signing gratitude he let share knowledge of scholars here!"

And extended what was in fact his best remaining seed.

For an instant the Count seemed afraid to touch it. Then one of his treasurers, who stood by, darted forward to examine it. He reported that it was indeed first-class.

Finally the Count condescended to take it into his own claw, and a murmur of surprise passed around the company. Jing realized he must have committed another breach of etiquette. But there was no help for that.

"You have no manners, fellow," the Count grunted. "Still, if your knowledge is as valuable as your pearlseed, you may consider yourself welcome. I'll talk with you when Twig has taught you how to address a nobleman!"

He hauled himself to his pads and lumbered off.

"Well, you got away with that," Twig murmured, arriving at Jing's side. "But you've pressurized a lot of enemies. Not one of *them* would dare to stand full height before the Count, and they claim to have authority from the Maker Himself!"

Indeed, the three sacerdotes he had earlier designated charlatans were glowering from the far side of the hall as though they would cheerfully have torn Jing mantle from torso.

III

"And here is where we study the stars," said Lady Rainbow.

It had been a long trek to the top of this peak, the northernmost of those girdling the round valley. Their path had followed the river which eventually created the channel used by boats from the south. It had not one source, but many, far underground or beyond the hills, and then it spread out to become a marsh from which issued bubbles of foul-smelling gas. Passage through a bed of sand cleansed it, and thereafter it was partitioned into many small channels to irrigate stands of fungi, useful trees, and pastures on which grazed meatimals and furnimals. Also it filled the castle fish-ponds, and even after such multiple exploitation it was warm enough to keep the channel ice-free save in the dead of winter. The whole area was a marvel and a mystery. It was even said that further north yet there were pools of liquid rock which bubbled like water, but Jing was not prepared to credit that until he saw it with his own eye.

Despite her deformity, Rainbow had set a punishing pace, as though trying to prove something to herself, and Twig had been left far behind on the rocky path. He was in a bad temper anyway, for he had hoped to show off his laboratory first, where he claimed he was making amazing transformations by the use of heat, but Rainbow had insisted on coming here before sunset, and Jing did want to visit the observatory above all else.

However, he was finding it a disappointment. It was a mere depression in the rock. Walbushes had been trained to make a circular windbreak, and their rhizomes formed crude steps enabling one to look over the top for near-horizon observations. A pumptree whose taproot reached down to a stream of hot water grew in the center where on bitter nights one might lean against it for warmth. A

15

few lashed-together poles indicated important lines-of-sight. Apart from that—nothing.

At first Jing just wandered about, praising the splendid view here offered of Castle Thorn and the adjoining settlements. There were more than he had imagined: almost a score. But when Twig finally reached the top, panting, he could contain himself no longer.

"Where your instruments?" he asked in bewilderment.

"Oh, we bring them up as required," was the blank reply. "What do you do—keep them in a chest on the spot?"

Thinking of the timber orrery which had been his pride and joy, twice his own height and moved by a pithed water-worm whose mindless course was daily diverted by dams and sluices so as to keep the painted symbols of the sun, moon and planets in perfect concordance with heaven, Jing was about to say, "We don't bother with instruments small enough to carry!"

But it would have been unmannerly.

Sensing his disquiet, Twig seized on a probable explanation. "I know what you're tempted to say—with all that steam rising from our warm pools, how can anyone see the stars? You just wait until the winter wind from the north spills down this valley! It wipes away mist like a rainstorm washing out tracks in mud! Of course, sometimes it brings snow, but for four-score nights in any regular year we get the most brilliant sight of heaven anyone could wish for, and as for the aurorae...!"

Touching Rainbow familiarly, he added, "And you'll be here to watch it all, won't you?"

"You must forgive Twig," she said, instantly regal. "He has known me since childhood and often treats me as though I were still a youngling. But it's true I spend most of my time here during the winter. I have no greater purpose in life than to decipher the message of the stars. I want to know why I'm accursed!"

Embarrassed by her intensity, Jing glanced nervously at her escorting prongsman, without whom she was forbidden to walk abroad, and wished he could utter something reassuring about Twig's abilities. But the words would have rung hollow. He had pored over Jing's star-maps, cursing his failing sight which he blamed on excessive study of the sun—in which Jing sympathized with him, for his own eye was not as keen as it had been—and exclaimed at their detail, particularly because they showed an area of the southern sky which he had never seen. All he had to offer in exchange, though, were a few score parchments bearing scrappy notes about eclipses and planetary orbits, based on the assumption that the world was stationary, which had been superseded in Ntah ten-score years ago, and some uninspiring remarks about the New Star. It was clear that his real interest lay in what he could himself affect, in his laboratory, and his vaunted theory of the fire above was plausibly a scrap from a childhood dream. Jing was unimpressed.

He said eventually, "Lady, where I from is not believed curses anymore. We hold, as sky tend to fill more with star, so perfectness of life increase down here." And damned his clumsiness in this alien speech.

"That's all very well if you admit the heavens change," said Twig bluffly. "But we're beset with idiots who are so attached to their dreams they can go on claiming they don't, when a month of square meals would show them better!"

He meant the sacerdotes, who—as Jing had learned—had been sent to Castle Thorn unwillingly, in the hope of winning the Count back to their "true faith," and were growing desperate at their lack of success even among the peasants, because everyone in this valley was well enough nourished to tell dream from fact. One rumor had it that they were spreading blight on the trencher-plants, but surely no one could descend that far! Although some of the lords of Forb...

Disregarding Twig, Rainbow was addressing Jing again. "You say I can't be cursed?"

"Is not curse can come from brightness, only darkness. More exact, is working out pattern—I say right *pattern*, yes?—coming towards ideal, and new thing have different shape. You noble-born, you perhaps a sign of change in world."

"But if change is coming, nobody will prepare to meet it," Twig said, growing suddenly serious. "With the trunks of Forb and other ancient cities rotting around them, people shout ever louder that it can't be happening. They'd rather retreat from reality into the mental mire from which—one supposes—our ancestors must have emerged.

You don't think Lady Rainbow is accursed. Well, I don't either, or if she is then it's a funny kind of curse, because I never met a girl with a sharper mind than hers! But most people want everything, including their children, to conform to the standards of the past."

"My father's like that," Rainbow sighed.

"He's a prime example," Twig agreed, careless of the listening prongsman. "He thinks always in terms of tomorrow copying today. But our world—I should say our continent—is constantly in flux; when it's not a drought it's a plague, when it's not a murrain it's a population shift . . . Where you come from, Jing, how does your nation stay stable even though you admit the heavens themselves can change? I want to know the secret of that stability!"

"I want to know what twisted my father!" snapped Rainbow. "Bent outwardly I may be, but he must be deformed within!"

Aware of being caught up in events he had not bargained for, Jing thought to turn Rainbow a compliment. He said, "But is still possible to him descendants, not? Surprise to me lady is not match often with persons of quality, being intelligent and of famous family."

Later, Twig explained that to speak of a noblewoman being paired was something one did not do within hearing of the party concerned. For the time being he merely changed the subject with an over-loud interruption.

"Now come and see what's really interesting about the work we're doing!"

Yet, although she declined to accompany them to the laboratory, the lady herself seemed rather flattered than upset.

This time their path wound eastward to the place where the hot river broke out of shattered rocks. Alongside it a tunnel led into the core of a low hill, uttering an appalling stench. Yet the heat and humidity reminded Jing's weathersense of home, and inside there were adequate glowplants and twining creepers to cling to when the going became treacherous. Sighing, he consented to enter.

When he was half choking in the foul air, they emerged into a cavern shaped like a vast frozen bubble, at whose center water gushed up literally boiling. Here Hedge, Bush and the rest were at work, or more exactly directing a group of ill-favored peasants to do their work for them. They paused to greet their visitor, and Twig singled out one husky fellow who sank to half his normal height in the cringing northern fashion.

"This is Keepfire! Tell Master Jing what you think of this home of yours, Keepfire!"

"Oh, it's very good, very safe," the peasant declared. "Warm in the worst winter, and food always grows. Better here than over the hill, sir!"

Jing was prepared to accept that. Anything must be preferable to being turned loose to fend for oneself in the barren waste to the north, where no plants grew and there was a constant risk from icefaws and snowbelongs, which colonized the bodies of their prey to nourish their brood-mass. Twig had described the process in revolting detail.

Having surveyed the cavern and made little sense of what he saw, Jing demanded, "What exact you do here?"

"We're testing whatever we can lay claws on, first in hot water, then on rock to protect it from flame, then in flame itself. We make records of the results, and from them we hope to figure out what fire actually can do."

To Jing, fire was something viewed from far off, veiled in smoke and to be avoided, and flame was a conjurer's trick to amuse children on celebration days. More cynically than he had intended—but he was growing weary and dreams were invading his mind again—he said, "You are proving something it does?"

Stung, Twig reached up to a rocky ledge and produced a smooth heavy lump which shone red-brown.

"Seen anything like this before? Or this?"

Another strange object, more massive and yellower.

Realization dawned. "Ah, these are metals, yes? You find in water?" Sometimes in the streams which fed the lake of Ntah placer-nuggets turned up, softer than stone ought to be, which after repeated hammering showed similar coloration.

"Not at all! This is what we get when we burn certain plants and then reheat their ash. Don't you think some of the essence of fire must have remained in these lumps? Look how they gleam! But I should have asked—what do you already know about fire?"

"Is to us not well known. In dry land is danger for

plants, homes, people. But in Ntah is air damp same like here. Is down in this cave possible flame?"

His doubt was plain. Twig snorted.

"I thought so! The more I hear, the more I become convinced we must be the only people in the world seriously investigating fire. Either they think it's blasphemous because it's reserved to the heavens, or they're as wrong as you about the way it works. Let a humble peasant show you better. Keepfire, make a flame for the visitor!"

Chuckling, the peasant rushed to a recess in the cavern wall. From it he produced articles which Jing's poor sight failed to make out in the dimness.

"Long before anyone came here from as far south as Forb," Twig said softly, "Keepfire's ancestors were priests of a cult which now has vanished—based on dreams, of course. But they found out some very practical techniques."

"What he do?"

"It's so simple you wouldn't believe it. I didn't when I first came here. He uses dry fungus-spores, and a calamar soaked in fish-oil, and two rocks. Not just ordinary rock, a kind that has some of the fire-essence in it. Watch!"

Something sparkled. A flame leapt up, taller than himself, and Jing jumped back in alarm. He risked tumbling into the hot pool; Twig caught him, uttering a sour laugh.

"Doesn't that impress you?"

"I guess so..." Jing was trembling. "But what to do with? Is not same fire and in—*as* in sky! Is under the ground!"

Twig said with authority, "The idea that fire belongs to the sky is false. Using it, we've made—not grown but made—things that were never in the world before."

"Did you make Count's blade?" Jing ventured, prepared to be impressed.

"Oh, no. That's a natural rock you find a lot of around here. But it too must have fire in its essence, or heat at any rate. It seems to be like this stuff." Twig reached to another ledge and brought down a clawful of smooth transparent objects shaped like half a raindrop, most bluish, some greenish, one or two clear. "The peasants' children use these for playthings. They hate me because I take away the best ones for more important use. On a fine day

you can catch sunfire with them and set light to a dry
calamar or a dead leaf. What better proof could there be
of my opinions? Look, here's a particularly clear one!"

To Jing's touch the droplet was relatively cool, so he
could not imagine how fire could be trapped within. All
of a sudden, however, as he was inspecting it, he noticed
something remarkable. At a certain distance he could see
his claw through it, only enlarged.

"It make big!" he breathed.

"Oh, that too! But it's no use holding it up to the sky.
Every youngling in the valley must have tried that, and
me too, I confess. But it won't make the moon or stars
any plainer, and as for looking at the sun—well!"

"I can have, please? Not to start fires. Is good for look
my star-maps."

Twig started. He said in an altered voice, "Now, why
didn't I think of that? But of course I never saw maps
like yours before, with such fine detail...Sure, take it.
We keep finding them all the time. Now we'd best get
back to the castle."

He padded away, exuding an aura of annoyance.

This was no astrologer: Jing was satisfied on that point.
Maybe when it came to trying this or that in a fire Twig's
record-keeping might be accurate, but given he could
overlook such an obvious use for a magnifying drop it
seemed unlikely. Anyhow, what value could his data have?
It was inconceivable that fire in heaven could be identical
with fire underground!

So perhaps there were several kinds of fire? And surely
there must be *some* way of enlarging the heavens if it
could be done at close range...?

Jing sighed heavily. He had to make an immediate
decision: whether to remain here in the hope that studying
the stars uninterruptedly for longer than he had imagined
possible would bring unexpected insights, or leave by the
final autumn boat. But the continent was already in the
grip of winter; he could scarcely reach home any sooner,
if he left now, than if he stayed until spring. And Waw-
Yint would certainly not forgive him for abandoning his
mission. He was not one to be bought off with such petty
marvels as a magnifying drop. True, he was old, and by
now might well be dead—

Shocked at his own disloyalty, Jing firmly canceled

such thoughts. No, he must remain, and if necessary next year carry on beyond the ocean, riding one of the half-legendary giant barqs of which they spoke in Yown and Forb... if they were not compounded of dreams.

Besides, this magnifier... It had seized his imagination, an ideal tool for astrologers hampered only by its present imperfection. He had been brought up to believe that perfection inhered in everything, even people; it needed only to be sought out.

Just before entering the castle again, Twig turned to him and said bluffly, "Put what I know about the world below together with what you know about the sky, and we might get somewhere one of these days, right? Shall we try?"

It was a formal invitation not just to collaborate but to make friends. Jing felt obliged to treat it as such, despite his reservations concerning Twig's researches. They locked claws accordingly.

Later, Jing reflected it was as well they concluded their compact at that juncture, for the first person to meet them within the castle reported Drakh's death; the best of Twig's cleanlickers had failed to purify his wound. Grief at being shorn of his last Ntahish companion might have driven him to dreamness and made him reject Twig-friend because of Twig-physician. Yet no blame could attach save to those who had stabbed Drakh a month's journey ago.

When, in compliance with local custom, they consigned Drakh's remains to a pullulating pond surrounding a handsome blazetree, Twig spoke much about loneliness and isolation, and Jing was touched and grateful.

As though the funeral were a significant occasion, the Maker's Sling delivered a cast of long bright streaks across the zenith.

But that was apt to happen any night.

IV

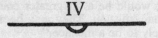

Next day distraught peasants came crying that a snowbelong had killed a child from the furthest-outlying village, and the Count hauled himself out of his sitting-pit and set off to hunt it down with hoverers and canifangs. Twig predicted it might be several days before he returned, and Jing looked forward not only to improving his Forbish but also to cleansing his mind of the nostalgic dreams which since the death of Drakh threatened to overwhelm him.

Taking advantage of his absence, however, the sacerdotes promptly summoned Jing to their chapel, an enclosure within the north wall of the castle which they had been granted because the Count, despite being well fed, was sufficiently at the mercy of his dreams to half believe their dogma.

"You'll have to go, I'm afraid," sighed Twig.

"Here I thought had they no power. How they force me?"

"Hmm! It isn't quite like that. True, the Count's rule is absolute here, and the people, if they have a religion at all, adhere to superstitions even more absurd than the sacerdotes', though some of their knowledge, especially where fire is concerned...Excuse me. The point is, the Count has opened up this place to trade with the south, and that means contact with southern believers. Most of the summer there are at least half a score of the faithful here, and the sacerdotes incite them to put pressure on the Count, who's growing senile. What I'm afraid of is that sooner or later he may conclude that they're right after all, and hoping to escape the curse he'll go whining to them for forgiveness, and you can guess what'll become of the rest of us then! At all events they're getting bolder, and if you don't obey their summons you could well find your food poisoned or a prong stuck in your back."

Jing would have dismissed the idea as ridiculous but for what had happened to Drakh. Sensing his dismay, Twig added, "If it's any comfort, though, you should bear in mind that it would be a far greater coup for them to convert you than kill you. They may be a nuisance but they're not likely to be a menace."

At least these sacerdotes were less determined to execute what they held to be the Maker's will than their counterparts at Forb. They greeted him politely as he entered the chapel, which was decorated with makeshift symbols: the Sling, of course, shiny with glitterweed; a pile of the seared rocks which were held to be what the Sling cast, but looked much like any other rock except for superficial melt-marks; some rather repulsive models of victims of the Maker's wrath, struck down from on high.

For a while there was ordinary conversation, about his homeland and his various travels. Jing answered as best he could, wishing he had asked Twig their names, for they had not offered them and direct inquiry might be rude. There were a chief, a middle and a junior; that would have to do.

Finally the chief broached the main subject. He said, "What god is worshiped in your land?"

"Most people not," Jing said. "Is some old and sick folk think of pleasing gods, but to rest of us is imaginary thing. We tell easily dream from fact, same as here."

"You don't believe in a creator at all?" the middle one demanded. "You don't think the world *was* created?"

"Is certain," Jing said. "But very long past. We think"— he groped for words—"world is made as path for us to go on as we choose. Important is to learn from sky whether we take right or wrong way. Creator is watch us, but not for punish, not for want offerings, just for see how done by us. When well done, more star come in sky. Perhaps in farthest future all sky is starry, and all here below walk in light all time."

He hated to give this bald account of the system Ntahish philosophers had evolved over many score-of-score years, but it was the best he could manage.

The junior, who was better-favored than his colleagues, spoke up eagerly. "But the New Star did light the whole of the night sky! For a while it could even be seen by day! Do you think—?"

"There is no New Star!" the chief snapped. "It's an illusion!"

Humbly the junior said, "Sir, I'm aware of that. But with respect it seems our visitor is not. I only wish to learn what explanation his people have—well, invented for it."

Gruffly, the chief granted permission for the question.

"We not have explanation," Jing admitted. "Never saw so much bright star appear in past, not at any rate to stay so long. In Ntah is no great change to explain it. Here why I am sent to ask in foreign lands."

"You actually imagine there have been other new stars?" asked the middle one. "Dreamstuff!"

"Can show you true. I bring copies of old sky-maps to make proof. Is also much difference in time of rise and set from old days. Will explain meaning of maps when want you!"

"Your star-maps," said the chief sacerdote coldly, "are of no interest to us. Any apparent change in the heavens must be due to the working of evil forces passing off dreams as reality. Bring your maps, yes, but so that we can burn them and save other people from your mad ideas!"

That was more than Jing could bear. Rising to his full height in the most disrespectful manner possible, he said, "Is your belief, anyone make use of fire is companion of evil, yes? You just propose that same! I say plain: I better tell dream from true than you! And anyway, is not place of you to order foreigner, guest of Count!"

The middle one scowled a warning, aware his chief had gone too far. After a moment the latter rose, glowering.

"The Count is not yet back! He is a reckless hunter and may well not come back at all! And if he doesn't, then we'll see about *you!*"

He stormed away.

Greatly distressed, the junior sacerdote escorted Jing to the exit, muttering apologies. And, as soon as they were out of hearing, he did the most amazing thing. Leaning confidentially close, he whispered, "Sir, *I* would like to see your sky-maps! Since coming here, I no longer think the heavens never change! I think new stars signal the birth of righteous persons, and the most righteous of all must now be among us!"

Before Jing could recover from his startlement, he was gone.

At first Jing was inclined to hasten straight back to Twig, but a moment's reflection changed his mind. Even in peaceful Ntah there were such things as court intrigues, and while in his profession he had been largely insulated from them, he was well aware of the need to protect himself. Given the Count's absence, might his daughter offer a degree of help, or at least advice? From a passing prongsman he inquired the way to her ladyship's quarters.

They proved to be in a large and comfortable bower on the west side of the castle, where she sat poring over a table of Ntahish mathematical symbols he had prepared for her. He was relieved to find she did not resent interruption; on the contrary, she declared herself delighted, and sent her maids to bring refreshments.

"I'm so pleased you're here!" she exclaimed, speaking as directly as a man. "Here at Castle Thorn, I mean. I'd never say so in Twig's hearing, but I long ago learned all he had to teach me about the sky, and it didn't even include the idea that the sun stands still while we move around it. It makes everything so much simpler when you look at things that way, doesn't it? I look forward to having you as my constant companion at the observatory this winter."

"To me will much pleasure," Jing affirmed. "But if to explain correct meaning I want say, must I very more Forbish learn."

"I'm sure you'll learn quickly, and if you have problems, turn to me. I have little enough to occupy me," she added in a bitter tone.

Thus emboldened, Jing said, "Is of problem I come now. See you..." And he summed up his encounter with the sacerdotes.

"You're right to beware of them!" Rainbow asserted. "How can I but hate them for claiming that my birth was the sign of a curse on my father? For him I have small love either, since he sent my mother away, but at least he had the kindness to bring me with him when he left Forb instead of abandoning or even killing me, and he provided for my education by offering Twig a refuge here. Without *him* I think I would have lost myself in dreamness. If only he hadn't more or less quit studying the sky when his eye began to fail . . . Still, he had only himself to blame for looking directly at the sun. He told you, did he, how he saw dark markings on it?"

"I hear of it in Forb, but he not say himself."

"Do you think it's credible? Sometimes when there's thin gray cloud, so the sun doesn't hurt your eye, I've imagined that I too . . . But what do you think? Is it possible for dark to appear out of bright, as bright may out of dark?"

"Is not in the knowledge of my people. Where I lived, is either clear day-sky or thick rain-cloud. Was to me new, see sort of thin cloud you mention."

"Is that so?" She leaned forward, fascinated. "I should ask you about your homeland, shouldn't I, rather than about stars and numbers all the time? Have you been away long? Do you miss it very much? Is it a place of marvels? I suspect it must be, particularly compared to this lonely backwater . . . But quickly, before my maids return: I'll assign you one of my own prongsmen to replace Drakh. I'll say it's because you need someone to practice Forbish with. I'll give you Sturdy. With him at your side you need fear nothing from the sacerdotes."

"Am not sure all to be feared," Jing muttered, and recounted the odd behavior of the junior sacerdote.

"Interesting! That must be Shine you're talking about. I realized long ago he was too sensible to deprive himself of the good fare we can offer, but I'd no idea he'd become so independent-minded. Cultivate him! It could serve us well to have a split in the enemy's ranks."

Jing noted in passing how swiftly she had begun to say "us."

"Tonight in hall sit with me," Rainbow continued. "I'll feed you from my own trencher-stump. That is, unless you're afraid of offending my father's wives. But they have no power; he takes and dismisses them according to his mood, and until one of them buds I remain his sole heir. Now here come my attendants. Let's change the subject. You were telling me about your homeland. The very weather is different there, I think you said. In what way?"

With infinite gratitude Jing slipped into memory, purging the risk of dangerous dreams. He described the subtropical climate of Ntah, and then progressed to a general account of the Lake and its environs—the creeper-bridges stranding out from island to island; the Lord's palace at the center, a huge tree sixty-score years old, whose sides were draped with immense waxy blossoms that scented the air for miles around; the western cataract where a broad river plunged over a cliff and kept the Lake from growing stagnant; the delectable flesh of the nut called hoblaq, enclosed in a shell too hard for anyone to break, which people gathered on the hillside and pitched into the river so that the falls would do the work for them and send the shattered kernels drifting across the water for everybody to enjoy; the game animals large and small which haunted the copses, the shallows and the water-meadows; the venomous insects and noxious berries which were obliging enough to advertise themselves by distinctive coloring, so even children might avoid them; and of course his prized observatory, with its orrery and its transits and its levels and its gnomons and its great trumpet-shaped viewing-funnel of dried pliobark, which blanked off all light from below and permitted the eye to adjust completely to its task of registering the stars . . .

"And we think we're advanced!" Rainbow cried. "How could you have brought yourself to leave such a place?"

It was a question Jing was to ask himself countless times during the next few months, particularly after the last boat of autumn had come and gone and the sun had set for the last time in six-score days.

V

The slopes and branchways of the castle were eerie in the long darkness, although the glowplants drew enough warmth from underground to provide faint luminance right through until spring. They were, Jing thought, like a model of his mind, a pattern matching himself alone as the sky matched the entire world. Some areas were darkly red, like those deep-lying mental strata concerned with fundamental processes such as digestion, where one might venture only in emergency and at the cost of immense concentration; others were pinker and brighter, like the levels where one might issue commands to oneself about sitting or standing, walking or climbing—or fighting; others again tended to be bluish, like the dreams harking back to childhood incomprehension of the world which could so easily overpower a person when weary, sick, frightened, grief-stricken or undernourished, and which sacerdotes and other fools deliberately cultivated because they had never learned to prize dreams less than memory; yet other levels were greenish as memory was; more still gleamed clear yellow like imagination; and just a few, including the great hall itself, shone with the white brightness of reality.

Contrary to what the chief sacerdote had hoped, the Count had a successful hunt, and his prongsmen dragged back enough snowbelong meat to garnish a score of winter meals. But he had fallen into a crevasse and ruptured some of his interior tubules. More bloated than ever, he summoned Jing to attend him under the misapprehension that all foreigners were skilled physicians. Jing, having seen a similar case when an elderly man slipped on the approach to the cataract at Ntah, offered suggestions which appeared to give relief from pain, if nothing more. Impressed, the Count made a vague attempt to engage in

29

debate concerning the patterns in the sky, but after that he seemed to lose interest.

Much the same could be said of Twig. Once he realized that Jing's star-maps were not only in an alien script but based on a sun-centered convention, he gave up. It was not because he shared the sacerdotes' conviction that the sun was only the Maker's Eye and therefore could not be the focus around which the planets revolved; enough observations had been amassed here in the north to indicate to him how far superior the Ntahish system was. No, the problem arose from a wholly unexpected source: Keepfire.

As the story came back to Jing, the elderly peasant whose ancestors had been a priesthood was angered by the fact that certain substances resisted change in his hottest flames. He therefore set about interrogating the oldest of his kinfolk in search of ways to make them even hotter. Siting a fire at the spot where a crack in the rock, leading to the outside, was aligned with the prevailing wind made the fuel blaze up violently. Winds, though, were unpredictable; how to cause an artificial one? Well, when a barq's bladder burst... Suppose one made a giant bladder out of hide? But that wasn't the answer by itself. It needed to be filled, and refilled, and refilled, and... How about tethered hoverers?

The problem engaged Twig's total attention. Sighing, Jing left him to get on with it, feeling lonelier than ever.

In absolute contrast, Rainbow was desperate for the information contained in Jing's maps. The regular winter wind had set in, but actual star-study was out of the question; there were constant snow-flurries, and whenever the gale died down the water was warm enough to generate fog. Jing, though, was in no mood to complain. He was taking a long while to adjust to the loss of his last Ntahish companion, and until he had rid his mind of intrusive dreams he was content to tutor Rainbow. He was greatly impressed by her quick wits. She had realized at once how much simpler a sun-centered system made it to keep track of the outer planets, and the inner one which was so rarely visible. Moreover, when she ran across a technical term in Ntahish for which she knew no equivalent, she simply adopted it. Within a few days she was using words nobody else at Castle Thorn would have understood.

Except one...

It astonished Jing when the young sacerdote Shine lived up to his promise and shyly came to beg a sight of the star-maps. Instantly fascinated, he set about matching the names they bore with their Forbish equivalents. Soon his colleagues were openly quarreling with him. One evening only the authority of the Count prevented a fight breaking out in the hall.

Quite without intention, Jing thereupon found himself the center of interest throughout the castle. He could go nowhere without some wench accosting him to demand a favorable horoscope for her family, or a prongsman wanting to be told he would be promoted chief-of-guard over his rivals, or peasants seeking a cure for trencher-plant blight—though luckily the latter had been less virulent of late.

As soon as the air cleared, therefore, he and Rainbow went to the observatory as often as possible. All Twig's extravagant claims proved justified. The stars shone down sharp as stabberclaws, from a background so nearly black Jing almost could not believe it. Even the square surrounding the New Star was barely a contrast to the rest. As for the Bridge of Heaven, it gleamed like a treasury of pearlseeds.

A faint suspicion trembled on the edge of his awareness. But it refused to come clear as he strove with chill-stiff claws to prepare for the portion of the sky not seen from Ntah maps and tables as exact as those he had brought from home. Often dreams threatened to engulf his consciousness, and then he had to break off and embrace the warm trunk of the pumptree until he regained his self-possession.

It was a marvelous juncture for observation, though. Time had brought all five outer planets into the same quadrant—an event which might or might not have significance. A year ago he would have insisted that it must; now he was growing skeptical. But there was reddish Swiftyouth, currently in a retrograde phase of the kind which had led Ntahish astrologers to center their system on the sun; there was Steadyman, almost white, lagging behind; there was Stolidchurl, somewhat yellower; there were Stumpalong and Sluggard, both faintly green, the latter markedly less bright...

Why were there moving bodies in the sky, and of such different sizes? And why were they so outnumbered by the stars? Shine was eager to explain the teaching he had been brought up to: that each corresponded with a region of the world, and moved faster or slower according to whether the people of that region obeyed the Maker's will. One day they would all rise together at the same time as the sun rose in eclipse, and—

Patiently Jing pointed out the fallacies in his argument. Clacking his mandibles, he went away to think the matter through. Apparently it was news to him that a solar eclipse was not simultaneously observed everywhere, a fact one might account for only by invoking distances beside which Jing's journey from Ntah to Castle Thorn was like a single step. It hurt the mind to think in such terms, as Rainbow wryly put it when she showed her how to calculate the circumference of the world by comparing star-ascensions at places on the same meridian but a known distance apart. He found the remark amusing; it was the first thing that had made him laugh in a long while.

Plants which swelled at noon and shrank at midnight were used in Ntah to keep track of time if the sky was clouded over and the weather-sense dulled. Whenever it snowed, Jing occupied himself by hunting the castle for anything which might exhibit similar behavior. The effect the long night was having on his own weather-sense was disquieting; without sunlight to prompt him back to rationality, he found dreams creeping up on him unawares when he was neither hungry, tired nor upset.

He was engaged in this so-far vain quest when he was hailed by a familiar voice. Turning, he saw Twig, filthy from pads to mandibles with blackish smears.

"*There* you are! I was surprised not to find you in Rainbow's quarters—they tell me you two have grown very close lately!"

For an instant Jing was minded to take offense. But Twig knew nothing of his being compelled to celibacy so long as Waw-Yint lived. And lately he had felt pangs of regret at not having left offspring behind in Ntah. Rainbow and Shine were about half his age; talking to them, he had realized how much happier he would have been had he passed on his knowledge to a son and daughter before setting forth on his travels...

Before he could reply, however, Twig had charged on, plainly bursting to impart information. "Take a look at this!" he exclaimed, proffering something in his left claw. Jing complied, hoping it was not something as irrelevant as Twig's last "great discovery": a new kind of metal, grayish and cold, which broke when it was dropped. This one, however, he thought he recognized.

"Ah! You found another magnifying drop. It's especially clear and fine, I must say."

"Not found," Twig announced solemnly. "Made."

"How? Out of what?"

"Sand, would you believe? Yes, the same sand you find beside the hot marsh! Keepfire's flames are getting better and hotter—oh, I know people are complaining about the smell, but that's a small price to pay!—and this time he's excelled himself! And there's more. Look at *this*!"

He produced what he had in his other claw. It was of similar material, equally clear, but twice the size.

"Hold them up together—no, I don't mean *together*, I mean—Oh, like this!" Twig laid claws on Jing in a way the latter would never normally have tolerated, but it was certainly quicker than explaining. "Now look at something through both of them, and move them apart or together until you see it clearly. Got it?"

Jing grew instantly calm. There presented to his eye was an image of Twig, albeit upside-down...but larger, and amazingly sharp except around the edges.

Very slowly, he lowered and examined the two pieces of glass. They were not, as he had first assumed, in the regular half-droplet shape; they were like two of the natural kind pressed together, but considerably flatter.

"You made these?" he said slowly.

"Yes, yes!" And then, with a tinge of embarrassment: "Well—Keepfire made them, under Bush's supervision. All I was hoping for was better magnifying drops. I never expected that when you put one behind another you'd get even more enlargement the wrong way up! At first I thought I was in a dream, you know? But you agree it works?"

"Yes—yes, no doubt of it!"

"Right! Let's go and look at stars!"

"It's snowing. That's why I'm here."

"Oh, is it? Oh. Then—"

"Then we'll just have to force ourselves to wait until it blows over. But I promise you, friend Twig, I'm as anxious as you are to inspect the heavens with such amazing aids!"

The moment the weather cleared, he and Twig and Rainbow and Shine—for the secret was so explosive, it had to be shared—along with Sturdy, who hated coming here in the cold and dark, plodded to the observatory, forcing themselves not to make a premature test. Then it turned out that the lenses had misted over, and they had to find something dry enough to wipe them with, and...

"Jing first," Twig said. "You're the most knowledgeable."

"But surely you as the discoverer—"

"The credit is more Keepfire's than mine! Besides"—in a near-whisper—"my eye's not keen enough."

"My lady—" Jing began. Rainbow snapped at him.

"Do as Twig says!"

"Very well. Where shall I look first?" He was shaking, not from cold, but because excitement threatened to release wild dreams to haunt his mind like savage canifangs.

"At Steadyman," she said, pointing where the gaps in the cloud were largest. "If there's a reason why some stars are wanderers, it may be they are specially close to us. You've taught me that our own world whirls in space. Maybe that's another world like ours."

It was a good, bright and altogether ideal target. Jing leaned on the walbush stems, which were frozen stiff enough to support him. It took a while to find the proper position for the lenses, and then it took longer still for his sight to adjust to the low light-level—particularly since there were curious faint colored halos everywhere except at the dead center of the field. Eventually, however, he worked out all the variables, so he had a clear view. At last he said:

"Whether it's a world like ours, I cannot say. But I do see two stars where I never saw any before."

"Incredible!" breathed Twig, and Jing let go pressure

from his limbs with a painful gasp and passed the lenses on. In a while:

"Oh! Oh, *yes*! But very indistinct! Rainbow, what do you see?"

She disposed herself carefully, leaning all her weight on her crippled side. Having gazed longer than either of them, she said, "Two stars beside the planet. Sharp and clear."

Turning, she sought Stolidchurl, and did the same, and exclaimed. "Not two more stars, but three! At least I think three . . . I—Shine, you look. Your sight is very keen, I know."

His mandibles practically chattering with excitement, the young sacerdote took his turn. "Three!" he reported. "And—and I see a disc! I always thought the planets were just points, like the stars! But I still see *them* as points! And what do you make of the colored blurs these lenses show?"

"Could it be that we're seeing a very faint aurora?" Rainbow ventured. "Jing, what do you think?"

Jing ignored her, his mind racing. If one put such lenses in a viewing funnel—no, not a funnel, better a tube—of pliobark, or whatever was to be had here in the north, and made provision for adjustment to suit different observers . . .

He said soberly, "Twig, this is a very great invention."

"I know, I know!" Twig clapped his claws in delight. "When I turn it on the sun, come spring—"

"You'll burn out what's left of your sight," Rainbow interjected flatly. "Making the sun as much brighter as the stars now appear will blind you. But there must be a way. Apply your genius to the problem, while the rest of us get on with finding unknown stars. Perhaps they hold the key to what's amiss with cripples like me."

VI

For the rest of the winter all four of them were embarged on a fabulous voyage of discovery. The world receded until they could wander through it unheeding, like a thin mist; all that mattered was their study of the sky. Shine abandoned his duties altogether, and his superiors threatened to kill him, but he put himself under Rainbow's protection and with Sturdy and her other prongsmen ready to spring to his aid they dared not touch him.

Growing frightened because his ruptures would not heal, the Count occasionally sent for them to demand how their work was progressing, but during their eager attempts at explanation his mind tended to stray, and he invariably wound up by raging at them because they cared more for star-lore than medicine. Nobody else in the castle—not even Twig's aides like Hedge and Bush, who refused to venture forth when the wind was bitter enough to build frost-rime on one's mandibles—seemed to care that a revelation was in the making. Twig said it was because the cold weather had sent their minds into hibernation, like the dirq and fosq which were so abundant in the summer and vanished into burrows in the fall.

There was one signal exception: the peasant Keepfire.

Throughout his life he had scarcely seen the stars. It was a tradition in his family that at winter sunset they should retreat to their cavern until spring reawoke the land. Twig, however, was sure it could not always have been so, and because he was so excited by what the lenses were revealing he patiently taught Keepfire how to store warm air under his mantle and persuaded him to the observatory at a time when the air was so clear the brilliance of the heavens was almost hurtful.

Such was Keepfire's amazement on learning that the glass he had melted from sand could show sparks of light where to the naked eye was only blackness, he returned home full of enthusiasm to improve on what he had already done. It being impossible to find fuel for new and hotter fires at this season—and hard enough at any time—he set about collecting every scrap of glass he could, whether natural or resulting from their experiments. For hours on end he sat comparing them, wondering how each differed from the rest. At last, in what the jubilant Twig termed a fit of genius, he thought of a way to shape the ones which were nearly good until they outdid those which were excellent.

Using the skin of a fish which was sown with tiny rough crystalline points, hunted by people but scarcely preyed on in the wild because swallowing it tail-first as it fled was apt to rasp the predator's gullet, he contrived to grind a poor lens into a good one, at least so far as form was concerned. But then it was seamed with fine scratches. How to eliminate them? There was no means other than rubbing on something softer than the glass, until the glass itself shed enough spicules to complete the task. This he set himself to do.

Nightless days leaked away, and Jing and his companions almost forgot about Keepfire, because every time they went to the observatory some new miracle presented itself.

At first Jing had thought it enough that, in the vicinity of the bright outer planets, there should suddenly appear new starlets which—as time passed—clearly proved to be satellites of what Shine had been the first to recognize as actual discs. But then they looked at the Bridge of Heaven, otherwise the Sling, and save at its midline it was no longer a band of uniform light; it was patently a dense mass of individual stars.

And there were so *many* stars! Even when the lenses were directed towards the dark square surrounding the New Star, at least a quarter-score (Shine claimed eight) other points of light appeared. At the zenith, near the horizon, it made no odds: wherever they looked, what had always been lightless zones turned out to be dotted with tiny glowing specks.

The New Star itself resolutely refused to give up any secrets. Even Shine's keen vision, which far surpassed the others', failed to reveal more than a bright spot with

a pale blur around it, a cloud lighted as a fire might light
its smoke from underneath. Was it a fragment of the Maker's Mantle, the aurora which at unpredictable intervals
draped the sky in rich and somber colors? In Jing's view
that was unlikely. Before coming to Castle Thorn he had
only heard of aurorae. Now, having witnessed several,
he was satisfied they must partake more of the nature of
clouds than of stars, for they affected the weather-sense,
as stars did not; moreover they did not necessarily move
in the same direction as the rest of the sky. Were they
then looking down on starfire from above? The image
came naturally to folk whose ancestors had been treetop-
dwelling predators, but by the same token "up" and "down"
meant one thing to them: towards or away from the ground
underpad.

Jing and Rainbow debated long about the matter as
soon as they realized that the little stars shuttling back
and forth beside the planets must in fact be revolving
around them, moon-fashion. By that stage Jing's prized
star-charts were little more than memoranda; he already
knew there was a lifetime's work in filling the gaps the
unaided eye had left. The perspectives opened up to him
were terrifying. Because if there were any number of different up-and-downs, then not only must the planets be
worlds like *the* world, with their own—plural!—moons,
but the sun, whose planets circled it like moons, might
be circling something greater yet, and...and...It was
dizzying to contemplate!

At least the moon lent them clues. Observations at the
full showed that the sparkles visible on the dark part of
its disc were only a fraction of what was actually going
on. Flash after brilliant flash came and went seemingly
at random, lacking even the momentary trace which followed a meteor. And here again Keepfire proved to possess unexpected insight. Shown the moon through his
original lenses, he said at once, "It's like when I make a
fire!"

And it was. By this time they had all watched his trick
of striking rocks together and catching a spark on a tuft
of shredded calamar.

Striking...

Jing felt he was being not so much struck as battered.
It had been hard enough to accept the distances he had

been taught about in childhood, necessary to let Sunbride
race around the sun, the world stride around it, and the
outer planets follow at their own respective speeds. What
to make of a cosmos in which scores-of-scores-of-scores-
of-scores (but it was pointless to try and count the stars
in the Sling) of not just suns but their accompanying planets
must be allowed for? If the sacerdotes were right in claiming that their sacred stones had fallen from heaven, and
they were so tiny, could those brilliant lights above also
be minute? Shine suggested as much, for he desperately
wanted not to forsake all his former beliefs; in particular
he clung to the notion that the New Star must indicate
some great event in the world below. During a late snow-
storm, however, Jing set him to making calculations based
on the new observations, couched in the Ntahish symbols
which were wieldier than what obtained in the north, and
the results overwhelmed the poor ex-sacerdote, even
though he had been properly fed for moonlongs past and
learned to separate dream from fantasy as never before
in his young life. They demonstrated beyond doubt that
in order to leave room for planetary motions the lights in
the sky must be not only far off but enormous. Did not
a lantern fade to imperceptibility, no matter how skillfully
you bred your gleamers, almost before its bearer was out
of hearing? And when one added in an extra fact which
Shine himself had drawn to their attention—that Swiftyouth sometimes appeared out of round, as though attempting phases like the moon's—there was precisely *one*
explanation which fitted the evidence. The universe must
be full of suns, and therefore presumably of planets too
faint and far away for even their precious lenses to reveal.

A cosmic hierarchy of fire evolved in Jing's imagination: from the Sling compound of giant stars down to the
briefest spark made by clashing rocks. Something pervaded all of them, something luminous, hurtful, transient,
imponderable, yet capable of being fixed and leaving
traces. Perhaps it penetrated everything! Was it the same
force which made treetrunks strong enough to lift gigantic
boulders, the same which brought forth blossoms, fruit
and nuts? It might be, surely, for fire shone brightly and
so did glowplants and glitterweed although they were cold
to the touch and in color much like Stumpalong or Sluggard. So was there a connection? Suppose it was a matter

of speed; suppose the slowness of plant-growth, and of the outer planets, meant *cool*, and the rapidity of flame meant *hot*: what did that imply about the stars? Remaining visibly the same for countless scores of years, must they not also be cool? Yet did not some of them now and then flare up? What about the bright streaks that nightly laced the firmament—must they not be cool, because manifestly the air was warm only when the sun had long shone on it? Yet Shine declared that those who had come on one of the Maker's slingstones immediately after it landed invariably stated that it was too hot to touch, and indeed the surrounding area was often charred! What fantastic link was there between light and heat?

Vainly Jing sought to convey his thinking to his companions. He was as fluent now in spoken Forbish as Rainbow in the use of Ntahish numbers. She, though, had not yet escaped her original obsession; she had only come around to the view that it was pointless to try and read from the heavens the true reason for her deformity, because if there were so many invisible stars there might be one for everybody, and you could waste a lifetime seeking out your own. Before leaving home, or even as recently as the first time he looked at the sky through lenses, Jing might have considered such an argument valid; since getting over Drakh's death, however, he had experienced preternatural clarity of thought, and ideas which for half his life he had treated as rational had been consigned to memory, reclassified as imaginary or as dreamstuff. Perhaps this was due to the plain but nourishing diet he was eating; perhaps it had something to do with the monotonous environment of the long night, when he was free from the cyclic shock of sunrise and sunset; it didn't matter. What counted was that he could now clearly envisage other worlds. What a plethora of individuals might not inhabit all those planets, seen and unseen! What marvels might lie yonder in the dark, more astonishing to him than Ntah to those who knew only Castle Thorn!

And what daunting celestial oceans of knowledge remained to be traversed, when by happenstance a humble peasant could open people's eyes to the miracles inherent in plain sand!

"We'll learn more of the answers," Twig kept promising in what he intended as a tone of comfort, "when the sun rises again. Darkness makes one's mind dull ... as the saying goes!"

Yet Jing's was not, nor Shine's. Could this be due to their constant intake of starfire? Could the mind as well be driven by the mysterious force? Was that why Keepfire, shut away in his foul-smelling cavern, believing in nothing and nobody save his traditional lore, was able to choose and pursue a course of action when Jing's mind was foggy with whirling symbols? Hedge and Bush became angrier and angrier with him, and subsided into sulky grumbling, so that no more new results emerged from the laboratory. Yet Keepfire worried on, and polished and pondered and talked to himself and polished some more, and ...

And on that spring day when the sun's disc cleared the horizon entire for the first time since fall, he came in triumph to Twig and Jing and Rainbow, and unfolded a scrap of the softest icefaw-hide, and revealed a pair of lenses of such impeccable shape that all the results of nature, or of early pourings, faded into insignificance.

Proudly he said, "Do I not bring the gift you wanted most? So I'll ask for what I want. You have shown me stars. They are little fires like the ones I understand. Now I want to see the biggest fire. Show me the sun!"

"But—" Rainbow began, and clipped off the words. Mutely she appealed to her companions, who could envisage as well as she the effect of looking at the sun through nearly perfect lenses.

Twig, however, was oblivious. He breathed, "To see the sun once with these would be enough to sacrifice my sight for!"

"Oh, shut up!" Jing roared. They shrank back as he erupted to his full height, every muscle and tubule in his body at maximum tension. "You're talking like a senile fool, and I speak to you as a sworn friend! Don't you think your eyesight will be useful tomorrow, too? What we need is a way to look at the sun without going blind!" He rounded on Keepfire. "Would you give up all vision for one fleeting glimpse of the sun? You'd rather see it over and over, wouldn't you?"

Alarmed, Keepfire signaled vigorous agreement.

"Very well, then!" Jing relaxed into a more courteous posture, but still tenser than his usual stance among friends.

"What do we know of which makes a scene darker without blurring detail? In Ntah old folk sometimes protected their sight on a sunny day"—he used the past tense unconsciously, and later thought of it as a premonition—"by using thin gray shells. But those deformed the image. Well?"

There was a long pause. At last Rainbow said, "You find membranes inside furnimals that are no good for parchment because you can see through to the other side."

Shine clacked his claws. "Yes! And stretching them can make them thinner still, yet they diminish light!"

"They make everything yellower!" Twig objected, and at once caught himself. "Ah, but the thinner, the clearer! So if we put several one behind another, and take away each in turn until the eye hurts . . . Jing, I'm pleased to be your friend! Once again you see to the core of the matter when I spring to premature conclusions."

"If you want to honor someone, honor Keepfire," Jing said, and reached a decision not foreshadowed by intention. Taking the new beautiful lenses one in either claw, he shrank from his overweening posture to the lowest he could contrive without pain, and remained there while he uttered unpremeditated words.

"You know and I know, without putting it to the test, that these will reveal to us yet more amazing private knowledge. It should not be private; it would not be private, had anybody else within this castle shared our interest. But it *is* so, and must not *remain* so. Already we have learned so much, I want to share our findings with Ntah. The dullwits of Forb and every other city I traversed to come here ought to have their eyes opened—no? Even if like your fellow sacerdotes, Shine, they decline to take advantage, do they not deserve to have this knowledge pointed out to them?"

Shine shouted, "Yes—*yes!*"

Thus encouraged, Jing yielded to a half-guilty, half-ecstatic temptation and let his mind be taken over by the dream-level. Imagination was not enough; it was handicapped by rational considerations like distance, delay, expenditure of effort, the obstinacy of other people. But already their new discoveries had made it plain that everyday knowledge was inadequate to analyze the outcome.

For once his dream faculty might be wiser than his sober and reflective consciousness.

Suddenly his head was roaring-loud with revelations, as though he had tapped the sap-run of time. He marveled at what he heard himself say—or rather declaim.

"*Oh-hya-na-ut thra-t-ywat insk-y-trt ah-bng-llytr-heethwa ibyong hr-ph-tnwef-r heesh-llytr-kwu-qtr-anni-byong*—ah, but I tackle poorly this speech of foreigners and wish I could say what is needful in the speech of the folk I grew up among! But I am far away and lonely beyond bearing so now my community is these who welcome me as friends and I speak to them and to the world because I overflow with knowledge born of fire! I have been set alight like dry crops on a distant hill and the scent of smoke from what I know must carry on the wind and warn the world of what's in store when heaven's fire descends to burn the densest wettest jungle and boil the Lake of Ntah! Vast fires surpassing number or belief loom yonder in the dark and we are cast away upon a fragile barq, this little world, and more and more fires loom and every night the dark is pierced with streaks of fire and what it is we do not know but we must master it or it will utterly consume us! We must pledge ourselves to spare the world the doom of ignorance, not keeping any knowledge private that we've found, but spreading it about to last beyond our lifetimes! You three and I must make a vow together, and in token of it take half another's name. The half is *fire*! It leaves a crust of dirty ash but in another season it may turn to life anew and so our world must do although the prong of heaven strike us down! Take the vow, I beg you, I beseech you, and let not our secret knowledge vanish from the minds of those who on this lost and drifting orb hope to make something greater than themselves!"

He was almost screaming with the fury of his visions, for the countless stars were crashing together in a colossal mass of flame, and the world itself was ripe to be their fuel.

Fuel—?

Abruptly he was back to normal consciousness, and wanted to say something quiet and ordinary, though perfused with unexpected insight, but he could not, for Shine was clutching his claw and crying at the top of his voice.

"I know now what the New Star signified! One is come among us who has wisdom we have never guessed! I'll take the extra name and vow my service!"

"I too!" Old Twig was lowering himself, though his agony was plain. "You have united fire above and fire below and we must tell the world your teaching!"

Last, Rainbow, awkwardly, with her lopsided gait, drew close and said, "I vow the same. For what it's worth I'll bind my followers as well."

There was a pause. She looked at him uncertainly and said at long last, "Jing . . . ?"

The tempest of impressions was fading from his mind. He rose, a little shyly, as though embarrassed. She said again, "Jing!" And continued: "What did you see? What did you see?"

But it was useless to try and describe everything that had so briefly stormed into awareness. He said eventually, "If stars are fire, then new stars happen when fresh fuel is fed to them. What fuel is there, barring worlds like ours? If we would rather not be fuel for a star, there's no one who can save us but ourselves . . . I've dreamed. It's made me weary. I must rest."

VII

That evening Rainbow sent for Keepfire to share food publicly with them and cement their compact, which the peasant did nervously yet with obvious glee. This act made Shine a formal enemy of the other sacerdotes; it was, however, scarcely necessary, since he had long disdained the asceticism they relied on to make their dreams vivid. Afterwards Jing found his companions hanging on his every word as though he were indeed the ultimately righteous person harbingered by the New Star. He did his best to dissuade them, but the force of his vision had profoundly affected them, and it was useless. He resigned himself to being adulated. When they pressed him for some new revelation, all he was able to say was what they must already have known: "It will be spring tomorrow."

Further revelations from the sky, though, were delayed. Warm air from the south, drawn in by the constant thermals rising above the valley, met the still-frozen ground beyond the mountains, and fog and cloud veiled the sun. The ice which had temporarily blocked the access channel began to fracture with noises like a gigant snapping trees, and Jing was moderately content to occupy himself by preparing a detailed report of their discoveries for the doctor in Forb, which he planned to send south by the first barq of spring.

It arrived, and like the one which had brought him and Drakh, it carried a sick passenger.

Leaving Rainbow to polish his final draft, Jing went to the wharf to see the barq come in. He was unprepared to hear a voice hail him in Ntahish.

"It is the Honorable Jing? Here am I, Ah-ni Qat!"

Supported by two youthful aides, a boy and a girl, a stooped yet familiar figure limped ashore. Jing said disbelievingly, "The son of my dear friend the Vizier?"

For he remembered Qat as a sprightly youth, and this personage looked so old and moved so slowly . . . and his skin was patched with ugly scars.

"Indeed, indeed! All winter I've struggled across this snowbound continent because at Forb I heard rumors concerning your whereabouts. I'd not have had the endurance to continue but that my father laid on me the duty of seeking you out and telling you: Ntah is no more!"

For an instant Jing stood frozen. Then he said uncertainly, "Young friend, you're sick. You're ruled by dreams."

"Would that I were," Qat whispered. "After your departure plague ran wild among us. Never were such horrors witnessed by a living eye! People died where they stood, their bodies fell into the lake and river until the water grew so foul the very fish were poisoned. Those who survived lost their reason and fled under the lash of horrid dreams. Most went south. I doubt they escaped like me and my companions. Our northern route must have saved us. It seems the plague loves heat."

"Your father—" Jing began.

"Died among the first. So did Lord Waw-Yint. There is no use in speaking of his heir. Ntah is a land of rotting carcasses, and all who used to live there have run away."

Qat's girl companion uttered a groan of misery. Jing said slowly, "We must find you quarters. The Count has treated me kindly, as has his daughter. You will be made welcome."

Surrounded by the high-piled parchments on which he was recording their discoveries, Jing sat blindly staring at the overcast sky. His mind was fuller of despair than ever in his life before; he wanted to renounce consciousness and retreat to dreams, where Ntah would last for all eternity and its glory never fade.

Behind him creepers rustled. A soft familiar voice said, "Is it true about your homeland?"

He did not turn. "Yes, Lady Rainbow. If Qat says so, he speaks the truth. I no longer have a home."

"You have made one here," she said. "By your kindness to me from the beginning, when first you told me I was not after all accursed; when you said you were surprised I had not found mates in spite of my misshapenness; when you opened my sight to a heaven full of so many stars it's absurd for any one of us petty beings to count on reading his or her fate up yonder—Oh, Jing!" Spreading her mantle, she embraced him as he made to rise. "You have caused me to love you, poor twisted creature that I am! Let me prove that you have a home wherever I am and for as long as I may live!"

She hesitated, and added in an altered voice, "That is, if you do not find me totally repulsive."

There was a moment of absolute stillness. Jing looked at her, and saw through her outward form, to the bright keen mind within. And his oath of celibacy was to lost Ntah...

They were both very clumsy, but they found it funny, and afterwards he was able to say, in full possession of his rational faculties, "But your father? He cares nothing for our work, and may despise me."

"He is sad and sick and this winter has shown him he

too can grow old. He has spoken much about over-close breeding, as one sees with canifangs, and has even mentioned the idea of a grandchild. Inwardly I think I may be normal, and most certainly you and I cannot be cousins to any degree. We shall find out. If not—so be it."

She refolded her mantle about her. Checking suddenly, she said, "Jing, if tomorrow you decide you never want to see me again—if you feel it was only misery which made you desire me—I shan't care, you know. You've given me such a gift as I never hoped for."

"And you," he said fondly, "have given me such courage as an hour ago I thought I'd never enjoy again."

"So you want my ill-starred daughter?" grunted the Count, when with difficulty his attendants had roused him from the mist of dreams in which he now passed most of his time. His ruptured tubules had been unable to heal, owing to his corpulence, and he slumped in his sitting-pit like a half-filled water-bladder. "Well, I always thought you were crazy and now you're proving it. Or have you scried something in the stars to show she's fitter than she looks? Wish you'd do the same for me!"

"I want her," Jing said firmly, "because she possesses a sharp mind, a keen wit and an affectionate nature."

"More than I could say of most of the women I've taken," the Count sighed. "Had I been gifted with a son... You want a grand celebration? You want mating-presents?" Suddenly he was suspicious.

"Nothing but your authority, Father, to continue our work together as mates as well as friends," said Rainbow.

"Hah! Work, you call it! Wonderful benefits it's brought us, all your gabble about stars the naked eye can't see—and the same goes for your people, Jing! Wiped out by plague, so they tell me! Still, you're of good stock, and maybe cross-breeds are what's been lacking in our lines. I'd rather believe too many cousins mated with cousins to keep control of the best homes and richest land, than that I was cursed by the Maker!"

"You are perfectly correct, sir. We too, after all, are animals."

"Hah! What animal could find more stars in the sky than the sacerdotes say were put there at the Beginning?

Oh, take her, and bring me a grandchild if you can. For myself, I'm beyond hope, And—" He hesitated.

"Yes, Father?" Rainbow prompted, taking his claw in hers.

"Dream of me as long as you can after I'm dead. Try not to let the dreams be ugly ones."

"Look, Jing!" Rainbow exclaimed as they left the Count's presence. "The skies are clearing! In a little we shall see the sun!"

But there were other matters to attend to. Qat was weak, and his servants in scarcely better shape. All of them bore plague-scars. Apparently the illness began with sacs of fluid under the skin, accompanied by fever and delirium. If they burst outward, the patient might survive, at the cost of being marked for life. If they burst inward, the victim died. Applying cleanlickers was useless; none could digest the foul matter exuded by the sores. Neither Jing nor Twig had heard of any disease remotely similar.

"Maybe this was what the New Star heralded!" said Qat in an access of bitterness.

"Were that so," Jing responded stonily, "would not I, the most dedicated seeker of its meaning, have been the first to be struck down?"

Thinking how pleased the sacerdotes would be to hear of such a notion.

By then it was midday, and the sun shone clear, albeit not very bright, being at this season close to the horizon. Rainbow was eager to get to the observatory, and Jing—reluctant though he was to abandon these three who might well be his last surviving compatriots—was on the point of consenting to accompany her, when Keepfire came hurrying with news that settled the matter.

"Sir, Scholar Twig is at the observatory with Shine, and they have shown me yet more marvels! Come at once!"

All else forgotten, they rushed in his wake.

"I was right!" Twig crowed. "I did see dark patches on the sun! Now Shine has seen them too!"

"It's true," Shine averred. He had stretched layers of furnimal membrane across branches of walbush so that one might look at the sun through them. Even so, long

staring with the tubed lenses had made his eye visibly
sore. "And something more, as well!"

"What?" Jing seized the tube.

"Look to right and left of the sun's disc, and you'll
notice little sparks! They're very faint, but I definitely
saw them. Perhaps they're distant stars, far beyond the
sun, which just happen to lie in that direction, but your
charts show that some of the brightest stars in that area
of sky must lie near the sun right now, and I can't see
any of *them*!"

Jing did not need to consult his maps to know what
stars were meant. Bracing himself on a stout branch, he
aligned the tube. At first his sight, after the low light-
levels of winter, would not adjust, and he saw only a blur.

"Too bright? I can add another membrane," Shine proposed.

"No, I'm getting a clearer view now..." Jing's ocular
muscles were adapting with painful speed. "And—oh,
that's incredible!"

What he saw was not a blank white disc. There were
three dark spots on it. How could that be?

"Do you see the bright sparks?" Shine demanded.

But his vision was overloaded. He stood back, relin-
quishing the tube, and for a long while was unable to make
out his immediate surroundings.

"I was right, wasn't I?" Twig exclaimed.

"Yes," Jing said soberly. "Yes, friend, you were right."

This too must be added to his report on their discoveries. And, given the delay caused by his grief, it could
not possibly be ready for the barq presently in harbor
here. At all costs, however, it must be sent by the next
one. He said so, and Twig objected, "But if we have to
take time to write up our findings—"

Jing cut him short. "Did we not pledge to share what
we learn with as many other folk as possible?"

"So we did," Twig admitted humbly.

"Well, then! Let's have a score, a score-of-scores, of
keen young eyes like Shine's at work on this! I want a
full account of our fantastic news in circulation during the
coming summer. Even without the resources of Ntah,
there must surely still be people on this continent who
will respond and imitate what we are doing—and some
of them, with luck, may do it *better*!"

Shine had reclaimed the lenses and was staring through them again. Now he gave a gasp.

"I see half of Sunbride!"

"What?" The others turned to him uncertainly.

"Half!" he repeated obstinately. "Tiny, but perfectly clear—half a disc, like half the moon, and as far from the sun as she ever wanders! Our conclusions must be true! They *must*!"

VIII

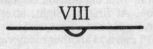

Parchments in one claw, pearlseed in the other, the steersman of the barq about to depart said, "So you want this delivered to your doctor friend in Forb, do you?"

Something about his tone made Jing react with alarm. He said, "The price is fair, surely! If you doubt the quality of the seed, come and see what a jeweltree the Count sprouted from one I gave him last fall. Even during the winter—"

"So you can still grow jeweltrees, can you? When your trencher-plants rot in the ground!"

It was true; with the return of warm weather, the blight which had affected last year's crop was spreading again, and trencher-plant was their staple diet.

"What does that have to do with—?" Jing began. The steersman cut him short.

"Your doctor had better be cleverer than most! We aren't going as far as Forb this trip. The Maker knows whether anyone will want to go there ever again!"

"What are you saying, man?" Jing advanced, clenching his claws.

"The plain truth! Some filthy plague spawned of the far south is rife in Forb, and a murrain is abroad among the livestock, and the very bravetrees are wilting! We've been here three days—how is it this is the first you've heard?"

"I've . . . uh . . . I've been preoccupied," Jing muttered.

"Dreamlost, more like it!" The steersman returned the parchments with a contemptuous gesture and—more reluctantly—the pearlseed too, adding, "You'll need this to pay for medicine, I've no doubt! If you yourself plan on returning to Forb, which I don't counsel!"

He turned away, shouting orders for his crew to pry loose the barq's tentacles and head down-channel.

"Sure we came by way of Forb," Qat husked. "I told you so. But we aren't sick any more, none of us. Maybe I'm still softer than I should be, but that's a matter of time."

"Yes—yes, of course," Jing muttered comfortingly. He nonetheless cast a worried glance at all three of them: Qat still limp enough to hobble rather than walk, and the boy and girl with their disfiguring scars. Not, according to rumor, that that had prevented their being taken up as curiosities by the younger members of the staff. When even the Count presently approved of outcrossing, and had let his own daughter choose a foreigner for her mate, it was the fashionable thing. Besides, the sacerdotes maintained that no plague could smite those who defied it boldly, so . . .

Their influence was rising again since news of Ntah's downfall. Was this not, they declared, perfect proof of the Maker's vengeance against those who defied His will? In any normal year, such a claim would have been laughed out of conscience; now, though, the blight on the trencherplants meant that many families were facing a hungry summer, and famine went claw-in-claw with madness, even when no plague exacerbated the victims' predicament.

Jing had witnessed, on his way hither from Ntah, how precarious was sanity among his folk—how a single year's crop-failure might entrain surrender to the tempting world of dreams. When he paid full attention to his imagination, he was chilled by the all-too-convincing prospects conjured up. The Count's illness was withdrawing one psychological prop from the minds of the people of the valley; it was certain that when he died some of his old rivals from Forb, or their descendants, would come to squabble over his legacy—that was, naturally, if they weren't caught by the plague already. Hunger and sickness might withdraw the others, and then...

Jing trembled at the threat the future held.

Yet his companions declined to worry, even about a means of getting their knowledge spread abroad. If this barq's crew refused to return to Forb, they said, another steersman could be found more susceptible to a handsome payment, more prepared to run risks. It was with some reluctance that they agreed to make extra copies of the parchments Jing had already drafted; Keepfire, of course, could not write, and Twig was constantly on call to administer medicine to the Count. Shine and Rainbow, however, did their best, and by the time the next barq arrived there were six copies of the report at least in summary outline—enough, with luck, for learned folk elsewhere to repeat their studies.

But they, and Jing too, would far rather have continued investigating the dark spots on the sun, and the bright nearby sparks which so far Shine alone had actually seen. Only their sworn pledge, Jing sometimes thought, made them obey his orders. How quickly they were defecting from their brief period of professed admiration!

Could it be because—?

He roused one morning from reverie with a firm and fixed dream-image in his mind, and it was shocking in its import. At once he rushed in search of Twig, and found him coming away from the Count's chamber with a grave expression.

Not waiting for an exchange of greetings, he said in a rush, "Twig, I believe the plague is at work among us!"

Twig gazed soberly at him. He said at length, "How did you know? I thought you said the disease was new to you, and you were unacquainted with its preliminary symptoms."

Jing tensed in horror. He said, "But I guessed it from a dream!"

"Then your weather-sense is far sharper than mine! Did you know the Count attempted to mate with the girl your friend brought here?"

"I'm not surprised, but—No, I didn't know!"

"It was futile, of course, but . . . Well, today he exhibits all the signs Qat said we should watch out for. I'm on my way to check out the other partners she and her brother have engaged with. Have you—? No, forgive me. I'm sure neither you nor Rainbow would consider the idea. But I must ask you a physician's question. Is the Lady Rainbow successfully in bud?"

Jing nodded. "We realized yesterday. Last night we went to the observatory, but there was a bright aurora, so we talked about the future. We're both afraid."

"Internally she's as sound as any woman," Twig assured him. "All the normal pressures are there; only her stance is distorted. But given that the Count, already weakened . . . Your weather-sense informs you of what I mean?"

"Even more. Even worse."

"Very likely." Twig hesitated. "Tell me: how did you decide the plague had got a grip here?"

"Because you in particular—forgive my bluntness—seemed to forget your enthusiasm for my leadership so quickly. A pledge is given with full rationality; dreams erode the recollection of it. I don't speak now of your duty to the Count, of course, but it was never my intention to prevent you serving him. It's a matter of priorities."

"You're right," Twig said after reflection. "In my present mood of calm, I see what you mean. Service to the whole world, which can be performed by spreading our knowledge, is more important than service to an old man whose life I can't prolong with all my skills. We must get those reports away at once, in all possible directions. I'd have realized this truth myself but that—yes, you guessed correctly: I'm being pestered by hideously persuasive dreams such as I haven't known since long before I came to Castle Thorn. And fever due to the onset of the plague would best explain that."

"I think I must believe the same," Jing muttered.

"Oh, no! You of all people! No, you must survive! It would be unbearable to think that the greatest discoverer of our age must be struck down randomly! Far better you should escape to tell the world your tale!"

"But I've kept company with Qat," Jing said stonily. "Out of nostalgia, I've spent half-days at a time talking with him and neglecting my own greater duty. Miraculously I believe Rainbow still to be unaffected. She and the child she buds must go away and take our reports.

Might I beg you to attend her before you continue with other matters?"

"Yes! Yes, certainly! But I must warn you that nothing I say or do can alter an established fact. She may already—"

"I know there's a risk. I want to diminish it. We'll buy the steersman of the next barq, give him all my pearlseeds so he can make for the great ocean and find one of the monster barqs that legend says can ply across it to another continent."

"Legend? You want to trust in legends now? Surely you must after all be afflicted!"

"I speak out of imagination rather than dream—though the two sometimes become so intermingled . . . Yes, I think there's no alternative. In one of the visions which haunted me this morning, I saw the bravetrees of Forb rotting from the base wherever a corpse had been deposited. What manner of sickness can attack trees as well as people?"

"A new kind," Twig said slowly.

"As new as the New Star?"

"Ah, but it was only a dream-guess!"

"I think we'll see the same when the first victims die at Castle Thorn."

Clenching his claws, Jing added as he turned away, "I wish with all my might it may just be a dream. But I fear it may well be correct imagining. The blight upon our trencher-plants, at any rate, is real enough."

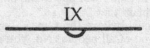

IX

When next they heaved the Count out of his sitting-pit to cleanse and salve him, there were the betraying sacs beneath his skin. And they were readily recognized, for a girl at one of the outlying villages who had partnered the boy from Ntah had died from their inward rupturing that very day.

Instantly the sacerdotes announced that this was the doom pronounced by the Maker against anyone who harbored heretics from foreign lands, and in the grip of the fever which preceded the visible outbreak of sores the peasants forgot what those same sacerdotes had been saying only days earlier about confronting the risk of plague with boldness. Keepfire managed to prevent his family and followers from being deluded; from one of the confusing visions that now beset him, part sane imagination and part lunatic dream, Jing almost extracted a clue concerning life below the massive layers of rock that sheltered Twig's laboratory, but it evaded him at last because he cared more about the survival of his wife and child.

For a little it seemed that Hedge and Bush were certain to escape, which would have dealt a logical blow to the sacerdotes' argument, especially since Twig's sole ulcer had burst outward and his cleanlickers proved able to deal with it. All three had been particularly close with Jing, and it was being claimed that associating with the Ntahans was the key to guilt and the Maker's punishment. But the day came when Bush succumbed, and admitted contact with the Ntahish girl, and a frenzy of hate exploded like one of the geysers that snowbelong-hunters reported far to the north.

"On the way to the observatory they set their canifangs at me," Rainbow said. "Only Sturdy's quickness with his prong prevented me from being badly hurt."

They sat in her bower, high in the castle and well defended, at a time when normally the night would be quiet but for distant icefaw screams and maybe a little music.

They all cast uncertain glances toward Sturdy. Were a trained prongsman to become delirious before he was restrained there could be considerable slaughter, especially when reflex due to killing had already been established in his mind. And killing canifangs was normally no part of an escort's duty.

Still, there were no marks to be seen on him.

"It's essential now for you to get away," Twig said to Rainbow. Her condition was barely perceptible, fortunately, owing to her lopsidedness. But her attendants could not be trusted to keep such a secret. Let the sacerdotes once get news of it, and they would no longer be confronting angry peasants, but a systematic series of clever attempts to frustrate the budding.

Jing drew a deep breath. "You don't yet know how essential," he said, and spread the right side of his mantle in a manner he would never normally do in anybody's presence except hers...but these were intimate friends.

"You too!" Twig blurted as he recognized what Jing was now revealing.

"It would appear," Jing said with all the detachment he could command, "that even those who make a good recovery, like Qat and his companions, still carry the plague with them."

"I'll kill him! I'll *kill* Qat!" Shine screamed, erupting to his full height. "He's going to deprive us of—"

"You will do no such thing," Jing decreed. It was strange, he reflected, how cold he felt, when he knew abstractly that he must be in the grip of fever. Just so long as he could continue to separate dream from reality..."You will hew to your oath. You will undertake the protection of Lady Rainbow and her bud and all the parchments on which we have copied details of what we have discovered. You will escort her away from Castle Thorn before the peasants storm it, which will doubtless be the day after they notice its bravetrees rotting where corpses have been consigned to feed the roots." This, with a meaningful glance at Twig. "I have no homeland. I have no future. I have used my life as it befitted me to do. You have sometimes appeared to look on me as a substitute for the imaginary Maker who so long ruled your life. I'm not a god. If there is one, He watches us but does not interfere. He speaks to us, perhaps, but if His voice is couched in the language of the stars it's up to us, not Him, to spell out the message...Oh, I ramble!"

"Not at all!" cried Shine. "You tell me what I most need to be told!"

"Believe it when I'm gone, and you'll do well," Jing said. Already he could feel the sac he had exposed starting to throb. "Now, take the future in trust. You here—you, Shine; you, Scholar Twig; you, Keepfire, who made us the tools to reveal unknown truth; you, my lady, who bear something of me which would otherwise be as hopelessly lost as Ntah itself—*all* of you must listen to my words and cherish what I say as proudly and as fiercely as when we took our oath. And by the way, Shine!"

Humbly the ex-sacerdote looked a question.

"Don't ever speak again of killing. Qat will die young; he was weakened anyhow by his suffering. Or if not, some crazy fool with a mindful of lunatic dreams will dispose of him. But this is neither justice nor vengeance. No, we must speak always and forever of life instead of death; we must fight the foolishness of dreams and concentrate on sanity. We must feed and shelter and educate our people, until the day dawns when we know how to conquer sickness and famine, blight and murrain. Then, and only then, shall we be fit to understand the message of the sky. Then, and only then, will the tools Keepfire created for us fall into the proper claws. And yours too, Twig, and mine—the star-charts created by my people . . . my *former* people."

He was briefly silent, and the pause was full of sorrow.

"But let nothing that has been well done go to waste!" he resumed at length. "Not that it can, if it's recorded in the stars . . . but we don't speak that language yet, and maybe it will be a long time before we do. Knowing now how many more stars there are than we believed, we must never be arrogant again! In all humility, going as it were in a mental crouch, we must patiently await the time when we are entitled to stand up to our full height, *and that height shall reach the stars to take them in our grasp like ripened fruit*! I say to you—"

At that moment he felt the sac under his mantle rupture.

Inward.

While they looked at him in wonder, for his peroration had been charged with the same power which persuaded them to join him in their common pledge, he said gently, "I am as good as dead, my friends. Tomorrow I shall surely be insane. I speak to you with the last vestige, the last shred, of what was Ayi-Huat Jing, court astrologer to His Most Puissant Majesty Lord Waw-Yint of Ntah, who set forth upon a journey longer than any of his nation previously, and must now die as my nation died. Dream of me. Make others dream of me. Or all my work will go for naught."

He added silently, "Would I had said that in my own speech. I could have expressed it so much better..."

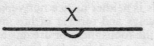

The day after the Count's death, another of the regular barqs came to the castle wharf. Her steersman was horrified to learn that the plague was here ahead of him, and was in mind to put about at once and risk her starving under him on the return trip. But Twig ceded him all the pearlseeds left in Jing's store—enough to buy the barq and her crew a score of times over—and he was reassured that at least this journey would not be as fruitless as he had feared. The peasants were in the grip of delirium; only the precarious loyalty of Sturdy and the other prongsmen kept them at bay while Rainbow and Shine, in obedience to Jing's order, scrambled on board with the precious parchments.

"But where shall we go?" the steersman cried. "Forb is rotting like a blighted fungus! I saw its bravetrees lean towards the river as though they had been snapped by gigants!"

"Any place the water carries you away from plague!" Twig retorted. "Do they not tell of folk who ply the ocean aboard barqs that make yours look like half-grown pups?"

"We'd have to chance the rapids of the Sheerdrop Range!"

"Then chance them, on a route you never dared before! It's better than the certainty of plague!" Rounding on the prongsmen, Twig ordered them to prod loose the barq's tentacles despite her groans of hunger.

"Won't you come with us?" Rainbow shouted. "Even if—"

"Your father's dead. Your husband told me he would rather you did not watch him follow the same course."

Twig descended to the wharf's edge and gently touched her claw. "No, Shine is to take care of you now. I've had my life, as Jing had his. If only we could read the stars more clearly, we might know why. But what you bear with you will instruct the future. You are the wife, my lady, of the greatest man it's been my privilege to know. Create a posterity for him. If the bud fails, then do so anyhow. I cannot; I'm old and weak and I must resign myself to facts."

"If by some miracle—"

"Qat has told us positively there are no miracles with this disease. Only if the sac ruptures to the outside like mine . . . and Jing's did not."

"Couldn't you have *made* it rupture?"

"That too was tried, in Ntah. It always failed."

The steersman was glancing nervously from one to other of them. He said, "If this woman has the plague-mark on her—"

"No, she does not!" Twig flared. "That's precisely why we want to get her out of here! You have pay for twenty voyages! Go as far as you can, go anywhere you can, and deliver our message to the world. Next time, perhaps, we may know enough about the universe to conquer such a plague! But without the information that you carry, someone else in the far future will have to start all over again! Oh, get under *way*, will you? The castle will be stormed within the day!"

The steersman flogged the barq's tentacles, and they unwillingly let go their grip; she put about and made down-channel. Watching, Keepfire—who had had the chance to travel with Rainbow, but refused because he feared the water more than fire—said, "Do you think, sir, that our work has gone to waste?"

"I sometimes fear it, sometimes think it can't," was Twig's reply. "Sometimes I feel it's like the seed funqi sow on the spring wind, so numerous that a few at least must find a lodging in good ground; sometimes I can imagine it being like a trencher-plant, at risk from unknown kinds of blight predicted or maybe not predicted by the New Star . . . At all events I know one thing. We are to consign the remains of Master Jing to your hot pool, instead of to a pool with fishes in or the roots of a tree."

Startled, Keepfire said, "This is to do more honor to me and my family? Sir, it's already been enough!"

"Not honor," Twig sighed. "He said when he still possessed some trace of rationality that he'd been told how hot pools can break up a dead animal. Did Hedge or Bush mention this, or was it you?"

"I think I did!" said Keepfire with a trace of pride.

"He wants to die more completely than anyone before, dissolved if possible into his finest shreds. He wants to leave a legacy of health and information, and not a rotting body to convey more plague. Come with me. He said he had chosen to die on the departure of his wife, and when we enter his chamber we shall find a corpse for sure."

"But we shall dream of him," said Keepfire, following. "We shall make sure he is dreamed of for all time."

PART TWO

FUSING
AND
REFUSING

I

After half a score of days the storm was over. Weather-sense and a familiar, reassuring noise lured Skilluck back from the dreamness whither he had been driven by exposure, privation and sheer terror. Slackening his mantle, he relaxed his death-grip on the pole he had clung to while he was reduced to primitive reflexes, concerned only to escape the fury of the elements as his ancestors might have hidden from a predator larger than themselves.

The sound he had recognized was the unmistakable munch-and-slurp of Tempestamer feeding.

Weak exultation filled him. Surely she was the finest briq ever to set forth from Ushere! He had pithed her personally with all the expertise at his command, leaving untouched by his prong nerves which other Wego captains customarily severed. At first his rivals had derided him; then, however, they saw how docile she was, and how fast she grew, and in the end came begging a share of his knowledge, whereupon it was his turn to scoff. Now she had proved herself beyond doubt, for she had defied the worst weather in living memory and—he looked about him—brought her crew to a safe haven, in a bay landlocked among low hills and sunlit under the first cloudless sky he had seen in years.

But where that haven was, the stars alone could tell.

With agony stabbing through his every tubule, he forced himself more or less upright, though it would be long before he regained his usual height, and uttered a silent blessing for his name. Those of his companions who had been called by opposites—Padrag and Crooclaw—had been lost overside on the third day of the storm. But the rest, better omened, were in view, though still unaware: the boy Wellearn, whose first voyage had come so near to being his last, and Sharprong, and Stronggrip, and Chaplain Blestar... Was the chaplain also alert? His voice could be heard mumbling, "Let each among us find his proper

star and there add brightness to the heavens in measure
with his merit in the world..."

But—no. His prayer was mere reflex. He was still lost
between dream and imagination. And in a bad way physically, too; his mantle was bloated and discolored, a sure
sign of cresh. The same was true of the others, and Skilluck himself.

For an instant the captain was afraid he might be
dreaming after all, that he was so near death he could no
longer distinguish reality from fantasy. But in a dream,
surely, he would seem restored to health.

His pain was receding, although the areas where he
had rubbed against the pole during the storm would remain sore for a long while. He forced himself to set out
on a tour of inspection. One piece of essential equipment
remained functional: the northfinder, tethered in its cage,
responded weakly to his order and uncoiled itself in the
correct direction. Also his precious spyglass had been so
tightly lashed to a crossbar, all the gales and waves had
not dislodged it. That apart, things looked grim. Most of
Tempestamer's drink-bladders had burst, the trencher-
plants had been so drenched with salt water they looked
unlikely to recover, the vines had been torn bodily away
leaving raw scars on the briq's hide, and—as he already
knew—their reserves of fish and pickled weed had been
used up.

He sipped a little water from an intact bladder, struggling to make plans. Food must come first, and more
water. Were there edible plants on this strange shore?
Was there any chance of trapping a game-animal? He
needed the spyglass to find out. But his claws felt weak
and clumsy, and the rope was swollen with wet; the knots
defied him.

A shadow fell across him. He glanced round, expecting
Sharprong or Strongrip. But it was young Wellearn who
had joined him, hobbling along at barely half his normal
height.

"Where are we, Captain?" he croaked.

"No idea, but I'd rather be here than in mid-ocean.
Take a drink—but slowly! Don't try and put all your fluid
back at one go, or you'll burst a tubule. Then help me
untie the spyglass."

Despite the warning, he had to stop Wellearn after several greedy gulps.

"There are three more of us, you know, and only three full bladders!"

Wellearn muttered an apology and turned his attention to the knots. After much difficulty they loosened, and Skilluck unwrapped the hide around the tube.

"Take drink to the others. But be careful. The state they're in, they may not know the difference between you and food. Or themselves, come to that. I guess you never saw anyone with cresh before, hm?"

"Is that what we've got?" Wellearn's eye widened in horror. "I heard about it, of course, but—well, what exactly is it?"

"Who knows? All I can say is, I've seen a lot of it at sea when our trencher-plants got salt-poisoned and our vines were blown away, same as now. Most people think it comes of trying to live off stale pickles. Makes you leak, drives you into dreamness, kills you in the end... Oh, curse the weight of this thing!" Skilluck abandoned his attempt to hold up the spyglass normally, and slumped forward in order to rest its end on the ridge of the briq's saddle. "I bet we'll be seeing cresh on land again one of these days, if the winters go on getting longer and harsher and seeds don't sprout and fish don't run... But you shouldn't worry too much about yourself. It always hits the biggest and strongest first and worst. Dole out a sip at a time and be specially wary of Blestar—he's delirious."

Carefully filling a gowshell from the drink-bladder in use, Wellearn heard him continue, mainly to himself: "Not a trencher-plant to be seen. Don't recognize a single one of those trees, don't spot a single animal. No sign of a stream unless there's one behind that cape..."

The boy shivered, wondering whether his own mantle was as patched with creshmarks as the others', and the captain was speaking only to reassure him. All things considered, though, he felt remarkably well after his ordeal: weak and giddy, of course, so that he wondered how he would fare if he had to leap clear of a cresh-crazed crewman; thirsty in every fiber of his being; and hungry to the point where he wished he could browse off floating weed like Tempestamer. Yet he was still capable of being excited about their arrival in this unknown region, and that was an excellent sign.

So Skilluck must be telling the truth. Sharprong, on the other claw, was almost too ill to swallow, and neither he nor Strongrip had the energy to attack a helper. Ironically, Blestar was worst off of them all, his mantle cobbled with irregular bulges as though it were trying to strain outward through a badly patterned net. He was talking to himself in a garbled blend of half a dozen learned idioms. Wellearn recognized them all; it was his quickness at language that had earned him a place among the crew. Their mission was to trade hides for food-plant seeds in the hope of cross-breeding hybrids which would grow very quickly during the ever-shortening northern summer. Many briqs this year had scattered on the same quest. If it failed, the Wego might have to move south en masse, and the hope of finding habitable but unpopulated lands was dreadfully slim. So there would be fighting, and the weakened northerners might lose, and that would be the end of a once-great folk. At best they might leave behind a legend, like Forb or Geys or Ntah...

Tormented by the sun, Blestar was reflexively opening his mantle as though to roll over and cool his torso by evaporation. Wellearn had never been in such a hot climate before, but he knew enough to resist the same temptation; in their dehydrated state it could be fatal. Anxiously he wondered how he could provide shade for the sick men, and concluded there was no alternative but to untie one of their precious remaining bales of hides. The outer layers were probably spoiled, anyway.

He contrived to rig two or three into an awning; then he distributed the rest of the fresh water and returned to the captain, dismayed to find him slumped in exhaustion.

But he was alert enough to say, "Good thinking, young'un. Give me a little more water, will you? Even holding up the spyglass has worn me out. And I don't see very clearly right now. We'll have to wait until Tempestamer has finished feeding and see if we can make her beach herself."

"Sharprong told me she hated that," Wellearn ventured.

"Oh, she does, and I'd never try it normally, of course. But that's our only hope; we've got to get ashore! Maybe while she's digesting she'll be tractable. Otherwise I'll have to pith another of her command nerves, and if I miss my mark because she bucks and bolts, then the stars alone know how we'll find our way home—Did you give water to the northfinder?"

"I didn't think of that!" Wellearn exclaimed, and hastened to remedy his oversight.

Returning, he looked at the ruptured drink-bladders, wondering whether any were likely to heal. But they were past that, hanging in salt-encrusted rags. In time Tempestamer would grow new ones, but it might be a score of days before they were full enough to tap. There was only one thing to be done.

"I'm going to swim ashore," he announced.

"You *have* got cresh! You'd never make it." Skilluck brushed something aside. A strange kind of winget had settled on him; others, all equally unknown, were exploring the briq, paying special attention to the scars left by the uprooted vines. It was to be hoped they were not in breeding phase, for the last thing Tempestamer needed right now was an infestation of maggors.

It occurred to Wellearn that in these foreign waters there might be creatures as hostile as the northern voraq, but Tempestamer showed no sign of being pestered by any such. He answered boldly, "There's no alternative! If I don't find water I can at least bring tree-sap, or fruit, or—or something."

"Then unlash a pole to help you float," Skilluck sighed. "And take a prong in case a waterbeast attacks you."

After that he seemed to lose interest in reality again.

The water was deliciously cool as Wellearn slid overside, but he was aware how dangerous salt could be to someone with a weakened integument, so he wasted no time in striking out for shore. His mantle moved reluctantly at first, but he pumped away with all his strength, and the distance to land shrank by a third, by half, by three-quarters...It was more than he could endure; he had to rest a little, gasping and clinging to the pole. To his horror, he almost at once realized he was being carried seaward again, by some unexpected current or the turn of the tide.

Although fatigue was loosening his grip on reality, he

resumed swimming. The sunlight reflected on the ripples hurt his eye, and salty splashes stung it; countless tubules cried pain at being forced to this effort without sufficient fluid in his system; fragments of dream and all-too-vivid imaginings distracted him. He wanted to rest again, relying on the pole, and knew he must not. At last he let it go, and the prong with it, for they were hindering too much.

After what felt like a lifetime, smooth rock slanted up to a little beach, and he crawled the rest of the way as clumsily as a new-budded child. Cursing his bravado, he forced himself across gritty sand that rasped his torso, and collapsed into the shade of bushes unlike any he had ever seen before. Some sort of animal screamed in alarm and branches fluttered as it fled; he could not tell what it was.

In a little, he promised himself, just as soon as he recovered his pressure, he would move on in search of water or a recognizable plant, or risk sampling something at hazard, or . . .

But he did not. After his exertions, cresh had him in its deadly grip, and he departed into a world of dreams compound of memory, so that the solid ground under him seemed to rock and toss like the ocean at the climax of the storm. He did not even have the energy to moan.

From the briq Skilluck saw him fall, and let go the spyglass with a curse, and likewise slumped to his full length. The pitiless sun beat down and, all unheeding, Tempestamer went on gulping weed to cram her monstrous maw.

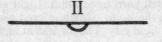

II

He was looking at himself.

Wellearn cried out. He had seen his reflection before, but only in still water, which meant he should be lying down on the bank of a pool. Every sense informed him he was in fact sitting up. Yet his image was confronting him. He was certain it must be confect of dreamness.

Suddenly it swerved aside and vanished. Struggling to accept he was not after all lost in sickness-spawned delirium, he discovered he was now seeing two people taller, slimmer, and with paler mantles than his own folk: a grave elderly man and a most attractive girl.

The former said something Wellearn did not quite grasp, though a tantalizing hint of meaning came across. Then, touching his mandibles with one claw, he said, "Shash!"

Imitating him, the girl said, "Embery!"

Clearly those were their names. Wellearn uttered his own, followed by greetings in his native speech. Meeting no reaction, he switched to others, and as soon as he tried Ancient Forbish Embery exclaimed in amazement.

"Why, you speak what we do!" she said, her accent strange but her words recognizable.

How then could Wellearn have failed to understand before? And now again, as she said something too rapid to follow?

"The language changes," Shash said slowly and clearly. "It has been a score-of-score years since our ancestors settled here. Use only the oldest forms. Wellearn, you comprehend?"

"Very well!"

"Do you remember your voyage hither?"

"The greater part of it." But where was here? Wellearn looked about him, realizing for the first time that he was in a noble house. Never had he seen such magnificent bravetrees—except they weren't exactly bravetrees—or such a marvelous array of secondary plants. Had he been hungry, which to his amazement he was not, he would at once have asked to sample the delicious-looking fruits and funqi which surrounded him. Light slanted through gaps between the boles, which offered glimpses of what looked like a great city. The air was at high pressure and very warm, though not so oppressive as when he swam ashore, and the scents borne on it were absolutely unfamiliar. But one matter must take precedence over the curiosity that filled him.

"My companions! Did you save them too?"

"Oh, yes. They are sicker than you, but we hope to cure them soon."

"But I had cresh..." Wellearn hesitated. In his people's knowledge there was no remedy for that affliction. Sometimes it went away of its own accord, no one knew why; more often its victims were permanently crippled.

"No longer. You saw for yourself. Where are the marks?"

"I saw," Wellearn agreed slowly. "But I didn't understand."

"Ah. Embery, show him again."

This time he was able to make out how it happened. She held up a large disc, very shiny, which gave back his reflection. Touching it diffidently, he discerned a peculiar coolness.

"Metal?" he ventured.

"Of course. But your people understand metal and glass, surely? We found a telescope on your briq, as good as our own."

"Captain Skilluck got it in trade," Wellearn muttered. "I can't say where it was made."

"Do you not know and use fire?" Shash demanded in surprise.

"Of course, but in our country there is little fuel and it's too precious to be used for melting rocks. Long ago the weather, they say, was warmer, but now in winter the sea freezes along our coasts, and then it's our only means of staying alive."

"Winter," Embery repeated thoughtfully. "That must be what we read about in the scriptures, the time of great cold which happens once a year and lasts many score days."

And yearly it grows longer...Wellearn suppressed a pang of envy. What a privilege to live in latitudes where winter never came! He had heard tales about such places from boastful old seafarers, but he had never expected to wind up in one on his maiden voyage.

Yet those same travelers always claimed that they found something grand in the country of their budding, something noble and challenging about its harsh landscape. He must not think of *worse* and *better* until he knew much more.

"May I see my companions?" he requested.

"Certainly, if you're fit enough," Shash answered. "Can you stand?"

Wellearn concentrated on forcing himself upright. He managed it, though he could not regain his normal height. Even had he done so, he would still have been overtopped by these strangers, who must be as tall as mythical Jing— or maybe not quite, for he was said to have been taller than anybody.

"Let me help you," Embery offered, moving to support him. Contact with her was very pleasant. He wondered what the local customs were concerning mating. The Wego themselves welcomed visitors in the hope that outcrossing would bring more and healthier children, for they were barely keeping up their numbers, and he had been told that many foreign peoples felt the same. But it was too soon to think of such matters.

In an adjacent bower Skilluck lay in a crotch made comfortable with masses of reddish purple mosh; he was still not alert but the creshmarks were fading from his mantle. Others beyond held Strongrip, Sharprong, and Blestar, who was visibly the worst affected.

"I've never seen such a severe case," sighed Shash. "One could almost imagine he had weakened himself deliberately."

Wellearn nearly admitted that in fact he had. It was the custom of chaplains, in face of danger, to fast in the hope of being sent a vision from the stars that would save them and their comrades. There was no recorded instance of it happening, but the habit endured.

These people, though, might have no faith in visions, and he did not wish them to mock the strangers who had

fallen among them. Instead he voiced a question that was
burning in his mind.

"What manner of place is this?"

"A healing-house," Shash replied, and added wonder-
ingly, "Do they not have such in your country?"

"A great house like this, solely for sick people? Oh,
no! We're lucky to have enough for those who are well.
Sometimes they die, and the occupants must take refuge
in caves, or pile up rocks for shelter . . . I'm amazed! When
we arrived in the bay, we thought this region was uninhabited!"

"Ah, you were the wrong side of the cape. People
rarely visit that bay except for glassmakers needing sand
or fisherfolk like the ones who spotted your briq."

"Tempestamer!" Wellearn clenched his claws. "What
of her?"

"We have small knowledge of matters of the sea, but
we have guarded against her wandering off by fixing strong
cables across the mouth of the bay. However, she's so
huge . . . Will it be long before she needs to feed again?
She's practically cleared the bay of weed."

"I'm afraid you'll have to ask the captain. Usually she
only feeds by night as she swims along, but she must have
been half-starved after the storm that drove us here."

"Hope then that the captain recovers shortly. We're
doing our utmost for him. Look, here come curers with
more creshban."

Wellearn turned in the indicated direction, but almost
literally while Shash was speaking, it grew dark. He
gasped. Then festoons of luminous creepers reacted, faster
than any gleamers he was used to, coming up to full brightness nearly before his vision adapted to the lower light-
level, and he saw two husky youths each bearing a round
object like an immense nut. There was a sudden pungent
smell, which reminded him of a taste that had haunted
his long period of dreamness. Also he recalled terrible
hunger, and having to be restrained for fear he might
attack those who were holding him . . . But that belonged
to the past, and in the present Shash was saying, "You
must continue the medicine for several days yet. Drink
some more now."

Wellearn complied. The nuts were hollow, and contained a bitter liquid of which he managed a few gulps.

"If we could only plant such nut-trees on a briq!" he muttered.

"It's not their natural juice," said the curer who had given him the drink. He spoke without Shash's deliberateness, but by this time Wellearn was adjusting to the local accent. "It's mixed with sap from half a score of plants."

Visions of saving the lives of countless future mariners bloomed and wilted in Wellearn's imagination. He said grumpily, "And I suppose not one of them grows in the north?"

"Later we can show them to you and let you find out," Shash promised. "But now I think you should return to rest."

"I couldn't! I'm too eager to see the marvels of your city, and meet more of its people!"

"In two or three days' time, perhaps. Not right away."

"May I not at least look out at the city, and question someone about it?"

"I'll oblige him, Father," Embery said, and added self-mockingly, "That is, if he can understand me."

"In my young days," Shash sighed, "people your age were wise enough to know when their elders were giving them advice for their own good...Oh, very well! But remember, both of you, that the workings of cresh are insidious, and over-excitement is as fast a route as any into dreamness!"

Embery guided Wellearn to the top of the highest tree in the house, which offered a clear view in all directions. The moon was down and the sky was clouding over in a way that upset his weather-sense, but he was too eager to worry about the risk of a lightning-strike. From here the outline of the city was picked out by glowing creepers and funqi, and he was shaken by its huge extent. It even marched over the crest of a hill inland, beyond which faint redness could be seen.

"That's where the fireworkers live," Embery explained. "They make glass and metal—they made the mirror you've seen. The area is sheltered, the wind almost always carries the smoke away from us, and it's easy to find fuel in that direction. They use vast quantities, you know. Some of their furnaces...But you have to see them."

Over and over she said the same, when describing the outlying farms, the giant nets which fish-hunters hurled by means of weights and long poles far out to sea from the nearby capes and islands, the work of those who bred mounts and draftimals—"like your briq," she added merrily, "only smaller and going on land!"—those who trained new houses to replace old ones or spread the city on fresh ground, and more and more until Wellearn could scarcely contain himself. How desperately he wanted to explore every nook of—

"I haven't asked your city's name!" he exclaimed.

"Hearthome."

It was apt. "How many people live here, do you know?" he pursued, thinking perhaps not a great number, if each of five sick strangers could be allotted a separate bower, and then yes a great number, if so many extra houses had been sown.

"Nine score-of-scores, I think, though some say ten."

It was unbelievable. The Wego numbered perhaps a fifth as many. Oh, this *must* be a better land to live in!

"But there are far larger cities inland and all along the coast," Embery said. "Many have a score-of-score-of-scores. None is as rich as Hearthome, though."

"Why is that?"

"Because we are the folk who work hardest at discovering new things. Travelers from a moonlong's journey away come to learn from people like my father, and my uncle who lives yonder"—she pointed in a direction diametrically opposite the furnace-glow—"and devotes his time to studying the stars."

Among Wellearn's people the stars were of little save religious interest. During his entire life at home he had seen a clear sky so seldom he could almost count the total. Before the adoption of the northfinder—a creature which, properly pithed, would always seek out the pole—it was said mariners had been guided by the stars on outward voyages. The return, of course, was never a problem; briqs like Tempestamer could be relied on to retrace their course. Though after such a tremendous storm even she...

Dismissing such gloomy thoughts, albeit making a firm

resolution to utter thanks, just in case, to the ancestors who—according to the chaplains—must have been watching over him during the voyage, he made shift to repeat a traditional Forbish compliment which Blestar had taught him when he was first apprenticed to the trade of interpreter, and of which mention of the stars reminded him.

"Ah!" he said. "Starbeams must shine on Hearthome even when the sky is cloudy!"

"Why not?" Embery returned. "After all, we are honest followers of Jing."

Wellearn drew back, startled.

"But he was only a legend! Tales about him are compound of dreamstuff!"

"Oh, no!" She sounded scandalized. "True, there is a great dream in his scriptures, but even that is in perfect accord with reality. Have you never studied his teaching?"

At the same moment thunder rolled, but it was not the shock to his weather-sense which made Wellearn's mind reel.

"Your father was right after all about my need for rest," he husked. "Kindly lead me back to my bower."

Where he spent long lonely hours wondering what—after teaching and believing all his life that tales about folk who conjured secrets from the stars were mere superstition—Blestar was going to say when he discovered himself in a land where Jing was real.

III

Skilluck's shattered mind crawled back together out of pits of madness and he could see a figure that he recognized. It was Wellearn, addressing him anxiously: "Captain, you're alert again, aren't you?"

Beyond him, unfamiliar plants hanging on what were not exactly bravetrees, immensely tall strangers whose mantles were astonishingly pale . . . They coalesced into a reality, and he was himself and whole and able to reply.

"Tell me where we are, and how Tempestamer is, and how these people treat us."

He was proud of being able to phrase that so soon after regaining normal awareness.

Wellearn complied, but half the time he was almost babbling, plainly having been cozened by the wonders of his first foreign landfall. Skilluck was a mite more cynical; he had spent half his life traveling, and more often than not he had been cheated by the outlanders he tried to deal with. The harsh existence led in northern lands was no school for subtleties of the kind practiced by those who dwelt in southern luxury . . . and it had been obvious, when Tempestamer came to harbor, that she had been driven further than any of the Wego had wandered before, perhaps to the equator itself.

So he merely registered, without reacting to, most of what Wellearn said, until a snatch of it seized his interest.

"—and they have a certain cure for cresh!"

At once Skilluck was totally attentive. Cautiously he said, "It works on everybody, without fail?"

Mantle-crumpled, Wellearn admitted, "Not on all. Blestar, they say, may well not survive. But for me and you, Sharprong and Strongrip, it's proved its worth!"

"Do they understand what we're saying to each other?"

"N-no! And that's something else amazing!" Wellearn blurted. "I have to speak to them in Ancient Forbish!"

Skilluck was unimpressed. His explorations had often brought him to places where relics of that once wide-spread speech survived. Blestar even maintained that many Forbish words had found their way into Wegan, but since they all had to do with fire and stars—things everybody knew about, but in which the chaplains claimed a special interest—sensible people dismissed such notions as mere religious propaganda. Wego seafarers took chaplains along much as they carried pickles: just in case. The best trips were those where they weren't needed.

Of course, their services as interpreters . . .

He forced himself to sound very polite when next he spoke to Wellearn.

"It seems we should behave to our hosts in the friendliest possible fashion. I guess at something we might do for their benefit. How goes it with Tempestamer?"

"That's what I'd just been asked to tell you! She has grazed the bay where we landed clean of weed, and the cables they've strung across its mouth won't hold her much longer, and they fear for their inshore fishing-grounds."

"Let the cables hold but one more day, and I'll put her to sea and feed her such a mawful as will content her for a week. And I'll come back, never fear. A cure for cresh—now that's something worth making a storm-tossed voyage for!"

"There's more," Wellearn said after a pause.

"So tell me about it! Anything we can trade for, I want to hear!"

"I'm not sure it's the sort of thing one can trade," Wellearn said. "But...Well, these people have shown me Jing's original scriptures. Or not exactly the originals, which might rot, but accurate copies. And they tell about how the stars are fire and our world will one day go for fuel to make the sun brighter and ourselves with it unless we—"

Skilluck had heard enough. He said as kindly as he could, "Boy, your brush with cresh has affected your perceptions. I counsel you to concentrate on growing up. A little worldly wisdom would do wonders for you."

Wellearn bridled. "Captain, do you know Forbish?"

"I've never taken lessons, if that's what you mean!"

"I have! And the documents I've been shown while you were lying sick have satisfied me that Jing was real!"

Worse and worse...Skilluck forced himself to an upright position. He said as emphatically as he could, "Since you oblige me to prove that our people are not all crazy, tell our hosts that I shall at once reclaim command of Tempestamer!"

"But you're not fit!"

"Let me be the judge of that!" Skilluck was struggling to bring his pads under control. "I must—"

But his pressure failed him. He was compelled to slump back to a sitting position, whence he glared at Wellearn as though it were the boy's fault he was so weak.

There was a rapid exchange in Forbish, and Wellearn stated authoritatively, "Shash is the curer-in-chief here.

He says you must drink creshban for at least another day before you leave this healing-house."

With a trace of mischief in his tone, he added, "I didn't tell him that was how long you already estimated would be necessary."

At home, mocking his briq-captain in that way would have led to punishment—perhaps lasting punishment, such as having one of his tubules punctured where it would never heal. Since arrival here, though, Wellearn had regretted his oath of fealty, and decided that if all else failed, he could put himself under the protection of the Hearthomers. What did he have to look forward to if he went back to Ushere? More and more hunger, more and more misery! He had never seen cresh on land, as he had told Skilluck, but he had seen old folk lose their minds, reduced to such a state that they scarcely reacted except when they were fed like hoverchicks or barqlings, or when some young'un was brought to them to be mated because a wise'un claimed there was still virtue in that line despite appearances. It had been happening to Wellearn since it became obvious that he was among the lucky bright few, and there were no memories so revolting in his short life as those which reminded him of the foul mindless gropings he had undergone with starvation-crazy ancients. Not one—praise the stars!—of his encounters had so far led to offspring, but if he went home he would certainly be compelled to do the same again, and once the smell and touch took over...

He shuddered. And wondered much about the nature of the stars which could dictate so cruel a doom for a person as well intentioned as himself, then pay him back— for it seemed to him to be a reward—with the gentle sweetness of Embery. She had received him twice already, and her father thoroughly approved, for as he said, "We too in this delicious land are plagued by forces we don't understand, and it has been nearly a score of years since one of our family bred true: myself with the lady who gave me Embery and died."

What, on the other claw, they did understand had not yet ceased to astonish him.

Leaving Skilluck's bower, he was overcome by memory.

...Behind the inland hills, a valley lined with smoke-blackened rock; heaps of charcoal, even blacker, surrounding cone-shaped furnaces; piles of sand and unknown minerals, green and brown and white and red; sober folk all of whose names ended in -fire, claiming spiritual if not physical descent from Jing's legendary friend who lived underground yet brought the light of heaven forth from a cave—Wellearn knew all the stories, for he had been told them as a child, but later he had been taught to think them fabulous, whereas the Hearthomers took them literally, and by their guidance produced incredible ingots of metal and unbelievable quantities of pure glass. Beyond, a desolation as complete as though a hurricane had laid the vegetation low for a day's walk or more, which was being systematically replanted with oilsap trees that grew quickly and burned hotter than even the best charcoal.

...In a fine house overlooking the sea, an elderly couple possessed of tiny miracles in the shape of roundels of glass no larger than a raindrop, but perfectly shaped, through which they showed him the secret structure of plant-stems, funqi, his own skin, immensely magnified, as though a telescope were to look down to the small instead of upward to the large.

...In a grove just outside the city, folk who selectively bred meatimals, burrowers, diggets, mounts, draftimals, and a score of creatures he could put no name to, seeking to make them fatter or more docile or in some other way more useful. Their cleanlickers were said to be unique, capable of ridding any wound of its poison within days and making a swift recovery. To take a few of those home to the lands where so often a daring fish-hunter died for his temerity in defying a rasper or a voraq: that would be an achievement! But what to trade for breeding-stock? Did Embery know about northfinders? It seemed not; alas, though, Tempestamer carried only one, which wasn't in brood-phase this year. Besides, they seldom bred true, a problem that plagued the Hearthomer animal-breeders too.

...On the highest of the nearby hills, the one Embery had pointed to from the crown of the healing-house, her uncle Chard—older and fatter than his brother—complaining about the difficulty nowadays of studying the stars because the sky was cloudy so much more often than in his youth, and boasting about the knowledge of ice which he had acquired only a few days' journey from Hearthome. There was, apparently, a range of mountains whose peaks were snowcapped even in these latitudes, a fact which dismayed Wellearn, for if the mountains were closer to the sun, how could they be so much colder than the land below? Surrounded by telescopes which made Skilluck's look like a toy, Chard launched into a lengthy lecture concerning reflectivity and absorption, conduction and convection, aurorae and shooting stars and a score of other concepts which Wellearn failed to grasp but which filled him with tantalizing excitement: so much knowledge, so much to be found out!

. . . In a giant tree at the heart of the city, hollowed out deliberately and ornamented with the finest and handsomest secondary plants, a glass container sealed with wax, through which could be glimpsed the original of Jing's scripture. It was uncapped only once in a score of years, so that a fresh copy might be made, but even so it was starting to rot, and next time they planned to make two copies, of which one would be incised on rock instead of perishable wood. In any case, though, by this time the Hearthomers had added many new discoveries to those of Jing and Twig. Everything he was told fascinated Wellearn, and above all he was seized by the tales of the New Star which Chard and Shash and Embery recounted. And, over and over, he pondered the central teaching of Jing's followers: that the stars were fire, and one day the planets would go to feed them, as charcoal was added to a furnace, to make them blaze up anew.

"We do not believe," Embery told him soberly, "that we are here solely to endure until the world falls into a dying sun. We believe it is our duty to escape that fate. Out there are countless worlds; until the end of time, some will remain for us to live on."

"But how can one travel there?" was Wellearn's natural riposte.

"We don't know yet. We mean to find that out."

Everywhere he went Wellearn had a sense of being watched and weighed and scrutinized. Until the captain regained his health, he was the Wego's sole ambassador; he did his best to behave accordingly.

And the day after Skilluck took Tempestamer to sea and brought her back content with what she had engulfed in open water, he found out that his conduct had impressed the citizens. For Shash came to tell the strangers they were invited to a gathering of the general council, to discuss a mutually advantageous proposition.

"What they mean," was Skilluck's cynical comment, "is that they've figured out a way to rob us blind. Well, we have to go along with the deal; we have no choice."

Wellearn bit back his urge to contradict. Time would tell.

IV

"It grieves us all to learn of the death of our visitor Blestar," Chard said to the assembled council. The foreigners dipped in acknowledgment, although Strongrip and Sharprong were reluctant and only a glare from Skilluck compelled them. Wellearn was still recovering from the shock of having to conduct his first-ever funeral, and in a far-off land at that. But the ceremony had been decent and respectful, even though the Wego tradition of committal to the ocean was unknown here, so Blestar's corpse was fertilizing a stand of white shrubs.

Now it was his duty to interpret some of the most complex statements he had ever heard in any speech. Chard and Shash had given him a rough idea in advance; nonetheless . . . !

Still—he brightened—none of the others spoke Forbish, let alone this modern descendant of it, although he had the distinct impression that Skilluck often understood more than he let on.

At all events, he had the chance to trim the list of the debate. He was determined to do so. He wanted his people and the Hearthomers to be friends; he wanted, in particular, to spend the rest of his own life here . . . not that he would dare risk admitting it. What he hoped was to be appointed resident agent for the Wego, and oversee a regular trade between north and south. So many benefits would flow from that!

But he must concentrate, not rhapsodize. The discussion was likely to be a long one. The Hearthomers took refuge from the hottest part of the day, but the assembly had gathered in late afternoon, and might well continue throughout the succeeding night. He composed his mind and relayed Chard's next remarks.

"We have been told that winters grow colder and longer in your land. Since according to our observations the sun is growing brighter and hotter, we are faced with a paradox."

("What in the world is he on about?" grunted Sharprong. "It doesn't make sense!")

But Wellearn was gripped by Chard's statement and anxiously awaiting what was to follow.

"We know this because we have carefully calibrated the way in which certain substances change after exposure to concentrated sunlight under identical conditions, that's to say, on a completely clear day. Cloudless days, of course, are growing fewer"—and several present glanced anxiously at the sky where yet more thunderheads were brewing—"but we keep up our experiments and we can be nineteen-twentieths sure of our conclusions."

("Is he ever going to come to a point?" was Strongrip's acid reaction.)

"We can only deduce that more solar heat causes more clouds to reflect it and more moisture to fall at the poles as snow, which in turn reflects still more light and heat. At my laboratory the possibility can be demonstrated using a burning-glass and a block of white rock half-covered with soot."

Wellearn had seen that demonstration; he had not wholly understood what he was meant to learn from it, but suddenly a blinding insight dawned on his mind.

("Come on, boy!" Skilluck rasped. "You're falling behind!")

"At a time when mountains here in the equatorial zone can remain snowcapped throughout the year, this is clearly a worrisome situation. Those among us who have never experienced ice and snow may doubt what I say, but I have felt how cold can numb the pads, seen how it affects the plants we here take for granted!"

("Why does he have to go *on* so?" growled Strongrip, but Skilluck silenced him with a glare.)

"We must therefore anticipate a time when mariners from the far north will arrive, not driven hither by a fortunate storm, but because their home has become uninhabitable. Yet this need not be an unmitigated disaster. For if there is one thing we lack, then... But I'll leave the rest to Burney."

("I've been told about him!" Wellearn whispered in high excitement. "He's the one-who-answers-questions, their most distinguished administrator! But I never saw him before!")

Burly, yet as tall as his compatriots, Burney expanded to full height as Chard lowered. He uttered a few platitudes about the visitors before picking up Chard's trail.

("I know his sort," Skilluck said contemptuously. "The politer they are, the more you need to brace yourself!")

"What we lack, and in lacking neglect our duty, is access to the oceans!" Burney stated at the top of his resonant voice. "Oh, we've done well by our founders in spreading their teaching across this continent; travel a moonlong overland and you won't find a child of talking age who doesn't grasp at least the rudiments of what Jing bequeathed! But we know there's more to the globe than merely land, don't we? Proof of the fact is that our visitors came to us from a country which can't be reached from here dry-padded!"

("You told them that?" Skilluck snapped at Wellearn. "Oh you threw away a keen prong there!")

("I did nothing of the sort!" Wellearn retorted, stung. "Listen and you'll find out!")

"Suppose, though, we were to combine the knowledge we've garnered with the skills of these strangers," Burney went on. "Suppose the brave seafarers of the Wego could voyage free from fear of cresh; suppose on every trip they carried the knowledge which Jing instructed us to share with everybody everywhere, so that every one of their briqs was equipped not just with a northfinder—I'm sure you've been told of their brilliant development of that creature which can always be relied on to point the same way? Though it does seem," he added with a touch of condescension, "they don't realize that if they really had crossed the equator, as Wellearn appears to imagine, it would reverse itself."

(Amid a ripple of knowing amusement Skilluck fumed, "It doesn't surprise me! After the flattery, the put-down!")

Burney quieted the crowd. "Perhaps that remark was unworthy," he resumed. "At all events, we know these are an adventurous people, who take the utmost care to ensure that when they set out on no matter how risky a voyage they can find their way home by óne means or another. Suppose, as I was about to say, they carried not only telescopes useful for sighting a promising landfall, but better ones suitable for studying the sky, and the means to prove to anyone they contacted how right Jing was in what he wrote!"

(Applause... but Wellearn had to cede a point to Skilluck when he mused, "So they want to overload our briqs with chaplains worse than Blestar?")

"We therefore offer an exchange!" Burney roared. "I hope Captain Skilluck will accept it! We will share with his folk everything we know—yes, everything!—if the Wego will put their fleet at our disposal every summer for a score of years, to return laden with southern foods and southern seeds and southern tools, after carrying our message to lands as yet unknown! Now this is a grand scheme"—his voice dropped—"and there are countless details to thrash out. But we must first know whether the principle is acceptable."

(Skilluck looked worried. Wellearn whispered, "They do things differently here!"

("That's obvious! *He* never tried to preside at a captains' meeting!")

"I see there are doubts," Burney said after a pause. "Let me add óne thing, therefore. Assuming they accept our offer, then—if the winters at Ushere do become intolerable, as we may apparently fear according to what Chard has said—their people can remove hither and settle around the bay where their briq first made landfall. We would welcome them. Are we agreed?"

A roar of enthusiasm went up, and among those who shouted loudest Wellearn was proud to notice Embery. But Skilluck gave a brusque order.

"Tell him we need time to discuss this idea. Say we will be ready no sooner than tomorrow night!"

Perforce, Wellearn translated, and the assembly dispersed with many sighs.

"It's a trap," said Strongrip for the latest of a score of times. "There must be some snag in it we don't see!"

"I've been everywhere in the city and met many of the most prominent of these people!" Wellearn declared. "They take Jing's teaching seriously—they really do want to spread his knowledge around the globe!"

"That's what frightens me most," grunted Skilluck. "Blestar was bad enough; embriqing with a stranger who has absolute rule over what course I choose is out of the question!"

"That isn't what they have in mind!" Wellearn argued. "These people never travel the oceans—they want to hook on to someone who does, and that could be us!"

"Budlings!" Strongrip said, and turned away in disgust.

That was too much for Wellearn. Rising to his maximum height—which, since arriving here, imbibing vast quantities of creshban, and eating the best diet he had ever enjoyed, had noticeably increased—he blasted, "I invoke the judgment of my ancestors in the stars!"

And bared his mandibles, which normally he kept shrouded out of ordinary politeness.

Skilluck said hastily, "Now just a moment, boy—"

"Boy?" Wellearn cut in. "Boy? I haven't forgotten my oath of fealty to my captain, but if you can't recognize a man who's just become a man I'll consider it void!"

Following which he opened his claws to full extent, and waited, recklessly exuding combat-stink.

At long last Skilluck said heavily, "It was time, I guess. You're not a young'un anymore. But do you still want to challenge Strongrip?"

"I'd rather we were comrades. But I must. Unless he accepts me for what I am, with all my power of judgment. I did," Wellearn added, "invoke the honor of my ancestors."

There were still creshmarks on Strongrip's mantle, but Wellearn's was clear. Skilluck studied each of them in turn and said finally, "I forbid the challenge. Your ancestors, *young man*, are honored sufficiently by your willingness to utter it. Strongrip, deny what you last said."

He clenched his body into battle posture, mandibles exposed, and concluded, "Or it must be me, not Wellearn, you take on!"

The stench of aggression which had filled the air since Wellearn rose to overtop his opponent provoked reflexes beyond most people's control. Only someone as sober and weather-wise as Skilluck could master his response to it.

Strongrip said gruffly, "He speaks this foreign noise. I admit he knows things I can't."

"Well said, but is he adult, worthy to be our comrade?"

The answer was grumpy and belated, but it came: "I guess so!"

"Then lock claws!"

And evening breeze carried the combat-stink away.

"Captain!" Wellearn whispered as the general council of the Hearthomers reassembled.

"Yes?"

"Did you know I was going to be driven to challenge—"

"Silence, or I'll call you 'boy' again!" But Skilluck was curling with amusement even as he uttered the harsh words. "You haven't finished growing up, you know!"

"I'm doing my best!"

"I noticed. That's why I didn't let Strongrip shred your mantle. He could have, creshmarks or no! So you just bear in mind your talent is for reasoning, not fighting. Leave that sort of thing to us seafarers, because at pith you're a landlubber, aren't you?"

"I—I suppose I am," Wellearn confessed.

"Very well, then. We understand each other. Now translate this. It's exactly what Burney most wants to hear. Begin: 'We can't of course speak for all the briqcaptains of the Wego, but we will promote with maximum goodwill the advantages of the agreement you suggest, *provided* that at the end of summer we may take home with us tokens of what benefits may accrue therefrom, such as creshban, better cleanlickers, useful food-seeds, spyglasses and so on. Next spring we'll return with our captains' joint verdict. In the event that it's favorable'—

don't look so smug or I'll pray the stars to curse you for
being smarter than I thought but not half as smart as you
think you are!—'we shall appoint Wellearn to reside here
as our agent and spokesman. Thank you!'"

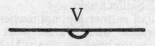

V

At every summer's end the Wego captains came together for a bragmeet where the wise'uns too old to put
to sea might judge whose briq had ventured furthest, who
fetched the finest load of fish ashore, who brought the
rarest newest goods traded with chance-met strangers. It
was the high point not only of their year, but the chaplains'
also. For generations the latter's influence had been
shrinking, particularly since too many stars fell from the
sky for most people to look forward to inhabiting one
after death. But when it came to matters of ancient tradition, naturally they were called on to preside.

This meet, though, was different. Now there was no
boasting, only mourning. On land things had been bad
enough, what with crop-failure, floods and landslips, but
at sea they were infinitely worse. Braverrant had not returned albeit her master was Boldare, wily in weather-
ways. No more had Governature with Gallantrue and Dry-
mantle, nor—next most envied after Tempestamer—
Stormock, whose commander had been Cleverule, sole
among them to make two-score voyages.

Nor Wavictor, nor Knowater, nor Billowise . . . and even
Tempestamer herself had not reported back.

Yet weather-sense warned them: the summer was done.
The customary congress must convene.

Frost on every tree, snow on the beach above the tide-
line, even icefloes—but it was too soon! As Tempestamer
closed the last day's gap between her and the waters
where she had been broken, uncertainly as though aware

something was amiss, Wellearn gazed in horror at the
shoreline through drifting mist.

"Captain!" he cried. "Have you ever seen so much ice
at this season, or so much fog?"

"Never," answered Skilluck sternly. "Maybe what your
friends at Hearthome spoke of is coming true."

"I thought—*our* friends . . . ?"

"Those who have knowledge sometimes batten on it
to gain power," Skilluck said.

"They spoke of partnership, not mastery!"

"What difference, when we are weak and they are
strong? Count me the briqs you see at Ushere wharf and
argue then!"

Indeed, the fleet numbered half its usual total, and the
houses were white with rime and some were tilted owing
to landslips, and the sky was dense and gray and the wind
bit chill into the inmost tubules of those who lately had
enjoyed the warmth of Hearthome.

"What's more, there's nobody to welcome us!" Skilluck blasted, having surveyed the city with his spyglass.
"They must have called the bragmeet, giving us up for
lost!"

Seizing his goad, he forced Tempestamer to give of
her utmost on the final stretch towards her mooring.

Shivering in the branchways, more of the Wego attended the bragmeet than ever in history, and while the
wise'uns tried to present the summer's achievements in
a flattering light, kept interrupting to ask, "What use is
that to us? Can we eat it? Does it help to keep us warm?"

In vain the senior chaplain, by name Knowelkin, strove
to maintain formality. The folk mocked the claims of those
who had survived the unprecedented summer storms by
staying close to home, like Senshower whose Riskall had
belied her name by scurrying from inlet to sheltered inlet,
like Conqueright who had pledged the reputation of his
Catchordes on the chance of garnering vast quantities of
fish only to find the schools weren't running where they
did. Almost as though they were hungry for news of doom
the assembly listened in silence to Toughide and Shrewdesign, who told of icebergs sighted all season long further
south than ever known before, fisherfolk driven into mid-
ocean clinging to barqs unfit for any but fresh-water work,

great trees torn loose by gales and set to drifting with the current, some bearing signs of habitation as though they had formed part of a house, a town or even a city. And when eventually they did make landfall, they reported, they found long tracts of coast abandoned to the dirq and fosq, the icefaw and snowbelong, whose normal range was half-a-score days' journey poleward.

"What we brought home from our voyage," Toughide concluded soberly, "was no better than what we'd have got had we made due north."

The company shifted uneasily, but the chaplains preened. Now the meeting had settled down, they could remind themselves how hunger and anxiety invariably drove folk back to the faith and customs of their ancestors.

But suddenly a roar cut through the soughing of icy wind among the boughs.

"Who *dared* to summon a bragmeet without Skilluck? What misbudded moron told you Tempestamer would not ride out the worst of storms? Let him stand forth who called the meet before I came!"

And the furious captain stomped into the center of the gathering, healthy-tall—taller than any Wego mariner in living memory—followed by Strongrip and Sharprong and someone whom the company had difficulty in recognizing: Wellearn. But a Wellearn transformed, bigger, huskier, and infinitely more self-confident than the callow youth who had set forth in spring.

Knowelkin shrank reflexively at Skilluck's intrusion, all the more because he and his companions were so obviously in good fettle. The captain fixed him with a glare.

"You!" he said accusingly. "*You* took it on yourself to say I must be given up for lost!"

"Not I!" the chaplain babbled, casting around for a way of escape, for combat-stink from Skilluck filled the air and he was weakened by fasting.

"Liar!" hurled Toughide. "You insisted on the meet being held when we captains said to wait a while! You understand the calendar—you know the normal end of summer!"

"But summer this year ended early! Surely a skilled seafarer—"

"We've been in latitudes where there is no winter!" Wellearn shouted.

"That's right!" Skilluck set himself back on his pads, claws poised. "Nor any hunger, either! Look at us! Think we're sick—weak—crazy—dreamlost? See any cresh-marks on us? But I see one on you!" Reaching out quicker than Knowelkin could dodge, he nipped the chaplain's mantle and provoked a squeal of pain.

"Thought so," the captain said with satisfaction. "Always the way, isn't it? When things get hard, instead of reasoning and working, you prefer to retreat into dreamness! Strongrip, make him drink a dose of creshban and see sense!"

"Best thing any briq from Ushere ever carried home," the seaman grunted, holding aloft a Hearthomer nutshell. "A certain remedy for cresh!"

That provoked a stir of excitement among the crowd.

"But," Strongrip continued, "do you think we should waste it on this idiot? After all, he's been starving himself like Blestar—deliberately—and Blestar was the only one of us it didn't save!"

"That's a point," said Skilluck ruminatively. "Very well, let them be the ones to go without. It'd be a fit punishment for the way they've insulted us."

"You have a cure for cresh?" Knowelkin whispered, voicing what all present wanted to hear.

"Not we, but allies that we've made in the far south. They've offered us as much as we need—they have plenty!—in return for letting some of their wise'uns travel on our briqs to spread their knowledge. And don't think creshban is the only trick they have under their mantles! *Oh* no! We've brought back marvels which ... But move over, you! Senior chaplain or not, you're a dreamsick fool and it's your own fault and Wellearn is worth a score like you! *Move*, before I rip your mantle into tatters!"

For an instant it seemed that Knowelkin would defy the captain out of pride; then he humbly crumpled to half normal height and padded aside. Wellearn found himself at a loss. Was he really meant to take over and preside at a bragmeet, youth that he was?

"Well, go on!" Skilluck rasped. "Or I'll start thinking you're as silly as Knowelkin! Speak out!"

"What shall I tell them?"

"Everything! Everything! I never imagined things would come to so grievous a pass this year. Next year maybe, or the year after... but it's upon us, and the land is in the claw of ice, and if another summer comes it could be our last chance to move to friendly country. The briqs which survive may already not be enough to shift us all! Hadn't you thought of that?"

Wellearn hadn't, but he pretended, and gave a grave nod of acquiescence as he took over the spot vacated by Knowelkin. After so long among the Hearthomers he felt like a giant compared to his own people... as tall as Jing!

And that gave him his opening. Maintaining his maximum height, trying to imitate in Wegan the style and manner of Burney and others who addressed council meetings at Hearthome, he began.

"Teachers like Knowelkin—and even my late mentor Blestar who has gone, let's hope, to make a star shine brighter!—told us to believe there never was a real person called Jing! They've encouraged us to be obedient and small-minded by saying there never was a man who understood the stars and made their nature manifest by transforming dull rock into marvelous new substances! With the evidence of spyglasses and metal blades to contradict it, we chose to accept this nonsense!

"But we have met followers of Jing who actually possess his scriptures, and I've read them and copied extracts for our use! Thanks to what Jing taught, the city of Hearthome is the richest on its continent! By studying Jing's principles the folk there have arrived at creshban and other medicines—they've bred mounts that go on land as our briqs swim the sea" (*thank you, Embery*! he added silently) "—they live in houses which make ours look like hovels—they have such wealth that a bunch of sick seafarers stranded there by accident might each repose in his own bower, recovering with the aid of a cure their own folk might not need in five-score years of which they yet keep stock for chance-come travelers..."

Gradually, as he talked, Wellearn let himself be taken over by imagination, sure that in his present state of vitality it would not shade into mere dreamness. He painted a picture of a glorious future to grow from the joint seed of the Hearthomers and the Wego. Some of his audience, he noted with dismay, had ceased to listen the moment he spoke of Jing as a real person; others, however, less parched by cold and shrunken by privation, were clinging with their remaining strength to wisps of hope.

Concentrating on the latter, he concluded with a splendid peroration that sent echoes ringing among the rigid branches and ice-stiffened foliage.

Yet only a few of his hearers clacked their claws, and after a pause Toughide said, "So you're asking us to pile aboard our remaining briqs and set forth now?"

"Of course not!" Skilluck roared. "But next year could see our last and only chance to move to a warm and welcoming land! If you won't hark to the boy—excuse me, Wellearn!—if you won't hark to the *young man*, then trust in me who came home after Knowelkin told you I was dead!"

For a moment Wellearn thought his forcefulness had won the crowd over, but the idea of quitting the land where the Wego had lived since time immemorial was too great to be digested all at once, and the assembly dispersed without reaching a decision. Vastly disappointed, Wellearn slumped to four-fifths height while watching them depart.

"Excellently done," said Skilluck softly at his side.

"I thought I'd failed!" Wellearn countered. "At any rate I don't see them clustering around us to vote Tempestamer the wise'uns' prize for the past summer!"

"Oh—*prizes!*" Skilluck said contemptuously. "To be remembered in a score-of-score years: that's something else. Until I saw how few briqs had made it back to Ushere, all I could think of was how the Hearthomers might cheat us. Now I've felt in my tubules how right they are about the grip of ice. It's time for a heroic gesture, and since someone's got to make one, it might as well be us. If we can get enough of the folk to emigrate next spring, one day they'll talk of us as we do of Jing. I felt this as truth. I couldn't have expressed it. You did. That's why I say you made a great success of it."

"Captain," Wellearn muttered, "I never respected anything so much before as your present honesty. I'm glad to find I guessed right after all, but what you've just said—"

"Save it," Skilluck broke in. "And don't worry about

persuading the rest of the folk around to our course. A few score days of cold and hunger will take care of that."

"I wish I could share your optimism," Wellearn sighed. "Yet I greatly fear that some of those who refused to listen did so not because they suspected us of lying, but because misery has already taken them past the reach of reason."

VI

"Uncle," Embery said musingly to Chard, "do you think Wellearn will come back?"

Grousing at the annual need to adjust the mountings of his telescopes because the branches they rested on had swollen in the rainy season, her fat and fussy uncle finally pronounced himself satisfied with the work of his apprentices. Since it was again too cloudy at the zenith for serious star-study, he ordered the instruments to be trained on the skyline.

"Hush, girl," he said absently. "In a little I can show you moon-rise like you never saw it before."

"But *do* you?" Embery persisted.

"With all the joint advantages that will flow from our alliance with his folk, why not?"

"Father says he doesn't think the captain trusted us."

"Just as long as that briq carried them home safely—and who's to say she couldn't if she lived out the awful storm which drove her here?—then you may rely on the powers of persuasion displayed by your young friend to bring more of their fleet here, and, if nothing else, the captain's greed...Ah, thank you!"—to the senior apprentice for advising him that the first telescope was properly set. "Now, my dear, come here. Before moon-rise, because this direction is fairly clear, I'd like to show you what they used to call the New Star. Ever since, more than a score-of-score years ago—"

Embery stamped her pad. "Uncle, I'm not some ignorant youngling from the city school, you know!"

He blinked at her. "No need to be offensive, niece! Of course I know you've looked at it before, but I want to share a new discovery with you, and I don't believe you've understood half the implications of what I've tried to teach you."

"I have so!"

"Then tell me how the world can grow cooler even though the sun seems to be getting warmer—and I've worked out why!"

"For the same reason it's better in full sunlight to have a light mantle than a dark one! Reflection!"

But Embery's mood changed even before he could compliment her on a lesson well remembered, and she said, "You think you've worked out why? You never told me *that*! Go on!"

And she cuddled up alongside him much as she used to do when she was barely strong enough to stand upright, so that he had to lift her to the ocular of his telescopes.

Chuckling, Chard said, "That's more like my Baby Rainbow! I used to call you that, you know, until you took offense and said it was ridiculous to use the name of Jing's lady—"

"I still think so!" she interrupted. "Come to the sharp end of the prong!"

"Very well." Chard settled back comfortably. "My line of reasoning goes this way. We have seen, in the place of the so-called New Star, nothing but a cloud of bright gas for many generations. Yet every now and then we have recorded a sort of *wave* passing through it, and comparison of notes made recently with those made just after the first proper telescopes were constructed allows us to hypothesize that the sudden addition of a large amount of new fuel to the fire of a star causes an outburst of colossal proportions, as when one drops a boulder into shallow water. There are splashes!"

"You've told me this before!" Embery complained.

"Ah—but what about the matter that gets splashed?"

She thought about that for a little. Eventually she said, frowning with concentration, "It must spread out, over huge distances. And it must get thinner as it goes."

"Correct! Even so . . . ?"

"Even so, when it reaches another star—Oh!" She stared upright in excitement. "You think a splash from the New Star has got this far?"

"It would explain a lot of things," Chard murmured, looking smugger than an astronomer of his age and distinction had any right to. "Above all, it would explain very well indeed why there are more and more stars falling from heaven—which of course aren't actually stars—at the same time as the sun is growing warmer."

"But this could be terrible!" Embery exclaimed. "Because the matter must have spread out very thin on its way here, so if it's only the first bit that's got to us, then—"

"There may be more to come," Chard confirmed. "And we have no way of telling whether there will be so much that it screens out sunlight, or enough to heat up the sun so that ice will melt again, or as much as we've had already with nothing to follow. Whatever happens, though, the Wego are due for the most appalling trouble. So could we be if the ice melted after forming, all at once. We'd need their help to rescue us if the level of the sea rose. Who knows how much water has already been frozen up? But we keep hearing from the fisherfolk that they have to go further and further every year to cast their nets deep . . . Oh, every way it makes sense to ally ourselves with the Wego! Whether they agree is another matter. I mean, they may be as ignorant of the effects of a polar melting as most of our own folk are of the effects of freezing! When I climbed the Snowcap Range . . ."

Embery sighed. Her uncle was about to launch into one of his self-congratulatory reminiscences. There was no hope of hearing more, as yet, about his new theory, so it would be best to distract him.

"Isn't it time for me to look through the telescope?" she offered.

"Of course! Of course! And I want you particularly to take note of—"

He bustled about, issuing orders to the apprentices, but they were superfluous; all her life, Embery had been accustomed to sighting and using a telescope. She applied her eye.

And tensed. The tropical night had not yet fallen; the sun, behind a patch of western cloud, still turned the sky to blue. In a few moments it would vanish, but for the time being its rays slanted across the ocean.

"That's not the New Star rising, or the moon either!" she exclaimed.

"Patience, my dear!" said Chard indulgently. "Wait for nightfall. Then, just above the horizon—"

"Not above! *On!*"

"Are you sure?"

"Oh, don't be so silly! Look, *quickly!*"

Sliding aside, she almost dragged him into position behind the eyepiece.

After a long pause he said, "My dear, I owe you an apology."

Upside-down in his field of vision was something like a giant fang, neither white nor blue nor green but a shade between all three.

"I wish them well in the far north," he muttered. "That's all I can say."

"Why?" Embery was almost crying.

"I never saw one before, but I recognize it from the descriptions I've read and heard." Chard glanced at his niece. "I think you must have done the same."

"Yes, but I was so much hoping you would say I'm wrong!" Embery clenched her claws. "Is it—"

"I'm very much afraid it must be. Further south than anybody has ever met one: that's an iceberg."

"You mocked me publicly before the folk!" charged Knowelkin.

A sky full of racing black clouds leaned over Ushere; a bitter gale lashed the wharf, the harbor; snow turning to hail battered land and water like a forestful of spongids uttering their pellets of spawn in an evil season. Behind him ranged the muster of surviving chaplains: those who sacrificed bulk to tallness, who had been infuriated when Skilluck and his companions overtopped them. And all of them were exuding combat-stink of such loathsomeness that even the frigid blast of the wind did not suffice to protect those nearby.

What could protect anybody in the clutch of this terrible winter, when not even seaqs or dugonqs were to be trapped beneath the ice because there were no floes thin enough to stab through, when icefaws and snowbelongs rampaged into the middle of Ushere?

The chaplains said: the stars. But nobody had seen a star in four-score days...

Somewhat reduced from the great height they had attained at Hearthome, Skilluck and his comrades confronted them. The crew were at the wharf perforce, for Tempestamer had to be taken to sea once in a while to eat, there being no pickled weed or fish to spare from feeding folk. To the surprise and satisfaction of his captain, Wellearn too had volunteered to turn out, regarding himself now as a full member of the company.

More than one briq was unlikely to live until spring, being already too weak to face open water thanks to the neglect of her captain, but Tempestamer remained fat and energetic, and they meant to ensure she stayed that way.

"Who did the insulting?" Skilluck rumbled, rising to the bait. "Who declared that Tempestamer was too weak to swim through storms? Who said I was too bad a navigator to find a way home?"

"Who said we were crazy to trust to visions sent by the stars?" Knowelkin countered. "Who brought a benefit for all the folk and now is keeping it himself?"

"We're doling out our creshban to those most in need!" roared Sharprong, clenching into fighting posture. "Those who have nothing to offer the folk may mock—like *you*!—and we shan't care!"

"Scores will! Scores-of-scores! You're traitors to the Wego!" Knowelkin shrieked.

Standing a little apart, Wellearn suddenly realized what made the chaplains' stink so harsh: fanaticism. They were so far into the maw of dreamness, reason would not convince them. And already they had deranged Skilluck, normally so self-controlled...

"Captain!" he shouted. "They've taken the windward of us! Shift round—*shift round or they will make us mad*!"

Startled, Skilluck shook himself as though emerging on land after a swim. "You're right, by Jing!" he exclaimed. "Sharprong! Strongrip! *Quickly!* Follow Wellearn!"

And with short but menacing strides they marched into the snap of the gale before turning and confronting the chaplains anew.

That put a very different color on the mantle of the situation. The exudate of righteous anger was accessible to those not breathing their own wafts of madness. It made the chaplains think again.

"How fragile is our sanity!" Wellearn whispered, not meaning anyone to hear.

"Once more you're ahead of the rest of us," Skilluck muttered. "But most of them are well and truly dreamlost!"

"Dreamlost?" Wellearn cried, straining to make himself heard against the howling of the wind. "No! They're frightened! And I'll tell you why! It's because if we steer the only sensible course and remove to Hearthome, they'll meet people who can contradict their lies about Jing!"

Skilluck clutched at his mantle. "If you provoke them any more—"

"They outnumber us," Wellearn returned softly. "Surely our best hope is to make them quarrel among themselves?"

Skilluck's eye widened. "Neat!" he approved, and went on at the top of his voice.

"That's right! Now suppose instead of Knowelkin, someone like *you*, Lovirtue, or *you*, Grandirection, had been in charge of the bragmeet: you'd not have insulted me, would you? You wouldn't be so afraid of meeting strangers, either, I'm sure!"

"Of course not!" they both exclaimed.

"Nonsense!" Knowelkin roared, turning on them. It very probably was nonsense, but all their tempers were set to snap like saplings in the path of a gigant.

Grandirection, whom Skilluck had picked on because he was visibly near breaking-point, immediately raised his claws and bared his mandibles and began to pad around Knowelkin seeking an opening for attack. In the meantime, several people had emerged from nearby houses and were gazing in wide-eyed astonishment at these chaplains making ready to disgrace their calling.

"Now's our chance," Skilluck whispered. "And—and thank you, Wellearn! Much more of this, and I'll come to think you *are* as smart as you imagine!"

A few moments later, the crew were able to pry Tempestamer's cold-stiff tentacles free of their mooring and goad her towards open water. Such was the violence of the wind, she was already tossing before she quit the harbor-mouth.

"What a disgusting spectacle that was!" shouted Wellearn against the blast.

"There's nothing wrong with them that a mawful of decent food wouldn't cure," Skilluck replied. "If only more of the Hearthomer seeds had taken . . . !"

"How could they," Wellearn sighed, "in a year when even the pumptrees are chill?"

They stood in a grove at the center of Ushere; it had been because of them that the Wego made their original decision to settle here, rather than the harbor, which was like half a score others nearby. Their taproots were known to reach an underwater spring, far below the level where a storm could stir the sea, which brought heat from deep-lying rocks. Carefully pierced and plugged, they furnished a year-round supply of warm fresh water. It was said that in the old days the chaplains denied that heat could come from any source except the sun, holding the stars to be cool because the spirits of the righteous dead departed thither after separating from the unrighteous in the moon— whose phases showed the division taking place—and that it had been the start of their decline when brave divers wearing capsules under their mantles for a store of air reported that the sea-bed was warmer than the surface at this spot . . . a fact for which they had no explanation.

Accordingly the seeds and spawn from Hearthome, all of secondary and parasitic or symbiotic plants, had been carefully planted in crevices of pumptree bark, not because that was the species most resembling their usual hosts but because they were the only trees likely to remain sap-swollen.

However, the diet didn't suit the strangers; some died off completely, some seemed to be lying dormant, and of those which had sprouted, none yielded the harvest that could be relied on at Hearthome.

Still, any extra nourishment was welcome . . .

Already, though, as the chaplains bore witness, voices were being raised against Skilluck and his crew, blaming them for what was not in their control: bringing the wrong sort of seeds, not insisting on being given more creshban, wasting space on spyglasses and articles of metal instead of food. It would be hard to keep their tempers in face of such taunting. Nonetheless it must be done. No other plan made sense than removal to Hearthome; no briq but Tempestamer could lead the fleet thither. There were no charts for her storm-distorted course.

So she must be fit and lively four-score days from now. Or they were doomed.

VII

For a while longer the fact that Skilluck and his comrades—surviving on what they had stored during their season of good eating but otherwise, save mentally, in little better shape than anyone else—struggled along the frost-rimed branchways to deliver doses of creshban, together with what scraps of fruit or leaf or funqi-pulp their exotic plantings on the pumptrees yielded, counted heavily in their favor, while the chaplains, who had disgraced themselves by their affray on the wharf, lost countenance.

Then the creshban started to run out, while the number of victims multiplied, and even some who had declared support for the idea of emigration took to accusing Skilluck of lavishing the medicine on himself at others' expense. By that stage it was useless to argue. People were taking leave of rationality and slumping into stupor from which a few at least would never revive.

The sole consolation was that, undernourished and sickly as they were, none of the Wego any longer had the energy for fighting. But that meant, of course, they would have none to prepare for a mass exodus when the weather broke, either.

"Why did we come home?" Wellearn mourned more than once. But Skilluck strictly reprimanded him.

"We had no way of knowing how bad this winter was to be! Nor would we have felt easy in our minds had we abandoned our folk to face it without help!"

"At least we needn't have found out until next summer," Sharprong grumbled.

"By which time our kindred and our young'uns could have been dead! As things are, we stand some slender hope of keeping a clawful of the folk alive."

"Slender . . ." Strongrip muttered, gazing at the drifts which blizzard after day-long blizzard had piled against the bravetrees. Many upper branches and almost all their fronds had frozen so hard the wind could snap them off, and every gust was greeted with their brittle tinkling.

"Next time we take Tempestamer to sea we'll hang a net while she feeds," Skilluck sighed. "Even a load of sour weed could save another briq or two."

"Captain, you can't keep our fleet in being single-clawed!" Strongrip began. Skilluck silenced him with a glare.

"Name me another captain who's fit enough to help?"

There was a dismal pause. At length Wellearn ventured, "Maybe Toughide?"

"One might well try him, sure. Wait on him and ask if he will join us. If he won't, I'll still do what I can to feed his briq, or anyone's!" Skilluck stamped his pad. "How many summers to catch and pith and train the briqs we need to replace Stormock and Billowise and the rest? For all we know, there may not *be* another summer!"

So it was done, and Toughide goaded his weak and weary Watereign forth in Tempestamer's wake the next clear day, and though she was less elegantly pithed, a lucky mawful of fish revived her and he was able to make it back to shore with a mass of weed caught on curved prongs, lacking nets such as Skilluck had preserved.

When it was noised abroad that those briqs too feeble to risk the winter ocean were nonetheless receiving fodder, a few score folk made their way to the wharf and watched the spectacle in silence. It was unprecedented. Never in history had any captain of the Wego acted to aid his rivals; rather, he should frustrate them so they would not win the wise'uns' prize.

It was a new strange thing. The onlookers dispersed and reported it. Next time the weather cleared not two but seven briqs put out: Riskall came, and Catchordes, and Shrewdesign's Neverest, and two more so young their captains had not named them, which seemed barely strong enough to quit the harbor.

Towards these last Tempestamer behaved most

strangely, for she slowed her pace instead of exulting in
the water, and kept them in her lee as though they were
of her own budding. By now Wellearn was informed concerning the manner of pithing and breaking a briq, and
therefore he exclaimed in amazement.

"Captain, had I known when I first joined your crew
that you'd left Tempestamer with *those* nerves intact . . . !"

He left the rest unsaid. There was no need to explain
he meant the nerves governing a briq's response to briql-
ings. It was generally held to be a recipe for disaster to
do as Skilluck had done, for such a briq might fall in with
a wild herd and become ungovernable.

Dryly Skilluck made reply, "Most likely my Tempestamer would cut younglings out of the herd without orders
and drive them home with her! It's something I've always
wanted to try. Is she not huger, even now, than any
wild'un?"

It was true. There was no record, not even any legend,
of a briq's surpassing her, and she was still growing despite the dreadful winter.

"We'll find a wild herd off the coast near Hearthome,"
said Skilluck dreamily. "We'll let her pick the young'uns
she personally likes. We'll raise such a fleet as will conquer any ocean, any season. Before my time expires, I
hope to see the Wego travel round the globe!"

"Captain!" said Strongrip with a sharp reproof. "We
have to live until the summer first!"

"Agreed, agreed," the captain sighed, and raised his
spyglass to search for weed among the random floes.

They returned with not only weed but plumpfish, for
Tempestamer sensed a school of them and patiently circled until they had to approach the surface again where
she and her companions could feed and nets haul up what
was left. The other captains were loud in admiration, and
Skilluck seized his chance to exact a pledge: were spring
to be delayed, were the fields to lie under frost a moonlong
past usual, they would take aboard whomever of the Wego
wished to come and head south, following Tempestamer.

Hearing the vow taken, Wellearn almost collapsed from
relief.

"Captain, we're saved!" he whispered.

"Didn't I tell you? A few score days of hunger and cold, and then a mawful of good food... But we aren't on course yet. So many of us are too lost in dreamness to work out what's best for our salvation."

For at least a while, though, it seemed Wellearn's prediction was assured of fulfillment. Revived by the gift of fish, half the Wego came to watch the next departure of the fleet—and help carve up the carcass of a briq that had died at her moorings, a tragedy for her captain but valuable food to the folk—and among them were Knowelkin and Grandirection, who had composed their quarrel. They made shift to chant a star-blessing on the departing briqs, and the crowd settled into familiar responses even though a few budlings, too young to have seen a clear sky, were heard to ask fretfully what stars might be.

Two calm days followed, and the nets were quickly filled, suggesting that warm water was working up from the south in earnest of springtime and bringing bounty with it.

But on the fleet's last night before returning home a fiery prong stabbed out of heaven and exploded on a berg, raising a wall of water high enough to swamp the smallest briq. There was a thunderclap, followed by a cascade of ice-chips, but this was not hail and that had not been lightning.

Tempestamer gave forth a cry such as no tame briq had ever been heard to utter, and for hours ran out of control, seeking the lost young'un. Although Skilluck finally mastered her again, and set course for Ushere well before dawn, it was obvious that some captains were regretting their pledge. After all, if despite the chaplains' blessing the sky signaled its enmity, what hope was there of carrying out Skilluck's plan?

"That was an omen!" was his retort. "If we *don't* move south, that's what we can look forward to more of! Wellearn, do the skies hurl such missiles at Hearthome?"

"Not that I was ever told!" Wellearn asserted.

"But you said the stars look down on Hearthome more than us! Maybe we should stay here, cowering under cloud!"

Wellearn was taken aback until he saw what Skilluck was steering towards. Then he roared, "Safe? Did that prong strike from clear air? More likely the stars are warning us to move where we can see them and be seen, instead of hiding from them all the time!"

The force of his logic told to some extent, but what counted most was that their weather-sense had given no warning of that blow from heaven. Had it been a lightning-strike, it would have been preceded by a sense of uncomfortable tightness and uncertainty. As things were, the discomfort had succeeded the impact. The sensation was weirdly disturbing.

Shortly thereafter the chaplains, whose duties included keeping track of the calendar, marked the usual date of spring. Weather-sense contradicted that, too. Traces of a thaw did occur; many beaches were cleared of ice as warm water washed against them. But uplands to the north which ordinarily caught the early sun-heat remained capped with snow, and even in low-lying valleys there were places where the drifts endured. As for the ground where new crops should be planted, it was stiff as stone a moonlong later.

"I hold you to your vow," Skilluck said when that day dawned, and the other captains shuffled their pads noisily. "But for me, would your briqs be even as healthy as they are?"

"Ask the storm-lost," someone muttered.

"They're not here—*we are*!" Skilluck snapped. "So are what's left of the Wego. Must they stay and starve because the bravetrees are frosted and nothing grows on them, because the fields are hard as rock and all seeds die at the sowing?"

"To risk cresh on a crazy course to nowhere?" another cried.

"To suffer cresh right here, when creshban is to be had at Hearthome and Tempestamer can guide us thither?" Wellearn countered.

Of all the various arguments advanced, that struck deepest in his listeners' tubules. Even those who had best planned to cope with the winter were showing creshmarks now, and saw little hope of escape before the sickness claimed their powers of reason.

"We'll follow you," said Toughide finally. "With all the family and friends our briqs can carry. And let those who choose the other way be cast upon the mercy of the stars."

"Then get to work!" Skilluck rose to what was left of his former height, and despite his shrunken mantle still overtopped the rest. "Tomorrow's dawn will see the Ushere fleet at sea, and our landfall will be in a kind and gracious country where we shall be helped by allies—helped by *friends*!"

"Uncle!" Embery cried, rushing up the slope that led to Chard's observatory. "Uncle, great news!"

Worried, absent-minded, owing to old age and the problems of the past few months which had so much interfered with his study of the stars, the old man nonetheless had time to spare for his brother's daughter. He beamed on her indulgently.

"Good news is always welcome! What have you to tell me?"

"Strangers are coming over the northern hills! It must be Wellearn's people at last! Did you not calculate that their spring must have begun by now?"

"Yes, at least a moonlong ago!" Suddenly as enthused as she was, Chard ordered one of his telescopes trained on the high ground to the north, and exercised an old man's privilege by taking first turn at its ocular.

And then he slumped. He said in a voice that struck winter-chill, "My dear, were you not expecting the Wego to arrive by sea?"

"Well, sure! But given how many of them there are, perhaps they had to ferry their folk to the nearest landfall and . . ."

She could hear as she spoke how hollow her words rang.

"This is no question of perhaps," her uncle said. "This is a fact. The fireworkers' district is being attacked. If that's the Wego's doing, neither you nor I want any truck with them!"

VIII

Heavier-laden than ever before, yet seeming utterly tireless, and with her back sprouting trencher-plants and vines as luxuriant as though this were an ordinary summer voyage, Tempestamer beat steadily southward on the trail which only a briq could follow through the currents of the ocean. Some said it was a question of smell; some, a matter of warmer or colder water; others yet, that briqs could memorize the pattern of the stars though they were invisible by day or cloud-covered at night. After all, maintained these last, a northfinder could be carried anywhere, even in darkness, and always turn the same unfailing way.

But most were content to accept a mystery and exploit it.

Certainly Tempestamer had learned from last year's storm. Now, if clouds gathered threateningly, she altered course and skirted them without Skilluck needing to use his goad, or when it was unavoidable hove to and showed her companions the way of it, even to locating masses of weed shaken loose by gales from coastal shallows. This gave much food for thought to both Skilluck and Wellearn, who served this trip in guise of chaplain because the passengers they had aboard would not have set forth without one. The former wondered, "Perhaps one shouldn't pith a briq at all. Perhaps there's a way of taming them intact. Could we be partners?"

While Wellearn mused, "The directions she chooses when she meets a storm: they imply something, as though the storm may have a pattern. At Hearthome I must study the globe that Chard offered to explain to me, because watching the sky..."

The other captains, though, grew afraid on learning how much of Tempestamer's weather-sense had been left intact. All of them had had the frustrating experience of trying to drive a briq direct for home when bad weather lay across her path, but rations had run so low that only a desperate charge in a straight line would serve the purpose of survival.

So too had Skilluck, as he said, and he preferred to come home late with vines and trencher-plants intact. What then of last year?—countered the others, and he could give no answer, except to say the fortune of the stars must have been shining on him.

Knowing him for a skeptic, they dismissed that and went on worrying.

Still, the weather continued fair. Despite the fact that they had met icebergs further south than even Toughide and Shrewdesign last summer, there had been whole long cloud-free days and nights, and the children had exclaimed in wonder at the marvels thereby revealed, especially the great arc of heaven composed of such a multitude of stars it never dwindled regardless of how many fell away in long bright streaks. Those riding Tempestamer kept begging for a peek through Skilluck's spyglass, and Wellearn amused them with fantasies based on something Embery had said, about the time when folk would travel to not just another continent, but another world.

One, though, acuter than the rest, demanded seriously, "Where do we find the kind of briq that swims thither?"

"If we can't find one," Wellearn answered confidently, "then we'll have to breed one—won't we?"

"She's slowing," Skilluck murmured. "That means landfall, if I'm any judge." Keeping his spyglass trained on the horizon, he swung it from side to side.

And checked.

"Wellearn, did the Hearthomers mention a people around here who consign their dead to the sea?"

Startled, Wellearn said, "That's a custom of seafaring folk like us! They said there were none on this whole coast! That's why when Blestar died we—"

"Oh, I remember," Skilluck interrupted. "But there are bodies floating towards us. Five of them."

It was in Wellearn's mind to ask whether he was mistaking some unfamiliar sea-creature, when his own eye spotted the first of them. No chance of error. Here came five light-mantled people of the Hearthome stock, and none was making the least attempt to swim...

"Stop Tempestamer eating them at all costs!" Skilluck roared to Strongrip. "It could be one of them is still alive!"

His guess was right. The last they hauled out of the water, while the passengers gazed in awe and terror, was still able to speak, though salt-perished and on the verge of death. Wellearn's mantle crumpled as he translated.

"We thought they were your people!" the stranger husked. "Even though they came to us by land! We thought maybe you were short of briqs to carry everyone..." He retched and choked up salt water.

"Go on!" Skilluck urged, aware how all the other captains were closing their briqs with his to find out what was wrong. Wellearn continued his translation.

"Beyond the mountains, land won't thaw this year! Except along the coasts, snow is still lying and the ground is hard as rock! That's what we found out from a prisoner we took. Never expecting an attack, we met the strangers with courtesy, but they were dreamlost and frantic and wrecked half of Hearthome before we managed to stop them. I never thought to see such slaughter, but they had started to eat us—yes, *eat* us!" A sound between a moan and a laugh. "And some of them were worse! They tried to eat *themselves*!"

"What of Hearthome now?" Wellearn cried, clenching his claws.

"I—we..."

The effort was too much. Salt-weakened, one of his lower tubules ruptured, and the victim saved from the sea leaked out his life on Tempestamer's back.

After a long dread pause Skilluck straightened. He said grayly, "We must go on. We can't go back. From what he said it's clear that if Ushere isn't doomed already it will be by next year. We've come south across a fifth of the world, and if even here we find that people have been driven off their lands by cold and hunger..."

There was no need to finish the statement. Those around him nodded grave assent.

"But if we can't settle here after all—" Wellearn began.

"Then we'll survive at sea!" Skilluck exploded. "The way the wild briqs do!"

"Not even Tempestamer can bear a load like this indefinitely!" Sharprong objected, indicating the puzzled and frightened passengers. "We've had an easy voyage compared with last year, but if there are going to be more storms—"

"Are there not uninhabited islands with springs of fresh water we can put into when our drink-bladders won't suffice? Aren't there capes and coves to offer shelter? And don't we have more seafaring skill in this fleet than ever was assembled outside Ushere?"

Wellearn shivered despite the warmth of the day. Here was a vision more grandiose than his—indeed, than any save Embery's, which pictured travel through the sky.

But what about the rest? Would they agree?

Strongrip said heavily, "We must at least make landfall, Captain. If our companions don't see with their own eyes what you and I might take on trust, there'll be recriminations."

"Those will follow anyway, the first time we run short of food," said Skilluck. "But you're right. We go ashore with all prongs sharp, if only for the chance to rescue wise'uns who know the secret of creshban. All else from Hearthome may go smash—who's going to light a fire in mid-ocean, let alone carry sand or stone to melt for glass and metal? Burn my Tempestamer's back? Never! Safer to use the stuff of life than the stuff of death! *But I want creshban!*"

Breathing heavily, he turned to Wellearn. "You stay here and keep the passengers soothed. The rest of us—"

"No," said Wellearn firmly. "I'm going ashore, too. If Embery still lives, I want her with me."

"Now you listen to me—" Skilluck began, but Wellearn cut in.

"Here come the other captains! We'd best present a united front."

"Stars curse it, of course! But you can't expect us to load up with every single survivor—"

"Then take her, if I find her, and I'll stay!" Wellearn flared.

"You're being unreasonable—"

"No, Captain. Much more reasonable than you. I've thought this through. If we do take to a nomad life at sea, what are we to do about keeping up our numbers? Already people from Ushere and Hearthome are overbred. We shall have to copy what roving tribes do on land: leave part of our company at the places where we stop in exchange for strangers who want to learn the arts of the sea. It had been in my mind to propose such a policy anyhow, because of a talk I had with Shash. But if we do as you suggest..."

Skilluck clattered his mandibles glumly. He said after a pause, "Well, perhaps there will be some among the passengers who want to take their chances on land, even so far from home, rather than carry on at sea. Salt water isn't in the ichor of us all the way it is in yours and mine."

Wellearn wanted to preen. How short a time ago it seemed that Skilluck had called him a landlubber at pith!

Yet he still was, and it required all his self-control to accept that his hopes of settling at Hearthome had been shattered the way the prong from heaven shattered that berg. Maybe after seeing the city in ruins the idea would come real for him. Until then, he must compose himself. Here came Toughide and Shrewdesign to demand what was happening.

"You expect us, in our condition, to plod ashore and win back Hearthome from its invaders?" Toughide snapped.

So much was to be expected. After the long voyage, few of the briqs were as fit and flourishing as Tempestamer.

"Not at all," was Skilluck's wheedling response. "We only expect the combined talents of the Wego to salvage something from the landlubbers, and above all what's going to be most valuable to ourselves: creshban, of course, but also..." He paused impressively. "Wouldn't you like spyglasses, all of you, better than this one of mine? The Hearthomers have them by the score! I never admitted it, but I craved one myself! Only they wouldn't part with the one I wanted until we'd concluded our alliance... Still, that's water past the prow. But the observatory where the glasses are kept is nearest the ocean and stands the best chance of having been defended! If we can only attain that hill before we're forced to retreat, and hold a bridgehead long enough to gather provisions, we shall retire with the finest treasure any Wegan could imagine!"

Rearing up to his full remaining height, though that strained his voice to shrillness, he brandished his beloved spyglass for all to see.

"If we don't come back with something better for us all, then you may cast lots for who's to have this!"

Uncertain at the prospect of a battle, for the Wego had never been collectively a fighting folk, Shrewdesign said, "We shan't try to retake the city by force?"

"It would be dreamness to attempt it! But what's of use to us, that the invaders would simply smash because they're starved insane—we must take that!"

Unheeded while the debate was raging, the sun had slanted towards the horizon. Suddenly the tropic night closed down, and there were moans from passengers who had not yet adjusted to the speed of its arrival.

During their last day's travel the fleet had broached a latitude further south than any on their course, and it was now for the first time they saw, at the western rim of the world just above the thin red clouds of evening, a great green curving light, edged like a shuddermaker's rasp.

Silence fell as they turned to gaze at it, bar the slop of water against the briqs' sides and the crying of frightened children. The redness faded; the green grew ever brighter.

"What is it?" Skilluck whispered to Wellearn.

"I heard of such things before, and never saw one," was the faint answer. "There are tales about the Blade of Heaven which comes to cut off the lives of the unrighteous—"

"Tales!" Skilluck broke in. "We can do better without those! How about some *facts*?"

"It's said at Hearthhome that when a star flares up—"

"Oh, forget it! Leave it to me!" And Skilluck marched towards Tempestamer's prow, where he could be heard on all the prow-together briqs.

"Chaplains! Stand forth! Tell me if that's not the Blade of Heaven!"

A ragged chorus told him, yes it was.

"Tell me further! Is it poised to cut off the lives of the unrighteous? And is it not unrighteous to leave those who offered to ally with us to suffer at the claws of crazy folk?"

The instant he heard any hint of an answer, he roared, "Well, there's our sign, then! Captains, prepare to moor your briqs! Against that cape there's a shelf of slanting rock where one may bring in even so large a briq as Tempestamer and not make her beach herself! And it's exactly below the observatory we're making for!"

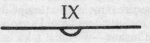

IX

Among the many stories Wellearn had been told when he was a young'un, then taught to disbelieve as he grew up, was a description of what went on in the moon when the righteous and unrighteous were separating. Gradually dividing themselves according to whether they found dark or light more alluring, folk were said to yowl and yammer in imaginary speech; those following star-blessed visions pursued a straight path towards the light, those who doubted kept changing their minds, while only those who had arrived at righteousness by reason were able not to collide with others and be beaten or tripped up and so delayed on their way to the glory of full moon. It was a child's impression of the adult world, perhaps, not stressing what the wicked must have done to deserve the dark.

Skilluck would have been deemed wicked by all the chaplains Wellearn had known, including Blestar, inasmuch as he often mocked and occasionally defied them.

But he was glad to be beside the captain when they went ashore, for what they found was like an actualization of that terrifying childhood story.

No concerted attempt was made to drive off the Wegans who landed; there was neither rationality nor shared insanity to generate resistance. Wild-eyed, stinking, often with their mantles leaking, a horde of starvation-maddened victims ran hither and thither, some sufficiently aware to try and alarm their fellows, many more so distraught that they reacted only to the scent of oozing ichor and under the impression "here's food" began to clap their mandibles excitedly before attacking those who meant to warn them.

It might have been different had the newcomers been exuding combat-stink, but none of them was. They were serious, determined, and—most of all—afraid.

Wellearn was too calm to pretend otherwise. Wherever he glanced, he saw new horrors. One image in particular sank barbs in his memory. There was an elderly man who must have walked, he thought, as far as Tempestamer had swum to get here. For his pads were completely worn away, and he was hobbling along on the under-edge of his mantle with vast and painful effort, no taller than a new-budded child, leaving a broad wet trail like a giant sluq...

For the first time Wellearn realized: there were some dooms far worse than death.

Beating back those who got in their way, using poles from their briqs' saddles in preference to prongs, Skilluck's party breasted the slope below the observatory and obtained their first view of the entire city. Wellearn repressed a cry. The trails of luminous vines which he had seen in Embery's company were being torn loose and waved madly around until they died, as though the bravetrees of all the houses had suddenly developed palsy. Northward, in the quarter of the fireworkers, there was a vast glare on the underside of a pall of smoke, suggesting that all the stored fuel had been set ablaze at once. And the night breeze carried not just fumes but the sound of screaming.

"Looks to me as if they're even crazier over yonder!" Skilluck muttered. "So who's going to want to quit the briqs and settle *here*? If we can't carry all the sane survivors...That's the spyglass-house, is it?"

His answer came in the shape of a well-aimed throwing prong, which missed Strongrip by a claw's-breadth. At once they dropped to the ground, prepared to crawl the rest of the way.

"The defenders are still on guard," Wellearn whispered. "I must let them know who we are!"

"But—"

"I know what I'm doing!" And he began to work his way uphill, soilover-style, using his claws and the edges of his mantle instead of his pads.

Sharpening his hearing to its utmost, he caught faint cries up ahead.

"Looks like a well-organized attack! Stand to!"

Another few moments, and a half-score of prongs flew over him. Somewhere behind was a strangled moan.

Moving as fast as he could, he closed the distance to the side of the observatory: that great complex of brave-trees and countless other plants where he had been shown marvels beyond belief. At every gap between their boles protruded a cruel spike instead of the former telescopes, and from roots to crown prongsmen waited to deliver death like a blow from the sky.

He gathered all his force and shouted, *"Embery!"*

And instantly doubled over, offering the toughest part of his mantle to any missile.

It came—but he felt only a blow, not a stab. The throwing prong skidded away into the undergrowth.

"Someone called my name!" he heard...or did he? Had tension allowed him to mistake imagination for reality? Straining perception to the utmost, he waited.

And almost rushed to dreamness with relief. No doubt of what he heard *this* time.

"No, daughter, it isn't possible. The stress has been too much for you—"

"Embery! Shash! Chard!"

Wellearn had to straighten out again to deliver his words with maximum force, and for an instant could imagine the prong that was going to lodge in his mantle. But he went on, "The Wego are here! *The Wego are here!* Don't—!"

One of the defenders high in the observatory's treetops heard the warning too late. He had taken aim and let go. Wellearn screamed.

But the prong sank into soft ground...so close, he could feel the quivering impact. After a little, he was able to recover himself and return to normal pressure as Shash and Embery and half a score of their friends rushed to meet him.

Shamelessly embracing Embery under his mantle, as though they were about to mate in public—but she was showing his bud, *his* bud!—and anyway nobody would have cared if they had, Wellearn translated the conversation going on softly among the trees of the observatory, trying to make himself believe in his own heroism. That was what they were all calling it, Skilluck too...but it wasn't, it was just that he had done what the situation called for, and anyway most so-called heroes turned out to have been temporarily crazy, living a dream instead of reality.

He forced aside the relics of the chaplains' teachings about reliance on visions, and composed himself to concentrate on his duties as interpreter.

"We saw no signs of organization on the way here," the captain was saying. "Does it break down at night, or is it always the same?"

"At the beginning there was some semblance of order among the invaders," Shash said. He was tired but coherent; his older brother Chard was slumped to the point where he looked as though he needed a sitting-pit, and paying scant attention. "They were able to confront us and—well, that was how we lost Burney. We were fit and rational, and thought they would be too. We now believe they must have been the first of their folk to work out what was happening, to decide that they must leave home and take over someone else's territory. And we assume that others fell in behind them when they realized this was their only hope, but by then they were—well—disturbed. And on the way I guess they infected others with their craziness."

"That fits," Skilluck muttered. "Any idea how far north they came from?"

"What few people we've been able to capture and feed up to the stage where they can talk normally—and there aren't many of those—all agree that the cold weather reaches down to the very pith of this continent. If my brother were better he could tell you more. But he's exhausted." Shash spread his claws helplessly. "The further from the sea, it seems, the worse the cold! We know that water retains heat longer than dry land, but even so, this is terrifying! Are we due for frost and snow here in Hearthome? We've never seen such things! One could imagine the whole world turning into a frozen ball!"

"I don't think we have to fear that," Wellearn said, a little surprised at himself. He parted from Embery and leaned forward. "The way Chard explained it to me, warmth at the equator turns water into vapor, so clouds turn into ice at the poles. But if the sun goes on getting warmer—"

"Quite right!" said Chard unexpectedly, and lapsed back into distraction.

"Forget the theories!" Skilluck snapped. "We need to decide on a plan of action! I have one. We should simply—"

"But what about the Blade of Heaven?"—from Tough-ide.

"Oh, that!" Chard roused himself completely. "We know about such phenomena. When a star—like the famous New Star—explodes, it throws off gobbets which cool down in the interstellar void. If one approaches another sun, it warms up and boils off part of itself. All this follows from the teaching Jing bequeathed."

"Is this going to save our lives?" Skilluck shouted, erupting to full height. "Are you coming with us? Are you prepared to give us what you want to preserve from Heart-home? Make your minds up *now*!"

He was so patently correct, Wellearn found himself upright alongside him.

"Yes! And whatever else you give us, we must have the whole of Jing's scriptures!"

"Creshban!" Skilluck shouted, and the other captains echoed him. "If nothing else, we must have the secret of creshban!"

The wind had shifted; there was something menacing in the air that affected their weather-sense, making tempers raw, and it wasn't just smoke.

After a pause filled only by the noise of the crazy folk smashing and ripping through the city, Shash said heavily, "There's no secret to creshban. We don't know why, but fresh sour juices of new-budded fruits or even new-sprouted leaves will do the job so long as they have no animal matter at the roots. Nothing from a briq's back—nothing from a cemetery—only shoots that spring from new bare ground. I'll give you seeds that produce the most suitable plants, but . . . Well, essentially it's like eating a proper diet at home, instead of wandering across a desert or an ocean and living on stored food."

"That simple?" Skilluck whispered. "If we'd known—"

"If you'd known you'd never have come back," said

Chard unexpectedly. *"You said that in Forbish, didn't you?"*

There was a thunderstruck pause, while Wellearn registered the fact that he had not actually translated the last statement, and the rest of the Wego captains were looking blank.

"When you first came here, I thought you were better informed than you pretended," said the fat old astronomer. He squeezed himself upright, and even though the effort slurred his speech he overtopped Skilluck, for his was the taller folk. "Did you wonder on the way home last year why we didn't give you all of everything at once? Did you wonder whether we realized your intention was to cheat us if you could?"

Skilluck cowered back in a way Wellearn had never imagined he would see, not in his wildest fantasies. Chard blasted on.

"But it doesn't matter anymore, does it? You kept your pledge to return, and *you* didn't know you were going to find us in these straits! You've met your honorable obligation, and it remains for us to match the bargain! Take what you can—everything you can, including people!— from this doomed city! Take telescopes and microscopes, take vines and blades and seeds and tools and medicines, and flee at once! Until dawn the attackers will be sluggish, but if you delay past then—! Leave us, the old ones! Leave everything except what your briqs can carry without sinking! And above all, take Jing's scriptures! Wellearn, *here*!" He bowed himself to a dark corner and pulled out a glass jar.

"Take the originals! We salvaged them first of all, of course, and here they are. Now they're yours. Use them as best you can. If you must, leave them where they will freeze. But *don't destroy them*! As for us, of course..."

"No! No!" Embery cried, hastening to his side. "I won't leave you, I won't leave father!"

"You'll have to leave me," Chard said gently. "But you'll go, won't you, Shash?"

"They've turned our healing-house into a jungle," the chief curer said. "They've rooted out our medicinal plants. If I stay, the stars alone know what use I could be to our folk."

"Go, then. Me, I'm much too old." Chard settled back

comfortably where he had been. "Besides, I'm fat and I'd probably sink even a handsome briq like Tempestamer. Take your leave and let me be. And dream of me kindly, if you will."

Soberly, the visitors prepared to depart. As they were clasping claws with him, he added, "Oh, captain, one more thing, which might be useful to you in your navigation—that is, if you haven't already noticed it. The end of the comet which you call the Blade of Heaven always points directly *away* from the sun. It might amuse you, Wellearn, when you have nothing better to occupy your mind, to devise a theory which will account for that."

"I'll try," Wellearn said doubtfully. "But without the means to conduct experiments—"

"There are always means to conduct experiments. And aren't you part of the greatest experiment of all?"

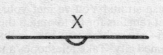

During the hours of darkness some of the briqs' passengers had indeed decided they would rather settle on shore and take their chances. As dawn broke they were heading south, together with several score refugees from Hearthome, in search of a site that would be easier to defend.

Meantime Skilluck's party was working out what of their loads—hastily collected in the city—would be least useful, and ruthlessly discarding whatever they did not regard as indispensable. Before the day's heat had fully roused the crazy invaders, the booty had been distributed and so had the two-score Hearthomers who were prepared to risk the ocean.

Skilluck prodded Tempestamer with his goad, and she withdrew her mooring tentacles and made for open water.

"What did uncle mean when he called us an experiment?" Embery asked her father.

"We're mixing like different metals, to see what alloy

will result," Shash answered, clinging anxiously to the briq's saddle as they felt the first waves. "It's the start of a new age, whatever the outcome."

"I liked the old one," Wellearn muttered. "And I've been cheated of my share in it."

"Don't think like that!" admonished the old man. "Even the stars can change! And what are we compared to them?"

"We don't yet know," said Embery. "But one day we shall go there and find out."

Overhearing as he issued orders to his crew, Skilluck gave a roar of sardonic laughter.

"Bring me the briq you want to swim to heaven on, and I will personally pith her! Me, with a northfinder I can trust and Tempestamer under me, I'll be content. Now let's go find a herd of wild briqs and start recruiting our new fleet. It's going to be the grandest ever seen!"

But despite the hotness of his words and the bright rays of the morning sun, the wind struck chill from the north.

PART THREE

THE OUT-POURING

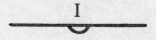

I

When northern summer ceased, the weight of ice leaned hard on those gnarled rocks which fearful wanderers had named The Guardians of the Pole. Slanting up either side of an underwater shelf that grudgingly permitted the highest tides to wash over it, they resembled prongsmen turned to stone, their mantles drawn aside and weapons clutched in both their claws.

Few were the mariners who braved the channel they defined; fewer still the ones who returned to tell of a colossal valley surrounding a land-locked sea so salt that what ordinarily ought to sink there was buoyed up. It was a foul and poisoned zone, though life endured. Chill and salt conspired to make its growths disgusting in the maw. Desperate commanders who imagined their junqs would nourish themselves off such weed as the water sustained watched in horror how first the drink-bladders burst, then the floats, and finally the major tubules, so they died.

By then, of course, the crews that clung to their haodahs were for the most part much too mad to care.

For a while after the last summer the Salty Sea remained liquid, roiling under hail and gale. At length, however, ice filled the valley and beset the Polar Guardians, shattering the rock they were composed of, and down it sped to gather on the shelf. In a single season boulders and ice were too high-piled for any warmer flow to pass. After that glaciers shed bergs until the isolated sea was covered; then it froze also.

The last foolhardy travelers who let a poorly-pithed briq carry them into such latitudes, thinking that because they had rounded Southmost Cape they were safe from the enmity of the stars, unaware that the briq knew nothing of this ocean dominated by junqs and was lost and panicking, struggled ashore on a desolate beach with the precious secrets it was their task to spread around the world, and sought shelter in a cave which became their tomb.

II

The water was rising, or the land was sinking. Either way the event spelled trouble for the people of Ripar, despite the work of their far-famed inventor Yockerbow.

Some of the inhabitants claimed that their city was the oldest in the world. Others, more cautious, admitted that its records might have been—as it were—revised, because the rotting trunks of sweetwater trees had been found too far out in the lagoon for them to date back to the age of the alleged foundation, when salt tides rolled a long day's walk inland and Ripar River was as yet unfed by its giant tributary, the Gush.

It was thanks to the latter's change of course that the city had flourished. Reason, and relics exposed when mud was being pumped away from the harbor, combined to suggest that originally it had been a mere hamlet, huddled on a narrow flood-plain constricted between dry plateaux. Only when (and this was attested not by legend alone but by recent discoveries) a ball of blazing rock fell out of the sky and blocked the old channel of the Gush was there enough fresh water for dense roots to lock up silt and build a delta, forcing back the sea.

Now a score-of-score-of-scores of people, at the lowest estimate, swarmed along its branchways, got on one another's pith and cursed and sometimes fought and always schemed to secure more than their proper share of the goods attracted to this uniquely sited entrepôt, whether they arrived by junq or were carried by a caravan of droms. The majority cared nothing for the past and little for the future. Their homes grew of their own accord, did they not? There was always sustenance, though it be dull, to be snatched from an overhanging bough or filched from a plot of funqi or—if all else failed and they must endure actual work—dragged up on a line from the lagoon. Fish did not abound as formerly, of course, but even mudbanks supported crupshells and other edible mollusqs.

So they were as content as the folk of any big city.

That was the majority. There were, however, others whose traditional obligation was to view Ripar in the context of the world: not only of the globe, but of the universe which comprehended all time and all space. It was said they possessed arcane knowledge dating back before the Northern Freeze. Always there were half a score of them; always they were presided over by the incumbent Doq; always they were collectively disliked because they levied duty on cargoes passing from sea to land or vice versa, and because they enforced the ancient laws with neither fear nor favor. Were one among their own number to succumb to a plague brought by strangers, for which no cure was known, he would quit the city himself before prongsmen came to expel him; were one of his relatives to enter into an unauthorized mating, he would be prompt to bring the new-budded youngling before a eugenic court to determine its fitness to survive; were it his own home that became infested with teredonts, or boraways, or a putrefying mold, he would be the first to pour the poison at its roots.

And it was among these notable and austere personages—short of their customary total by one, for the doyen Chelp had died a few days earlier—that the inventor Yockerbow was summoned to stand today, beneath the interlaced branches of the Doqal Hall, with water plashing underpad. Acutely conscious of being no more than half as old as anyone else present, he strove to reason out why he had been sent for. Surely it could not be, as his beautiful spouse Arranth insisted, that he was to be invited to replace Chelp! His weather-sense informed him that the idea was ridiculous, for the peers were exuding a distinct aura of incipient panic.

But the fact was in no way reassuring.

He sought some kind of signal from Iddromane, spokesman for those who worked with fire and metal, and the only one of the peers he could claim close acquaintance with, but the old fellow remained stolidly imperturbable.

Yockerbow trembled a little.

Then the period of waiting was over, and the Doq rose to his full height.

"Greetings to my brothers, and to Yockerbow the stranger, who is uninformed concerning the reason for his attendance. All will be made clear in moments.

"Since time immemorial"—catching on, Yockerbow glossed that as meaning, in practice, a few score-of-score years—"the Great Fleet of the Eastern Sea has enjoyed harborage rights at Ripar. It has been a considerable while since those rights were exercised. Today, however, notice has been served that the Fleet is to call here very shortly."

So *that* was it! Making no attempt to maintain a stoical demeanor like the others, Yockerbow clenched his claws. He was schooled in history, and knew that there had been times when a visit by the Fleet was welcome; then the folk boasted how they on land shared ancestors with the People of the Sea, and clamored to trade and intermarry. On the other claw, there had been occasions when the Fleet arrived storm-bedraggled and half-starved, and crazed mariners stole what they could and spoiled the rest, whereupon the folk vowed they could never be called kin to such monsters.

Yockerbow's lifetime had elapsed without a sight of the Fleet; it was working the broadest equatorial waters. Reports from travelers indicated that it had a new commander—land-budded, they said as one—who, having deposed the former admiral, was interesting himself more than any of his predecessors in what the continents could offer.

His name, they said, was Barratong, and his shadow fell across the day-half of the world at every dawn. In Yumbit he had agents who seized the sharp spice remotaw and made it a monopoly for those he favored; in Clophical his prongsmen guarded the giant trees beloved of the spuder, and each autumn they rolled up as many webs as a junq could carry and used them for rope to snare wild junqlings and increase the Fleet; in fabled Grench—yes, he had ventured so far!—he held the sole right to export the fine wax known as cleb.

And he was coming here!

Briefly, alarm drove Yockerbow into imagining an unrealized threat. His lovely Arranth had never made any secret of how, as a youngling, she had dreamed of being traded to the Fleet, of touring the globe as the favorite partner of its admiral. Still, after so many years together... He had never, though, quite understood why someone like her, so fascinated by the skies, so able to make the dead past come alive, should want to be a partner in his own mundane toil...

"The Fleet's new commander," the Doq was saying in a rasping voice, "has sent word that he wishes to examine the famous novelties of our city: to wit, the pumps which have enabled us to withstand the encroachments of the sea. But that is not the only reason for the presence of a stranger. Immediately on the demise of our late brother Chelp, our brother Iddromane advanced Yockerbow's claim to be his replacement. Without his aid, the boles of this hall might be shriveling under the impact of salt water. Moreover, he is city-born and none has been found to speak a word against him. It would certainly be fitting were he to join us in the ranks of the Jingfired."

But this was incredible! How could Arranth's prediction possibly be right, when the aura of everybody present was so wrong? Besides, Yockerbow had no ambitions in that direction, whatever plans his spouse might have.

A murmur of conversation had broken out. Enjoining silence with a clatter of his mandibles, the Doq continued.

"There is, however, an alternative opinion. Because it is without precedent we have agreed that Yockerbow shall be present when it is put to the vote. It has been suggested that Barratong be inducted to make up the minyum. Some say he is of the commonalty. True, but he has attained the counterpart of noble status. It is known that the Great Fleet is increasing so fast because from every continent—let alone the islands—folk are flocking to him like cloud-crawlers at migration-time. His declared intention, we are told, is to make us all citizens of a global community. Those among us who are concerned with the future limitations of Ripar, its dependence not only on what others bring us from inland or abroad but on the natural process of weather and climate, faced with the undeniable rise in sea-level which is now putting us to such shifts, should be the first to applaud! And nowhere in the ancient scriptures is it laid down that our Order must be confined to city-budded persons!"

Chill certainty pervaded Yockerbow. He had been drawn into an argument the rights and wrongs of which the Doq had already decided in his own mind, but which other of the peers had doubts about. Now all were looking at him expectantly. What should he say? Should he risk the disfavor of the Doq? Knowing nothing of the intrigues of the Order, he felt hopeless. Hoping for guidance, he glanced at Iddromane, but—as ever—he was preserving perfect impassivity.

Well, then, he must trust to his own feelings, and even though he was sure Arranth would be angry with him afterwards, he could deal with that problem when it arose.

"Speak freely!" the Doq urged. "In meetings of the Order neither dissimulation nor subterfuge is permitted!"

Thus instructed, Yockerbow had the temerity to rise to his full height.

"Within or without the compass of your Order," he declared, "you can rely on me to serve our city. So if by inducting Barratong you may hope to enlist his support for our welfare in the future, I say do it!"

The resultant exudations, in the close air of the hall, made Yockerbow feel as though he were lost at sea and a storm were bearing down on him. Yet, though there was still no sign from Iddromane, the Doq was regarding him benignly.

"Well said!" he announced. "Iddromane, you deserve credit for proposing to the Order someone who can take the long view! Be it then resolved that during his visit we invite the admiral of the Greet Fleet to join the Jingfired, inasmuch as what he is doing is in accord with our ultimate aims!"

When the Doq had retired, some of the Order came to clasp claws with Yockerbow and compliment him on his selflessness; others departed wearing scowls. Bewildered, he made shift to answer politely, having only the vaguest notion of what he was supposed to have done right.

III

Never had Arranth been in such a rage! It was futile for Yockerbow to try and calm her; all she could say, over and over, was, "You had the chance to join the Order of the Jingfired, *and you turned it down*!"

He countered in his most reasonable tones that he had had no assurance of being elected—that if he had been by a bare majority he would have made himself enemies for life instead of, as it turned out, enjoying the patronage of the Doq—that the administrative duties such rank entailed would have interfered with his work. She refused to listen. She merely repeated facts which he already knew, as though he were some dull-witted youngling who should have been spotted by the eugenic courts.

"The Order is so old, no one can tell when it began! They say it dates back before the Northern Freeze! Its articles have been copied and copied until scarcely anyone can read them—but I'm sure *I* could, if I had the chance, and I'd have had it if you weren't a fool! Or maybe I ought to call you a coward! The path to secret wisdom lay before you, and you turned aside!"

"My dear, what's supposed to be so secret?" he rejoined. "You told me how your cousin Rafflek, who was then attendant on the Doq, reported what he overheard them saying during an induction rite: 'The stars aren't fixed, and sometimes they blaze up!' So much you could be told by any of your friends who study sky-lore!"

"That's not the point!"

"I say it is! All right, some stars aren't stars but only planets, and our world is one of them. All right, other stars may be suns with planets of their own—I see no reason why not! But saying they're inhabited is about as useful as telling me that something's happening in the Antipads, or something happened in the far past! Without

129

means of either communicating with these folk, or visiting them, what good is there in making such a statement?"

"That doesn't mean they don't exist!"

"Well, no, of course it doesn't—"

"And even if we can't communicate with the past, the past can communicate with us, and often does so without intention! Your pumps have sucked up ancient tools in the harbor, and scholars like Chimple and Verayze have worked out how the folk of that distant day employed them! So I'm right and you're wrong!"

As usual, Yockerbow subsided with a sigh, though he still wanted to attack her logic. It was, after all, true that his spouse was highly regarded in intellectual circles, though he did sometimes wonder whether it was because she really displayed such an outstanding knowledge of astronomy and archeology, or whether it was due rather to her slender grace and flawless mantle...

No, that was unworthy. But, for the life of him, he could not share her obsession with the unprovable! You didn't need a telescope to discern how the moon's turning, and to some extent the sun's, affected the tides, for instance. But the planets obviously did not; records of water-level had been kept for so long that any such phenomenon must by now be manifest. Therefore the night sky was a mere backdrop to the world's events, and even if there were reasoning beings on other planets, without a way to contact them their existence was irrelevant. Certain authorities claimed there were creatures in the sun, what was more! They argued that the celebrated dark spots on its brilliant surface indicated a cool zone below a layer of white-hot air. And there were dark and light areas on the moon, too, which the same people held to be seas and continents. Given their chance, as Arranth wished, they would have imposed their convictions as dogma on all Ripar!

Perhaps he should wait on the Public Eugenicist and accuse his predecessor of authorizing a mistaken pairing. Things would have been so much simpler had they budded...

Yet he could not imagine living alone, and what other spouse could he find who was so stimulating, even though she was infuriating in equal measure?

Finally, to his vast relief, she lost patience, and made for the exit.

"I'm going to Observatory Hill!" she announced. "And while I'm up there, you can think about *this*! I look forward to meeting Barratong! I gather he recognizes merit in a female when he finds it! Maybe I can still fulfill my old ambition, and tour the globe aboard his banner junq!"

And off she flounced.

As the screen of creepers around their bower rustled back into place, Yockerbow comforted himself with the reflection that in the past a night of stargazing had always calmed her mind.

He could not, though, wholly persuade himself that the past was going to be any guide to the future.

But there was work to be done if the admiral was to admire the latest achievement of his beloved city. And he did love Ripar. He could conceive of no more splendid vista than the parallel ranks of giantrees which flanked its access to the ocean, no more colorful sight than the massed bundifloras ringing the lagoon, no sweeter perfume than what drifted up at nightfall from the folilonges as they closed until the dawn.

And he, for all his youth and diffidence, had saved Ripar, thanks to nothing better than sheer curiosity.

At least, that was his own opinion of what he'd done. Others seemed awestruck by what he regarded as obvious, and talked about his brilliance, even his genius. Yet anybody, in his view, might have done the same, given the opportunity. He was not even the first to try and protect Ripar by means of pumps. All along this coast, and far inland, folk made use of syphonids. Their huge and hollow stems could be trained, with patience, so that they might supply a settlement that lacked nothing else with fresh water from a distant lake, albeit there was higher ground between. But in cool weather their action grew sluggish, and sometimes air-locks developed in the stems and the flow failed.

On the coast, cutinates had also long been exploited. These were sessile creatures like immobile junqs that fed above the tide-line by trapping small game in sticky tentacles, yet to digest what they caught required salt water, which they sucked up from inshore shallows and trapped by means of flap-like valves. Fisherfolk would agitate one of them at low tide by offering it a scrap of meat, then gather stranded fish from drying pools as the water was pumped away.

Yockerbow's interest had been attracted to cutinates when he was still a youngling barely able to hold himself upright, by the odd fact that no matter how far inland the creatures might reach (and some attained many score padlongs) they never exceeded a certain height above sea-level, as though some invisible barrier extended over them.

Once, long ago, someone had thought of forcibly connecting a cutinate to a syphonid, so that any air-bubbles which formed in the latter would be driven out by the water-pressure. The project failed; for one thing, the syphonid rotted where it was connected to the cutinate, and for another, the cutinate would only pass water so salt it was useless for either drinking or irrigation.

But the young Yockerbow was excited by the idea of finding practical applications for these abundant creatures. When he discovered that air-locks in syphonids always developed at exactly the same height above water-level as was represented by the limit of the cutinates' spread, he was so astonished that he determined to solve the mystery.

The key came to him when, after a violent storm, he found a cutinate that had been ripped open lengthways, so that its internal tube was no longer watertight. Yet it was far from dead; still having one end in the sea and—fortuitously—the other in a pool left by the heavy rain, it was pulsing regularly in a final reflex spasm.

Yockerbow contrived a blade from a broken flinq with two sharp edges, cut away the longest intact muscles, and carried it home, along with a mugshell full of seawater. To the surprise of his family, he was able to demonstrate that the cutinate's activity depended less on its intrinsic vitality, as the scholars of the city were accustomed to assume, than on the simple relation between salt and fresh water. And then he discovered that, if vegetable material or scraps of meat were steeped in the fresh water, the muscle could actually be made to grow...

Lofty and remote, Iddromane came to hear about his work, and sent a messenger to inquire about it, who was sufficiently impressed to suggest that his master invite

Yockerbow to wait on him. That was their only private meeting; they had crossed one another's path frequently since, but always at formal events such as season-rites or disposition-meets.

Iddromane's influence, however, was such that when he timidly put forward his idea that detached muscles might do useful work in pumping away flood-water from the city's outermost sea-wall, Yockerbow was overwhelmed with offers of assistance. There were several false starts; at first, for example, he imagined he could overcome the height problem by arranging the muscles to squeeze a succession of ascending bladders with flap-valves in between. That worked after a fashion, but the bladders kept rupturing and synchronization proved impossible. After a year of trial and error—mostly error— he was about ready to give up when one disconsolate day he was wandering along the shore and noticed a long thin log which the retreating tide had stranded so that its heavy root end lay on one side of an outcropping rock and its thin light spike end on the other. The rock was closer to the root than the spike; as the water withdrew, there came a moment when the log was exactly balanced, and hung with both ends clear of the ground.

Then a mass of wet mud fell away from the roots and the balance was disturbed and the log tilted towards its spike end and shortly rolled off the rock. But Yockerbow had seen enough.

A month later, he had the first pumping-cluster of cutinate muscles at work. Grouped so close together they had to synchronize, they shrank in unison to half their normal length, then relaxed again, exerting a force that five-score strong adults could not outdo. By way of a precisely fulcrumed log, they pulled a plunger sliding inside a dead, dried syphonid, which led to the bottom of a tidal pool. At the top of its travel, the plunger passed a flap-valve lashed to the side of the tube, and water spilled through and ran off back to the ocean.

Much development work followed; in particular, the cords attached to the plunger kept breaking, so that Iddromane had to authorize the dispatch of an agent to bargain for a batch of spuder-web—doubtless thereby arousing the interest of Barratong, for only his factors were entitled to market the webs on this side of the ocean.

That problem solved, means had to be found of ensuring that the plunger dropped back to the bottom of its course without jamming halfway; again, that called for an agent to travel abroad in search of cleb, the astonishing wax which, pressed upon from the side, was as rigid as oaq, yet allowed anything to glide over its surface be it as rough as rasper-skin.

With a ring of flexible hide around it, the plunger on its web-strand slid back and forth as easily as might be hoped for, and every pulse of the combined muscles could raise the volume of a person in the form of water.

But the purchase of cleb had also been notified to Barratong, and beyond a doubt that must have been what decided him to call here after so long an absence of the Fleet. For now travelers came to gape at the ranked batteries of pumps which, working night and day, protected Ripar from the ravages of the ocean. As often as the tide flooded salt water into the outer lagoon, where it was trapped behind a succession of graded banks, so often did the pumps expel it and allow fresh water back to keep the giantrees in health. A few were wilting, even so, but very few, and the routine difference in water-level was a half-score padlongs.

To Yockerbow's intense annoyance, though, people who ought to have known better—including some members of Iddromane's entourage—expected him to increase this margin indefinitely. To them he spoke as vainly as to Arranth. He said, "I've tried to raise water further than the height represented by the limit of cutinate growth, and it *won't work*." Not even Arranth believed him; she was more and more rude to him nowadays, and he felt certain it was because he "wouldn't" improve his pumps.

And nobody shared his excitement at the probable implications of his discovery. It seemed to him that the only explanation must be that air was pressing down the water in a pump-tube, so when the weight of water lifted matched the weight of the overlying air, it would rise no further. He had contrived some elegant demonstrations of the theory, using clear glass tubes supplied by one of Iddromane's associates, but not even Arranth would take them seriously. She believed, as everybody did, that air had neither weight nor—what would follow—limitations to its upward extent. Solid substances had much weight; liquids, rather less, because they incorporated more fire; but air's must be negligible, because it filled the universe and neither obstructed nor slowed down the planets. And if the stars were fire, and fire could not burn without air—as was proven by covering good dry fuel, after setting it alight, with something impervious—then there must be air around the stars.

"But just suppose," he argued vainly, "that starfire is different from regular fire—"

"Now you're asking me to believe something much more ridiculous than that the planets are inhabited!" Arranth would crow in triumph, and that was always where the discussion ended, because he had no counter to that.

So, having improved his pumps as far as they would go, he was turning his attention to other matters. He was trying to make a connection between fire and mere heat; he was testing everything known to create warmth, especially rubbing, and he was approaching a theory to explain the brightness of the stones that fell from heaven. It was generally accepted that the glowing streaks which nightly crossed the sky were of the same nature as the lumps of hot rock that were sometimes found at the probable point of impact of one of them. Burning rock? Well, rock could be melted, and if air contained more of the principle of fire the higher one went . . .

It was tolerably logical, that idea. Yet it failed to satisfy Yockerbow, and on the occasions when he had joined Arranth at the observatory on the high hill to the east of Ripar, where there were many good telescopes and files of records extending back nine-score years—it should have been far longer, but a disastrous winter had flooded the pit where earlier records were stored, and they rotted—he always came away disappointed. Some of the astronomers listened to his ideas politely, but in the end they always made it clear that to them he was no more than a lowly artisan, whereas they were refined and erudite scholars.

It was their disrespect which had hardened his view of them, rather than any secure belief that their explanations of the stars were wrong. Essentially, he could not accept the probability of such people being completely right.

And, little by little, he was formulating concepts which

he knew made better sense. Suppose he had broached them to the Order of the Jingfired, after insisting on being inducted as Iddromane proposed . . . ?

No, the outcome would have been disastrous. He knew little of the web of intrigue in which the peers held Ripar like a catch of squirmers in a fish-hunter's basket, but he had the clear impression that mastering its complexities must be like trying to weave a net out of live yarworms. Had he uttered his heretical notions in such august company, means would have been found to replace him prematurely. Radicals, revolutionaries, had no place in the deliberations of the Order.

Yockerbow felt caged and frustrated. What he had expected to flow from the acceptance of his pumps, he could not have said. Certainly, though, it had not been anything like this sense of impotence and bafflement. In a word, he was indescribably disappointed by the reaction of his fellow citizens.

Suddenly he found he was looking forward as keenly as Arranth to the arrival of Barratong. Maybe someone who had traveled half the globe would be more open to new ideas than those who sat here smug behind the defenses he had contrived but paid scant attention to the inventor's other views.

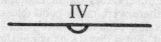

IV

First there was a pale line of phosphorescence on the pre-dawn horizon, so faint only the keenest-eyed could detect it. Then it resolved into individual points of light, each signifying the presence of a junq festooned as lavishly with glowvines as any palace in Ripar. And at last, just as the sun cleared the horizon, the entire Fleet came into sight of land, and the city's breath seemed to stop collectively.

The Fleet was *huge*! Records indicated it had never exceeded four score junqs; now there were seven score,

and another score of younglings followed behind, secured
with hawsers made of spuder-web until they were safely
broken. Each of the adults carried an enormous haodah
beset with edible funqi and other useful secondary plants,
and each haodah was aswarm with people, from those so
old their mantles were shrunken with age down to children
who could not yet stand upright, and nonetheless clambered with infinite confidence from pole to creeper to
outlying float.

"It looks more like a mobile city than a Fleet!" marveled Yockerbow, and he was not alone.

And the resemblance was magnified a scorefold when,
responding to a perfectly drilled system of signals issued
by gongs and banners, the junqs closed on the place allotted for their mooring and came to rest, prow against
stern, so that one might walk dry-padded from each to
the next and finally, by way of the leading junq, to shore.

"That must be Barratong!" Arranth exclaimed, surveying the wondrous spectacle through a borrowed spyglass.

"Where?" Yockerbow demanded. Passing the glass to
him, she pointed out a tall, burly fellow at the prow of
the lead junq.

"I think not," Yockerbow said after a pause.

"What? Oh, you're always contradicting me!" She
stamped her pad.

"He doesn't match the descriptions," was his mild reply. "The person directly behind him does."

"Are you sure? He looks so—so ordinary!"

And it was true. Apart from combining northern shortness with a southerner's pale mantle, he looked in no way
exceptional, but he wore crossed baldrics from which
depended the ancient symbols of his rank, a spyglass and
an old-style steersman's goad, and his companions de-
ferred to him even in their posture.

The Doq and the eight peers were waiting for him,
surrounded by their entire retinue, and moved to greet
him the moment he climbed down from the junq. After
that he was invisible from where Yockerbow and Arranth
stood, and the group moved off towards the Doqal Hall
where a grand reception had been prepared.

"We should be going with them!" Arranth said accusingly. "If you'd asked Iddromane like I suggested, I'm sure he—"

Yockerbow fixed her with a rock-hard glare.

"No! Am I to wait on him, like a humble underling? Has it not occurred to you, my dear, that *he* is coming to see *me*?"

Her eye widened enormously. After a moment she began to laugh.

"Oh, my clever spouse! Of course you're right! It's much more remarkable like that! It's going to make us famous!"

As if we weren't already . . . But it didn't matter. He had made his point, and there was work to do.

It was not long before the mood of excitement generated by the Fleet's arrival started to give way to annoyance. This was not because the visitors were discourteous or rapacious; they traded honestly for what they found on offer, and conducted themselves with tolerable good manners albeit some of them, especially those who hailed from the distant south, had very different customs.

More, it was that they seemed somewhat patronizing about even the best that Ripar had to show, and in this they took after the admiral himself. Blunt, plain-spoken, he refused to be as impressed as the peers expected by anything about the city, including its alleged antiquity, for—as he declared in tones that brooked no denial—his Fleet could trace its origins back to within a score-score years of the inception of the Freeze, when briq-commanders from the west were storm-driven into what was for them a new ocean and found not wild briqs but wild junqs, which none before them had thought to try and tame, yet which proved far superior: more intelligent and more docile, not requiring to be pithed. He even had the audacity to hint that Ripar had probably been a settlement planted by the early seafarers, and that contradicted all the city's legends.

He compounded his offense when, having enjoyed the greatest honor they could bestow on him and been inducted to the Order of the Jingfired, he made it unmistakably plain that that too was delaying fulfillment of his chief purpose in calling here: inspection of Yockerbow's pumping-system.

The peers seethed. That anyone should find the work of a commoner, a mere artisan, of greater concern than their most ancient rituals . . . !

They yielded perforce, thinking what the Fleet might do were its commander to lose his temper, and sent urgent messages to Yockerbow to meet them on the outer harbor bank.

To the intense annoyance of Yockerbow, but the huge amusement of a crowd of bystanders who had come here to catch a glimpse of the famous admiral, Arranth was rushing up and down in a tizzy of excitement, like a girl waiting to greet her first lover. Not until the procession of the peers and their attendants actually stepped on the high bank did she suddenly realize how unbefitting her behavior was. Speech—fortunately—failed her long enough for Barratong to pace ahead of his companions and confront Yockerbow person-to-person.

"So you're the celebrated inventor, are you?" he said, gazing up at the Riparian who had clean forgotten that, according to normal rules of politeness, he should have reduced his pressure so as not to overtop the distinguished visitor. "I like you on sight. You don't pretend to be what you are not—a stumpy little fellow like myself!" He added in a lower, private tone: "That Doq of yours must be aching in all his tubules by this time! Serve him right!"

At which point, while Yockerbow was still overcome with astonishment, Arranth recovered her self-possession and advanced with all the dazzling charm at her disposal. From somewhere she had obtained thick, fine strands of sparkleweed and draped them about her body in rough imitation of the admiral's baldrics; this, she hoped, would not only be taken as a compliment but maybe start a trend among fashionable circles.

"Admiral, what an honor you've bestowed on us by coming here! I so much crave the chance to talk with you! You know, when I was a girl I used to dream the Fleet might call here so I might beg the chance to make a trip with it and see the stars of the far southern skies for myself—astronomy, you see, is my own particular interest!"

"Then you should talk to Ulgrim, my chief navigator," said Barratong, and deliberately turned his back. "Now, Master Yockerbow, explain your pumps! I came here specially to see them, because—as you can probably imagine—every now and then the Fleet at sea runs into the kind of waves we can't rely on riding, and often our junqs are weighed down by water which we have to bale out with our own claws before they can swim at full speed again. In the wild state, as I'm sure you know, they never experience such swamping, because their flotation bladders always bear them up, so they have no reflexes of their own to cope with such a situation. Still, we've taught them to endure and indeed nourish all sorts of parasitic plants, so maybe we can add something more. Do we go this way?"

He made for the nearest working pump, and Yockerbow hastened to keep pace with him. Nervously he said, "I believe I should congratulate you, shouldn't I?"

"What for, in particular?"

"Were you not just inducted into the Order of the Jingfired?"

"Oh, that!"—with casual contempt. "Sure I was. But I gather its teaching is supposed to be secret, and I can't for the life of me see why. If it's true, then the more people who know about it, the better, and if it isn't, then it's high time it was exposed to ridicule and correction."

The peers who had remained within earshot stiffened in horror at the prospect of this rough intruder revealing their most sacred secrets. Barratong paid no attention. His aroma had the tang of one accustomed to bellowing orders into the mandibles of a gale, and his self-confidence was infectious. Yockerbow found he was able to relax at last.

"Now here you see a pump actually working," he said. "The tide being on the turn, there's relatively little water left beyond this bank. If you want to inspect a dismounted pump, we have one available . . ."

Barratong's ceaseless questioning continued all day and long past sunset, while Arranth hovered sullenly nearby and kept trying to interrupt. At last she managed to make him angry, and he rounded on her.

"If you're so well grounded in star-lore, you can tell

me the interval between conjunctions of Swiftyouth and Steadyman!"

"It depends on our world's position in its orbit! The year of Swiftyouth is 940 days, that of Steadyman is 1,900, and our own—as you may perhaps know!—is 550." Clenching her claws, she positively spat the words.

Softening a little, Barratong gave a nod. "Very good! Though I still say Ulgrim is the person you ought to be talking to, not me, a common mariner."

"The most uncommon mariner *I* ever met!" blurted Yockerbow.

Pleased, Barratong gave a low chuckle. "I could honestly match the compliment," he said. "For such a big city, it has precious few people in it worth meeting. I was introduced, though, to some folk called Chimple and Verayze, who do at least base what they say about the history of Ripar on solid evidence."

"We found it for them!" Arranth exclaimed, then amended hastily, "Well, it turned up in the mud the pumps sucked..."

"Yes, of course: they told me so." Barratong shook himself and seemed to return to reality from far away. "As it happens, I'm engaged to dine with those two, and it's dark now. You come with me. I find you, as I just said, interesting."

Neglected, insulted, the peers had long ago departed in high dudgeon. There was no one else on the sea-bank except a few dogged onlookers and a couple of Barratong's aides.

"It will be an honor," Yockerbow said solemnly, and could not resist whispering to Arranth as they followed in the admiral's brisk pad-marks, "Isn't this better than being on the outer fringes of some banquet in the Doqal Hall?"

Her answer—and how it carried him back to their time of courting!—was to squeeze his mantle delicately with her claw.

They met with Chimple and Verayze at Iddromane's bower on the south side of the city, where the plashing of waves mingled with music from a flower-decked arbor. It was blessed with the most luscious-scented food-plants Yockerbow had ever encountered, many being carefully nurtured imports. Even the chowtrees had an unfamiliar flavor.

Yet the admiral paid scant attention to the fare his host offered, and at first the latter was inclined to be offended. Yockerbow too began by thinking it was because, after voyaging to so many fabulous countries, Barratong had grown blasé. In a little, though, the truth dawned on him. The signs, once recognized, were unmistakable.

Barratong was in the grip of a vision budded of his vivid imagination, yet founded securely upon fact—a vision of a kind it was given to few to endure without slipping into fatal dreamness. Yockerbow trembled and lost his appetite. Now he understood how Barratong had attained his present eminence.

Musing aloud, the admiral captivated everyone in hearing with words that in themselves were such as anybody might have used, yet summed to an awe-inspiring total greater than the rest of them would dare to utter.

"The ocean rises," he said first. "It follows that the Freeze is ending. If it began, it can just as well end, correct? So what will follow? We've tried to find out. The Fleet has put scouts ashore at bay after cove after inlet and found traces of the higher water-levels of the past. How much of the ocean is locked up in the polar caps we shall discover when the continued warming of the sun releases it. You here at Ripar, despite your wealth and cleverness—despite your pumps!—will have to drag your pads inland and quarrel for possession of high ground with the folk who already live there. You!"—this to Iddromane—"with all your ancient lore, in your famous Order, why did you not speak of this when you inducted me?"

Iddromane's notorious composure strained almost, but not quite, to the bursting point. He answered, "Truth is truth, regardless of when it was established."

"I don't agree. Truth is to be found out by slow degrees, and the world changes in order to instruct us about truth, to save us from assuming that what was so in the past is necessarily bound to be the case tomorrow, too. I'm sure our friends who study relics of the past will support me, won't you?" This with a meaningful glare.

Chimple and Verayze exchanged glances, then indicated polite assent.

"And how say you, Master Inventor?"

Yockerbow hesitated, seeking a way to offend neither Iddromane nor Barratong, and eventually said, "Perhaps there is more than one kind of truth. Perhaps there is the kind we have always known, truth about ourselves and our relations with each other, and then maybe there's the kind which is only gradually revealed to us because we actively seek it out by exploration and experiment."

"Most diplomatically spoken!" said the admiral, and exploded into a roar of laughter. "But what's your view of the origin of the universe? In Grench they hold that once all the stars were gathered right here, in the same world as ourselves, and the advent of unrighteousness caused them to retreat to the furthest heaven in shame at our behavior. In Clophical they say the departure of the stars was a natural and inevitable phenomenon, but that that was the cause of the Northern Freeze, and hence, if the ice is melting again, the stars must be drawing closer once more!"

"If only we could tell one way or the other!" sighed Arranth. "But though it's suspected that the stars move, as well as the planets—if not so visibly—our astronomers have so far failed to demonstrate the fact. Am I not correct, Master Iddromane?"

"Not entirely," was the judicious answer. "Careful observation does indicate that certain stars must be closer to us than others. As the world progresses around the sun, a minute difference in position—relative position, that is, of course—can be detected in a few cases. They are so few, however, that we are unable to decide whether the shift is solely due to a change of perspective, or whether part is motion proper to the stars themselves. The distances involved are so great, you know, Admiral, that if your Fleet could swim through the sky it would take a score-of-score-of-score years to pass the outermost planet Sluggard, and twenty times as long again to reach the star we have established to be nearest."

"Hah! If means were given me, I'd do it! I'd spin a rope of spuder-web and catch the moon, and swarm up it to see what's going on out there! But since we can't, I must be content with my current project. You see, although you may view the rise in water-level as an unmitigated disaster, I say we shall be amply repaid by the recovery of some of our ancient lands. Already at the fringe of melting glaciers we have found frozen seeds, wingets, animal-hides and mandibles, even tools belonging to our remote ancestors. This year I purpose to venture further north than anyone since the Freeze began. It's an ideal time. So far this season we haven't seen a single berg in these latitudes. What's more, there have been many fewer storms than formerly—to my surprise, I might add, because if the sun is heating up I'd expect the air to roil like water meeting hot rock... Yockerbow, I detect a hint of wistful envy."

Yockerbow gave an embarrassed shrug. It was true he had been dreaming for a moment, picturing to himself the new lands Barratong described.

"Come with me, then," the admiral said. "The Fleet has the ancient right to select a hostage from among the people of Ripar, exchanged against one of our own as a gage of amity. This time I choose you. And we already know your spouse fancies a sea-voyage; she may come also."

"But—!" Iddromane burst out.

"But what?"

"But he is our most notable inventor!"

"That's exactly why I picked him; he has the sort of open mind which permits him to see what happens, not what one might expect to happen. If you refuse, it will be a breach of our long-standing treaty, and you need not count on us when the time comes—it will, I promise you!—when your folk find you can neither stay here nor flee inland, and require my Fleet to help in your removal to safe high ground! But in any case it will be only for this season, unless Yockerbow decides to opt for a life at sea. It has been known for people to make such a choice... Well, Yockerbow?"

There was one sole answer he could give. All his life he had been led to believe that sea-commanders were no more than traders, glorified counterparts of the subtle, greedy folk who thronged the Ripar docks. Barratong, though, was none such. He was a visionary, who shared the passion that drove Yockerbow himself, the lure of speculation, the hunger for proof, the delight to be found in creating something from imagined principles which never was before on land or sea.

How much of this came logically to him, and how much

was due to Barratong's odor of dominance, he could not tell. He knew only that his weather-sense predicted storms if he did not accede.

"Arranth and I," he declared boldly, "would count it a privilege to travel with you."

There was a dead pause during which Arranth looked as though she was regretting this fulfillment of her juvenile ambition, but pride forbade her to say so.

"Then there's nothing more to be said," grumbled Iddromane, and signaled his musicians to play louder.

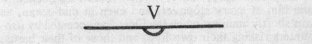

V

Yockerbow and Arranth were not the only new recruits to depart with the Fleet. Here, as at every city the junqs had visited since Barratong assumed command, scores of other people—mainly young—had decided that life at home was too dull for them, and they would rather risk the unknown dangers of the sea than endure the predictable monotony of Ripar.

Seventeen of them had survived interrogation by Barratong's deputies, and the peers were not averse to letting them go; the city's population was beginning to strain its resources, so they did not insist on an equal exchange.

Dawn of the fifth day saw the junqs turn outward-bound again—vibrating with hunger by now, yet perfectly drilled. Sedate, majestic, they adopted an echelon formation such that when they came on schools of fish or floating weed there would always be at least a little left even for the younglings that held the rearmost station. Thus impeccably aligned, they beat their way north.

"Is this like what you were expecting?" Yockerbow murmured to Arranth as they clung to the haodah of the banner junq and wondered how long it would be before they could imitate the unfeigned self-confidence of the children who casually disregarded the motion of the waves.

"Not at all!" she moaned. "And I persuaded Iddromane

to let me have a first-rate telescope, too, thinking I might make useful observations! How can one study stars from such a fluctuating platform?"

The greatest shock of all, however, was to follow. Who could have guessed that the admiral of the Great Fleet of the Eastern Sea was bored and lonely?

Oh, bored perhaps. After one's sub-commanders had flawlessly executed every maneuver required of them for half a lifetime—after putting in at ports of call on every shore of the world's largest ocean—after dealing with people of different cultures, languages and customs for so long—yes, one would expect him to lose the sharpness of his prong. Yet . . . lonely? When volunteers flocked to join him at every stopover, and even in mid-ocean, as was shortly manifest when the Fleet was accosted by fish-hunters risking their own lives and those of their barqs, only to be turned back to shore disappointed? No, it was incredible!

Nonetheless, it proved to be the case. Yockerbow found out the second dark of the voyage, when chief navigator Ulgrim—amused, apparently, to meet not only a landsider but a female with at least a smidgin of sky-lore—had taken Arranth to the stern for a practical discussion. It was a fine clear night, with little wind, and only a clawful of falling stars. The Great Branch gleamed in all its magnificence, and the Smoke of the New Star was clearly discernible, at least as bright as the glowvines of a city they were passing to the westward. The glowvines on the junqs themselves were shielded, for fear of attracting hawqs or yowls; they were rarely fully exposed, as Yockerbow had been told, except when approaching shore or when the fleet needed to keep in contact during a gale.

And there was Yockerbow, more from courtesy than choice, alone with Barratong at the prow, while the rest of the crew amused themselves with a game that involved casting lots.

"Chance . . ." the admiral mused, making obvious reference to the gamesters. "Well, one can see why people tossed on the ocean by a lifetime of storms may hew to notions such as luck, but—You, Master Inventor! Do you believe your great achievements were the fruit of accident?"

Cautiously, for the "great achievements" were far behind, Barratong having concluded that his pumps could not easily be adapted for use on a junq, Yockerbow answered, "I think luck must be a different phenomenon from chance. I think the world goes about its own business, and those who are ripe to respond do so, much as a fertile plant catches the spores of its kin from a favorable breeze."

"Diplomatic as ever!" said the admiral sourly. "How I wish you'd speak your mind openly! If you only knew how I hunger for someone who might amaze me—startle me by voicing one of my own ideas without being prompted! Better yet, mention something I never dreamed of even when I was half-starved as a youth, plodding from city to city in search of knowledge and instruction!"

"Is that how you began your career?" Yockerbow ventured.

"What else but the quest for knowledge would tempt a sane person away from a comfortable home? What else would persuade a landsider to take to the ocean, except the chance of getting to meet more strangers in a shorter time? Oh, I've sat with scholars in a score of famous cities, listening eagerly to what they purported to teach the world, and after a few years I realized: no one is making new discoveries any more! My sub-commanders long refused to visit Ripar, because last time the Fleet came so far north the junqs were set on by a gulletfish following the drift of the bergs, and two were lost. I acceded for a while, until I heard rumors about the Order of the Jingfired, and even then I held back until reports of your pumps reached me. *I* never expected them to be useful aboard a junq, but it was an excuse to swing the support of other commanders behind me. Then the absence of bergs during our trip this year came to my aid, and now they are agreed that if I've been successful so far the chances are good that I'll continue to be so. Myself, I can't but doubt it. And I have no one I can turn to for sane counsel."

The last words were added in so low a tone that at first Yockerbow was unsure whether to reply. At length he made his mind up.

"Admiral, I recognize you for a visionary. Such folk have always encountered difficulties. In my humble way,

I've done the same. But—well, since it wasn't truly news of my inventions which drew you to Ripar, I deduce it was the hope that the Order of the Jingfired possessed data that you lacked."

"Was I to know there would be a vacancy in the Order when I chose to turn up? The decision to head north this year was already taken."

"Then"—boldly—"how did you plan to obtain the Order's secrets?"

There was a long interval during which one of the outlying scouts reported a huge float of qrill, and the entire Fleet altered course fractionally to take advantage of it. When Barratong replied, there were loud squelching noises in the banner junq's maw, and now and then the whole of her body rippled longitudinally and let go a puff of foul-smelling gas.

"Had I not been inducted to the Order," the admiral said at last as though the interruption had not happened, "I did plan to choose Iddromane as my hostage for this voyage, or some other scholar well grounded in the so-called 'secrets' of the Order. I'd have relied on his terror during the first storm we met to make him reveal—"

Pride in his own city made Yockerbow risk breaking in. "It wouldn't have worked!"

"It wouldn't have been worth it," Barratong retorted sourly.

Yockerbow was shaken. "You mean there's nothing worth knowing in what they teach you?"

"I wouldn't say *nothing*," came the judicious answer. "I do accept that, acting as they do to preserve lore garnered in the far past, they have succeeded in assuring the transfer from generation to generation of certain indispensable facts. Of those you meet on the branchways of Ripar, or Grench or Clophical, come to that, or any city, or even as you pass from junq to junq of the Great Fleet, how many folk would you rely on finding whom you could talk to about what really matters—the nature of the universe, the fires of heaven and how they correspond with those down here, the beginning and the end of everything? Hmm? Many would be prepared to debate with you on any such subject, but how few would have solid evidence to back their views!"

"I always thought," Yockerbow admitted, "the Order of the Jingfired did have evidence."

"They claim to have, but when you ask for it, it can't be produced!" Barratong exclaimed. "I'm ready to believe, for instance, that long ago one of the stars in the sky blazed up until it outshone the sun. I can see the cloud of glowing gas they still call its Smoke—it's right there, isn't it? What I want to know, though, is *why* that happened, and why it hasn't happened since! And then there are elderly folk among my own people who say that when they were budded certain stars were not so bright as they are now . . . but who's to define what 'bright' means? Can the members of your Order tell me that? They swear in principle they could—if only they had certain ancient star-maps which were spoiled by a flood! But when I asked for them they hadn't even kept fragments and tatters which I could have shown to Ulgrim!"

He concluded that tirade on a fierce tone, and a second later continued in a much milder voice, as though reminded about Arranth by his reference to his chief navigator.

"They said at Ripar that your buds don't take."

Yockerbow curled his mantle before he could stop himself, and a waft of combat-stink fouled the salty air. Aghast at his bad manners, he was on the point of prostrating himself when he realized that the remark had been made in the matter-of-fact fashion of an equal speaking to an equal. Flattered, he confirmed its truth.

"Nor do mine," said Barratong, staring across the water where the new-risen moon was creating a path of brightness for others to follow—not the Fleet. "Your lady wishes me to join with her, and I shall with pleasure, but don't expect the offspring you can't give her. Were I capable, my line would be among the greatest in history. But the only thing that keeps the Fleet in being—the only thing that helps so many cities to survive around the shores of the eastern ocean—is the fact that a first-time mating between strangers takes more often than not, so your seventeen from Ripar will engender enough progeny to keep us going for quite some while . . . Oh, Yockerbow, I almost look forward to the tumult the great melting will entail! We must stir the folk around more! Little by little, thanks to our habit of choosing *either* sea *or* land, *either* drom *or* junq, *either* this *or* that, we are breeding apart! And the same holds for the inventions made in one place or another! Do you know about the longwayspeakers that they have at Grench? No? I thought not. But think what use you could have made at Ripar of a means to communicate simply by beating on a distended bladder in a patterned code, comprehensible to somebody the other side of a mountain range: they can do that! And they can signal orders at Clophical by using trained and brightly colored wingets which make patterns that are visible from end to end of the valley, but they don't survive being taken out to sea. And the use they could make of your pumps at Gowg...! Do you see what I mean?"

Yockerbow certainly did, but already he was lost in contemplation of the possibilities. He stood silent for a long while, until Barratong roused him with a nudge, pointing to the north.

"Look yonder! What can the Jingfired tell me about that—*hmm*?"

For an instant Yockerbow thought he must be watching a drift of cloudcrawlers on their migration route; some species displayed bright flashes from time to time, and occasionally they synchronized to make bright polychrome bands. But this was much too blue, and too near the horizon, and anyway the season was wrong.

"Tonight the sky is clearer than I ever saw it," said Barratong. "You're looking at the aurora round the pole. I've been told that when one draws close enough it reaches to the apex of the sky. Not that anyone has seen it in all its glory since the Northern Freeze—*but on this trip we shall*! Even my sub-commanders don't know what I have in mind, friend Yockerbow, but on this voyage I mean to break all records for a northern swim, and go where nobody has dared to venture since the ice claimed what was habitable land. I want to witness the rebudding of the continents! Don't you?"

VI

After a few days of steady northward travel, they made the first of many detours. Fog and mist did not deceive the northfinders carried by the Fleet, but this time a violent storm lay across their course. At about the same time the sea became noticeably cooler, as though chilled by melting ice. Paradoxically, however, at the same time it started to teem with a wider range of life-forms than could be found in the waters nearer Ripar, from the tiniest qrill which Barratong scooped up in a shell and showed to Yockerbow through a single-lensed microscope that magnified better than ten-score times, up to giant schools of sharq. The Fleet accorded these a respectfully wide berth also, not because they were a threat themselves, but because they in turn were hunted by the fiercest predator in these waters, the huge and solitary gulletfish whose mindless charge could rupture the tubules of even the largest junq. For amusement, elderly mariners jelled the ichor of the new recruits by regaling them with tales of what it was like to meet a gulletfish in mid-ocean and try to make it charge a barbed prong. It was worst in the dark, they said, when all one had to guide the eye was the ripple of phosphorescence as it rounded to for yet another onslaught.

"How rich in life the planet is!" murmured Yockerbow, and Barratong gave him a sardonic dip.

"Who says only this planet? Some think the stars may be alive, or harbor life, because living creatures are always warmer than their environment! Myself, though, I suspect the reason we don't find such a plethora of fish in tropical waters is that life requires a differential of heat, the way your pumps require a differential of level, and as the water becomes warmer the task of survival grows harder, just as when it grows extremely cold. What about that?"

Yockerbow felt he would never grow accustomed to the way the admiral kept tossing out provocative ideas, even though he was modest about the source of them, and always gave credit to anonymous scholars said to have been met in distant places. By this time, however, Yockerbow was beginning to doubt their existence. Barratong combined his restless genius with a diffidence more proper to a shy young apprentice.

He said after a pause for thought, "It makes sense to invoke a limit at either end of any scale of events. Just as there is no life in solid ice, so there is probably none in the stars. After all, a living creature which is trapped in wildfire dies, and certain persons have conducted experiments wherein a small animal and some burning fuel were closed up together, and the animal died and the fuel did not burn out."

"I've heard of such cruelty," Barratong said musingly. "I personally would not care to witness it, but I'm glad in a sense that someone could bear to . . . Ah, there is so much to know, my friend! And so much that has already been discovered in one place, yet never conveyed to another! But we have spoken of such matters already."

"As we have," rumbled Ulgrim, approaching from the stern with Arranth—somehow shyly—following him. "Admiral, do we plan to put in at any harbors before we reach the polar circle? The lady has convinced me that it would be of interest were I to peek through her big spyglass on stable ground."

Behind his back Arranth gave a moue, as to tell Yockerbow, "See? There are some who respect my learning even if you don't!"

Whether Barratong noticed or not, he gave no sign. He merely chaffed Ulgrim, who was still tall but whose mantle showed the tell-tale wrinklings of age.

"What youth and good looks may do to reform a character! You never cared to come ashore with me in other climes to hear what the local philosophers had to say, or view their instruments and their experiments! Lady Arranth, I bow to you; whatever else you may be schooled in, you certainly display a vast knowledge of people's nature! But the answer's no!"

Abruptly he extended to his maximum height, a third or more above his usual stature, and even though this brought him barely equal with Yockerbow and Ulgrim, the effect was as shocking as though he had grown taller than mythical Jing. One more element was added to Yockerbow's understanding of this admiral's dominance over his enormous Fleet.

"We go ashore next time on land newly exposed by the retreating ice! We stocked the junqs with food enough to see us through the trip—their drink-bladders are bulging—no blight or mold afflicts the food-plants—and we have medicines for every conceivable ill! For all I know, the landfall we next make may be shrouded under so much cloud you can't see stars—but never mind! We already know how the ice when it melts reveals wonders from far distant in time, so the wonders that are distant in space may take care of themselves for this season! The stars are slow to bloom and fade, but you and I are not. Time enough for your observations next winter, if the Fleet remains in the far north and we are compelled to lie up a while, which I suspect . . . But tell me, though, old companion"—this as he imperceptibly resumed his normal pressure—"what's excited you anew about the stars you've known so well for so long?"

Embarrassed, but putting a bold countenance on matters, Ulgrim said bluffly, "She speaks of stars which I can't see, and yet they're there. More than once since leaving Ripar, when the water was most calm, I've thought I could discern them—an eleventh in the cluster of the Half-Score Wingets, another at the focus of the Welkin City . . . And of such a color, too: a strange deep red! Yet when I look again—!"

"Master Navigator," Yockerbow said, "have you ever seen a bar of metal heated in a fire until it melts?"

"I never had time for such landsiders' tricks!"

"I know: one dare not carry or use fire aboard a junq. Yet fact is fact. The metal starts to glow in the dark red; afterwards it becomes orange, and yellow, and green—which we see clearest—and then shades through blue to white, just like the rainbow. Eventually it can be made to glow like the sun itself. It follows that a hotter or a cooler star . . ."

His words trailed away, for Barratong was scowling.

"I thought you were never inducted to the Order of the Jingfired!" he said in an accusatory tone.

"What does that have to do with it?" Arranth demanded before Yockerbow could reply. "Had I but the means, I'd show you all this with a glass prism!"

"It is as I feared!" Barratong raged, and began to pace back and forth along the poop of the haodah, spinning at every turn so violently one thought he might blister his pads. "Your vaunted Order possesses no truly *secret* knowledge! Do you realize that the heating of a metal bar is the chief symbol of their most private ritual?"

There was a moment of dead silence, save for the slap-and-hush of waves against the junq's broad flank and the *meep-meep* of a flighter and its young which were following the Fleet in hope of scavenging carrion or floating dung.

All of a sudden Yockerbow started to laugh. As soon as he could he recovered his voice and said, "Admiral—excuse me, because this is truly too silly—but you were right the first time, and this time you're wrong. It doesn't matter that someone else knows the inmost secret of the Jingfired ritual. *What counts is that Ulgrim didn't.*"

"I think I see what you mean," said Barratong, and a waft of anger-stink blew away as he mastered himself. "Clarify!"

"How long ago was such a truth discovered, that may prove to be valid even in the case of the stars? Well before the Northern Freeze, we may be sure! What happened following the onset of it? Why, people driven crazy by hunger and despair felled great civilizations which otherwise might well by now have shown us things we regard as impossible—you might, for instance, have your spuder-web to catch the moon! But nobody among the Fleet would dare to undertake the necessary research because a fire literally cannot be lighted on a junq! Hence no metal—no glass—no melted rocks—no anything of the kind which pertains to such realities!"

He was downwind of Barratong as the Fleet bore into a strong northerly breeze. Whether it was because he scented the admiral's enthusiasm, or because the newly exposed lands which the ice had reluctantly let go were emanating signals from those who had once occupied them, he never knew. But in that moment he was as great a visionary as the admiral.

"Yet we *can* bring our knowledge all together!" he

declared, and his weather-sense confirmed that he had
safely picked a course into imagination, steering well clear
of dangerous dreamness. "Knowledge borrowed from past
time will guide us to the future we deserve for all the
troubles we've endured! There must be suffering—would
I knew why! I don't believe the stars decree it, for they're
so remote they might as well be cool and stiff like arctic
rocks, yet they *can* blaze up, and I don't want to think
it's simply because they suck into themselves the vital
force from planets like ours where life exists between the
limits set by ice and fire!"

"Say it's because of ignorance," offered Ulgrim, and
at once looked surprised at his own improbably philo-
sophical suggestion.

"Yes! Yes!"—from Barratong. "Have we not found
remains of animals such as none of us had seen or heard
of? Have we not then encountered similar beasts in strange
new waters? And are we ourselves not different from our
ancestors? It follows that if the stars blaze up it must be
for a reason we shan't comprehend until we work out why
there are creatures—or were—unknown to us on this small
planet!"

"We understand each other," Yockerbow said soberly.
"I was so afraid when you invited us to come with you ..."

"Ah, but we're all bound on one quest," Barratong
stabbed. "Some of us seek an answer to a single mystery—you, Yockerbow! You wanted to find out why syphonids and cutinates could never pump water above a
certain level. On the way to a solution, you saved your
city from being washed away. You still don't know all
the reasons why the original phenomenon presented, but
you have suspicions, don't you? And Arranth has just
drawn my dear old partner whom I've trusted in storm
and floe-time, trusted under the onslaught of heaven's
crashing meteorites—drawn him too by some miracle into
the charmed circle where I hoped to lure him long ago"
(this with a dip to her) "and for that I thank you,
ma'am—"

Yockerbow was half-afraid the admiral had lost track
of his own peroration, but he was wrong, for he concluded
it magnificently.

"And here we are together on the sole straight course
which any of our people ought to choose! All of us a little

angry with the universe because it seems to want to mislead us—all of us determined to find an answer to at least one mystery before our time runs out—all of us resigned to the certainty that we shall uncover many other mysteries in the solving of our own! Perhaps the time may come when there are no more questions to be asked; if that is so, that's when the world will end!"

VII

Cooler it became, and cooler... yet not cold. No frost-rime formed this season on the rigging of the haodahs, and the junqs themselves responded briskly to the increasing iciness of the water, as though they needed by activity to keep the ichor coursing in their tubules. Awed, those who rode them as they trespassed among bergs and floes under an amazing pale blue sky watched the bare brown land on either side slip by, and marked where it was suddenly not bare, as though the sun had charmed plants out of rock.

"We are approaching the polar circle," Barratong said. "We are the first to come by sea in who can say how long? But we are not the first of all. See how the flighters whirl who brought new life to these mud-flats!"

Watching their graceful swoops, as they glided back and forth and sometimes failed of their prey so they had to whip the water and achieve enough velocity to take off again, Yockerbow said, "How can they eat enough to fly?"

"Sometimes," said Barratong, "they can't, or so I was informed by a fisherman whom we rescued in mid-ocean the summer before last. They breed on high bluffs and launch their offspring into air by laqs at a time when they burst the brood-sac. Those which catch enough wingets and flyspores grow; they soar and mate on the upgusts; then they hunger for what's in the water, and if they're large and fast enough they snatch the surface-breeding fish. If not—well, they can use up what fat they've stored and spring back into air from the crest of a rising wave. But this fish-hunter had many times trapped those which did so, and always found them lean and scant and taint of flesh. It's my view that flighters' natural zone is the air; by contact with either land—except to breed—or sea, they are diminished of their powers. Witness the fact that out of every brood-sac a score or two survive. And is not the same phenomenon apparent in ourselves? Had you and I, and all the other so-called worthy persons, bred at every pairing, would we not by now by laqs and craws have overswarmed the pitiful resources of the Age of Freeze? How many more of the folk could Ripar have supported before either they started to starve off into dreamness or some epidemic sickness rushed through them like a flame in dry brushwood? Hmm?"

Yockerbow, after a second's pause, admitted, "It is in the records of the city that Ripar came close to that."

"As did our Fleet," the admiral rasped. "How think you I—a landsider—was able to assume command? I was better fed than old Grufflank, and that's all! *He* dreamed away his days in nonsense visions! There was I fit and strong and offering suggestions so practical the captains' meet recognized the common sense of them. Yet, given a season's decent diet, any of them might have done the same, and more, for they had sea-experience, while I did not..."

He brooded for a moment; then he concluded, "At least I can say this. I'm still in the domain of imagination and not dreamness; my weather-sense assures me of it, and that's the sense that fails us last, even though the eye or the very mantle may be fooled. A sweet taste may deceive you; a fair odor; a sleek touch...but weather-sense extends into your very pith and being, and even if you starve it's last to go. Moreover it's what leads us to trust our junqs more than ourselves. At Ripar, do they know the legend of Skilluck?"

Yockerbow looked blank, but to his surprise Arranth, standing by as usual but less bashfully than before, said, "If the name is Skilq, we have the same tale, probably."

"Who swam a wild briq across the western ocean when all others had lost their way, and salvaged something of a now-lost city?" Barratong rounded on her with excitement.

"They say he saved the telescope for us," Arranth concurred. "All younglings at Ripar are told the story."

Having dismissed fables of that sort from his conscious mind because his preceptors so ordered him when he entered into adult phase, Yockerbow was acutely embarrassed. He said, "I too of course heard such stories, but in the absence of evidence—"

"To starfire with your ideas of evidence!" roared Barratong. "For me, it's enough that someone in the Fleet should remember hearing a vague tale! It's because I want to turn the legends of the past into a new reality that we are here! Those which don't stand up to present discoveries may be dismissed as spawn of dreams! But anything I take in claw and hold and *use*—!"

He broke off, panting hard, because he had involuntarily tallened again. Relaxing, he concluded in a milder tone, "Besides if the same tales survive on land as we know among the People of the Sea, there's a double chance of them being based on fact. Do inland folk recount the stories, too? If so, are they just borrowed from contact with mariners?"

The ebb and flow of talk surrounding Barratong was such as Yockerbow had never dreamed of. Once he dared to ask what mix of ancestry had given him rise, and met with a curt—though plainly honest—answer.

"I inquired about that, right up until I found I was a muke, and got no details; there was a famine which affected memory. And after I discovered that my line won't take, there seemed no point in pursuing the matter. I can only suggest and instruct; I cannot breed."

Timidly Yockerbow ventured, "A—a—what did you call yourself?"

"A muke! Take junqs from a northern and a southern herd, and they will mate eagerly enough, and often throw a bunch of first-class younglings. Yet when you try to make the strain continue, it's like me, and you, and—given she's tried me and Ulgrim and a score of others in the Fleet—Arranth as well. We call those mukes, and hope against hope the wild strains will continue to furnish us with the next generation . . ."

With an abrupt shrug of excitement, he added, "Yet there *is* hope! Suppose our heritage has lain under a mantle of impotence as the northern continent lay under ice: the end of the Northern Freeze may signal salvation for us mukes! I couldn't begin to tell you why I foresee this; it may be leaked from dreamness to my mind. Still, the border between dreams and imagination might very well fluctuate just as the boundary between ice and ocean does... Oh, time will judge. Now watch the way the land is changing on this coast. Look not just for the flighters that bore back southern seeds when they quested their prey into these waters, because as you know some seeds pass clear through the digestion of a flighter and are nourished by the dung they're dropped in, nor for what they brought when it foliates and blossoms, but for what lay hid till now when the sun came back and released it... Ah, but darkness falls. Tomorrow, though—!"

And he was right. He was astonishingly right. Next dawn revealed what he predicted, and Yockerbow decided—though he could not convince Arranth he was correct in saying so—that among Barratong's chief gifts must be the art of assessing whether someone who relayed a story to him told the truth.

For their course came to a dead end in a wide bay whose northern shores were still blocked off by a huge glacier. Some drifts of mist hung about it, but it was a fine morning and a brisk wind disposed of most of them within an hour.

And, either side of the steep bluish mass of ice, life was returning. Not only were the drab gray sand-slopes nearby aweb with creepers and punctuate with burrowers: the air was full of unexpected wingets. The mariners caught as many as they could, for some were known to lay maggors which infested junqs, and brought them to Barratong for examination.

"They're unlike any in the south," he stated. "Even if they are similar, then the colors vary, or the size, or the limb-structure. Is the Fleet still thriving?"

"As ever!" came the enthusiastic report. "We didn't expect to fare so well this far north, but the junqs' maws are crammed and we ourselves enjoy the food we reap from the sea!"

"Then here's our landfall, and our harvest will be knowledge!" cried the admiral. "Report to me whatever you find unusual—"

Something shot past him with a whizzing sound. A moment later, Ulgrim, who stood nearby, cursed and clapped a claw to his upper mantle. Withdrawing it, he displayed a pointed object with a pair of vanes on the after end. Similar noises continued, and complaints resounded from all the nearby junqs.

"What in the world—?" began Yockerbow, but Arranth cut him short.

"Those must be seeds!" she exclaimed. "Did you never play the game we did as younglings—placing seeds like those on a rock and shining sunlight on them through a burning-glass until they flew away?"

Once again Yockerbow found himself at an embarrassing loss. When he was a youngling, he had known nothing of such miracles as lenses, or indeed any form of glass. Attempting to recoup his pressure, he said, "You mean heat bursts them?"

"Burst? Not in the sense a bladder bursts, dear me! They emit some sort of stinking gas from one end, and that makes them leap through the air."

All this time, a horde of the things was descending on them, and Barratong—who else?—was reasoning about the strange phenomenon.

"They must be coming from up there," he said, and pointed to a bluff a little above their own level, where a dark shadow was growing more and more visible as ice melted and water cascaded down the lower rocks. "That's where we'll send explorers first. A sign of life is never to be overlooked."

"And the top of that bluff," said Arranth in high excitement, "would be just right to set up the telescope I brought! That is," she added hastily, "if the dark-time is as clear as this morning, and weather-sense indicates it may be."

Exuding an aura of puzzlement, Barratong said, "I fear you're right."

"Fear?"—from two or three voices simultaneously.

"Our whole voyage has been strange," the admiral said after a brief hesitation. "Too fair weather—no storms to mention—the bergs dissolving as we passed by . . . There is a real change taking place in the world, and it disturbs me. We must seize our chance, though! Overside with you!"

The Fleet having been instructed to make all secure, a small group of crewmen was detailed to follow Ulgrim and find a way to the cliff-top where the telescope might be sited. Meantime Barratong, Yockerbow, and Arranth, who was too impatient to concern herself with preparatory details, set off along a sloping miniature watercourse towards the source of the flying seeds. Its bed was pebbly, and the flow chilled their pads, but they were able to obtain a good grip on the gradient, and shortly they found themselves looking at a shadow behind a veil of ice.

"Now there's a cave!" declaimed the admiral, loudly enough to overcome the rushing of streamlets which was greeting the advent of renewed summer. (Had there been one last year? It seemed unlikely; Yockerbow was prepared to believe that Barratong's weather-sense had picked the very first possible year for folk to return to these latitudes.) "What icefaw or what snowbelong may have laired here! What refuge it may have offered to beasts we exterminated when the Freeze drove them southward! You realize, of course"—lapsing into his most condescending and didactic mode—"that up here there may still be creatures which cannot live off vegetation but devour other animals, as sharqs eat other fish?"

For once the others paid him no attention. They were seeking the source of the flying seeds, and shortly found it: an ice-free patch was exposed to sunlight on the side of the adjacent rock, and a small, tough, low-growing plant was exerting its utmost efforts to reproduce itself, though by this time its main arsenal had been expended and only a few weak flutterings resulted.

Standing back, Arranth began, "I think—"

"Look out!" Yockerbow roared, and dived forward to push her clear of impending disaster.

Whether it was the effect of sunshine, or whether—as they later wondered—the mere vibration of their presence sufficed, the ice-veil before the cave was starting to collapse. A web of cracks appeared; a grinding sound followed . . .

"Down!" roared Barratong, and set the example as

great frozen shards fell crunching and slid down the watercourse. They clutched at what they could, including one another, and somehow succeeded in not being carried bodily away.

And got uncertainly to their pads again, for nothing worse emerged from the cave than a most appalling and revolting stench, as of corpses shut up for uncountable years.

It blew away, and they were able once again to venture close, while the low northern sun beamed on them from a clear blue sky. At the cave-mouth things glistened wetly, and a few were instantly identifiable.

"There's a mandible," Barratong muttered, kicking it. "People too were here, you see?"

"Where there were people, I look for what people make!" shouted Arranth, and began to scrabble among the dirt at the opening. And checked, and said something incomprehensible, and rose, clutching a long rigid cylinder such as no creature in the world had generated naturally.

"It's a glass!" she cried. "It's a glass tube! And I hear something rattling inside!"

She made as though to crunch the crackly-dry wax that closed the tube's ends, but Barratong checked her.

"Not here! Whatever's in it must be fragile, for it's certainly very ancient. We'll take it back to the junq and open it with great care in a safe place. Are there any other relics like it?"

Reaching for the mandible, he used it as a scraper, and the others joined him in sifting through the foul mass of putrid matter at the cave entrance. Shortly they were satisfied there was nothing else as durable as the glass tube, and returned on board.

There, quaking with excitement, Arranth broke the wax and removed a stopper made of spongy plant-pith. Tilting the tube, she shook from it a tightly rolled bundle of documents, inscribed on an unfamiliar off-white bark. The moment she unrolled the first of them, she exclaimed at the top of her voice.

"I can't believe it! It's a star-map!"

"Are you certain?" Yockerbow ventured.

"Of course I'm certain!" Studying it feverishly, she

went on, "And either it's inaccurate, or...No, it can't be! It shows the stars as they were before the Freeze, and straight away I can assure you: some of the constellations aren't the same!"

VIII

The past can communicate with us...

Echoes of Arranth's repeated argument kept ringing through Yockerbow's mind as he and Barratong, and the senior Fleet sub-commanders, gathered to hear the result of her and Ulgrim's researches. In spite of aurorae and shooting stars they had been pursued through every dark-time until now, when their weather-sense warned of an approaching storm and indeed clouds could be seen gathering at the southern horizon. Every junq had been ransacked for writing-materials, and meticulous sketches were piled before Arranth, each adjacent to one of the pre-Freeze maps. Yockerbow shivered when he thought of their tremendous age. Yet they had been perfectly preserved in their airtight container.

Delighted to be the center of attention, Arranth could not resist preening a little, but when Barratong invited her to present her report, she spoke in a clear and businesslike manner.

"With only a single telescope and what crude instruments we could improvise, Ulgrim and I have not been able to make the sort of exact measurements that could be performed at a proper observatory. However, that is paradoxically fortunate. Whoever compiled these ancient maps can have had access to a telescope barely better than our own, if at all, so we have an excellent basis for comparison. In other words, we can be reasonably sure that the stars we see and those depicted on the old maps correspond. Thoughtfully enough, the map-maker indicated which stars were visible to the unaided eye, and which only with the aid of a glass. We have therefore been able to establish the following facts.

"First: the stars do change position—very slowly, but unmistakably—and some have certainly grown brighter.

"Second: there are not just a few but *many* stars now discernible which were not known to the map-maker, and all of them have something most disconcerting in common. They are all deep red, and they all lie in the same general area of the sky. Which leads me to the third point.

"What we have been accustomed to call the Smoke of the New Star can be nothing of the sort. We have traced the site of the New Star, which in the days when these old maps were prepared was still clearly visible, though now it takes a strong glass to detect it. Indeed, one does not so much see the star itself, as a faint and wispy cloud of glowing gas with a dot at its center. But this is *not* the large, widespread cloud we normally think of. It's too far away—several degrees distant. On the other claw, within it there are some genuinely new stars, which must be far newer than that fabled one which burst out without warning and became brighter than the sun, as the old legends claim—though, strangely, no reference is made to heat from it.

"Within the Smoke, as I was saying, we have counted no fewer than ten stars of which there is no sign on the old maps. Moreover, what reference is made to the Smoke is cursory and vague, and no outline is indicated for it, though we can see one fairly clearly. All these ten new stars, what's more, are reddish, even darker than the Smoke, as though they only recently lighted their fires. They are barely bright enough to make the surrounding cloud shine by reflection, and much too far away to account for the ending of the Freeze.

"And even that is not the most astonishing news."

Having helped as best they could with the observations, Yockerbow and Barratong were primed for the final revelation, and glanced covertly around to see what impact it would have on the unforewarned.

Using an image which Barratong himself had supplied, Arranth said, "Imagine the Great Fleet keeping station on a calm sea, and yourselves aboard a solitary junq making haste towards it. Would you not see the nearest of the

Fleet diverge to either side as you drew close, while the furthest remained at roughly the same angle?"

Puzzled at being reminded of something that everybody knew, her listeners signified comprehension.

"What disturbs and even frightens me," concluded Arranth, "is that scores of stars whose positions we can check against the old maps appear to have diverged outward from a common center, and that center is located in or near the Smoke. Either we, with the sun and all its planets, are hurtling in that direction, or the Smoke and its associated stars are rushing towards us. It makes no difference which way you look at it; the outcome is the same. And if, as certain astronomers believe, stars begin because they accumulate surrounding matter, be it whole wandering planets or mere dust like what comes to us as meteorites and comets, then there must be incredible quantities of it in any zone where ten new stars have started to burn since these maps were drawn!"

As though to emphasize her words, a meteor brilliant enough to shine through the daytime sky slashed across the zenith, and immediately thereafter Barratong cried, "Get those maps under cover! The storm will be upon us any moment!"

An echo of thunder confirmed his warning, and they scattered, the sub-commanders to their respective junqs, Arranth, Ulgrim, Yockerbow and Barratong to huddle beneath the shelter offered by their own's haodah.

Tucking the precious maps carefully into the tube again, Arranth said, "Do you think they understood?"

"Most of my fellow-navigators," Ulgrim grunted, "have never thought about stars except to figure out what use they are in guiding us, and most of our lives that hasn't been much, you know. The admiral's right: a real change is working in the world. This is more the sort of weather I'd have expected here in the far north, not the clear bright kind we've had since our arrival."

The first assault of rain rattled the canopy of interwoven reeds that formed the haodah's upper deck, and the junq stirred restlessly as the air-pressure changed.

"Will the fine weather return?" asked Arranth.

Her question was mainly addressed to Ulgrim, but before he could answer Barratong cut in.

"It's over-soon to guess, but either way we must get

these maps to where they'll be most useful. To begin with, I shall arrange to have them copied with the utmost care. I know who among the Fleet are most skillful at writing and drawing. Of course, I don't know whether we have enough writing-material left. But we'll do what we can, although we have to kill and flay one of the junqlings to make writing-sheets. Beyond that, though, there's the question of what we should do with the originals."

"Why, we take them back to Ripar, obviously!" Arranth burst out.

"It may seem obvious to you; it's not to me. They should go to the finest of modern observatories, and that's not at Ripar. Besides, Ripar is due to be flooded. Not all your spouse's pumps can save it—can they, Yockerbow?"

He made sober reply. "From the bluff where we've installed the telescope, we've seen ice stretching to the skyline. I wouldn't dare to calculate how far the level of the oceans will rise when it melts, but if it's going to be the same as before the Freeze, nothing can save Ripar or any other coastal city."

"Agreed. We should therefore present them to the observatory at Huzertol, inland from Grench and in a zone of clear skies." The admiral spoke in a tone of finality, not expecting to be contradicted.

"Won't do," said Ulgrim instantly.

"What?"

"Won't do," the navigator repeated. "Huzertol may have the best astronomers in the world, the best instruments—it doesn't matter. That far south, they can scarcely see the Smoke, and some of the other important stars nearby never clear its horizon."

Barratong gave a dry laugh. "You know something, old friend? Next year I think we ought to circumnavigate the globe, if only to impress on your admiral's awareness that we do live on a spherical planet! You're right, of course. We must find a northerly observatory."

"Or found one," said Yockerbow.

"Hmm! Go on!"

"Well, if there isn't any place in the northern hemisphere to outdo Huzertol, there ought to be. Ripar is wealthy, and Ripar is doomed. What better memorial than to create a city dedicated to learning and science on some suitable upland site, to which we could transfer—?"

But Barratong wasn't listening. Of a sudden, he was paying attention to the junq. Her back was rippling in a rhythmic pattern.

"The water's growing warmer," he said positively.

To Yockerbow, that seemed unsurprising, since the heavy rain must be raising its temperature. That, though, seemed not to be what the admiral meant.

A gong-signal boomed across the water. A pattern of banners, rain-limp but comprehensible, appeared at the prow of the junq lying furthest to the eastern side of the bay.

Barratong rose to his normal height as he stepped out from the haodah's protection. He said to Arranth, "Give me the map-tube!"

"What? I—"

"*Give it to me!* Bring cord to make a lashing and a bladder to wrap round it! There's no time to make a new wax seal!"

Ulgrim recognized the scent of authority before the rest of them, and scrambled to comply. While the others stared in astonishment, Barratong folded the tube with its maps inside a skin bag, and tied it tight with all his strength to the thickest of the haodah's multiple crossbars.

"Thus does the legend say Skilluck preserved his spyglass," he muttered, while the gong-signals multiplied and grew more frantic, and the junqs began to fret and buck. "And for the sake of imitating him, I'm risking the greatest fleet that ever was . . ."

The job was done. He turned back to them, claws clenched.

"*Now,* Ulgrim, give the signal! *Open sea!*"

And the Fleet incontinently turned and fled.

The order came in time, but only just. Wide though the bay-mouth was, the junqs jostled and tossed in their mad retreat, and the first huge slabs of the ice-wall were already sliding down as they escaped and their commanders regained control.

"Scatter!" Barratong yelled, and pounded the banner junq's gong. It could not be heard above the scraping, grinding, splashing noise from astern, and the rushing, pounding, battering racket of the new-budded waves that were smashing floes against the rocks. All of a sudden the world rocked and twisted and great hills of water erupted in their path, and sometimes the junqs ascended them at a giddying angle and came close to capsizing and sometimes they crashed into them prow-foremost so they broke and doused the crews and filled the back-wells, soaking the stored food. There was no need to order scattering; the alternative did not exist.

Out from the bay rushed bergs as keen as new-cut fangs, and the junqs panicked in their attempt to dodge. The haodah lashings creaked and the junqs screamed for pain, and some of the youngest sought to escape their burdens by rolling over, but their flotation bladders obliged them to right themselves, and if any riders were lost they were children and old folk too weak to cling on. Primeval reflexes bound the adults to whatever they could grasp, folding their mantles around to reinforce their claws and pressurizing the edges until they were stiff as stone.

In a moment of lucidity Yockerbow thought: *Just so must Skilq, or Skilluck, or whoever, have endured that legendary storm . . .*

Yet it was not the storm which had caused this. It went on pelting down, but it was trifling. No storm could make the ocean heave and seethe this way! Louder than thunder the noise of shattered ice conveyed the truth.

That warming of the water which Barratong had detected must have presaged the undermining of the high ice-wall. Once it collapsed, whatever was pent up behind it was turned loose, and the Fleet was washed away across the world as randomly as those vaned flying seeds . . .

"Has it only been a year?" mourned Arranth, her mantle shrunken by salt and cresh, when next they came to what had been the site of Ripar. There was no more trace of the sea-defenses, no sign of the pumps Yockerbow had been so proud of—only some wilting treetops bending to the water, and a trapped mass of what had been prized personal possessions that washed back and forth, back and forth, in time to the waves. Any corpses must have been devoured long ago, for now a horde of greedy sharqs ruled where the Order of the Jingfired had held sway.

Not all the destruction, of course, had been caused by a simple rise in water-level. Maps and charts explained why Ripar had been worse affected than so many other cities they had visited. Northward, an archipelago had focused the impact of the first gigantic wave, driving it into a single channel where it could no longer spread out relatively harmlessly. Some of the islands had been completely washed away; enough, though, had resisted to ensure that Ripar's fragile protective banks dissolved under the eventual onslaught. Once the city's roots were exposed to the intense saltiness of the warm northern water—warm!—they were doomed.

But the melting was certain to continue, as was betokened by the presence of countless bergs following the same currents as the Fleet, and when—if—all the polar ice returned to the liquid state, the world would be transformed unrecognizably.

They had talked long and long about the future as they strove to recreate the Fleet. Barratong had had the foresight to decree what none of his predecessors had thought necessary: a rendezvous in mid-ocean, near four islands with fresh water and ample vegetation. That was where they had waited out the winter, but one of the islands was shrunk to half its normal size and many of the edible plants were dying...as were too many of the reunited junqs. There was a loathsome taint in the air, and every gust of northern gale brought a drift of grittiness that revolted the maw and made the torso itch beneath the mantle. Sometimes the aurora towards the pole was blanked out not by regular clouds but by some kind of dust, not cleanly star-budded dust such as gave rise to meteors—few, come to that, had been seen this year, hidden no doubt by the same ghastly veil—instead, like the much-feared smoke which drifted from the world's rare drylands when a lightning-strike released wildfire, and could blind and choke those trapped downwind.

"But we saved something worth as much as any city," said Barratong, and pointed to the glass tube holding the old star-maps, which had miraculously resisted the worst the waves could do.

Embittered, Yockerbow as well as Arranth railed at him, and to all their complaining he responded imperturbably:

"You will die, and I, and all we can create—why not a city? But if there is one thing that deserves to be immortal, it is knowledge. Perhaps in the far future like my web to catch the moon a means will exist to unite past and present, here and there, abolishing distance and anxiety at a blow. We spoke a while back, though—did we not?—of an observatory, and a city we shall dedicate to science?"

"A while back" had been very nearly a full year, and Yockerbow, overcome with misery and privation, had long ago dismissed his proposal to the realms of fantasy. He was amazed to hear the admiral repeat it seriously.

"It's out of the question after a catastrophe on this scale," he muttered. "And it isn't over yet. It may take scores of years before the water-level stabilizes. If all the polar ice melts, there may be no dry land whatsoever."

"I don't believe it," Barratong responded. "But even if that's so, we shall build continents of floating weed! We'll not go tamely to an accidental doom! And if we can't learn about the stars, we'll learn about ourselves and the life around us!"

He drew himself up stern and tall, and now he did overtop his companions, for their dispirited mood had sorely shrunk them.

"This you must understand at least: *we* are the Jingfired now."

Eventually the implications of his words penetrated the dismal fog in Yockerbow's mind, and he too straightened. He said, "You intend it seriously?"

"Oh, not at once, of course. First we have other duties to attend to. I shall break up the Fleet, and dispatch it to every corner of the world, bearing seed and medicine and knowledge above all. At every port of call my commanders will be instructed to inquire after secure sites where people may remove to, and rescue whoever needs to be conveyed thither. Also they shall diligently search out scientists and scholars, so that when we choose the site for our new city—not this year, not next, perhaps not in our lifetime—our successors will know where to recruit a population for it. Then let them assemble with their books and instruments and do as you, friend Yockerbow, suggested: combine their knowledge so that none be lost."

"Will you be obeyed in this?" husked Arranth.

"Oh, I think pride will serve to persuade the ones I have in mind."

"Pride in independence, because they will be in command of their own Fleets, with the right to take wild junqlings and increase them?" Ulgrim's tone was cynical; for countless generations, it had been a punishable offense to do so.

"In part." Barratong was unperturbed. "More to the prong, however, pride in ancestry—which I, an ex-landsider, cannot boast of. Think, Ulgrim! Think of how the People of the Sea must already be reacting to the news that their forebears chose correctly! We face nothing worse than storms and tidal waves. If an island we're accustomed to put in at vanishes, we find another; if the waters rise and swamp what was dry land, so much the better, for where there were isthmi now we find new channels that will take us into undiscovered seas ... Oh, we shall be rulers of the western ocean too, and very soon! And will not it make for pride that we give aid to those who boasted of security on land?"

"You think more clearly and more distantly than anyone," said Ulgrim in a sober voice.

"Not I! Not I! But Arranth and her like. You chided

me for not reacting to the fact the world is round! She saw the very stars moving apart like local floes!"

He gave a little crazy laugh. "That's why I must break up the greatest fleet that ever was. There aren't enough of us to fight the stars, and after this long melting we'll be fewer still. We need a score of Fleets, a score-of-scores! We have to be so crowded and so crammed together that we can burst outward from the world—become like these!"

From one of his baldrics he produced a tiny object, dry and shriveled.

"Remember these?"

"One of the seeds that pelted us up north," said Yockerbow.

"Correct! Well, if a mindless plant can find a way to spread beyond its isolated patch, why shouldn't we? Did it ever strike you that there must have been a first person who pithed a barq or briq, just as there was certainly a first who tamed a junq? Then, folk were confined to continents or islands, and had to trudge wearily from place to place unless they had a drom—and someone, equally, must have been first to ride a drom!"

Ulgrim and Yockerbow exchanged worried glances. Sometimes nowadays Barratong spoke so strangely . . . Only Arranth seemed totally to understand him, as though he and she, during this dreadful winter, had found a skyward course into the future in their joint imaginations. But how sane was their shared vision, when the world itself was dissolving back into its primeval waters?

"I wish," said Yockerbow, scarcely realizing he had spoken audibly, "I'd never left Ripar. I'd rather have been here to tend my pumps, to learn their limitations and escape to high ground where I might have built them anew and much improved."

"Somebody will," said Arranth with assurance. "Now your task is to wander the world teaching those who need to know how it was done, just as mine is to explain the star-maps that—thanks to Barratong—have been preserved. You never respected the Order of the Jingfired, and you had some justification, I suppose, given that you devised new methods not envisaged by its ancient wisdom. But I always did, even when I was angry at the way intrigue and self-seeking tarnished its ideals. And if Barratong, who at first mocked it, has come around to my point of view—well!"

Acid rose in Yockerbow's maw. He was minded to utter cruel truths, for she had not truly respected the Order, only envied its members, wanted her spouse to be inducted for the glory of it. He meant to tax her with her ridiculous adoption of crossed strands of sparkleweed in imitation of an admiral's baldrics, seeking petty temporary fame by setting a trend.

Yet he could not. This last appalling year had altered her. The first signs had already been apparent when she spoke with such authority of the discoveries she had made with Ulgrim. Now she had grown used to being someone other than her old self. In a way not even she could have foreseen, she had fulfilled her ambition and become the admiral's lady.

Who was this new strange person who confidently claimed to understand the actions of the stars?

Not his spouse. Not anymore...

So leave her the luxury of self-deception, that she might the better convince the few who, like her and Barratong, could see beyond the current crisis. For his part, he had information about techniques that would be useful everywhere when folk settled on new lands and needed fresh water drawn from a distance, or irrigation systems, or means to lift a heavy load. Suppose, for instance, there were other creatures than cutinates whose muscles could be isolated and made to grow...

All of a sudden he felt as though a great burden had been taken from him. His mind cleared. Without his realizing, his life had been spent in the shadow of those allegedly greater than himself. They were nothing of the sort; they were merely more powerful. And the power they wielded was puny compared to Barratong's, yet the admiral was ultimately humble before the marvels of the boundless universe, which—Arranth said—now threatened them with something no Great Fleet, no member of the Jingfired, no person whatsoever could defy: a cloud of stars and interstellar gas that must be burning at temperatures unmatched by any furnace.

Compared to the cosmos, everyone was equal. Everyone was a bud of this small planet. Either everyone must work together, or in a few score generations there would be no one.

A flock of cloudcrawlers was passing. He looked up, wondering whether in their serial migration might be sought the secret of survival.

But he knew too little. Still, he had about half his life before him; there could well be time to find out what had been discovered or invented on other continents, as well as by the People of the Sea. The most amazing chance could, as he realized, lead to practical results, and whatever chance itself might be, it had already supplied the most important information.

"The past *can* communicate with the future," he said aloud. "And we're the past."

"Yes, of course," said Barratong. "We have to devise gongs and banners in order to signal our successors as the Fleet does. At every port we shall leave copies of the star-maps, ancient and modern; at every port we shall leave ashore folk who, having fled drowned cities, want to start anew on land with foreign knowledge... We dare not let blind fortune alter the world without hindrance. We too must play our part in changing it. Ulgrim, call a general meet. Today I purpose to divide the Fleet, and the planet."

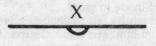

X

The ice's burden lifted swiftly from the northern lands, and new huge rivers carved their course through what had been dry plains. Gigantic floods drowned forests and the creatures living in them; meantime, the ocean-level marked new records every spring. What had been land-bridges turned to open channels; what had been island-chains were strings of shoals.

But most important of all, the weight of frozen water had held down a necessary, long-impending shift of one continental plate against another. Part of the Great Thaw was due to absorption by the sun of a wisp of interstellar gas which for a brief while had helped to mask its radiation. The local space was temporarily clear now, and extra warmth was piercing the atmosphere because fewer dust-motes were falling from the sky to serve as nuclei around which drops of rain or hailstones might develop, and the long ice-age had inhibited production of natural nuclei due to vegetation or the smoke of wildfire.

Another reason for the Thaw, however, was to be sought in the conversion of kinetic energy to heat. Around the north pole there were geysers and volcanoes testifying to the presence of magma near the crust. Patient, they had waited out the period during which so monstrous a mass of ice lay over them that all their heat could serve to do was make a glacier slide or melt a summer valley for migrating flighters. The continental plates which powered them, however, were on a different and grander scale. No ice could long have resisted their padlong-per-year progress, and the added solar warmth did no more than hasten what was inevitable.

The ice-cap shattered in a laq of seizures, each one casting loose a craw of bergs. Lava leaking from far underground met open water and solidified and then was cast high into the air when water turned to steam. Plume followed eruption followed temblor, and at every stage more water streamed back from the arctic plateau to the ocean.

Somehow the separated Fleets survived, even though their business became, first and foremost, mere survival, and their admiral's vision of immediate salvation was eroded by the giant waves that unpredictably rushed from the north and, later, from the south as well, where there was no such enormous valley as the one which had penned in the Salty Sea to deliver its new water all at once.

Often overloaded, so they were forced to land unwilling riders on half-sunken islands in the hope at least their mountain peaks might rise above the water when the oceans calmed; often driven off course by storms such as nobody had seen in living memory; often picking their cautious way over what had been a land-mass a scant year or two ago, searching for anything which might be useful, be it edible carrion or a batch of tools and instruments which would float; often rescuing survivors from a sunken city most of whom were starved into dreamness already and having to make the harsh decision that they must be again abandoned, for their sanity was poisoned past all hope of cure; often—once the barriers between the eastern and the western oceans had been breached—confronting herds of wild briqs, savage in a way that junqs had never been and panicked by an amazing explosion of gulletfish, so that they had to reinvent on the basis of legend and guesswork the means to pith a briq, with the minor consolation that if the attempt failed there would at least be food for the folk on board, and the major drawback that the taint of their own kind's ichor in the water drove the other briqs frantic with terror; often near despair and redeemed only by messages from another luckier Little Fleet, with an achievement to boast about such as the safe delivery of a group of scholars to an upland refuge...

The People of the Sea endured the horrors of the Thaw and by miracles preserved the vision Barratong bequeathed to them.

Meantime, the landsiders moved along the tracks and paths available. Confronted by the rising water, they summoned droms and other mounts and loaded them, and struggled up steep mountainsides, collecting useful seeds and spores. Again and again the caravans were overwhelmed by hunger or sickness caught from murrained water, or trapped on a valley path when floods came rushing down. Desperate, some resorted to the use of fresh-water barqs, only to see them wilt and die when salt afflicted their tubules.

A few, however, found a way to safety, and after cautious negotiation settled on high ground near existing hamlets, being eventually made welcome because they had brought new food-plants and, above all, because they offered the chance of fertile first-time matings to communities whose numbers were diminishing.

Following the caravans, though often having to invent new routes, discontented wandering scholars trudged from town to new town seeking their lost equals, each bearing something of what had been known in a city sunk beneath the waves or lost when a hillside slumped into the sea. Occasionally they borrowed the services of the tramp junqs which, after the dispersal of the Lesser Fleets, traveled in groups of three or four and traded as best they could along inlets of the sea that formerly had been mountain passes or river-valleys. The hegemony of the People of the Sea endured, but the mixing of the landsiders resulted, almost at once, in an explosion of population, for instead of one pairing in several score producing a bud, suddenly five took, or even seven, and wise persons argued about miscegenation, and proper diet, and the influence of privation, and it seemed that most of them must be at least partly correct.

The sea-level stabilized. Those fortunate astronomers who had access to long-term brightness records for the sun admitted cautiously that it looked as though the extra heat due to infalling matter was over. Those who had preserved their presence of mind during the period of violent quakes, devising means to mark and measure the trembling of the land, noted with satisfaction that it shook only now and then, and hilltops seldom broke loose anymore. Such scientists, when they met them, the People of the Sea declared to be Jingfired, and gave them copies of the ancient star-maps. It was a mere token, for the donors scarcely understood what the maps recorded, yet they were seeds of knowledge, after their fashion. The skies cleared, and there was no longer a gritty stench when the wind blew from the north. Daringly, a few started to maintain that an outburst of volcanic dust had protected life on the planet from the worst effects of increased solar radiation . . . but it was at best a guess, lacking evidence.

When the world settled back to an even keel, explorers set forth once more who employed techniques that once had been the private property of jealous cities: means to signal across vast distances, means to preserve knowledge by multiplying it in countless copies; medicines to cure common illnesses, others to master strange rare disorders; tools for tasks that most people had never dreamed of undertaking; seeds so treated they would yield edible fruit simply by being soaked in salty water when required; vegetable parchments that changed color when light shone on them, which placed at the proper distance from a lens would fix an image; juices and saps which served to bind together plant and rock, or glass and metal; vessels not of wood or hide but melted sand, not exactly glass but stiffer, wherein a fire might safely be lighted on the back of a junq without the creature suffering...

Tricks and ideas, hints and suggestions, cross-fertilized and bred faster than the population. A means was needed that would match one invention, to be exchanged, against another. After much fierce debate, it was agreed that persons schooled in the desired technique should be the unit, and the surviving Little Fleets should carry them for longer or shorter periods among the folk requesting the new knowledge. By now, however, many of the new cities had their own research groups, not to mention their own miniature Fleets, and the system rapidly broke down.

It made no odds. The time was past when one city might strive for superiority over its neighbors. The impulse was for sharing, because over all of them loomed the threat which they could now read directly from the sky. Even the southmost of the settlements, shielded from all the new stars in the Smoke, accepted it. Beyond a doubt the day would dawn when the folk, in order to survive, must quit their world.

How, naturally, none yet knew...

As for the banner junq of the Great Fleet of the Eastern Sea, her last recorded trace was when they brought to Yockerbow, old then and shrunken-mantled, a bundle found among jetsam on what had been the slopes of a mountain inland from Clophical, and now was a steep beach beset by trees. His name was inscribed on it three times. The finders located him without trouble; he was famous, because he had become the lord and leader of a scientific community not quite like what he, Barratong and Arranth had envisaged, but near enough. Scholars flocked to him from every land, and new discoveries and new inventions flooded out as water had poured forth when the ice-wall broke and loosed the Salty Sea.

"Here is," he said when he had opened the bundle—with assistance, for his pressure was now weak—"the original glass tube which held the ancient star-maps. I wonder what happened to the maps themselves. Not that it matters; we've found other better copies. What map, though, could show me where to find my lost lady Ar-ranth? What chart could guide me to my old friend Bar-ratong?...Oh, take this thing to the museum, will you? I have much work to do, and little time."

PART FOUR

BREAKING THE MOLD

I

Few communities on the planet were more isolated than the settlement at Neesos, a dark-and-a-bright's swim from the mainland. Once the island had been linked to it by a narrow isthmus passable even at high tide, but the Great Thaw had drowned that along with most of its fertile land, and for scores of years it was visited solely by fisherfolk riding kyqs with their trained gorborangs perched on the saddle-branches like dull red fruit. There were still sandbanks, though, and tradition held that in the past such sand had furnished excellent glass. A certain Agnis eventually made an expedition thither and, finding the tale correct, set about producing magnifiers.

However, he did so at a time when a chillward shift in the weather had led to a revival of religion. Made hungry by the failure of staple crops, the folk were as ever victimized by those who, by starving themselves voluntarily, claimed to obtain visions of a higher reality. In truth, so Agnis charged, what they craved was power over others, and they hoped to gain it by preventing the public from directly consulting the Jingtexts, wherein might be sought solutions to all worldly woes . . . not, naturally, that every humble person might aspire to read the ancient teachings without guidance, for they were couched in archaic symbols, a far cry from the crisp and simple script used for modern messages, and the speech itself had changed almost beyond recognition.

This did not content the relidges, eager as they were to draw down everybody to that mental level where reason was indistinguishable from dreamness. Sight was the first mode of perception to be diminished by famine, as weather-sense was the last, but it was in vain for Agnis to argue that by providing artificial aid he was encouraging the spiritual advancement of the folk. The relidges countered by saying it made them more vulnerable to the rationalist writings now being distributed in countless copies thanks to the invention, by some foreigner beyond the horizon, of a vegetable which could be made to ooze blackish stains on a dry absorbent leaf in exact imitation of any mark inscribed on its rind. Images had long been fixable, at least in one color; soon, it was claimed, means would be found to reproduce them as well.

Despairing, Agnis gathered his family and a few supporters and made for Neesos with the town's entire stock of burnable wood. The cool phase of the climatic shift, far from enough to reinitiate the Northern Freeze, did not prevent the sky being bright over this region for almost half the year, and when the sun was up its rays could be focused. Using his pilfered fuel, Agnis cast a giant mirror and with it melted colossal quantities of sand. This served to fabricate spyglasses of outstanding quality, such as lured not only fisherfolk but even the all-powerful People of the Sea. Shortly his village was better off than the town its inhabitants had quit, since the latter had little left worth trading for.

Sometimes the settlers found relics of the far past in the shallow waters around Neesos, and they too served for trading purposes, mysterious though their nature might be to the modern mind. In consequence, it was into a community more prosperous than its isolation might have suggested that Tenthag—half a score of generations in direct succession from Agnis himself—was budded in the year called Two-red-stars-turn-blue.

But the community was so small that the People of the Sea were rarely able to trade what they most wanted and needed at Neesos: stock with which to cross-breed themselves. They had sampled every genetic line on the island, and every line, in turn, was already spiked with some of the travelers' ichor.

Long-lived, reasonably content, the folk of Neesos were resigned to budding being rare. It was not until three quarter-score of years had slipped away that they began to notice:

There has been no new bud since Tenthag.

As soon as they realized he was "special" the folk of Neesos started to pamper the boy, which he found no fun at all, for it meant he was forever being prohibited from doing the things the other young'uns enjoyed. The old'uns said "protected," but it amounted to the same boring thing.

Yet his slightly older companions were contemptuous of his youth, and very shortly there was only one left for him to play with. The rest had gone on to the pretence of being grown-up, although their matings led to no offspring. Tenthag wished achingly that they would, to release him from his confinement in a web of concern.

Still, his father Ninthag was a perennial optimist and, despite the pleas of Sixthon who had budded Tenthag for him and never childed with anybody else, he was happy to turn a blind eye when his son did what in olden times all young'uns were accustomed to—go swimming out of storm-season on the northern coast—along with Fifthorch, who was next-to-youngest.

Here there were beaches sown with rocks defining the trace of what had been Prefs, the port serving crag-beset Thenai in the days before the water-level rose a score of padlongs. Great ocean-going briqs and junqs had unloaded here, revealing marvels brought from half the world away, and sometimes odd bits and pieces that had proved unsalable had been tossed overside before the fleets returned to sea. Young'uns sought for them, trapping as much air as possible beneath their mantles before they dived, in the hope of retrieving artifacts intact. But that had been in the old days. Now only scraps were to be found, at least at any level they could reach.

Nonetheless Fifthorch spent as much time as he was spared from his apprenticeship at the general trade of glassworking, plunging and basking around the northern shore, and perforce Tenthag tagged along. He did not really like Fifthorch, but there was no alternative; he so hated being fussed over and petted by the old'uns.

Eventually, they all assumed, he would fall into the standard pattern of the island's folk, and were its population to die out, someone else would take it over. That was the way it had been since time immemorial, and even though a few stars might turn color, life down here was not expected to alter very much. The age of changes seemed to be long past, bar the occasional shift of weather.

It did sometimes puzzle Tenthag why, if nothing was to change worth mentioning, there should be so many relics of a different past lying just off shore. But when he tried to talk about this to the old'uns they were always busy with something else, and if he voiced his private anxieties to Fifthorch, the latter mocked him, quoting what he had been told by his own father, who despised the Jingtexts.

"The form of now is permanent," he would insist. "If there were changes in the past, it must have been because what passed for people then were only animals. We were set here by the Evolver to use and exploit the lower orders. Now we know how to do it—we have gorborangs to catch fish for us, we have kyqs to ride on when we put to sea, we eat enough to let us tell reality from dreamness, we live a proper life that must not be disturbed! And nothing can, and nothing will, disturb it!"

Thereat, becoming bored, he would propose a diving expedition, and—not wanting to seem ungracious, nor to become bored himself—Tenthag would once more risk the effect of salty water on his tegument.

He relished the experience of plunging through the ocean shallows, as his ancestors must once have plunged through air from branch to branch of forests now lost beneath the waves, but he could never quite rid himself of awareness of what nightly he saw marked out on the sky. Since he quit infancy and was able to erect himself and raise his eye to the zenith, he had been fascinated by those brilliant spots and streaks... and started to wonder why his elders never paid them any attention except when there were unusual displays, and seemed almost to welcome the dull season—regardless of its storms—when clouds closed over land and sea alike. Did not the Jingtexts refer to changes which...?

But "change" and "Jingtext" were incompatible, they said, one necessarily contradicting the other. If a scripture spoke of change, it must be taken metaphorically, as parable. The year of his birth, when two stars turned to blue, was dated in the manner of a nickname.

And so it went, with Tenthag defeated at all turns, until the year whenafter the world could never be the same.

II

It wasn't kyqs that year which swam into the bay as soon as the spring hail died away, but junqs and briqs far grander than ever had been seen before at Neesos. Moreover, they arrived without the slightest warning.

Led by Ninthag and his deputy, Thirdusk, the folk assembled on the shore in mingled wonder and apprehension. Even the People of the Sea did not boast such magnificent steeds, so finely caparisoned with secondary life-forms. Who could these strangers be?

Very shortly the explanation spread, and generated universal amazement. Those who had come hither were not any sort of common trader, though prepared to pay for what they took; they hailed from a city far to the south, called Bowock, and they went by a name whose roots were drawn from Ancient Forbish, "archeologists"—which some of the more learned of the folk patronizingly rendered into today's speech for the commonalty, making it "pastudiers."

What they wanted, they declared, was to explore the underwater ruins, and they would offer either food and tools for the privilege, or new kinds of seed and animal-stock, or something abstract known as "credits" which allegedly would give the folk of Neesos privileges in return if ever they were to visit Bowock. Since nobody from here in living memory had voyaged further than the horizon, the latter were turned down at once, but the rest appealed, and a bargain was struck with which the majority of the folk were in agreement. What little wariness remained soon melted when the newcomers exclaimed over the fineness of the local glass and ordered magnifiers, microscopes and new lenses for a strange device used to find relative positions, hence distances otherwise impossible to measure. These they exchanged for the right to deepwater fish caught from their junqs and briqs.

Almost the sole person who continued to grumble about this intrusion was Fifthorch, because the strangers had occupied his favorite area for swimming.

Not wanting to lose his only friend, or what passed for one, Tenthag dutifully agreed with him, even though his pith wasn't in it. He was fascinated by the newcomers, above all because, for people concerned with the past, they had so many new gadgets and inventions at their disposal. They had set up a mainland base, where they were necessarily treating with the folk of the town the Neesans' ancestors had fled from—though time had healed most of the old wounds—and made some sort of connection with it to carry news faster than the swiftest briq could swim. A cable like a single immensely long nerve-strand had been laid along the sea-bed between the two places, and covered over with piles of rock carefully set in place by divers wearing things called air-feeders: ugly, bulging, parasitical organisms bred from a southern species unknown, and unhappy, in these cool northern seas, which somehow kept a person alive underwater. Also they had means to lift even extremely heavy objects, using some substance or creature that contracted with vast force.

Such matters, though, the Bowockers were secretive about. To those who asked for information concerning them they named an impossibly high price. Anyway, there was scant need for such devices here.

Otherwise they were not unfriendly, and came ashore by dark to chat, share food and otherwise socialize; a few of them knew songs and tales, or played instruments, and became tolerably popular. Inevitably, too, there were pairings, but none resulted in a bud, although Tenthag desperately hoped they might. He was tired of being the permanently youngest.

The same problem apparently beset Bowock, though. Now and then the divers, ashore to recover from the toll exacted by their work, would grow confidential after sampling the powerful local araq, and admit that at home there were too few buds to keep up the population, despite contacts with other cities and the People of the Sea. Some went so far as to wonder aloud what they were doing all this for, if in a few score-of-score years there might be no one left to enjoy the knowledge. But they kept on regardless.

What precisely the knowledge was that they hoped to garner from the broken fragments they brought up, the folk of Neesos could not imagine. Little organic material resisted the erosion of salt water; tides and currents had scattered what did endure, like blades, lenses and the burnt-clay formers used to compel houseplants to grow into the desired shape. Within a couple of months most people stopped wondering, and treated the strangers as a familiar feature of the locality.

Tenthag was almost the only exception.

Nonetheless, the day came when some most exciting discovery was made—to judge by the noisy celebrations the pastudiers spent a whole dark in—and shortly afterwards a single rider arrived mounted on a sea-beast such as nobody had ever sighted in these latitudes before. She was unbelievably swift in the water, casting up a snout-wave that broke in rainbow spray, and nearly as large as the smaller junqs, but with a tiny saddle and virtually no secondary plants. She had an appetite of her own, though, and a huge one. Cast loose to browse in the next bay to where the pastudiers were working, she gulped and chomped and gobbled and gulped again the whole dark long. When they were asked about her, the strangers said she was an unpithed porp, specially bred for high-speed travel.

The idea of a porp, even a tame one, in the local waters was not calculated to appeal to the folk of Neesos. Schools of such creatures were reputed to strip vast areas clear of weed and drive away the sorts of fish the folk depended on. However, the Bowockers promised that she would leave again at dawn, carrying important news. What kind of news, they as usual declined to say.

By now there was a feeling among the folk that they should be entitled to a share in the pastudiers' discoveries, and Fifthorch's parents were among the loudest with complaints, although they personally did nothing to cultivate the visitors' acquaintance and laid all the responsibility on Ninthag and Thirdusk. The night when the porp was feeding, Tenthag grew sufficiently irritated by Fifthorch's automatic repetition of his father's arguments to counter them with some of Ninthag's. The result was a quarrel, and the older boy went storming off.

Alone in the dark, under the bright-sown canopy which

was as ever shedding sparkling starlets, Tenthag turned
despondently towards the beach. He was so lost in a mix
of imagination, memory and dream that he was startled
when a female voice addressed him.

"Hello! Come to admire my porp? I understand you
people don't tame any sea-creatures but kyqs, right?"

Taken aback, he glanced around and spotted the person who had spoken: a she'un only some half-score years
his senior, relaxing in a pit in the sand.

This was the rider who had made so spectacular an
entry into the bay? But by comparison with the monstrous
beast she rode, she was puny! Even erect, she would be
a padlong below him, and he was not fully grown.

"We—uh—we don't know much about them," he forced
out as soon as enough pressure returned to his mantle.
"Certainly taming porps is a new idea to us."

"Oh, where I come from there's never any shortage of
new ideas! Our only problem is finding time to put them
all into practice. Are you going anywhere, or would you
like to talk awhile? I'm Nemora of the Guild of Couriers,
in case you hadn't guessed. And you are—?"

"Tenthag," he answered, feeling his courage grow.
"And... Well, yes, I'd love to talk to you!"

"Then make yourself comfortable," she invited.
"You've eaten, drunk, and so on?"

"Thank you, yes. We feed well here, and all the better"—he thought of the compliment barely in time—"because of the Bowockers who bring us deepwater fish."

"Yes, normally you only work the shallows, I believe.
Well, here's something from my homeland which may
tempt you even if you're not hungry. Try some yelg; it's
standard courier ration, but I have more than enough for
this trip because my lovely Scudder is so quick through
the water."

What she offered was unfamiliar but delicious, and
within moments he felt all temptation to slip into dreamness leave him. He was in full possession of himself.

"I hope I'm not keeping you from your friends," he
said.

"Friends? Oh, you mean the archeologists! No, I don't
know them. Anyhow, they're too busy to be bothered
with a mere courier. They hadn't finished preparing their
reports and packaging what they've found, because they

figured I wouldn't be here until tomorrow. But, like I said, Scudder is the record-breaking type...Oh, there goes a beauty!"

A wide and brilliant streak had crossed the sky, to vanish behind low cloud on the eastern horizon. For a moment it even outshone the Major Cluster, let alone the Arc of Heaven.

"There isn't much to do when you're a courier," she said musingly, "except to watch the weather and the sky. Yet I wouldn't trade my job for anyone's."

"I don't believe I ever heard of the Guild of Couriers before," Tenthag admitted.

"Really?" She turned to him in surprise. "I thought we'd pretty well covered the globe by now—but come to think of it they did warn me I was going to a very isolated area. Well, essentially what we do is keep people in touch with one another over distances that nervograps can't span, and transport bulky items which briq and junq trade would delay or damage. That's why I'm here, of course: they found what they were looking for, and the relics are extremely fragile. But you must know about that."

"I'm afraid they don't talk to us about what they're doing," Tenthag muttered. "Not even to the old'uns, let alone someone of my age."

"Oh, that's absurd! I'll have to mention it when I get home. We couriers have strict instructions from the Order of the Jingfired to maximize trade in information. The Guild was originally founded to spread news of the musculator...but I sense you aren't following my meaning."

By now Tenthag was emitting such a pheromone-load of incomprehension he was embarrassed. Nemora, in contrast, exuded perfect self-confidence and, impressed by her tact, he was shortly able to respond.

"The word is new to me," he confessed. "Same as—what was it you said?—nervograp?"

"Hmm! No wonder you still only hunt the shallows! But you must have seen the musculators working here, and you could trade something for a brood-stock. They say you make good glass, and—Oh. Never tell me these 'friends' of mine have bought your entire supply for much less useful goods!"

"I believe," Tenthag answered, quoting what he had

heard from Fifthorch, "they've commissioned a whole summer's output."

"For supposedly dedicated students of the past, they're far too mercenary, then. I'll report that, definitely. Well, a musculator is what you get when you breed a particular type of shore-living creature for nothing but strength—not even mobility, nothing else except the power to contract when one end is in fresh water and the other in salt. You feed it a few scraps, you can breed from it in turn, and you use it for—oh—pumping water where it's needed, lifting heavy weights, hauling a load across a mountain gorge where mounts can't go, and things like that. And a nervograp... But there's one in operation between here and the mainland, isn't there?"

"A way of signaling?"

"Ah, you know about that, at least. That's much newer than musculators, of course—in fact, so new that we're still stringing them overland between cities, and I think this is the first-ever underwater connection. I hope it's being done in time, that's all. We've got to link up everybody on the planet if we're ever to get away."

There followed a long baffled silence. Reacting to it, Nemora said eventually, "I'm sorry about that. I was just so stunned to realize you had no idea what I'm referring to. Aren't the Jingtexts available on Neesos?"

"Not many people can read them," Tenthag muttered. "I've never been allowed even to study the language of them."

"But this is awful!" She erupted out of her sitting-pit in a single graceful surge, and Tenthag had his first chance to see her entire. He was embarrassed all over again. She was perfectly lovely, and there was no way he could hide the exudate that signaled his reaction. Luckily she took it as a compliment.

"Hold that for a while, young'un!" she commanded. "There are some things more important than pairing, you know! You really haven't been told that our sun and all its planets are being drawn into the Major Cluster, and if we don't escape we shall wind up fueling a celestial fire? My goodness, how old are you?"

He had to answer frankly, though he could have wished to pretend he was older. Lying was pointless with anybody who had a weather-sense as acute as Nemora's...and would not someone who piloted a porp singleclawed across great oceans have been selected for precisely that talent?

"I was born in the year called Two-red-stars-turn-blue."

"Then you really ought to be better informed! Why did they turn blue?"

"People here don't pay much attention to the sky," he said defensively.

"That's obvious! Well, the answer is this." Padding up and down, so that her mantle rippled in curves it almost hurt him to watch, she launched into the sort of lecture he had always dreamed of being given by someone older and wiser than himself. "The fixed lights in the sky are suns like ours, but far away. We have records showing that some of them, the nearest, are moving apart; this proves that we're approaching them. I don't mean the ones that move visibly. They're planets like ours, revolving around our sun, and the ones that spill out of the sky are just odd lumps of nothing much which heat up when they fall into our air. But there are too many of them for comfort. We think we're drawing closer to a volume of space where there are so many of these lumps that some must be very big indeed, big as the nubs of comets, and if one of them falls on a city, or even in mid-ocean—! And eventually we think our whole world may be drawn into a sun and go up in another star-turned-blue. The more fuel you put on a fire, the hotter it gets, right? And we don't want to be burned!"

Once more there was a period of silence, but this time it was for reflection. Tenthag felt as though he had been afflicted with acute mental indigestion, but what Nemora had said made excellent sense. Besides, how could someone as ignorant as himself challenge her?

He wanted to ask another million questions, but suddenly one became more urgent than any other. He said faintly, recalling what he had heard about the Bowocker divers, "Just now you told me there were some things more important than pairing. But suppose we don't breed, and there aren't enough people left when we find out how to—what did you say?—escape? In any case, I don't see how we could! First we'd have to learn to fly like cloud-crawlers, and then..."

Speech failed him; he sat dumbstruck.

With a deep chuckle she dropped beside him, so close their mantles touched.

"There are people working on means to fly *better* than cloudcrawlers," she murmured. "One of these days I hope to carry the news of somebody's success in that endeavor. But you're perfectly correct. There must be people to enjoy the benefit of what we're doing now. Would you like to pair with me? I guess it may be your first time, and they do say a first time can be fruitful."

When she departed after dawn, she left behind a transformed Tenthag, who knew beyond a doubt what he wanted to make of his life. To the dark with glassworking! He was determined to be like Nemora: a courier.

III

Later Tenthag concluded ruefully that if he'd realized how much he had to learn, he would probably have changed his mind. Life on Neesos had not prepared him for the complexity of the modern world, and particularly not for Bowock with its eleven score-of-scores of people, its houses every one of which was different (for the city itself served as a biological laboratory and experimental farm), and its ferment of novelty and invention.

Despite its multiplying marvels, though, which rendered public notice-slabs essential—announcing everything from goods for trade through new discoveries seeking application to appeals for volunteer assistance—there was a taint in Bowock's air, an exudate of anxiety verging on alarm. It was known that scores-of-scores-of-scores of years remained before the ultimate crisis, and few doubted their species' ability to find a means of escape, were they granted sufficient time.

In principle, they should be. Disease was almost unknown here and in other wealthy lands; crop-blights and murrains were held in check; everyone had food adequate to ensure rational thinking; maggors and wivvils and slugs were controlled by their own natural parasites—oh, the achievements of the Bowockers were astonishing!

But Nemora had not taken his bud, or anyone's. His first frightened question, so long ago, so far away, on the dark beach of Neesos, was one which everybody now was asking. Indeed, it had been Nemora's commendation of his instant insight which had secured him his appointment as a courier-to-be.

Hence his excitement at the challenging future he could look forward to was tempered by the sad gray shadow of a nearer doom. He tried to lose himself in training and caring for the porp assigned to him, modestly named Flapper, but even as he carried out his first solo missions—which should have been the high point of his life so far—he was constantly worrying about the folk he had left behind on Neesos, condemned to grow old and die without a single youngling to follow them.

He felt a little like a traitor.

"It is Neesos that you hail from, isn't it?" said the harsh familiar voice of Dippid, doyen of the couriers.

Tenthag glanced round. He was in the pleasant, cool, green-lit arbor of the porp pens, formed by a maze of root-stalks where the city's trees spanned the estuary of a little river. Porps became docile automatically in fresh water, a fact first observed at Bowock when one of them was driven hither from the open sea for an entirely different purpose, and between voyages they had to be carefully retamed.

Alert at mention of his home, he dared to hope for a moment that he was to be sent back there. Giving Flapper a final caress, he swarmed up the nearest root-stalk to confront Dippid . . . who promptly dashed the notion.

"The stuff that Nemora brought back from the trip when she met you: it seems to have borne fruit. You know about the work that Scholar Gveest is doing?"

Tenthag scoured his pith, and memory answered. "Oh! Not much, I'm afraid—just that he's making some highly promising studies on a lonely island. It's an example of information trade in which has not been maximized," he added, daring.

But it was a stock joke, and Dippid acknowledged it with a gruff chuckle.

"People's hopes must not be inflated prematurely," was his sententious answer. "But... Well, we've had a message from him. He believes he's on the verge of a breakthrough. What he needs, though, is someone from Neesos to calibrate his tests against."

"Why? What sort of tests?"

"You know what it was that they recovered from the sea-bed at Prefs?"

"I'm not sure I do. I—ah—always got the impression I was supposed not to inquire. Even Nemora was elusive when I asked about it. So...."

Dippid squeezed a sigh. "Yes, you judged correctly. I sometimes wish I didn't know what Gveest is working on, because if he fails, who can succeed? But enough of that." He drew himself up to a formal stance.

"Here's your commission from the Council of the Jing-fired, boy. You're to make with all speed for the island Ognorit, and put yourself at Gveest's entire disposal."

"Did you say Ognorit?"

"I did indeed. What of it?"

"But that's south of the equator, isn't it—part of the Lugomannic Archipelago?"

"You've learned your geography well!"—with irony.

"But I've never been into the southern hemisphere before!"

"There's a first time for everything," Dippid snapped, and clacked his mandibles impatiently. "And if what Gveest is doing turns out wrong, it would be a great advantage to have the equatorial gales between us and Ognorit! Don't ask what I mean by that. Just put to sea. You'll find out soon enough."

It was by far the longest voyage Tenthag had undertaken, and he often wished that Flapper were as swift as Scudder. But each bright-time she pursued her steady way, and each dark she fed and gathered strength anew. She might not be particularly quick, but she was trustworthy, and never turned aside, not even when all her instincts tempted her to run off with a school of wild'uns, or follow a sharq's trail of murder across a shoal of errinq, or flee from the suspected presence of a feroq, the traditional enemy of porps. Little by little he was able to relax.

Cronthid went by, and Hegu, and Southmost Cape, and another day saw them entering the Worldround Ocean, that huge sea where currents flowed around the planet uninterrupted by continental masses. Once it had been different; the Great Thaw had altered everything. Tenthag watched the patterns in the sky change as they drove south, and felt in his inmost tubules, for the first time, that he did truly live on a vast globe adrift in space.

He had to apply all his navigational skills to the correction of Flapper's course; her impulse was to follow odor-patterns and temperature-gradients. He was obliged to ply his goad more often than he liked, but she responded, though she grew a trifle sullen.

Stars he had never seen were their guide now. But he had been well taught, and felt relieved to find his instructors' maps reflected in reality.

Islands loomed and faded, but he ignored them save to check his calculations. Then came a major problem: rafts of rotting weed, each alive with its own population of wild creatures, and uttering pestilential swarms of mustiqs. Someone had forgotten to advise him that it was the southern breeding-season . . . though, of course, he should in principle have known. Itching, swollen, worried by the way they clustered on Flapper's mantle, he was overjoyed when he raised a squadron of free junqs belonging to the People of the Sea. They were much less pleased than he by the encounter, for they regarded the Bowocker courier service as having cheated them of their ancestral rights; for scores-of-scores of years it had been their sole prerogative to trade in information, ever since the days of the Greatest Fleet created by Admiral Barratong.

Tenthag, though, was empowered to issue certain credits redeemable at Bowock and its allied cities, and some of them ensured the chance of pairing. Like every other branch of the folk, the People of the Sea were growing frightened at the fewness of their buddings, so he was able to convince them to part with a couple of spuderlets. Within half a day Flapper was protected from prow to tail by a dense and sticky web, and so was he; it made life easier to watch the baffled mustiqs fidget and struggle in their death-throes. Also they were a useful adjunct to his stock of yelg, and rather tasty.

Then came a storm.

It blew and poured and pelted down for a dark and a bright and a dark, and when it cleared Tenthag was more scared than ever he had been in his young life. He had clung to Flapper—who seemed almost to exult in the violence of the waves—and his stores were safe under her saddle and the spuderlets had made themselves a shelter out of their own web-stuff, and all seemed properly in order but for one crucial point:

Where had the tempest driven them?

There were islands low on the horizon when dawn broke. It was self-insulting for a courier to ask the way, but there seemed to be no alternative. He goaded Flapper towards a cluster of small barqs putting to sea under the wan morning sky, their riders trailing lines and nets for fish.

When he hailed them, they said, "Ognorit? Why, it's half a day's swim due south!"

Half a day? The storm had done him favors, then! Even the fabled Scudder—growing old now—could have brought Nemora to this spot no quicker!

He was already preening when his porp rushed into a narrow bay between two rocky headlands, and an old, coarse-mantled figure padded into the shallows to shout at him.

"You'll be the courier from Neesos that I asked for! It's amazing that you're here so soon—though I suppose you actually started from Bowock, didn't you? Welcome, anyway! Come ashore! I'm Scholar Gveest, in case you need a name to tell me apart from all the animals!"

IV

The meaning of that cryptic statement was brought home to Tenthag as soon as he had set Flapper to browse— a duty he discharged meticulously despite Gveest's obvious impatience.

Then, heading inland in the scholar's pad-marks, he found himself assailed by hordes of wild creatures. Some leapt; some slithered; some sidled; some moved with sucking sounds as they adhered and freed themselves. Gveest was not afraid of them, and therefore Tenthag was not. But what could they possibly be?

Abruptly he caught on. He recognized them, or at any rate the majority; it was just that he had never seen more than one or two of them before in the same place. Whoever heard of six vulps in a group, or nine snaqs, or a good half-score of jenneqs, or such an uncountable gang of glepperts?

His tubules throbbed with astonishment. Whatever Gveest was doing, it had resulted in a most amazing change of these species' usual habits!

And the house he was taken to, on a crest dominating the whole of the island, reflected the same luxuriance. There were trees and food-plants massed together in quantities that would not have shamed Bowock itself, or any rich city in the north. Suddenly reacting to hunger despite his intake of yelg and mustiqs, Tenthag could not help signaling the fact, and Gveest invited him to eat his fill.

"Be careful, though," he warned. "Some of the funqi in particular may be rotten."

Edible food, left to rot? It was incredible! Was Gveest here alone? No, that couldn't be the explanation; here came two, three, five other people whose names he barely registered as he crammed his maw.

Belatedly he realized that his journey had made him

sufficiently undernourished to exhibit bad manners, and
he quit gobbling in embarrassment, but Gveest and his
companions reacted with courteous tolerance.

"You got here with such speed," the scholar said, "we
can't begrudge recuperation time. My colleague Dvish,
the archeologist, informed me that the courier who brought
away his precious discoveries from Neesos also surprised
his party. The efficiency of the Guild remains admirable."

*Though as soon as they learn to string nervograps from
continent to continent, and convey images along them . . .*

Tenthag clawed back the thought. It was bitter for him
to admit that, in his amazement at the greater world, he
had committed his life to what might shortly become an
obsolescent relic of the past. But pretense was useless
when dealing with a weather-sense as keen as Gveest's;
the scholar must be a match for Nemora, for he was going
on, "And despite your worries, there will be need for
courier-service for a long, long while. Regardless of the
principle of maximizing trade in knowledge, some things
are too fraught with implications to be turned loose . . . *yet.*
That's why you're here."

Confused, Tenthag said, "I expected to bear away news
of some great discovery you've made!"

The party surrounding Gveest exchanged glances. At
length one of them—a woman, whose name he faintly
recalled as Pletrow—said, "It's not what you're to take
away that matters right now. It's what you brought!"

"But I brought nothing but myself!"

"Exactly."

After a pause for reflection, Tenthag still found no
sense in the remark. Moreover she, or someone, was
exuding a hint of patronizingness, which in his still-
fatigued condition was intolerable. He rose to full height.

"I am obliged to remind you," he forced out, "that a
courier is not obliged to wait around on anyone's con-
venience. Unless you have data in urgent need of transmission—"

"We sent for you not because you're a courier but
because you're from Neesos!" Ill-tempered, Pletrow strove
to overtop him, and nearly made it. The air suddenly
reeked of combat-stink.

"Calm!" Gveest roared. "Calm, and let me finish!"

Always there was this sense of being on the verge of

calamity, and for no sound reason... In past times, so it was taught, only male-and-male came into conflict; Pletrow's exudations, though, were as fierce as any Tenthag had encountered. But a timely breeze bore the stench away.

"We had expected," Gveest said in an apologetic tone, "that any courier sent here would be fully briefed about our work."

"Even the chief courier told me he wished he didn't know about it," Tenthag retorted. "So I didn't inquire!"

"Then you'd better make yourself comfortable, for when I explain you'll have a shock. The rest of you, too," Gveest added, and his companions swarmed to nearby branches, leaving a place of honor to Tenthag at the center.

Lapsing into what, by the way he fitted it, must be his own favorite crotch, the scholar looked musingly at the patches of sky showing between the tangled upper stems of his house. The fisherfolk's estimate of half a day's swim had been based on the southern meaning of "day"—one dark plus one bright—and the sun had set about the time Tenthag came ashore. Clouds were gathering, portending another storm, but as yet many stars were to be seen, and some were falling.

"Are you surprised to find so many animals here?"

"Ah... At first I was. I wondered how this island could support so many. But now I've seen how much food you have—some of it even going bad—I imagine it's all the result of your research, on plants as well as animals."

"You're quite correct. It seemed essential to improve the food-supply before—" Gveest checked suddenly. "Ah, I should have asked you first: do you know what Dvish recovered from the underwater site at Prefs?"

"The people who dived there wanted too much for the information," Tenthag answered sourly. "And since I joined the Guild the Order of the Jingfired have decreed it a restricted question."

"Hmm! Well, I suppose they have their reasons, but I for one don't accept them, so I'll tell you. During the years prior to the Great Thaw, the people there—presumably having noticed that ice could preserve food for a long time against rotting—became sufficiently starved to imagine that living creatures, including the folk, could also be preserved and, at some future time, perhaps resurrected. Nonsense, of course! But they were so deranged, even after the Thaw began, they went right on trying to find ways of insuring a dead body against decomposition. And one of their late techniques, if it didn't work for a whole body, did work for individual cells. We found a mated pair, sealed so tightly against air and water that we were able to extract—You know what I mean by cells?"

"Why, of course! The little creatures that circulate in our ichor and can be seen under a microscope!"

"Ah, yes—your people make good magnifiers, don't they? Good, that saves another lengthy exposition ... Excuse me; it's been so long since I talked to anyone not already familiar with our work." Gveest drew himself inward, not upward, into a mode of extreme concentration. Frowning from edge to edge of his mantle, he continued, "But that's only one kind of cell. Our entire tissue is composed of them. And even they are composed of still smaller organisms. And, like everything else, they're subject to change."

This was so opposed to what he had learned as a child, Tenthag found himself holding his pulsation with the effort of paying attention.

"And the same is true of all the creatures on the planet, that we've so far studied. Above all, there was one enormous change, which judging by the fossil record—You know what I mean by fossils?"

There had been few at Neesos, but other couriers had carried examples around the globe, including, now Tenthag thought of it, some from this very island. He nodded.

"Good. As I was about to say: there was one gigantic change, apparently around the time of the outburst of the New Star, which affected all creatures everywhere. We came to Ognorit because it's one of the few peaks of the pre-Thaw continents where many relics of lost animals can be dug up. Better still, some local species endured and adapted. They offer proof that we're descended from primitive life-forms. Marooned on islands like this one, creatures recognizable in basic form on the continents are changing almost as we watch, in order to fill niches in the ecology which were vacated by other species killed off by the Freeze or the Thaw. We mainly haven't changed because, thanks to the People of the Sea, we were protected against the worst effect of those disasters. But even though we don't know how some event far off in the void of space can affect our very bodies, something evidently *did*. There was a brief period when we were multiplying rapidly, owing to the miscegenation which the Thaw engendered. It served to disguise a terrible underlying truth, but now there's no more hope of fooling ourselves. We are afraid—aren't we?—that we may die out."

Hearing it put in such blunt terms, Tenthag could not prevent himself from shrinking.

Rising, starting to pad back and forth like Nemora on that distant beach at Neesos, the scholar continued with a wry twist of his mantle.

"Yet for a species that has the power to reason about a doom written in the stars, it's an unjust fate! Have we not thought—not *dreamed*, but *reasoned*—about surviving even if our planet goes to fuel a star? Have we not contemplated that destiny since the legendary days of Jing and Rainbow? That's what drove me here to work on my theory... which, I hope against hope, has proved to be valid."

Calm again, Pletrow said, "You're right, if anybody can be absolutely right in this chaotic universe."

"Thank you for that reassurance. But we must clarify our reason for demanding samples of a Neesan mantle."

"Mine?" Tenthag could achieve no more than a squeak.

"Yes, Master Courier: yours. It is imperative." Gveest turned half-aside, as if ashamed, although his exudates continued to signal arrogant self-confidence. "You are of the only stock on the planet isolated enough to let us make the comparisons necessary if we are to advance our success with lower animals and improve the reproduction of our own kind. We must know exactly what sort of changes have taken place, *because we intend to reverse them*."

Tenthag sat stunned. It was as grandiose a notion as he had ever dreamed of, and he was hearing it stated in real time, in real life, as cold potential fact.

He husked at last, "I'm not sure, even yet, what it is you want of me!"

"About as much of your mantle as Pletrow could scrape off with one claw... Ah, but a final and important question: do you recognize this lady as one of your own species?"

Gveest came to a halt directly confronting Tenthag, and waited.

"Of—of course!"

"But I'm not," said Pletrow, and descended from her branch to stand by Gveest.

"But I could pair with you!" Tenthag exclaimed, beginning to be more afraid than even at the height of the storm on his way hither.

"That's so. But we wouldn't bud."

"How can you be sure? I know mostly it doesn't happen nowadays, and I myself was the last on Neesos, but—Oh, *no!*"

Fragments of what he had learned by chance during his time as a novice courier came together in memory and made terrible sense. He waited, passive, for the truth to be spelled out.

Gveest announced it in a rasping voice.

"Here, and elsewhere around the planet, we have tasted the fossil record. We hunted above all for our common ancestors. We haven't found them. What we have found, and the discovery at Neesos was its final proof, is two separate species which evolved in total symbiosis. You and I, Tenthag, can't reproduce without the mediation of that species which evolved with us and gradually took over the role of bearing our young. We must have been in the closest competition, craws of years ago, equally matched rivals for supremacy. One species, though, opted for acceptance of the other's buds, while mimicking to perfection its behavior—as far as speech, as writing, as intelligence! And we aren't alone in this! Why, for example, does one only tame *female* barqs—briqs—junqs—porps? Those are the malleable, the pliant ones, who adopted the same course as what we call our females, at about the same time in the far past as we were establishing our rule over dry land! We are the highest orders of what some folk are pleased to call 'creation'—though if indeed some divine force called us into existence, I personally would have been glad to give that personage a bit of good advice!"

He was pulsing so hard, Pletrow turned to him in alarm and laid a friendly claw on his back. In a moment he recovered, and spoke normally.

"Well, anyway!" he resumed. "We hypothesize that in

the early stages it was approximately an even chance whether implantation of a bud resulted in offspring for the 'male' version, the implanter, or the recipient, whose hormones were provoked into reproductive mode by impregnation and sometimes outdid the invader, thereby budding a female. We know parasitic organisms, especially among jenneqs, which still depend on the host's hormones to activate their buds; sometimes they lie dormant for a score or more of years!

"But at just about the time the New Star is said to have exploded, wherever and whatever it may have been—*I'm no astronomer, but they say it was somewhere around the Major Cluster*—something provoked the 'female' species into yet another round of mimicry. It must have been a valid defense technique at some point in the far past, but extending it has cost them *and us* our reproductive capability. Tenthag, when Pletrow confronted you, were you not shocked at how male her exudates appeared?"

"I was," said Pletrow before Tenthag could answer. "It's the survival of us all that is at stake. New friend!"—she spoke as she advanced on Tenthag, mantle open in the most intimate of all postures—"do help Gveest! Don't turn him down! I cringe before you and invoke your aid!"

Suiting her actions to her speech, she shrank to two-fifths of her normal height, and bent to touch the courier's pads.

"It is other than my familiar duty," Tenthag achieved at last. "But I was instructed to put myself at Gveest's disposal absolutely, so—"

Pletrow uttered a cry of joy, and as she rose scratched the underside of Tenthag's mantle, which by reflex he had opened as to greet her. Before he could even react to the trivial pain, the threatened storm broke over Ognorit, and the house's retracted leaves unfolded, shutting out the sky, so as to channel the precious water to the ditch around its roots. Instantly there was a clamor from the animals outside, for they knew this gift from heaven would result in an explosion of funqi and other food.

"Long ago," said Gveest, during the brief dark before the house's luminants responded, "there must have been a clash between symbiosis and extinction. Our ancestors preferred symbiosis, so we have to accept it. But the natural system was so delicate, so fragile, that even the explosion of a distant star could ruin it. It's up to us to create a better, tougher one. And this gift from you, Tenthag"—he held aloft the scrap of mantle-skin which Pletrow had passed to him—"may provide us with the information that we need. If it does," he concluded dryly, "they'll remember you one day as a savior like Jing!"

"And if it does," Pletrow promised as the luminants grew brighter, "I'll make amends to you for that small theft of your own substance. I want—oh, *how* I want!— to bear a bud!"

She clutched him to her for a moment, and then the company dispersed, leaving Tenthag alone with his mind in tumult.

In its way, Ognorit proved to be a greater wonderland for Tenthag even than Bowock on the day of his arrival there. Never had he seen a place where everything was so single-mindedly dedicated to one common goal. The island was a maze of experimental farms, pens for live-stock, streams and rivers dammed to isolate breeding populations of fresh-water fish, salt-water pools above tide-level kept full by musculator pumps... and every-where there were exposed fossils, revealed when thin sheets of compacted clay or slate had been painstakingly separated. He was able to taste for himself how ancestral forms differed from modern ones, though the faint organic traces were evaporating on exposure to the air.

"If only we left behind something more durable than claws and mandibles!" said Pletrow wryly; to compensate for her irascibility she had undertaken to act as his guide, and was proving an agreeable companion. Gveest, once possessed of the tissue-sample he had asked for, had van-ished into his laboratory, barely emerging for a bite of food at darkfall. "Suppose," she went on, "we'd had solid shells like mollusqs, or at least supporting frames like gigants! But I suppose the lesson to be learned is that the plastic life-forms do better in a changing environment. Once you develop rigidity you're at risk of extinction."

But aren't we? Tenthag suppressed the thought, and merely requested evidence for Gveest's amazing claim about the male and female of the folk actually being separate species.

Much of what Pletrow offered in answer, Tenthag had already partly grasped. Until he went to Bowock, he had been unacquainted with ideas like "symbiosis" and "commensalism"; however, as soon as they were spelled out in terms of, for example, the secondary growths on a junq's back, he instantly recognized how well they matched ordinary observation. And the notion of plasticity was not at all foreign to him. Since childhood he had known about creatures which seemed not to mind what part of them performed what service. If one took care not to dislodge it from the rock where it had settled, one could literally turn a sponqe inside-out, and the inner surface that had been its gut would become a mantle, and vice versa. But he was astonished by a demonstration Pletrow performed for him with a brollican, a mindless drifting creature from the local ocean, avoided by the folk because of the poison stings that trapped the fish it preyed on. To indicate how far back in the evolutionary chain symbiosis must reach, she carefully peeled one of the things apart, dividing it into half a score of entities so unalike one could not have guessed at a connection between them. Then she tossed food into the pool, and within a day each portion had regenerated what it had been deprived of.

"But if you split them up so completely, how is that possible?" demanded Tenthag.

"Because you can't split them up *completely*. Enough cells from each of the components enter the common circulation to preserve a trace of the whole in every segment, but they remain dormant so long as suppressor chemicals are circulating too. When they stop, the cells multiply until they once again reach equilibrium. I'll show you under the microscope."

Sometimes dazed, sometimes dazzled, Tenthag thereupon suffered through a crash course in modern biology. On the way he learned about the invention of musculators and nervograps—a web of the latter, connected to various sensitive plants, reported results from outlying pens and plots and pools—and about the buoyancy of cloudcrawlers, whose gas-distended bladders had furnished the earliest proof that air was not one substance, but a mixture, and about a score of other matters he had previously felt no interest in.

Clacking his mandibles dolefully, he said at last, "And this incredibly complex, interlocking system could be put in danger by something happening out there in the sky?"

"Ridiculous, isn't it?" agreed Pletrow. "Almost enough to drive one back to astrology! But every line we pursue leads us to the same conclusion. Now we think it may have to do with the fact that some kinds of light can burn. You've used burning-glasses?"

"Well, naturally! I grew up with them."

"But do you realize there are kinds of light too wide to see, and also too narrow?"

After proving her point with a small fire and a black filter that allowed no visible light to pass, yet transmitted heat without any direct contact, she introduced him to mutated creatures from the rest of the Lugomannic Archipelago. This was her specialty, and she waxed eloquent over the creatures she kept in pens on the north shore: vulps, snaqs and jenneqs all somehow *wrong*—lopsided, or looking as though one end of an individual did not belong with the other, or missing some external organ, or boasting an excess of them. Tenthag found the sight repulsive, and with difficulty steered her away from the subject, back towards the crisis facing the folk.

If anything, what she told him next was even more disturbing, for she illustrated it with cells cultured from his own mantle, and invited him to compare them with those recovered from Prefs—and then calmly took a sample of her own tegument to complete the argument. All his life, like virtually everyone in the world, Tenthag had been conditioned against bringing anything sharp towards his own, or anyone's, body. A claw-scratch, such as she had inflicted on him, was nothing, but the risk of having a major tubule punctured, with consequent loss of pressure, was terrifying; it could lead to being permanently crippled. Among glassworkers this was a particularly constant danger. Yet here she was applying a ferociously keen blade to her own side—to judge by the scars already surrounding the area, not for the first time!

Sensing his disquiet, she gave a harsh chuckle.

"They say Jing's Rainbow was deformed, don't they? It can't be *too* disastrous to lose a little pressure . . . but in any case I've had a lot of practice. There we are! Now you can compare one of my cells with one from the female they found at Prefs. You'll notice it's far more like the male's, or, come to that, your own, than it is like hers."

Struggling to interpret the unfamiliar details exposed to him, Tenthag sighed.

"I'm going to have to take your word for it, I'm afraid. I simply don't know what to look for. Can't you tell me, though, what became of our original—uh—females?"

"There never were any," was the prompt response.

"What?"

"Females—that's to say, versions of what we're used to thinking of as females—seem to have occurred very early in the evolutionary process. But prior to their appearance, as is shown by primitive creatures like the brollican, the standard pattern was well established: clusters of simple organisms banded together for mutual advantage and shared a circulation, a chemical bath, which controlled the reproduction of them all. That, though, works only up to a certain level of complexity. If I chopped a claw off you, you couldn't regrow it, could you? And reproduction is only an elaborate version of regrowth. *But*—and here's the main problem—within any single organism there's always decay going on. To renew the stock, without aging, and to *evolve*, calls for some sort of stimulus, some infusion of variety; what, we don't yet know, but we're sure about the principle. We assume it comes from the use of the symbiotic species, whose chemical makeup is much more unlike the donor's than outward appearance would suggest. Or at least it used to be. Now we're back to the change dating from the New Star, and the latest outburst of mimicry, which seems now to be going clear to the cellular level. At all events"—Pletrow briskened, evading the subject that was closest to her pith—"there never were specific females for the folk. Our species evolved together from that stage, craws of years ago, when it became impossible for either of us to continue providing the necessary variant stimuli from our own internal resources. So to say, we'd become so completely efficient as a single organism that we could no longer be peeled apart, and identity had supplanted variety. Probably you males"—with a wry twitch of her mantle—"were essentially parasitic, but you must have been amazingly successful, or you'd never have attracted such a promising species as us females into dependence!"

Controlling himself with extreme effort, Tenthag said, "If Gveest's research is successful, and his techniques can be applied to—to us, what will it involve?"

"Modification of another permanent symbiote that will survive transmission into our own bodies by way of the food we eat, and then restore the original bud-reaction."

For a moment the scope of the plan took the air from Tenthag's mantle. Eventually he husked, "But what about numbers? Gveest himself has said it will be necessary to build up the food-supply—that he had to do it here before trying his methods on vulps and snaqs and so on. Suppose we do suddenly find we can produce buds, if not every time, then twice as often as before, five times, half-a-score times: might we not outstrip our resources?"

"Gveest plans to give us new delicious foods. You've tasted some. But in any case..."

She fixed him with so piercing a glare it transfixed him to the inmost tubule, and her voice was like a prong as she concluded:

"Let the future take care of itself! I only know one thing! *I mean to bear a bud before I die!*"

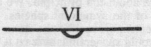

VI

After so long a delay that Tenthag was afraid he might lose control over Flapper, who should either have departed on a new voyage or been retamed in fresh water, Gveest emerged weary but triumphant from his laboratory to announce he had no further need of Tenthag's presence.

"We've successfully established a reproducible strain of your cells," he explained. "That will furnish us with all the data we require. You've performed an invaluable service, Master Courier! Permit us, in return, to re-equip your porp."

"Thank you, but I'm content with the growths that she already bears," was Tenthag's stiff reply. "Besides..."

He hesitated, not wanting to be tactless to this elderly scholar who was, after all, an uncontested genius and on the verge of a breakthrough which might benefit the whole planet.

Might...

It was pointless, though, trying to elude Gveest's weather-sense. Dryly he said, "You're concerned about the probable success of my work. Pletrow told me. That's why I'm disappointed that you won't let me refit your porp. Now we shall have to signal the People of the Sea and let them spread the first stage of our techniques."

"I—I seem to have misunderstood something," said Tenthag slowly.

"So you do, and I'm surprised." Gveest turned to pad up and down along the stretch of beach where they had met, glancing now and then towards Flapper, fretful at her long confinement in the shallows. "I know as well as anybody that, unless we vastly increase our food resources first, doubling or trebling the rate of budding could lead to dreadful consequences. But we're not the only people who've been working on this problem, you realize. There are outstanding scientists among the People of the Sea, just to begin with, who may be more anxious than we are for personal glorification because their traditional role has been undermined by couriers."

Tenthag clenched his mantle as the implications struck him.

"You want to start by publishing your methods of improving crops," he suggested at length.

"Naturally. But the People of the Sea don't keep farms, do they—save on certain islands that they use as temporary bases when the weather's bad? Besides, we landlivers far outnumber them now."

"Is that true? I had the impression—"

"Oh, yes. We've confirmed it over and over. Harvesting what they're used to thinking of as the inexhaustible resources of the sea, they grew very numerous indeed so long as they were benefiting from the interbreeding that followed the Great Thaw. But little by little their population has dwindled, too. Had it not, would there have been a chance to set up the Couriers' Guild, or a need to do so?"

"I've heard that they no longer recruit as many junqs and briqs as formerly," Tenthag admitted.

"They aren't there. Those are life-forms almost as advanced as we ourselves, and subject to the same worldwide problem. What we must do is publish news of what we now know how to do to mounts and draftimals—because improved transport will be imperative—and also to the creatures which our ancestors once used as food."

He uttered the concluding words softly and with reluctance. Tenthag instantly recognized the logic underlying them, but his inmost being was revolted.

"Are we to go back to the ways of savages?" he cried. "I know folk sometimes do in the grip of famine, but for scores-of-scores of years we've fed well enough from *civilized* resources—"

"You eat fish and wingets, don't you?"

"Well, yes, but they're as mindless as plants! I'd never kill a land-creature for food—or a porp like Flapper!"

"We may well have no choice." Gveest was abruptly stern. "We must decide between extinction—slow, but certain—and an increase in our breeding-rate. If we opt for the latter, we must make provision to save ourselves from famine due to overpopulation. Think, *think*! If twice as many buds appear in the next generation, those raising and catching food will just suffice to keep us all well fed—assuming, as I mentioned, better transportation. But if the figure isn't *twice*, but half-a-score times more ... what then?"

Tenthag's pulsations seemed to stop completely for a moment. He said in an awed whisper, "You think your work has paid off so completely?"

"Think?"—with a harsh chuckle. "Beyond my wildest dreams! I now see how to grow a bud from *every* pairing!"

"This is because of me?"

"Yes, what we learned from you made all the difference. You haven't seen Pletrow the past few days, have you?"

"Ah—no, I haven't! She said she was busy with some new research, and I'm used to being by myself, so..."

"She, who never took a bud before, has taken mine, and it's a female, exactly as my theories predicted. Now will you let us re-equip your porp? I should remind you: you're bound by the couriers' oath to distribute whatever information you are given, and there are folk the world around who could learn just by looking at what we plan to graft on her a means to multiply a score of different food-plants! We want—we *need* to have that information running ahead of any news about transforming animals ...like us!"

A terrible chill bit deep into Tenthag's vitals, but his voice was quite controlled as he replied.

"It is not, as you point out, my place to act as censor. I'll leave that to the Order of the Jingfired. I'm amazed, though, that you want to send off one courier, not laqs of us! Surely this is something every expert in life-studies ought to hear of right away!"

"All the experts on the planet may not be enough, but if we fail...Who'd care, if an unpeopled globe crashed on a star? We must have seen it happen countless times! Maybe the New Star itself was some such event! Come, bring Flapper to the fresh-water pool on the east coast. She will be tamer there, and you can retrain her while the grafts are taking."

And, as Tenthag numbly moved to comply, he ended, "But what I said about certain people being able, just by looking, to judge our achievement where plants are concerned, may also hold good for animals and for ourselves. The news you spread will be enough to bring the People of the Sea hither in a year or two. I hope it won't be sooner. The resources of the ocean are no less limited than those of the land, and I greatly fear what would happen were our nomads, already saddened by the fading of their ancient glory, to seize on my techniques before they understood the repercussions. For the time being, therefore, you will be our sole link to the outer world, and Bowock the sole place where all the facts are known."

"But," Tenthag confessed to the Council of the Jingfired a month later, "all Gveest's wise precautions went for nothing. On my outward voyage, beset by mustiqs, I had traded Bowocker credits for a pair of spuders, as you know. Returning, I was accosted by the same fleet, and it appears that rumors of Gveest's success had already reached them. I was faced with the choice between redeeming Bowocker credits against new knowledge—which, I respectfully remind the councillors, is the ultimate justification for their existence—or attempting to dishonor them, and Bowock, by making my escape. The fleet consisted of about a score of junqs, and a few were young and very fast. Not only would I have been trapped for certain; my action would have brought the credibility of Bowock into disrepute. I maintain I had no alternative but to honor the Bowocker pledge."

He fell silent, and waited trembling for the verdict. It was very quiet here in the Grand West Arbor of Bowock; the plashing of waves underpad, where only a mat of roots separated the assembly from ocean ripples, was louder than the distant sound of the city's business. A few bright-colored wingets darted from bloom to bloom; otherwise there was no visible motion beneath the canopy of leaves.

Until the Master of the Order stirred. He was very old, and spoke in a wheezing tone when he spoke at all. His name was known to everyone—it was Iyosc—but this was the first time Tenthag had set eye on him. For years he had been sedentary, like an adult cutinate, incapable of mustering pressure to move his bulk unaided. Yet, it was said, his intellect was unimpaired. Now was the time for that opinion to be confirmed.

"It would have been better," he said at last, "had the credibility of Bowock gone to rot."

A unison rush of horror emanated from the company. Tenthag could not stop himself from cringing to half normal height.

"But the courier is only a courier," Iyosc went on, "and not to blame. It is we, the Order of the Jingfired, who have failed in our duty. We, who supposedly have the clearest insight of all the folk, equipped with the best information and the most modern methods of communicating it, should have foreseen that a solitary courier crossing the Worldround Ocean might be accosted twice by the same squadron of the People of the Sea. Where is Dippid, chief of the couriers? Stand forth!"

Dippid complied, looking as troubled as Tenthag felt.

"We lay a new task on you," Iyosc husked. "Abandon all your others. News of what can be done, thanks to Gveest's research, with food-plants and—yes!—animals *must* outstrip news of what can now be done to people! I speak with uttermost reluctance; like Barratong, who forged the Greatest Fleet in the years before the Thaw, and created the foundations of the modern world, I have hankered all my life after the chance to plant a bud . . . and always failed. Now it's too late. But the notion of two, three, *five* taking in place of one fills me with terror. Long have I studied the history of the folk; well do I comprehend how, when starvation looms, our vaunted rationality flows away like silt washing out of an estuary, to be lost on the bottom mud! Nothing but our powers of reason will save us when the claws of the universe clamp on our world and crack it like a nut! For the far-distant survival of the species, we should have risked loss of confidence in the credits that we issue. Now we are doomed beyond chance of redemption!"

A murmur of furious disagreement took its rise, and he clacked his mandibles for silence. It fell reluctantly.

"Oh, yes! There are many among you who are young enough to benefit—as you imagine—from Gveest's achievement! But are you creating the farms and fields, the forests and the fish-pens, which will be needed to support the monstrous horde of younglings that must follow? Where would you be right now, if you had to support five times the population of Bowock from its existing area? And don't think you won't! As soon as the word gets abroad that the secret of fertility is known here, won't crowds of frustrated strangers quit the countryside and the service of the sea, and concentrate here to await a miracle? We're none of us so absolutely rational as to have forgone all hope of miracles! Besides, by this time it's beyond doubt that the People of the Sea must have landed on Ognorit and appropriated Gveest's techniques."

"No! No!" Tenthag shouted, but realized even as he closed his mantle that Iyosc had seen deeper than he to the core of the matter.

The Master of the Order bent his bleary old gaze on the young courier.

"Yes, yes!" he responded with gentle mockery. "And

I still say you were not to blame. You weren't brought up, any more than I or the rest of us, to react in terms such as the People of the Sea are used to. We tend to think more rigidly; we draw metaphors from rock and glass and metal, all the solid changes in the world that fire can wreak. Theirs is the universe of water, forever in flux, forever fluid. They will not heed the strict conditions we'd apply; they'll rush ahead as on the back of a swift junq, and exclaim with pleasure at the sparkle of her snout-wave. Yet some of them are clever scientists. I'll wager it won't be longer than a year before we learn that they are trading Gveest's discovery to just those poor communities which are least fitted to fill extra maws!"

VII

And those isolated settlements, naturally, were the ones the couriers must leave to last . . .

Obeying Iyosc's directive, the Guild mustered in force to distribute Gveest's data concerning food-plants and—against their will—animals that had once been used for food. Scores of volunteers were impressed to make more and ever more copies, enclose them in waterproof capsules, bind them to the saddles of the porps. Meantime the nervograps were exploited to their utmost and beyond; the two which stretched furthest overland shriveled and died. Therefore old techniques had to be revived, so messages were sent by drum, or tied to flighters, or to bladders cast loose on the ocean currents.

"It must have been like this during the Thaw," Tenthag said suddenly as he, Nemora, Dippid and other couriers readied their porps for departure. Dippid glanced round.

"How do you mean?"

"For the rising waters, put the People of the Sea."

"*Oh*, yes!" said Nemora with a harsh chuckle, giving Scudder a final tap on her flank before ascending the saddle. "Eating away at our outlying coasts, while we make desperate shift to salvage what we can on the high ground! I've always been in love with open water, but for once I wish I could be a landliver, doing something direct and practical to stem the tide!"

"There's nothing more practical than what we're doing!" Dippid snapped. "No matter how much land you culti- vate, no matter how many animals you help to breed, you can't withstand the onslaught singleclawed! We must alert the world, not just a chosen few!"

"Oh, I know that." She sounded suddenly weary as she secured her travel-harness. "But I have this lust for something basic instead of abstract! I want to puddle in the dirt and watch a chowtree grow! I want to see more life come into existence, instead of darting hither and thither like some crazy winget that doesn't even drop maggors!"

Her voice peaked in a cry, and to the end of the porp- pens other people checked and gazed at her.

Tenthag, remembering Pletrow at Ognorit, said sob- erly, "You mean you want a bud."

"Me?" She shook herself, like one emerging from a swim, and curled her mantle's edge in wry amusement. "No, since you I've grown too accustomed to my solitary life! But what I *would* like is a bud from Scudder. Never was there such a swift yet docile porp, and now she's old, and I must train a new one to replace her... Had it not been for this emergency, I'd have asked leave to try and breed her with a wild male. Probably it wouldn't take, but I'd have liked to try, regardless. As things are, how- ever—Oh, never mind my dreams! There's work to do!"

And, shouting farewells, she plied her goad and drove the porp to sea.

Watching her go, Dippid said softly, "That's one prob- lem I hadn't thought of."

"You mean her wanting to raise a youngling of Scud- der's as a—what's the word?—surrogate?" Tenthag sug- gested.

"Exactly. I suspect there may be many cases like hers, as soon as the implications of what the People of the Sea are doing have sunk in."

"But they don't take porps, only briqs and junqs," said Tenthag, missing the point. "So even if they multiply—"

"Of course they don't!" Dippid retorted. "Porps are

what we couriers have made our own, of all the creatures on the planet! But even before Gveest's discovery, we were looking forward to our own abolition. Have we not envisaged nervograps across the deepest oceans? Have we not heard of means to transmit images as well as symbols? And are there not scholars as brilliant as Gveest working on the idea of actual flight, with gas-bladders and musculators to carry folk aloft? Oh, I know what you'll say to that—I've heard it often from the youngest couriers! Given that our ancestors were flying creatures, we could adapt to the air! Maybe you could. Not me, not Nemora. Yet it would be something to have passed on certain skills, in navigation, for example . . . But that's not what threatens us now: not simple obsolescence. It's actual disaster, the risk that in two or three generations' time there won't be enough sane folk to make new discoveries, there won't be any news to carry, there won't be any reports to publish, there won't be scholars anymore, but just a pullulating mindless mass, alive enough to breed but not well fed enough to reason and to plan."

"It cannot happen," Tenthag said obstinately.

"Don't you mean: you won't admit it's likely?"

Dippid's self-control had slipped. Meantime, silence had fallen over the whole area of the pens, and everybody was listening to the argument. Abruptly aware of angerstink, Tenthag strove to prevent his voice from shaking.

"Even though I did let the People of the Sea redeem their credits—and nineteen in every score of us would have done the same!—I still say things won't be that bad. It calls for intelligence and planning to apply Gveest's treatment. Without that, our bud-rate will drop back to what it has been."

"But how long would it take before we could restore our food-supplies? *One* explosion in *one* generation would suffice to set us back a score-of-score of years, at least!" Dippid pulsed violently. "Have you not seen the madness due to famine?"

"No, never," Tenthag admitted.

"If you had, you wouldn't treat what you've done so casually! *I* saw it, when I was no older than you are now. There had been a crop-blight at the Southmost Cape. You know about that dreadful episode?"

"I've heard it mentioned, yes."

"That's not enough! You had to be there. I was among the couriers who brought away samples of infected food-plants for Scholar Vahp to study—the same Vahp who taught Gveest, by the way. And the folk were so desperate, we had to land with an escort of prongers because they didn't want us to take even a leaf, even a stalk, infected or not. They were just aware enough to remember that they needed more food, and they were prepared to fight for it. Yes, fight! Tear gashes in each other's mantles, slash each other's tubules if they could! They say everyone's entitled to one mistake, Tenthag, but it's given to few of us to make an error as immense as yours!"

"But I . . . !"

The attempted rejoinder died away. Turning to mount Flapper, he said humbly, "Only time can judge whether it was as grievous as you claim. Deliver my commission and let me go."

Memory of the hostility that had overwhelmed him haunted Tenthag until he was well under way. Objectively he knew that he was not at fault—Iyosc himself had exonerated him—but that didn't alter the impact he had had on the lives of his companions in the Guild . . . and everybody else.

He delayed long before studying his commission, afraid it might be some sort of punishment. On the contrary: the route assigned him was through familiar waters and to familiar ports, and the tour actually concluded at Neesos. Would the People of the Sea have reached his old home before him? He dared to hope it was unlikely. They would have started by selling the knowledge they stole from Ognorit among the islands of the southern and equatorial zones; perhaps they would not get as far as Neesos this summer. He cheered up.

But his optimism faded as he made his assigned stopovers, delivering to the local savants messages concerning plants and animals. Rumor, if not precise information, had outrun the couriers; wherever he called, the folk were impatient to the point of rudeness, and tossed aside his dispatches.

"We want to bud!" they shouted. "We want Gveest's secret of fertility! There are five-score fewer of us than this time a score of years ago!"

Or "two-score" or "half a score"... but always fewer.

It was in vain to insist that before more buds were brought forth there must be extra food. Even the wisest old'uns were in the grip of passion; they dismissed everything he said with a wave of one casual claw.

"We'll take more from the sea!" was a typical answer, or, "We'll go back to wild plants like our ancestors!"

Sharply he said, "It looks as though you already decided to!"

For everywhere he saw the symptoms of decline: parasitic weeds hanging about the eaves of the houses, blocking the sap-run on which depended edible plants and funqi; mold spoiling swatches of good fruit; clamps and copses abandoned in the surrounding countryside as all the folk converged on ports where the latest news was to be expected. The air was full of a dreadful expectation, and the reek had so permeated everyone, they no longer cared to plan for anything except that miraculous day when they too—even they—would parent buds.

Explanations of the dual-species theory met with mockery. Reasoned arguments about numbers versus resources met with boredom. Here and there a few people still remembered sanity and begged to be taken away on Flapper's back, but the couriers were forbidden to carry passengers, and anyhow it seemed better to leave them where they were in the hope that sense might after all prevail.

At Klong, a month after leaving Bowock, Tenthag first encountered an outburst of religion, and trembled to the core of his pith. So dreamness could take a new grip on the folk even before the actual onset of the population explosion. Mere rumor had sufficed, at least in this one land...

He fidgeted with the urge to make for Neesos, but defied it. He must make his own obeisance to reason—his own sacrifice, whatever a sacrifice might be.

By dark especially, while Flapper broke the water into glowing ripples as she fed on drifting weed and occasional fish, he stared achingly at the sky wherever it was clear of cloud and wondered about voyages across space. Were there living creatures in that ocean of oceans? Watching a comet bloom out of a dim and distant blur, it was hard not to make comparison with a plant sprouting under the

influence of summer. Marking the dark-by-dark progress
of the planets, it was tempting beyond belief to imagine
other beings capable of transforming inert matter into
something that could feel, and react, and devise and plan
and—make mistakes...

In ancient times, he had been told, some folk held that
when the welkin shed its fleeting streaks it was a means
of signaling, which no one here below could understand.
With all his pith he wished he could send back a message
of his own:

"Help us, strangers! Help us! We're in danger!"

Budded in the year called Two-red-stars-turn-blue,
Tenthag sought comfort in the unaltered patterns of the
sky, and found none. For they weren't unaltered.

As though to harbinger the shock the folk must bear,
the dark before the bright that saw him at his bud-place
was lighted by a singular event.

One of those very stars, on the fringe of the Major
Cluster, which had gone to blue from red, changed yet
again. A hint of yellow touched it. It seemed brighter... but
a cloud drifted across it, and there was no way of being
sure about the outcome before dawn.

VIII

But where was everybody?

Goading Flapper into the bay that covered the site of
Prefs, Tenthag surveyed the vicinity with his telescope.
Normally by dawn the fisherfolk would be launching gorborangs, and sand-collectors loading raw material for the
glass-furnace. Because it had been so long since he left
here, he had been prepared for some changes, but not for
this feeling of vacancy which set his weather-sense to full
alert.

Leaving the porp to browse, he waded ashore carrying
the last of his copies of Gveest's food-data. As soon as

he was clear of the water, he shouted with all the force of his mantle.

There was no answer.

Becoming more and more alarmed, he padded along familiar tracks—how often had he come this way with Fifthorch, to swim from the gentle beach and sometimes dive for relics?—noting with dismay how well-tended clusters of food-plants had been let run wild. He came across sleds of the kind used to bring home sand, abandoned by the path; creepers were twining over them in a way that indicated they must have been dumped a moon-long ago, at least. And his forebear's mirror, source of Neesos's prosperity, was pointing at nowhere.

Shortly, breasting a rise, he came in sight of the little town at the center of the island, sheltered in a hollow against the worst of winter weather. Here at last were people, though nothing like as many as he would have expected. Draped on slanting branches, or lying under rocky overhangs for protection against the morning sun-light, they were listening to someone talking in a loud rough voice. Before he drew close enough to make out what was being said, Tenthag had already discerned that they were surrounded by all the goods they could assemble, be it foodstuffs or glassware or seed-stock or objects salvaged from Prefs.

Something prompted him to great caution. Lowering to minimum bearable height, he stole among shadows cast by bushes until he reached a rocky niche where he could look on unobserved. Fortunately the wind prevented any-one from scenting him . . . but the stink it bore to him from the crowd was enough to make him quail. It uttered a whole history of greed and jealousy, and the speaker at the middle of the group was fomenting it.

And the orator was—

Recognizing him, Tenthag was almost snatched by dreamness. It was Fifthorch.

Who was saying, "—so *of course* they want to keep the secret for themselves! It's lucky for us that the People of the Sea aren't under the pads of the Bowockers and their precious Order of the Jingfired! Jing was never real! Jing was a figment to keep young'uns quiet! Well, some of us grew out of childhood tales! I wish we all had! The fact that supposedly adult people right here on Neesos still claimed that the Jingtexts must be truth—until we drove them out as they deserved!—isn't that enough to curdle your maw? It certainly did mine! Be thankful for the People of the Sea, who are coming to our rescue! I'm sure we've brought together enough goods to make them give us the secret of fertility! *They* care about the fact that we've been left without a single new bud since traitor Tenthag ran away! They aren't cold and cynical and cruel like the Bowockers, who weren't content to take our most valuable possessions from beneath the Bay of Prefs, but stole our youngest young'un as well! And what did they leave in exchange? Rubbish! Scraps and oddments any one of us could have got by making a voyage to the mainland! Things you trade for common seed or common glass! Not glass like ours, the finest on the planet! Did they offer musculators and nervograps? Did they give us anything useful? No, they robbed us of what we didn't even realize we owned, and laughed when they went away! Taking our last new-budded youngling with them, what is worse!"

His memory echoing with Nemora's comment about the archeologists who were far too mercenary for her liking, Tenthag found that more than he could endure. Rising to normal height, he padded forward, shouting, and all eyes turned on him with amazement... save for Fifthorch's, which was full of hate.

"I never dreamed you'd miss me so much, Fifthorch!" he roared. "Did it not suit you to become the youngest when I left—not stolen, but of my own free will?"

His diet of yelg, in spite of his lonely and inactive life aboard a porp, kept him fit and well pressurized; he was able to overtop Fifthorch without effort. Taking station higher on the branchway, where he could continue to dominate the other, he filled his mantle with air for the loudest possible shout. These people looked as though they needed to be startled back to reality.

But a shrill voice took the pressure out of him with a single question.

"Are you one of the People of the Sea, who are going to show us how to breed again?"

He turned, seeking the source of the inquiry... and was instantly deflated.

"Ninthag!" he blurted, scarcely recognizing the old, bloated, half-blind shape that clung to a slanting bough befouled with tatters of wild orqid—colorful, but unfit for food. "Ninthag, don't you know your own sole bud?"

"Are you pretending to be Tenthag?" the old man wheezed. "I'm not such a fool as to believe you! He went away, long, long ago, stolen by the Bowockers! I see him in visions now, and he's laughing at us—laughing at the poor folk he left behind while he rejoices in the best the world can offer! We stay here, wondering when if ever another bud will come among us, and—Keep away from me!"

Tenthag was scrambling towards him, but on the instant half a score of others rose to block his way. Their exudates took on the taint of combat-stink.

Slowly Tenthag retreated, recognizing what he had encountered at Klong and sundry places since. These folk were starved into dreamness...of their own volition.

He said, "Aren't you ashamed to deny your own? Fifthorch knows me—why don't the rest of you?"

"We know what we want to know," said one of them, and there was a rumble of agreement.

"But you can't! You're underfed, you're going crazy! Yet there's food all around you!" Tenthag clenched his claws in impotent rage.

"We have to keep everything we can spare to trade with the People of the Sea," said Ninthag obstinately. "Who knows how much they'll demand for the secret of fertility? We must be sure that there's enough."

"But here I am, who was at Ognorit where the secret was discovered, and I bring data due to Gveest himself— free of charge!"

With that shouted boast Tenthag broke through their apathy. They reared back and gazed at him with pitiable eagerness. Even Fifthorch was taken off guard, and gapped his mandibles.

"Is it truly you?" whispered Ninthag, staring blearily. "Your voice, your scent...But it has been so long!" He summoned a last trace of his old authority. "Show what you've brought, then! Not to me, for my sight has failed. Where's Thirdusk?"

"He betrayed us!" shouted Fifthorch. "He fled with the cowards who were prepared to let Neesos die!"

That statement made everything clear to Tenthag. He could picture how it must have been: one faction, the

more rational, counseling that life go on as normal, with
enough food eaten and enough new crops planted for next
year; the other so obsessed with the lack of new buds as
to forget the need to provide for them if they happened,
ultimately seizing the goods of their rivals and driving
them away. It was much like what had happened at his
other ports of call. But in his pith he had hoped that his
own homeland might be a little different, a little better . . .

He'd been wrong. He knew that even as he proffered
the documents he had brought, and a half-score of greedy
eyes fixed on them as Fifthorch spread them out.

"There's nothing here to touch the folk!" the latter
yelled. "It's all to do with plants and animals!"

"But if there's not enough food—"

"We manage well with half the food we used to gobble!
We must save the rest to pay the People of the Sea! You're
a coward like Thirdusk! You're a traitor!"

All at once they were pelting him with insults and tram-
pling his precious message underpad. He could do nothing
but turn and flee, or they would have torn him torso from
mantle in their fury.

Luckily—luckily!—they were too weak to overtake him
on his way to the bay where he had left Flapper. By the
time he stumbled into the shallows, he also was weakened
by his efforts, and his perception was diminished. Had it
not been, he would have reacted to what was happening
on the skyline before he remounted his porp and turned
her seaward.

Only then, though, and much too late, did he realize
what was looming towards Neesos.

Here came the visitors the relic of the folk were waiting
for: five junqs, four briqs, with bright banners hung on
poles to tell the world—

WE HAVE THE SECRET OF FERTILITY! AND IT'S FOR SALE!

He crumpled on Flapper's saddle, utterly dispirited,
and offered no resistance when they detached him from
his travel-harness, dragged him aboard the commander's
briq, and lashed Flapper to her side with yells of triumph.

He was too busy mourning for a world that never was.

IX

The commander of this raggle-taggle fleet still wore
ancient symbols of rank on thongs crossed about his body:
a spyglass lacking its objective, a briq-goad worn to a
stump. Crusty-mantled from bad food and long exposure
to the elements, he interrogated Tenthag about Neesos,
wanting to know whether any folk were left, or whether
they had all fled as from so many other lonely islands.

"They might as well have run away," was Tenthag's
bitter answer. "They took leave of their senses long ago.
But why ask me? I'm just a visitor, and there they are
who can answer for themselves!"

He pointed. Those who had rushed in pursuit of him
were milling about on the beach, amazed at the sight of
the fleet, and he could almost hear the arguments over
who must return to town and collect trade-goods.

"Hah!" said the commander with satisfaction. "Let's
go see what they can offer worth the taking! You!"—
handing a prong to a nervous she'un—"keep watch over
him, hear me?"

And, surrounded by his sub-commanders, headed
landward.

More miserable than ever, Tenthag was compelled to
look on as the Neesans delivered everything they owned
for the visitors' inspection. Meantime, however, a suspicion began to gnaw at the back of his mind. At first he
was too despondent to react; by degrees it overcame his
depression, and he roused himself enough to survey the
close-clustered briqs and junqs.

They still bore their complement of old'uns and she'uns.
But not a single one among the latter was in bud...

The monstrosity of the deceit these nomads were per-
petrating stabbed him to the pith, and he almost made a
leap for Flapper. But the she-guard was ready to spike

him, and he was in no hurry to become an underwater banquet.

He must match their deception without giving off a betraying odor, therefore. Would anger-stink cover up a lie?

Well, by now experience had made him cynical enough to try...

He and the guard were isolated near the briq's after end; the rest of her riders were gathered forward. He said softly, "What's your commander's name?"

She hesitated; then, finding no reason to refuse the information, muttered, "He's called Sprapter."

"And he is a good person to serve under?"

"He does well by us. He's clever. The proof's around you." Her tone was curt, but uneasy, as though she feared a trap.

Tenthag saw nothing special about the accoutrements of the briqs and junqs—indeed, they could have been matched by any kyq from his youth, and the latter would have been set about with useful gorborangs, as well—but now was no time to be patronizing. He said hastily, "And you are...?"

"Veetalya."

"Do you believe it to be part of Sprapter's plan that I must parch to death?"

Taken aback, she said, "You heard his order to me!"

"So I did. It made no mention of my being denied water. Oh, I know the People of the Sea hate us couriers nowadays, but our lives have much in common, and I take it that if Sprapter ordered you to guard me he'll expect to find me fit and well when he returns."

Alongside the briq Flapper was growing restive, as always in salt water. Why had they not turned her loose, or stripped and killed her? Did Sprapter cherish grandiose dreams of adding a porp to his little fleet? Or did he think she might prove useful for trade purposes when they headed south in search of the secret they claimed to possess, but did not? Whatever the reason, it was a stroke of luck. Tenthag said in his most wheedling tones, "Your drink-bladders are bulging, aren't they? And if there's one thing a porp lacks, it's adequate drink. A briq is far superior in that regard. You People of the Sea know ancient tricks that we ought really to have studied, but of course, as you know, we tend to be arrogant. With a few exceptions, like myself for example. But isn't that a fault you too display?"

She was nervously tightening her grip on the prong. With a reflex glance at the drink-bladders, she said, "I don't know what you mean!"

"Oh, it's plain as sunlight! You're not in bud, although your folk possess the secret of fertility, and I can only explain the fact by assuming that you angered Sprapter, and he refused to let you have a bud until you'd made amends for some offense you'd given. Well, if you give me drink, I'll speak up on your behalf when he returns."

By this time, as he had dared to hope, she was thoroughly confused. Providentially, a shout rose from the beach at the same moment. The distance was too great for Tenthag to make out exactly what was being said, but a fair guess suggested that one of the Neesans had complained about all their best possessions being taken, and one of the visitors had demanded what price was too high to pay for fertility.

The same might be asked concerning freedom. Accustomed, like almost everybody else, to imagining that the risk of being stabbed through a major tubule was sufficient to make anyone sit quiet, Sprapter had relied on Veetalya's possession of a good sharp prong a padlong distant to ensure his captive would obey her. But he had seen Pletrow calmly cut her own body with a far keener blade, and heard her casual dismissal of the risk...

"Oh, come now!" he said, as Veetalya glanced towards the row on shore, and took a stride that brought him within the range of her prong. "A drink is not too much to—"

And *snap*. At maximum pressure his claws closed on the prong and broke it off, and he was all over her, trusting to his greater weight to force her backward. She wasted her spare pressure on a scream, and that sufficed. He trampled on her as though she were not there and swarmed over the briq's side into Flapper's saddle, which the People of the Sea had not found time to dismount. With claws and mandibles and the stub of the prong he slashed at the bonds restraining her, and before the startled crewfolk at the forward end could get to him, he had weakened them enough for the porp to break the rest with one great heave and surge. Half-swamped in a deluge of water, he clung valiantly and jabbed her back with the prong in lieu of a goad. With all her well-fed force she rushed for open water, leaving his captors to fret and curse and hurl obscenities.

The breeze bore him one furious shout: "Well, a courier's no loss to us, any more than a porp!"

Wrong, promised Tenthag silently. *I'm going to cost you more than you can possibly afford!*

After so long a period of forced inaction, Flapper rushed straight for the horizon, and he let her go, glad that his provisions had not been pilfered. He drank a lot and ate a little, restoring his normality while calculating how long it would be before the trading on the beach came to an end. If tradition were anything to go by, it would last until dark, and some kind of celebration would follow. The People of the Sea would not dare risk departure without the regular formalities, or even in their debilitated state the Neesans might suspect the trick that had been played on them. Therefore he should have time to swing around on a long circular course and bring Flapper back to the island just after darkfall, when her return was least likely to be noticed.

Cold anger colored his mind gray. Stark facts like distant mountains marked the boundary of his thinking. He was possessed, for the first time in his life, by lust for vengeance.

As darkness fell, he sought the star which had caught his attention at the fringe of the Major Cluster. There was no mistake. It had turned yellower and brighter. Perhaps someone who had not watched the sky from the lonely vantage of a porp's back in mid-ocean might have overlooked the change, but to Tenthag it was past a doubt.

In ancient times they'd said the stars reflected what went on below. He was too well informed to swallow such deceits. But the image, nonetheless, was powerful, and struck chords in that level of his mind where dreamness ruled.

Perhaps that star was shedding bright new light on what had been dead planets, conjuring the force of life from them. It didn't matter. For him it was a symbol, and a challenge. He must cast light of his own on his own folk . . .

Luminants faintly outlined the island, but there were

wide gaps where they had not been properly tended and
he was able to steal ashore without being spotted. He left
Flapper to fend for herself. If he came back by dawn, she
would probably still be here; if not, she would shed her
saddle as soon as it rotted, but with luck keep the secondary plants Gveest had bestowed on her, which would
be an example to any other of the folk who ran across
her later on. Maybe, if she bred in the wild, some of them
might cross-take on her bud...

Who, though, would help the porps if the Guild of
Couriers all met the same doom as Tenthag? In a few
years, following the population explosion, they would
surely be hunted down for food!

Repressing all such horrible previsions, he crept over
the hill-crest on which stood the derelict solar mirror, and
found his guesses accurate. Reluctant to leave before
sharing refreshment with the local people, the visitors
were sitting under arbors of luminants and pretending to
be polite. Fifthorch, recognizable by scent and voice, was
lavishing on them what food and liquor remained, while
others waited in shadow, exuding the stink of greed... or
was it from the outsiders? At this distance he could not
be certain.

But that was irrelevant. Hastening down the old familiar path, he headed for the crowd—and was brought
up short, so that he clutched his sole weapon, the broken
prong, and spun around with a hiss of terror. He had
abruptly caught a waft of death, and there were overtones
to it that he recognized.

Beside the path, clearly having collapsed as he moved
away from the town, leaking his stale ichor on the ground
after a major rupture of a lower tubule... Ninthag.

He who had been the town's elder for so long, its guide
and counselor: left here to rot unheeded! Had he been
stabbed? But a quick tactile check confirmed that he had
simply died from stress. Well, that was a relief, of a sort—
but still an insult!

Tenthag drew himself together and put on the best
imitation he could contrive of his father's appearance.
Maintaining it, while imitating an old'un's hobble, he let
himself show in the circle of brightness shed by the town-
center lights.

It was Sprapter who first noticed him, accepting a shell

of araq. He was so startled that he tilted it and cursed as
the biting liquid spilled down his torso. Before he could
speak, while others were still turning to gaze at him, Tenthag said loudly enough to be heard by everyone, "Have
they shown you a female with a bud?"

Fifthorch, offering more araq to another of the People
of the Sea, started so violently he almost slumped, and
Tenthag, still posing as his father, padded towards him.
In a thin voice he repeated, "A female with a bud—have
they shown you one?"

"Drive him off!" Sprapter cried, struggling to full height.

"Why?" Tenthag countered. "You have the secret of
fertility, or so your banners claim! That means you must
have buds and young'uns in your fleet!"

"Of course they have the secret!" Fifthorch shouted,
while the hunger-sluggish minds of those around him registered what Tenthag was saying. "They've sold it to us,
and on fair terms, what's more!"

"But have they shown a single young'un, or a she'un
budding?" Tenthag abandoned his disguise and strode to
take station at Sprapter's side, his prong leveled. "I say
they haven't even met the southern fleets which raided
Ognorit, but stole everything you could offer in the hope
that when they do they'll get the secret! Truth, Sprapter—
tell the truth! And for every lie I'll let the pressure out of
one of your tubules!" He jabbed the commander's torso,
just enough.

Terrified, Sprapter babbled, "I swear we would have
kept our bargain! We needed to buy the secret and we'd
have come back and—"

"You mean you didn't give it to us?" Fifthorch said,
belatedly reacting to the commander's reek of guilt and
shame.

Without compunction Tenthag slit a minor tubule in
the trickster's torso, forcing him to fold over and compress the leak until it sealed.

"I don't know what they clawed off you," he said mildly,
"but as I tried to tell you earlier, I was at Ognorit, and
learned from Gveest himself what must be done. On the
briq where I was captive, I met a she'un who was ripe
for budding, and she had no bud. I saw not a single bud
or young'un in this fleet that claims to sell the secret!
What do you make of that, you fools who left Ninthag to

leak away his life on that path yonder? Who'd have the secret merely to sell to others, without using it to benefit themselves?"

A pulsation later he was frightened by the forces he had loosed, for Fifthorch roared with mindless rage and launched himself at Sprapter. Before the two could be separated the commander was as dead as Ninthag, and the air was foul with the stench of drying ichor and loud with screams of pain.

But within moments the seafolk were cowering to the ground, emitting the odor of surrender, and finding themselves about to slash or stab with whatever weapon came to claw, the Neesans recovered enough of their normal awareness to realize what they had done, and be horrified at it. Weak, but calm, they began to mutter among themselves that Tenthag had been right, and they were stupid not to have insisted on being shown a budded she'un before parting with their goods.

Suddenly Tenthag found them all looking to him for guidance, seafolk and Neesans alike... except for Fifthorch, who faded into the dark moaning about the need to wash off Sprapter's ichor.

He said after a pause for reflection, "Eat what there is. Give nothing more to the seafolk. You must restore your strength of mind and body both, because you're going to make these liars pay for their deceit. Not only are they going to return what they cheated you out of; they're going to be set to work recovering the plants you've let run wild, ridding the town of mold and orqid, bringing fish from deep water, and laying up great stores of food against the time when the real secret of fertility is brought hither. It won't be long, I'm sure. *But there must be food first!*"

The seafolk whispered among themselves. Eventually one sub-commander rose to normal height.

"It's fair judgment," he admitted sullenly. "I'm Loric. I've been chosen as Sprapter's successor. I'll abide by your terms, but I'll ask one thing in return."

"You don't deserve anything," Tenthag snapped. "Feel free to ask, though, as I shall to refuse."

"You do owe me something," Loric insisted. "Sprapter wanted to kill your porp, or at any rate drive her to open water. But I've been in charge of our food-plants for years, and I saw new ones on the porp which gave me ideas. That's why I insisted on her being lashed alongside the briq. I wanted to study and adapt them. They told us that was how you were able to escape, though I must admit none of us expected you to return. It was a brave thing to do, and your countryfolk ought to be proud of you. Instead, they described you as a traitor and a runaway, especially Fifthorch, and in the end they made us believe it, so you took us completely by surprise... Don't you owe me something, though, for saving your porp?"

"I guess so," Tenthag admitted gruffly. "Very well. When you leave here, which won't be soon, you'll have grafts of Gveest's new food-plants to help you on your way. But it may take months before there are enough for both Neesos and your fleet, and in spite of being foolish my people are still my people, and they get first call. By that time you'll have learned a lot about food-plants on land, I promise you."

"You're an honest man in spite of being a courier. You won't regret striking this bargain. How do you think I was able to persuade your folk that we did truly have the secret of fertility? Could I have convinced them without considerable understanding of all sorts of life-forms? Oh, I'm not a Gveest; I'm more the practical type. But if there's any connection between his work with plants and lower animals, and what he's discovered that will make us breed, then don't be surprised if I figure out the secret for myself eventually. I'd like to, obviously. It'd save us a trip south, into waters where there are already too many of us for the junqs and briqs available, not so?"

It was impossible not to be won over by this fellow's audacity. Tenthag tried to stop himself quirking into a smile. Loudly he said, "Work, then, if you want to clench the deal! We have two funerals to conduct immediately. Then we must tell the rest of your company the fate in store."

X

What Tenthag was doing was not in accord with his commission; he should have returned directly to Bowock. But after the hostility he had met on the day of his departure, he was in no hurry. Besides, his actions were consonant with his courier's oath, at least in his opinion. By summer's end there would be at least one fleet—small, admittedly—in possession not of the secret of fertility but of information far more essential, which it could then trade to supplement the couriers' efforts. And the seafolk would need to trade if they did begin to multiply; one bud per she'un would require at least two extra briqs or another junq, complete with food-plants, and this far north there were few young wild'uns nowadays.

He occupied himself not only with supervising the restoration of Neesos's fortunes, but with retaming and exercising Flapper, whom he took to sea almost daily with the fleet on its fishing-trips. Once they had grown resigned to the failure of their intended fraud, the seafolk proved to be friendly enough, and of course they had far more in common with couriers than they were usually prepared to admit. In the end even Veetalya recovered from the shame she felt at having let Tenthag escape, and their relations became very friendly. Loric, too, turned out to be likable, and interested not only in life-study but star-study also. Together they pondered the possible meaning of that star which almost nightly shone yellower, brighter, hotter. Through a good telescope it could be seen to be surrounded by a sort of aura, like drifting smoke.

"That's some of the cold matter massing to block our way to the future," Tenthag explained soberly. "But before we get that far, more of it will doubtless turn into stars, more will be drawn into our own sun, more will tumble out of space and crash into the oceans, raising huge waves, or smash down on land and burn forests to ash...Oh, Loric, we are caught in a trap worse than a gigant's claw! On the one side, the risk that there won't be enough of the folk for us to save ourselves; on the other, that there may be far too many!"

"Don't you think we'll make it?" Veetalya asked timidly.

Tenthag shrugged with his entire mantle. "When I see what we can do when we combine our efforts, as here on Neesos, I feel very optimistic. But when I remember how nearly my own people went insane, and how you tried to take advantage...Who can say?"

Turning the telescope curiously in all directions, for it was superior to any he had used before, Loric suddenly stiffened.

"Another fleet!" he whispered. "Look! See the glimmer on the water?"

"Where...? Oh, yes! Give me the telescope...But those aren't junqs or briqs! They're porps—you can tell by the way they move! And none but couriers use porps, and that must be half the complement the Guild can boast! Quick, to the beach, and signal!"

As he incontinently led the way, hoping no loose rock would betray his steps in the dark, he wondered silently what disaster had brought *this* about.

Within a very short time, as all the folk of the island gathered on the beach, he learned the terrible truth. First to land was Dippid himself, followed by Nemora, and then another score of his friends and colleagues. When they had got over their astonishment at finding Tenthag alive and well, they told their story.

"We thought you must be dead," Dippid rasped. "Many of the couriers have been attacked for not possessing the secret of fertility, by people convinced they did but were holding out for the highest price. It's a rumor started by the Major South Fleet. Iyosc was right; they did raid Ognorit and now they're trading what they're pleased to call 'the right to bud'...against everything they can lay their claws on, especially seed and food-plants!"

Tenthag exchanged glances with his companions, who by now included Fifthorch. He said slowly, "What's the situation like at Bowock? Have you been driven away?"

"Yes," was Nemora's simple answer, and she turned aside in grief. Dippid amplified.

"Iyosc was right about that, too. She'uns in bud and their companions, deprived of all their food-stocks by the greed of the People of the Sea, naturally started heading for the cities, not just Bowock, but any place where it looked as though there were still plenty of victuals. Bowock has been the chief magnet, obviously, because of that rumor that we were withholding the secret. And I regret to admit..."

He hesitated. Recovering, Nemora said curtly, "Some of the Jingfired betrayed their trust. Either they got hold of Gveest's technique, or they were able to work it out from what was already known. Anyhow, they applied it to themselves. It was impossible to keep *that* secret. As soon as the news got out...Well, you can imagine its effect. We clung on as long as we could, but when we learned that couriers were being hunted down and killed we decided to flee. I remembered coming to Neesos, all those years ago, and as near as we could calculate we believed it must still be well beyond the sweep of the Major Fleet. Besides, the closer we got, the more we heard rumors that the people of lonely islands like this one were abandoning their homes and making for mainland cities, where the bud-right might be theirs all the sooner."

"Some of the folk did leave here," Tenthag muttered, and went on to explain what he had found on his arrival.

"You were very sensible not to return to Bowock," Dippid pronounced at last. "It may not have been what you were supposed to do, but it's turned out for the best."

"Do you have the bud-secret?" Loric demanded suddenly.

There was a pause like the interval between the lightning and the thunder. At last Dippid heaved a sigh.

"Yes. We had to bring something we could trade for food."

"That's liable to draw crowds of crazy folk to Neesos, then!" cried Fifthorch, indicating how much he had learned about the real world since Tenthag's return. "We must think of ways to defend ourselves—"

"We must think of ways to feed ourselves," Tenthag corrected stonily. "Sane, well-nourished folk are always our friends and allies. Only the crazy ones are a threat. And now we have a vast stockpile of precious knowledge;

couriers are as well informed as anybody short of the Jingfired themselves, or scientists like Gveest. Is there news of him, by the way?"

Dippid clacked his mandibles. "Report has it that he and Pletrow and the rest are captives with the Major Fleet. But nobody knows for certain. It may just be another rumor put about to encourage folk to pay extortionate prices."

"I hope for his sake he's not," Tenthag said softly. "I got to know him pretty well while I was at Ognorit, and I'm certain he would be horrified to see the dreadful impact his discovery is having. He knew about it, he tried to guard us against it, and through ill-luck I was the one who was obliged to undermine his precautions."

"Iyosc forgave you for that," Nemora said, laying a claw friendly on his mantle-edge. "And what you're doing here is making further amends. What's more, perhaps the star—"

"We've been over that!"—morosely from Dippid. "More likely it's a harbinger of catastrophe, like the old New Star."

"It can't be! It's not at all the same!" Nemora hunched forward. "We know the other one outshone the Major Cluster, to begin with. No, I think this is more likely a stroke of good fortune. Changes like that going on in the sky are just what people will need to keep reminding them of Jingtruths. Things must have been equally bleak when the Northern Freeze began, and again at the time of the Great Thaw—yet here we are, and we have some achievements of our own to boast of!"

"There's no comparison," Dippid maintained. "This time we're breaking the very mold we were cast in by our evolution!"

Tenthag thought of Pletrow's collection of mutated animals, and shuddered as the chief courier went on.

"No, it's going to be a different world. Even during the famine at Southmost Cape I never saw anything as horrible as what's now happening at Bowock. For all we can tell, there's something in the radiation from the stars that drives us crazy now and then, and what can we do to withstand that? Grow a roof over the entire planet?"

"What use would a roof be against what's sure to fall on us one of these days?" said Tenthag wearily, and forced himself to full height. "No, we dare not try and hide from our doom. The universe will not permit it. We must carry on somehow, preserving at least a nucleus of reason... There's a tale about the legendary Barratong. When he realized the Thaw was bringing more and more of the planet under his people's sway, he didn't rejoice or boast about it. He accepted the duty which the past had laid upon the present. Do you remember what he said?"

"Of course," said Loric as he also rose. "All we People of the Sea are brought up to regard it as the finest principle of our heritage, though since it led to the foundation of Bowock and the Guild of Couriers—Never mind! This is not a moment for squabbling over what's past and done with. Barratong said, in fact, 'We are the Jingfired now!'"

"It's our turn to say the same," said Tenthag, and padded miserably away towards the first glint of dawn, wondering how much sorrow and insanity the sun must shine on before the folk recovered from the shock of being multiplied.

And if they would.

PART FIVE

BLOOM

I

The city of Voosla was allegedly approaching her land-fall, but Awb could scarcely credit it. There was too much dark on the horizon.

Wherever there was habitable ground there were people, and even more than food-crops the folk cultivated plants which, after sundown, either glowed of their own accord or gave back the light they had basked in earlier. Troqs who had taken to caves for refuge in desert regions where houses would not grow, squimaqs who eked out their existence around the poles where darkness could last for half a year—they knew that trying to manage without luminants was to risk being driven into dreamness as certainly as by starvation, if not so quickly.

And indeed, throughout the voyage until now, there had always been distant glimmerings: nothing like as bright, of course, as the lights of the city, but discernible with even a crude telescope like Awb's, which he had made himself and was very proud of. Thilling the picturist had ceded him a couple of lenses too worn for fixing perfect images, and fitted into a tube they afforded a view of the strange northern coasts they were paralleling.

However, they also showed, much too plainly for comfort, that blank gap on the edge of an otherwise populous continent. There was something so eerie about it that it made his weather-sense queasy. He found himself longing for the familiar scenery of the tropics which, since his budding, the city had never previously left.

To think that one new moon ago he had been beside himself with excitement at the prospect of this journey to the intended site of the World Observatory . . . !

Swarming along the branchways in search of distraction, he shortly discovered that a crowd had gathered on the lookout platform at the prow, including most of the

delegation from the University of Chisp. Their chief,
Scholar Drotninch, was conferring with Mayor Axwep.

Awb also found it disturbing to have so many foreigners traveling with them. Voosla was by no means a large
city, and he knew all her inhabitants at least by sight.
Before this trip he had been used to meeting strangers, if
at all, by ones and twos, not scores together. Still, the
scientists were polite enough, and some—like Thilling—
were positively friendly, so he decided to chance a rebuff
and draw close enough to overhear.

And was considerably reassured by an exchange indicating that he was not alone in worrying about this un-
naturally lightless shore.

"Amazing, isn't it?"—from Drotninch. "Last time I
came up here, this was the brightest spot for padlonglaqs."

To which Axwep: "The city's growing fractious, as
though she senses something amiss. Could be a taint in
the water; we're well into the estuarial zone. I'd be inclined to hold off until sunrise. It won't mean too much
of a delay, and it'll give us a chance to feed and rest the
musculators. I can send a pitchen ahead to explain why
we aren't landing at once."

Drotninch pondered, and one could almost scent her
indecision...but, like most landlivers nowadays, she
coated her torso with neutralizing perfumes. It had become a mark of good manners, and those—as Awb knew
from his few visits to shore—were far from a luxury in
the overcrowded conditions of a fixed city. Life at sea,
in his view, was superior; if Axwep noted an accumulation
of combat-stink she needed only to consult her weather-
sense about what course to set and let a fresh breeze calm
things down.

Finally the scholar signed agreement, and Axwep issued the necessary orders. The group dispersed, some to
tend the musculators, others to prepare the pitchen.
Slowly, owing to her colossal bulk, the city ceased to
thrash the water. The group of interlinked junqs around
which she was built exuded relief, for even in calm weather
they disliked being brought near land, perhaps owing to
some ancestral fear of being stranded on a beach or dashed
against rocks. Not, naturally, that they could do anything
against the resistless force of the musculators.

When it was uncaged the pitchen seemed equally unhappy, as though it too were alarmed by the dark shore, but that was fanciful nonsense, since it did not depend on sight—indeed it possessed no eye, and reacted solely to magnetic fields, like the ancient northfinders which had died off during the Northern Freeze. When it was dropped overside with Axwep's message tied to its claws, it set out obediently enough for the place it had been conditioned to regard as home, leaving patches of phosphorescence to mark each of its leaps. Watching it go, Awb reflected what a benefit its kind had proved to be, especially since they had been modified to follow canals and winding inland channels as well as pursuing a direct course across open water. He wished he knew who had been the first to domesticate pitchens, but during the Age of Multiplication people had been much more concerned with staying alive and sane than with keeping records of who invented what.

"That's much better!" said a she'un's voice behind him, and he lowered reflexively as Thilling swarmed down an adjacent branchway with, as ever, her image-fixer at the ready. "Maybe now I'll get the chance to cut a few new lenses! I've lost count of how many got spoiled when a wave disturbed me while I was trimming them, and I do so want to catch everything that happens when we go ashore ... And what's wrong with you, young'un? You seem worried."

"I never saw a coast so dark before!" Awb blurted.

"Hmm! I did! Once I was sent to cover an epidemic on Blotherotch—went in with a medical team looking for the causative organism, assigned to picture the victims for future reference. Some of the folk there had turned so dreamish, they imagined they could prolong their lives by eating luminants, and they'd absolutely stripped the area. It was ghastly. Still, we got away safely, and now we're all immune against *that* disease. On the other claw ..."

She hesitated. Greatly daring, he prompted her.

"Oh, I was only going to say: we've discovered cures for so many disorders including infertility, it seems incredible there should be a brand-new one, least of all one that can afflict an entire countryside—people and animals and plants as well!"

"Is that really what we can look forward to finding?"

"You're asking me? I never set pad here, haven't even had a sight of the nervograp messages that got through before the link failed. Phrallet must know more about those than I do; doesn't she tell you anything?"

"As little as possible," Awb muttered. He was always embarrassed when someone mentioned his budder, who flaunted her five bud-scars in a manner most people regarded as indecent and seemed to think that because Axwep only had four she had the better claim to be Voosla's mayor.

"Well, you should pester her more," Thilling said, loading a sensitive sheet into her fixer. As much to herself as him, she added, "I wish I'd had time to graft a new lens on this thing, because I'm sure there's a salt-water blister somewhere, but with dawn so close I'll have to make do . . . Keep your eye skinned, young'un. If what I've been told is reliable, we should be in for a treat. Look yonder, where I'm pointing."

Awb complied, but still all he could make out, even with his telescope, was a vague patch of black-on-blacker. In the south-east the first hint of dawn was coloring the air, not nearly enough as yet to dim the Arc of Heaven, let alone the Major Cluster. There was a bank of dense cloud to the north, veiling any aurora there might be, and that surprised him, for visibility in this region was reputed the best in the hemisphere; why else choose it for the World Observatory?

On the other claw, no place on the planet was immune from what happened next. A streak of yellow light slashed out of the east, and at its tip a fireball exploded, scattering trails of luminance across a quarter of the welkin. Caught by surprise, Thilling uttered a curse.

"That's spoiled my leaf good and proper! Young'un, keep looking, and warn me if I'm apt to miss anything!"

Hastily she threw away the sheet she had been mounting in the fixer, and peeled another from the stack.

By this time Awb was beginning to guess at what she meant. The flash of the meteor had revealed something outlined against the northern clouds. He had had too brief a glimpse to make out details, but there was only one thing it could be: Fangsharp Peak, on top of which the observatory was being grown. Of course, since it was so much higher than the surrounding land, it was bound to catch the sun's rays first. So—

"Quick!" he cried, suddenly aware that all about them the branchways were alive with folk scrambling to seek a vantage point and watch the unique spectacle. Barely in time Thilling leveled her fixer.

The sky grew brighter, though the land and sea remained virtually featureless. The world paused in expectation. And there it came!

On the very crest of the mountain, so high above them that it looked as though a huge and jagged rock were floating in mid-air, a single shaft of sunlight rested.

It was the most awe-inspiring event that Awb had ever seen. Without intention, he found himself counting his own pulsations to find out how long the sight would last: three, four, five, six—

It was over, and the sky was turning daytime blue, and he could see the whole mountain. Its flanks were scarred where the natural vegetation had been stripped away in favor of what would be needed to support the observatory. Guide-cables for construction floaters swooped down to either side. A passenger-carrying floater, five bladders glistening, was descending slowly from the top. Awb had never seen one so close; usually they passed over at pressure-height, mere sparkles to the unaided eye.

Axwep and Drotninch returned to the lookout platform, and waited along with everybody else until full daylight also overspread the shore, revealing a stark, discolored mass of shriveled foliage.

"That's *worse* than what we were warned to expect," muttered Thilling as she stored away her exposed sheets. Awb was about to reply, when—

"Look!" somebody screamed.

On the top of the peak something was moving. No: the top of the peak itself was moving! It was cracking apart, it was shedding chunks of rock, it was tilting, it was sliding and rasping and collapsing and slamming down with horrible slowness in an inexorable paradigm of disaster. The guide-cables snapped, the passenger floater leapt up the air like a frightened pitchen taking off from a wave-top, the new plants on the mountainside vanished in a cloud of dust and boulders, so all at once that Awb could not take everything in.

The avalanche subsided into a monstrous scree, blocking a canal that led from the base of the mountain to the shore along which, presumably, rubble had been carried to create the sheltering mole now visible between the city and the land, the first stage in preparation for a full-scale harbor. All the seafarers stood transfixed with horror as the dawn breeze carried off the dust.

But from the shore, incurious and dull as mere animals, most of them sickly and with their mantles ulcerated, a few natives gazed at the city before dismissing it as incomprehensible and setting off to seek food in the shallows.

What Awb found most appalling, as he strove to hold his telescope steady, was that not a single one among them made for the scene of the catastrophe, to find out whether anybody lay in need of help.

II

"Of course we know *what* happened," said Lesh, so weary she could scarcely flex her mantle, let alone stand upright. "It's another of the unforeseen disasters that bid fair to wreck our project! Without our noticing, a pumptree shoot invaded a slanting crevice and expanded there, turning the crevice into a crack and the crack into a split. Finally it sprang a leak. Water by itself might not have made the rock slide, but mixed with nice greasy sap—smash! You can see the way it must have gone quite clearly from the air. But what we now have to find out is *why*. Pumptrees simply aren't supposed to act like that!"

She was the resident chief designer for the observatory project. She and a couple of assistants had been all dark on the mountain-top investigating reports of irregular pulsation in the pumptrees. About the time Voosla hove in sight they had concluded the trouble was due to nothing worse than irritation caused by the topsoil they were carrying in the form of slurry, which necessarily contained a trace of sand and gravel. The roots of the toughtrees which would eventually form a foundation for the large telescopes needed more nutriment than they could extract from bare rock, at least if they were to grow to usable size in less than a score of years. Besides, the intention was to keep the peak in more or less its original form, and toughtrees certainly did erode rock, given time.

Down below there was plenty of rich fertile dirt, and it had seemed like a brilliant shortcut to mix it with water and render it liquid enough for pumptrees to transport it upward. This was not entirely a new technique; something similar had been attempted recently in desert-reclamation.

So Lesh and her companions had remounted their floater, to take advantage of the coolness of the gas in its bladders before sunshine increased its buoyancy and obliged them to have it hauled down, and that lucky chance had spared their lives. In fact, as things had turned out, everybody was safely accounted for, except perhaps a few natives, and they were so stupid they could rarely be taught to answer their names. Still, the harm done was severe enough.

"It's set us back years!" Lesh mourned.

"Well, I did warn in my original report, when the site was first surveyed, that there must be something amiss in this area!" That was from Drotninch's elderly colleague Byra, hunching forward.

"You didn't lay much stress on the point, then," Drotninch countered. "As I recall, you concluded that 'the abnormalities found fall within a range of normal variation comparable to that in the Lugomannic Archipelago!'"

Other voices were instantly raised. Awb recognized Phrallet's—trust her to poke a claw in, he thought morosely—but none of the others. It was dark again now, and even though a few luminants had been brought from Voosla it was hard to make out anybody's features, here on the gritty beach beside the unfinished mole.

In any case, he was too worn out to care. So much had happened, he was half-convinced he had wandered into dreamness and would recover to be told he was suffering from fever and delirium. He *wanted* to have imagined what he had witnessed today, the stench of shock and misery exuded by the people working here as they surveyed the ruin of years of effort. At his age he had scarcely begun to conceive ambitions, let alone put them into practice, and he had been stabbed to the pith on realizing how trivial an oversight could cause such a calamity. That vast mound of shattered rock blocking the canal; that dismal garland of carefully tended plants now dangling over the new precipice so high above; those tangled cables which only yesterday had guided massive loads up and down Fangsharp Peak...

Too many images, too much emotion. He let his mind wander and made no attempt to follow the discussion.

Then, unexpectedly, he heard Axwep's boom of authority, and reflex snatched his full attention, just as though they were in mid-ocean with a line-squall looming.

"Now that's enough of this wrangling!" the mayor rasped. "I thought we were bringing cool-minded scientists here! I'd like to see a bunch like you put in charge of a city when one of her incorporated junqs turns rogue and has to be shed because you can't kill her without attracting sharqs or feroqs! Fancy trying to keep your musculators working when rogue ichor's leaking through the circulation, *hmm*? If you can't cling to your drifting wits when you're not even in danger of your lives, it's a poor lookout for your project anyhow! So shut up, will you? And that goes for you as well, Phrallet! I don't care how much of the voyage you spent chatting up our guests while I was busy running Voosla—you can't possibly know enough about the problem to discuss it. Even Drotninch hasn't been here for two years, remember."

The direct insult provoked Phrallet to a reeking fury, and she rose to full height in a way that proved she had worked little, if at all, during the bright-time; none of the others present had pressure left to match her. For an instant she imagined she was at an advantage.

Then, suddenly, she realized that those nearest her were all landlivers, perfumed against such a naked show of emotion, and they were shuffling away from her in distaste. With a muttered curse she stormed back to the city, splashing loudly off the end of the mole.

And good riddance, Awb thought. He had long wished that something of the sort might happen. Of course, like everyone else, he would have hoped to love his budder...but did she like him? Had she liked any of her offspring? True, it was a custom in every floating city to trade off young'uns to communities where, for some reason, the fertility treatment had not properly taken, or been counteracted in emergency, but she never stopped boasting about what splendid bargains she had struck for her four eldest . . . all of whom were she'uns.

Awb's mantle clenched around him. So were three of Axwep's—and they were still in the city, one studying, two working on the secondary plants. The mayor didn't object to their presence. But Phrallet could all too easily have seen her buds as potential rivals, and that would explain so much, so much!

Oh, if only he had been budded to somebody like Thilling! But the picturist must be sterile; she had no bud-scars at all.

A faint idea hovered at the edge of his awareness, in that dim zone where memory, imagination and reason blurred together. He was far too tired to pursue it, though, and turned his mind back to the discussion. Axwep was presiding over it now, directing its course like a commander of old at the bragmeets recounted in ancient legend.

She was saying: "So when you first came here, and heard about peculiar plants and deformed animals, you found no actual evidence, correct?"

"The nearest reports," Byra confirmed, "were from several padlonglaqs away. The local vegetation displayed some unusual features, but that's often the way with modified Gveestian secondaries, isn't it?"

"What about the natives? I haven't seen much of them, but they strike me as very peculiar indeed!"

Axwep's thrust went home. Byra broke off in confusion. But Drotninch spoke up bluffly.

"It was regarded by the Council of the Jingfired as a great advantage that the folk hereabouts were unlikely to protest at our intrusion!"

There was a murmur of approval from the assembled scientists, growing restive at the mayor's intervention.

"I thought so too," Lesh said suddenly. "But now I don't. Oh, it's very well for you lot to argue in such terms, comfortable at home in Chisp! What do you think it's been like for us, though, surrounded by people we can't even talk to? It's been preying on my pith, I tell you straight, and I don't think I'm the only one."

Seizing her chance, Axwep said, "Can you relate the loss of your luminants to any particular event? Or the failure of your nervograps? After all, when you first arrived everything seemed normal except for the people. What did you do that might have—oh, I don't know!—imported a new infection from beyond the hills, say?"

There was a pause. Lesh said at last, with reluctance, "Well, I have wondered about . . ."

"Go on!"

"Well, we do require a lot of fresh water, you know, and we were running short the winter before last, because it freezes so hard around here, and one of our aerial surveys noted that a stream just the other side of the local watershed was still free of ice. So last spring we tapped it with some quick-growing cutinates, and by the end of the summer we had a good supply. It's lasted through the winter exactly as we planned. But in any case, what could that have to do with the sudden blight we've suffered? We're all trained personnel, and we have the most modern medical knowledge, and—"

"Nobody's told me," Axwep cut in, "but I'll wager that the local folk have long been accustomed to collecting food from beyond the watershed. Correct?"

"Ah . . . Yes, I believe so."

"Because the vegetation there is lusher, or better to eat, or superior in some other way? Or don't you know?"

"I already told you: some of the Gveestian secondaries are unfamiliar, but we're on the edge of a climatic boundary, so I suppose the cold—"

"It's time to stop supposing and start thinking," murmured a soft voice at Awb's side, and Thilling settled close to him. "No need to explain what's going on. I can guess, even though it's taken me until now to get all my images developed. They practically tell the story by themselves . . . Say, wasn't it Phrallet I sensed passing me on the way here? What's with her? She was reeking!"

Awb summed up the reason, and Thilling clacked her mandibles in sympathy.

"It's not going to be much fun for you on Voosla for the foreseeable future, is it?"

That was it. That was the hint he needed to complete

the idea which had been so elusive before. Even though
life at sea was preferable, life anywhere in company with
so foul-tempered a budder...

"Do you spend most of your time on land?" Awb whispered.

"No more than I can help. I like to travel, I'm good at
what I do and get plenty of commissions. Why?"

"Would you accept me as an apprentice?"

"Hmm! I don't know about that! But"—quickly before
he let his mantle slump—"you can help me on shore until
Phrallet gets over her present mood. Then we'll see. Fair?"

"I can't thank you enough!"

"Then please me by keeping quiet for a bit. Oh, if there
were a bit more light...! But this sort of thing needs to
be fixed in sound, really. You should be listening: all these
recriminations about who betrayed Lesh and her chums
by not exploring the far side of the watershed properly!"

Awb composed himself and did his best to concentrate.
But all he could think of was how suddenly the blight
must have struck if a mere two years before experienced
investigators like Drotninch and Byra had found nothing
in this area to worry them.

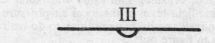

III

Finally a weak conclusion was reached. After the extent of the damage had been assessed, so a report could
be sent back to Chisp, an expedition must cross the watershed and test the plants there for infective organisms,
even though none had been found over here.

So much could have been agreed straightaway, in Awb's
view, but everybody was so overwrought, making deci-
sions seemed like excessively hard work. He was as affected as anyone else. He felt he ought to be doing
something, if only getting better acquainted with the observatory site, but it was still dark, and what could he
learn without adequate luminants? Voosla carried seed of

a recently developed type that rooted immediately in a shellful of soil and could be carried around draped over a pole, lasting for up to half a score of darks, exactly the kind of thing that was called for in a crisis like this. But nobody had expected a crisis, so none of them had been planted in advance, and even if they were forced now it would be days before they ripened.

In the end he remained inert, pondering a mystery that had often troubled him before.

Why was it that, when the world was generally calm by dark, it was always harder to analyze and act on important memories? Surely the opposite should have been true! Yet it never was. While the sun was down, memories lurked on the edge of consciousness like dormant seeds, only to burst out when there was so much else going on that one would have expected them to be smothered. Oh, they were accessible enough at a time like now... but they didn't seem to connect to activity.

Awb had been puzzled about this for a long time, for a reason he suspected people from fixed cities would not appreciate. Incomprehensibly, though, when he mentioned it to people on Voosla—Tyngwap the chief librarian, for example, who had custody of not only the city's history and navigation records, but also data concerning all the shores she had touched—they missed the point of his question too, brushing him aside with some casual reference to the light-level or the local air-pressure.

Which manifestly could have nothing to do with what he was trying to figure out!

Even though cities like Voosla were commanded by experienced weather-guessers, storms sometimes broke out unexpectedly across their course, perhaps precipitated by a meteor; nobody could forecast those, but the sparks they shed through the upper air did often seem to provoke foul weather. If such a thing happened in the dire middle of the dark, the people's response was as prompt and efficient as by day, and they were quite well able to put off their usual time for rest and reflection. But they never seemed to need to make it up later! Physical exhaustion due to lack of pressure was one thing; it demanded food and drink and that was enough. Mental exhaustion was something else; it gathered in the lower reaches of the mind, and eventually burst out in altered form. Take Phrallet as an example. What she had done this dark, by intervening in the scientists' debate without knowing the facts, was typical of her excessive need to be active, vocally or otherwise. It didn't render her unattractive to males, but her fellow she'uns didn't like her much, and as for the status accorded to mere males ever since it had been established that originally they had been parasitical on females and used them simply to bear their buds . . . !

Well, only the fact that inbreeding rapidly led to deformity had prevented cities like Voosla, and probably fixed cities as well, from reducing males to simple tokens, like certain lower animals whose symbiosis must go back so far in the history of evolution that even the finest modern techniques could not recover a single independently viable male cell. Luckily—from Awb's point of view—it had early been shown, in the light of Gveest's pioneering work (and he was male and some said had betrayed his kind!), that species lacking the constant chemical renewal due to symbiosis were precisely those most vulnerable to climatic change. Where were the snowbelongs of yesterday, hunted to extinction as soon as the Great Thaw overtook them? Where were the canifangs, pride of the earliest bioscientists—not that they called themselves by any such name in that far past? They had been deliberately made to specialize, and they died out. The list was long: northfinders, hoverers, fosq, dirq, some exploited by folk for their own ends, some simply unable to compete when their range was invaded by a more vigorous rival or even a rash of Gveest's new plants!

Beyond them, too, according to the latest accounts, there had been ancestral creatures without names, which pastudiers labeled using Ancient Forbish, receding to the very dawn of time.

Did they think? Did they reason? Certainly they left no message for the future, which was a mark of the folk; as long ago as the age of legendary Jing, means had been found to warn posterity about the menace looming in the sky. Without such aids, probably the Age of Multiplication would have proved a disaster—

No, not necessarily, Awb corrected himself. Eventually the truth could have been rediscovered. But perhaps there would have been less reason to go in search of it, and by the time it was once more chanced on it might have been too late: the sun might be being drawn inexorably into some new star, up there in the Major Cluster... He tipped his eye in search of it, and was astonished to realize that it was nowhere to be seen; the sky was blue, and everybody was dispersing to daylight duties.

What was Thilling apt to think of him if he stayed here mooning? Hastily he scrambled to his pads and set out after her. It was a vast effort to catch up, since his pressure yesterday had been so badly lowered, but he struggled on, reminding himself that all effort was made the more worthwhile by knowing how the ancestors had dedicated their lives to the survival of descendants they could never meet.

The first part of the bright was spent in making a careful record of the damage caused by the landslide, and Awb followed Thilling from place to place carrying bulky light-tight packs of the sensitized sheets she still referred to as "leaves" in memory of a more primitive technology. For the first time he gained a proper impression of the complexity of the work that had gone into creating the site for the observatory. Planning it must have been even harder than, say, founding a new fixed city, what with digging the canal to carry broken rock and make the mole, stringing the floater-cables, supplying food and accommodation for the workers, all of whom had had to be recruited at a distance and were used to a high standard of living. Several times he heard it vainly wished that the natives could have been enlisted, but today, again, they went about their own animal business, apparently incapable even of wondering about this intrusion into their placid world. If any of them had indeed been killed by the landslide, they showed no signs of grief.

Moreover there were mounts and draftimals to provide for, the musculators and cutinates, the floaters themselves constantly in need of the right nourishment to replenish the light gas in their bladders... Awb knew perfectly well that when they first joined Voosla the people from Chisp had occasionally had difficulty finding their way around on her numerous levels, but he couldn't help feeling that, if they were accustomed to places like this, they ought to have found so small a city comparatively simple.

When the sun was at its highest—not very high in these latitudes, of course—Lesh gathered her companions on the top of the scree caused by the landslide, and started working out how long it might take to clear away. Already draftimals were dragging musculators towards it, along with grabbers and scoopers.

This spot afforded a splendid prospect of the area including the bay where Voosla was lying, minus her giqs, all of which had been detached and were now spread as far as the horizon. Delighted, Thilling used up her stock of sheets in fixing a view in each direction, returned them to their pack, and asked Awb to take them back to the city and bring replacements. Nervously, because he had no wish to encounter Phrallet, but equally none to disappoint Thilling, he complied.

It took him a long time to regain the shore because the usual branchways were decaying, like so much of the vegetation on this blighted coast, and he had to stay on the ground most of the way. The stink of rotting foliage was all-pervasive, and he wondered how the people working here could bear it.

Coming in sight of the sea again, he discovered that a strange briq had entered the bay. She must have been just around the western headland when he looked before, because she was of a type by no means speedy, the broad northern breed called variously smaq or luqqra much in favor for carrying bulky freight. Voosla had crossed a number of them during the couple of brights prior to landfall.

As she touched the side of the city, Axwep came to greet her commander, and by the time Awb arrived they were deep in conversation.

"There's somebody who can probably tell us," the mayor said, interrupting herself. "Awb! Do you know where Lesh is?"

"When I left, she was on top of the rockpile trying to work out how long it will take to clear," Awb called back.

"Will you be going back there?"

"Yes, I'm on an errand for Thilling."

"Then you can carry a message. Come here. This is Eupril; she's from the quarry down-coast which we passed the dark before last."

Awb remembered that being pointed out to him, at a

spot where luminants grew normally. He had never seen a quarry, but he knew about such places where specially developed microorganisms were used to break up rock and concentrate valuable elements to enrich poor soil, or even to extract metals. In ancient times, it was said, the folk had employed fire for similar purposes: however, during the Age of Multiplication fire had fallen out of use except for very special purposes, because most burnable substances were far too valuable for other applications. Most people nowadays were terrified of it. Sometimes, far out at sea, one could smell smoke on the wind, and the Vooslans would mutter sympathy for the poor land-livers whose homes and crops were going up in flames.

"I don't suppose it'll do much good," Eupril said sardonically. She was thickset, with the forceful voice of one used to calling over long distances, rather like Axwep. "I've warned and warned those people that they picked a bad site for this observatory of theirs. We surveyed it when we first came up here, and though there were a lot of useful minerals we decided against prospecting further. We didn't like the look of the natives, nor what we found the other side of the ridge. People who won't listen make my pith ache, you know? Of course, when we saw a chunk had fallen off the mountain, we thought we'd better come and see if they needed help. We have no other way of finding out. Used to have a nervograp link, but it went bad on us."

"From the same blight that's spoiling everything else?" Awb suggested.

"Now that's the other reason I'm here," Eupril said. "We have news for Lesh. It's not a blight. It's a poison."

"How can you be sure?" Axwep demanded. "I mean, I know the people here haven't been able to isolate a causative organism yet, but there's a lot of talk about germs you can't see even with the best microscope, that go through the finest filters and can still do damage—"

"We're sure," Eupril cut in. "Who'd know better than a concentration specialist? Matter of fact, we've been worrying about something of the sort ever since they warned us they were going to tap water from beyond the ridge and discharge it here, because there's a current that follows the coast and washes right down to our place. Still, they claimed it was only going to be for a year or two, and a bit of extra fresh water might conceivably have been an advantage, because we use a lot of cutinates and even with our best salt-precipitators they tend to wear out pretty quickly. So we didn't raise as much objection as we should have, what with the delay involved in sending a delegation to Chisp *and* the rigid attitude of the Jingfired. Everybody knows they think they're incapable of making a mistake, hm? Bunch of arrogant knowalls, that lot!"

She shrugged with her entire mantle. "Anyway, nothing much happened last year, so we more or less stopped worrying. This season, though, our concentration-cultures have started to die off, and our cutinates are developing blisters like we never saw before, and just the other day we finally traced the problem. Of course we thought it was disease at first. It's not. It's definitely a poison that's coming to us in solution, in the water, and even diluted as it is when it reaches the quarry it's deadly dangerous. We don't have anything that can resist it. Our toughest precipitators turn black and rot within a month."

Stunned, Awb said, "Mayor, I think this is something Lesh ought to hear personally. I mean, I couldn't possibly repeat such an important message and be sure of getting all the details right."

"That's not the message," said Axwep with gentle irony. "The message I meant was simply a request to get here as quickly as she can. I'm sure you can manage to relay that much!"

"Probably not," said a harsh voice, and Phrallet appeared, swarming along the nearest slanting branchway. "Even if he is of my own budding, I wouldn't trust him to find his way from one side of Voosla to the other!"

Furious, Awb reared back, holding up the pack of image-sheets like a shield. "Thilling trusts me!" he blurted. "She sent me to bring a fresh batch of these for her!"

"Instead of which you're standing about gossiping?"

"But—!"

It was no good. All his life he had found it impossible to get his budder to take him seriously. Clamping his mandibles tight shut, he muttered an apology to Axwep, who seemed mildly amused—a reaction calculated to irritate Phrallet still further—and hastened in the direction of Thilling's bower.

IV

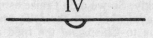

The first thing Axwep asked Lesh when the latter returned to Voosla—annoyed at the interruption even though Awb had done his utmost to explain its reason—was whether water was still being drawn from beyond the ridge; if so, the city should be moved.

"All our cutinates got crushed by the rockfall," was her curt reply. "They're not pumping anything right now, and in fact I'm not sure they'll survive. Now what's all this about, Eupril?"

The concentration expert sighed. "Oh, I know you suspect our people of wanting to drive you away because we have designs on this site for our own purposes, but that's untrue and unfair! I came with proof of the danger you're in. Carry on like you're doing, and those toughtrees you're planting on the peak will turn as rotten as everything else. Then what will become of your telescopes?"

"Proof? Let's see it!" Lesh snapped.

"I'd rather present the evidence in proper order. You're supposed to have a ripe bunch of experts here now, or so Axwep tells me. Maybe some of them will be a bit less—ah—emotionally committed. Let them be the judges."

For a second it seemed that Lesh was going to yield to rage; then, resignedly, she slumped to four-fifths height.

"Very well, I'll send for Drotninch and the rest. But where are we going to get the water we need if we can't take it from across the ridge?" With sudden optimism: "Maybe from the sea! You can let us have some of your salt-precipitators!"

"They're dead or dying," Eupril answered. "We've had to order fresh stock, and it'll be months before we have any to spare."

Thilling, never one to miss important news, had accompanied Lesh back to the city, and stood beside Awb listening keenly. Now, however, she muttered, "This could go on for ages. Come with me. You said you'd like to be my apprentice, so let's see if you can learn to trim a lens while I develop the images I've caught so far."

Excited, he followed her down into the very core of the city, where the junqs fretted and throbbed, dreamlost perhaps in visions of their ancestral freedom. Here a small dark bower had been assigned to the picturist, which she could make entirely light-tight. Judging by the stink of juices and concentrates which blew from it when she finished work, it must be very unpleasant in there. Awb began to have second thoughts. But he willingly accepted the blade she gave him, and paid total attention when she demonstrated how to cut loose the full-grown lenses that bulged from the plants she had hung to nearby branches.

"Here are the measurements for a mid-range lens," she said. "Try this kind first. If you spoil one I shan't mind. If you spoil two, I'll be disappointed. If three—well, I'll probably part you torso from mantle! Understood?"

Awb signed yes.

"Get on with it, then. Go back where there's better light. And take your time. I may not be through with this lot before sundown."

And indeed the sun was touching the horizon when she rejoined him. He had completed two of the lenses, and the second was flawless as near as he could tell, but he waited on her verdict nervously.

"Hmm! Very good!" she pronounced, surprised and pleased. "More than I can say about the one I have on the fixer at the moment. I mean, look at these, will you?"

She flourished a selection of the sheets she had exposed in the morning. Awb examined them. To his untutored eye they appeared satisfactory, and he said so.

"No, look again! Here, here, here!"—each time with a jab of her claw. "There's a blur, there's a smear, there's a streak... At first I thought the fixer must be leaking light, but I've checked and doublechecked. I suppose there must be a blister in the lens, but I can't locate it."

Awb ventured, "But then wouldn't the blurs always reappear in the same place? And these don't."

Taken aback, she said, "Give those back to me... Hmm! I wonder if it could have to do with the angle of incidence of the light—No, that wouldn't fit either. And most of the early ones, come to think of it, are all right. It's only from about the point where we climbed up the rockfall that I started having trouble. Maybe a wind-blown drop on the lens, but I was careful to shield it . . . Oh, *I* can't figure it out, unless . . ." She fixed him with a stern glare. "You didn't drop the leaf-pack by any chance?"

"No, I promise I didn't!" Awb cried, recoiling in alarm. "And if I had, surely the damage would show on one edge or one corner?"

"Ah . . . Yes, of course it would. I'm sorry." Thilling clattered her mandibles in confusion. "This makes no sense at all, you know. It's as though some trace of light—very bright light—got through the pack-wrap, and . . ."

"A fault in the making," Awb offered.

"I suppose so." All of a sudden she sounded weary. "But I never had trouble with my supplier before. I've been trying not to arrive at that conclusion, because if all the leaf-packs I have with me are faulty, I might as well not have come."

Startled to find himself in the unprecedented situation of having to reassure an adult, Awb said, "Please, you're making too much of this. As far as I could tell, those images were fine until you pointed out the flaws. Nobody is likely to notice what worries you so much, except maybe another picturist."

"I suppose you're right," Thilling sighed. "Let's go and eat something. I've had enough for one bright, or even two."

Because the scientists were still arguing, Axwep had suggested that Lesh and her senior colleagues, along with Eupril and some of her companions, should eat this evening on Voosla, where the food was better than on shore. However, although she made it clear that she could not repeat the invitation regularly, because any floating city was in a delicate balance with its inhabitants and the best efforts of the giqs could never gather as much nourishment as she collected for herself in open water, there were some who instantly accused the mayor of wasting public resources. Wasn't it bad enough to have brought these scores of passengers all this way?—that was their cry, and they took no account of the fact that Voosla had been specially replanted with new high-yielding secondary growths developed at the University of Chisp, which would continue paying her back long after the return voyage.

Prominent among those who complained, of course, was Phrallet. Axwep had finally lost patience with her, and ordered that she be forbidden access to the prime food zone. Tagging along behind Thilling, Awb managed to steal in and join the company, hoping desperately as he nibbled a bit here and a bit there that his budder would not get to hear.

Finding herself next to one of Eupril's fellow quarry-workers, whom she had seen earlier but not spoken with, Thilling said, "What's all this about a poison, then? Why can't it be a disease? Name of Thilling, by the way."

"Name of Hy," said the other. "Well, it's because of the way it acts in living tissue, of course. Ever hear of a disease organism that simply killed the cells around it, without spreading, or reseeding itself at a distant site? Oh, we've carried out all the tests we're equipped for, and we even managed to get our claws on the corpses of some of the natives. They don't seem to care about their dead, just leave 'em to rot. And in every single case we've found necrotic tissue, either in the digestive tract or quite often in the nerve-pith, and if you take the dead center—excuse me!—and triturate it and apply microscopic drops to a suitable test medium, like the partly flayed rind of a cutinate . . . Well, what would you expect to see?"

Thilling frowned with her entire mantle. "A whole series of infection-sites, obviously."

"That's exactly what we thought. Wrong. One and only ever *one* new patch of necrosis. The rest is unaffected."

Chomping solemnly, Thilling pondered that awhile. At last she heaved a sigh.

"It doesn't sound any more like a poison than a disease, in that case, does it? Still, it's not my specialty, so I have to take your word. But I always thought poisons worked by spreading throughout the system."

Awb was glad to hear her say that; it meant his own main question was likely to be answered.

"So they do, for the most part. I've been dealing with poisons much of my life, because you never know, when you feed new ore to a concentration-culture, whether it's going to survive on it. But I never saw the like before: a

poison so lethal that a particle too small to see with a
microscope can kill cells over and over. It doesn't dis-
solve, it doesn't disperse, it just sits there and kills cells!"

"Thilling!"

They all turned, to find Drotninch approaching.

"You are coming with us to check out this hot stream
tomorrow, aren't you? Yes? Good! We're going to leave
at first bright. Lesh is working out how many mounts can
be spared. Will you need a whole one for your equipment?"

With a wry twist of her mantle Thilling answered, "Not
a whole one. I have a volunteer helper now."

V

Slowly the expedition wound its way up the narrow
trail cut to facilitate laying of the cutinate pipeline. It had
remained alarmingly clear of overgrowth, though Lesh
said it had not been recut this spring. It was as though
the surrounding plants, both Gveestian and natural, had
bowed away from it.

The air was comfortably calm, and since the morning
of the city's arrival there had been scarcely a cloud in the
sky, let alone the threat of a storm. Nonetheless Thilling's
weather-sense was reacting queasily. She did her best to
convince herself it was because of her unpremeditated
decision to accept Awb as an apprentice. Taking on someone from so utterly different a background, and with such
an awful budder to hint at how he might turn out in the
long term ... Had it been wise?

Just to complicate matters, Phrallet was a member of
the party. Whether out of misplaced ambition, because
she fancied she might make a better impression on this
trip than usually at home on Voosla, or out of jealousy
of Awb, or simply out of bad temper because of what
Axwep had said to her last dark, she had insisted on
coming along. Drotninch, who had gotten to know her

slightly during the voyage, was no more in favor than was Thilling; however, Axwep was glad of the chance to be rid of her for a while, and she possessed sufficient charm as regarded strangers for Lesh to say with a shrug, "Why not? We can always do with an extra set of claws, and a volunteer is better than a draftee."

Thilling's view was that she was apt to be more of a nuisance than a help. And she was equally dubious about Awb. She still could not quite rid herself of the suspicion that her images might have been spoiled by his carelessness. Moreover she was moderately certain that his ambition to spend his future in light-tight bowers reeking of chemicals was due less to a genuine interest in the work than to the fact that if he became Voosla's first official picturist he would always have an excuse to shut himself away from his budder.

Still, there was little point in speculating. Determinedly she forced her attention back to the country they were traversing, only to find that the view made her more worried than ever.

From the canal which carried waste and usable rock to the new harbor, irrigation ditches had been ichored off for the crops that fed the work-force. So much was normal; so much was sensible economy.

Yet the point in time at which the crops began to fail coincided with the failure of the nervograp links to the outside world, and in turn followed the first use of water from beyond the watershed. How was it that supposedly rational people could have overlooked the connection? They definitely had! Even in the light of what Eupril and Hy reported, Lesh was still obstinately hoping to find that the water-supply had nothing to do with the—the blight, the poison, whatever it might ultimately prove to be.

Now, fixing images of the true extent of the devastation in the morning shadow of Fangsharp Peak, Thilling started to wonder whether those who had been living here for two or three years might not already be affected, already be on the way to matching the miserable mindless natives.

Then she noticed something else even more alarming as the mounts wound in single file up and over the ridge. During the first part of the bright, the beasts had too much sense to browse off the nearby foliage, sere and discolored as it was. About noon, however, when presumably they were starting to thirst, the one carrying among other loads her own equipment did begin to help itself now and again from the nearest branches. But the leaves were wilting, and the rind of the cutinates whose line they were following was patched with suppurating black.

She glanced at Awb, laboring along behind her under the burden of her spare image-fixer and a spare lens-plant, and realized that he too appeared uneasy. But neither Lesh nor Drotninch seemed concerned. Why not?

Well, perhaps she was worrying overmuch. She strove to make herself believe so.

Night fell late in these latitudes, and was short. They crossed the watershed before they lacked enough light to wait for tomorrow's dawn. The chance to rest was welcome; they all needed to accumulate pressure for the next stage of the journey. But Thilling was dismayed anew when she realized that Lesh, who had been responsible for organizing the expedition, expected everybody, and the mounts too, to subsist off the local plants because, as she said, "it would only be for a day or two." This was enough to startle even Drotninch and Byra, and a furious argument broke out in which—predictably—Phrallet was prominent.

True, there were plenty of edible secondary growths of the kind which that far-sighted genius Gveest had modified to provide for the folk during their traumatic population explosion. Possibly, as Lesh was now claiming, the planners of the observatory project had seeded them deliberately to furnish an emergency resource for the workers. More likely they had arrived of their own accord; their spawn was designed to drift on the wind and displace natural rivals when it settled. But those which grew close to the path were so unwholesome both in appearance and in odor...

Even though she had no luminants, and as yet only a shred of moon was visible, very close to the horizon, Thilling slipped away to a spot where a few cautious bites convinced her the food was safe, or at least safer. Glancing up on hearing a noise nearby, she was amazed to discover that Awb was here already. Good for him!

But he was tensing as though afraid of being reprimanded, and small wonder, for that was certainly how

Phrallet would have reacted. Suddenly full of sympathy for this young'un, Thilling said sharply, "All right, keep your pith from boiling! What made you come this way?"

"I just didn't like the smell of what the mounts were eating," he muttered.

"Nor do I. I think that worn-out old nag they assigned to us is going to rot in her pad-marks before we get where we're going... By the way!"

"Yes?"

"I'm sorry I accused you of dropping my leaf-packs. I've been watching you all this bright, and I'm satisfied that you've been taking great care of my gear. I'm also convinced that there's something in what Eupril says about poison. When you're through eating, come and set up my dark-bower. I expect all today's images to be faulty."

"Do you want them, then?" Awb countered in confusion.

"What I mostly want is to do Drotninch and Byra in the eye because I have an eye that they don't. If I'd been here with the original expedition that chose the observatory site—! But never mind that. I sense something's bothering you. Out with it!"

"Are you really going to spend all dark developing your—uh—leaves?"

"And why not?"

"Well, I'd have thought..." Awb shifted uncomfortably from pad to pad. "You know—review today into memory, build up pressure for tomorrow..." He subsided, more at a loss than ever.

"Oh, there's plenty of time for that while you're waiting for images to develop—"

It was her turn to break off, gazing at him with astonishment in the faint starshine. "Are you trying to tell me you've never been educated in dark-use?"

"I don't know what you mean!"

"Oh, dear!" Seizing a clump of funqi, she settled beside him. "It's no news to me that cities like Voosla are behind the times, but this is incredible."

"Sorry to appear so ignorant," Awb muttered resentfully.

"Oh, I don't mean to be matronizing, I promise. But... Look, young'un, I just took it for granted that you must have your own version of dark-use training. I mean,

I know the People of the Sea are contemptuous of land-livers who can't move to avoid bad weather or follow the best seasons, and the rest of it, and what's more I know they can turn to in mid-dark and cope with gales and storms, so... Well, surely we have to exploit all the time at our disposal if we're to meet the challenge of the future, right? You know what I mean by that, at least?"

"Of course!"

"That's a mercy... Oh, I'm starting to sound like Phrallet, and I'm ashamed. She's anti-male, by the rude way she treats you, and I'm not. I admit I'm sterile, and the fertility treatment won't take in me, but that's neither here nor there. Just makes me wonder about those it took in much too well! But I sense you have a whole branchful of questions, so I'll see if I can answer them without being told what they are."

She filled her mantle for a long speech; he heard the hiss.

"Why shan't I mind if my images are faulty? Because I think the faults may teach us something we never knew before. Why am I appalled that you haven't been trained in proper dark-use? Because I don't hail from where you think I do. You believe I'm from Chisp, don't you?"

"I—ah—I did assume..."

"Eat your assumptions, then. I was budded in the Lugomannic Archipelago."

"Where Gveest discovered the cure for infertility?" Awb burst out, and was instantly horrified at himself, because she had just mentioned her own sterility. But her only reaction was mild amusement.

"More to the point: where someone you never heard of, called Pletrow, realized after she'd finally had the bud of her own which she longed for that in order to cope with the consequences of Gveest's success there had to be a means of exploiting dark-time, instead of squandering it."

Exuding fascination, Awb hunched forward. "I've always resented that myself! I mean, one never really stops thinking, does one? It's just that by dark it always seems so much harder to make action match intention!"

He added self-excusingly, "I envy you the fact that you're going to spend this dark doing something constructive, you see. I don't know how."

For a long while Thilling remained indecisive. Should she broach her most precious secret to this chance-met stranger? Yet the magnitude of the catastrophe that was set fair to overwhelm the great observatory was daunting, and the need for the information it could supply was so urgent. Could she confront the insights she was burdened with entirely alone?

No: she could not. She needed to confide in someone, and none of the scientists from Chisp was right to share her private anxiety. At least Awb had fought back against the handicap of being Phrallet's bud...

She said after a small eternity, "Then I must teach you how to liberate consciousness from concern with digestion. That's the first of the mental exercises Pletrow developed for the Jingfired."

"You mean *you*...?" Awb's pressure failed him.

"Yes, I do mean!" Already she was half regretting her admission. "But if you so much as hint that you're aware of the fact, I'm bound by oath to leak you. Understood?"

Fervently he echoed, "Understood!"

"Very well, then. Now there's one other thing I ought to ask you. But I'm not going to. If you're the person I think and hope you are, you'll work it out yourself."

"Does it have to do with why Lesh doesn't want to consider any other site for the observatory?"

"Very indirectly I suppose it does. We all hope to bequeath some achievement to the future...No, that's not what I want you to say. Think it over. In the mean-time, what about setting up my dark-bower for me?"

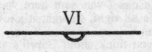

VI

Was Thilling truly one of the legendary Jingfired?

That question haunted Awb as the party wended its way down from the crest of the ridge, still following the line chosen for the cutinates, either side of which the trees were stunted and their secondary growths pale and sickly.

The stink of decay in the air was worse than where they had started from because it was older, as though even storms could not disperse it. Its impact was unnerving; one heard fewer voices raised to normal pitch, more murmurs of apprehension and more cries from unseen creatures in the overgrowth.

Along the bottom of the valley, where they were bound, ran a watercourse formed by the confluence of three streams half a day's journey to the east. It was the middle one which remained so warm during the worst of winter that it could keep the whole river free of ice. Nobody had explored it to the source, but presumably it must rise where there was hot rock of the sort well known on other continents, that created geysers or pools of bubbling-hot mud.

An earth dam had been built to make an artificial lake for the cutinates to draw from. Now and then they could glimpse the sunlight gleaming on its surface, wherever the vegetation had died back sufficiently.

That was disturbingly often.

Byra announced loudly, "This is far worse than what I recall from my first visit! If things had been this bad then I'd have argued strongly against choosing this site."

"I thought the Jingfired didn't make mistakes like that," was Lesh's snappish response. Close enough behind to overhear the exchange, Awb whispered to Thilling:

"Is *she* one of—?"

"Of course not!"—with contempt. "She's enjoyed giving herself the sort of airs she thinks might suit one of us ever since the first time she was assigned to a foreign survey team. She carries it off well enough to mislead the ignorant, but she's never dared to make the claim outright. One of the reasons I was sent here was to make sure about that. It's all right, though: it's a bit of harmless vanity, no more."

"What do you think about Eupril's attitude towards the Jingfired?" Awb risked.

Thilling gave a soft chuckle. "The more people who feel that way about us, the better we can achieve our aim."

Confused, Awb said, "But I always thought—"

She cut short his words. "The real Jingfired, young'un, are never who you think they are. You have to *know*."

And she hurried up a convenient branch to fix another image from the treetops.

Awb found himself wishing they didn't have to rely on mounts, for it would have been quicker and more pleasurable to swarm along branchways in the ancient fashion instead of padding along on the ground. Away from the water's edge, and away from these discolored cutinates, the overgrowth mostly smelled normal despite its peculiar tint, so—

His thoughts came to a squeaking halt.

Why weren't there any people in this valley?

Where else on the entire globe was there such lush terrain without a city, a town, even a hamlet?

This is what the world must have looked like before the Age of Multiplication.

The thought struck him so forcibly that he uttered it aloud. Some of those within hearing responded as though he had chanced on a profound truth.

But not all. Phrallet was close beside Byra; she had moved in to offer comfort after Lesh made mock of her. Now she turned and said loudly, "Ah, that's my youngest bud making noises again! I wish I'd had another she'un that I could have traded off to benefit Voosla, but who wants a he'un, particularly a useless lazy one like Awb?"

Clack: Awb's mandibles rattled as he rose in fury to maximum height, heedless of Thilling's gear which he was carrying. There was no case on record of a budling fighting his budder, but after that—!

Except, amazingly—

(As the pheromones mingled in the taut still air with what the rotting plants exuded, but far fiercer...)

Clackonclackonclackonclack: and abruptly climaxing—

"SHUT UP!"

It was Drotninch, fuming with chemical proof of the reason why she had been chosen to lead the university team.

"I don't want to hear any more arguments until we get to the lake and have something solid to argue about! In the meantime, save your pressure for moving your pads!"

Phrallet slanted her mantle as though to puff a blast of combat-stink directly at Drotninch, but Lesh, Thilling and even Byra signaled a warning of the consequences. She subsided, still angry, and let the rest of the party go by, falling in right at the end. As Awb sidled past, she glowered with her whole mantle, but said nothing.

He was indescribably relieved.

The sun was just at the zenith when they emerged on a flat bare outcrop of rock overlooking the artificial lake. The water-level was a little below maximum, as could be judged from the mud along the banks, some of which was a curious yellow color. There were automatic spillways to cope with the rise due to a spring thaw: a dense mat of small but coarse-stemmed plants along the top of the dam, designed to float upward and lift their root-masses just enough for the surplus to spill over without letting the dam erode.

At least, there should have been. In fact, the plants were decaying like everything else in the vicinity, and the mud along the banks was actually bare, whereas ordinarily it would have been fledged with shoots sprung from the riverside vegetation.

"Have you noticed," Byra said after a pause, "that you can tell at a glance which of the trees have taproots long enough to reach the river? They're dying off. Look!"

In a dull voice Lesh said, "So they must be sucking up the poison, if that's what it actually is."

"And the state of these cutinates!" Byra went on as she clambered over the edge of the rock and gingerly descended to the waterside. She prodded the nearest, and its rind yielded, soft as rotting funqus. A swarm of startled wingets took to the air, shrilling their complaint at being disturbed. Awb, with the quick reflexes of youth, snatched one as it shot past, and bent his eye to examine it.

"How long since you sent anyone to check out the cutinates?" Drotninch demanded of Lesh.

"As soon as the snow melted," was the muttered reply. "I was assured that everything was in order. At any rate the spillways were working properly, and above the water-level the cutinates looked pretty much all right."

"You didn't haul their ends to the surface and—?" The scholar broke off. "No, I don't imagine you'd have seen the need if they were still pumping normally. Were they?"

"Oh, they've been functioning fine. Though, now that

I've seen the state they're in, I'm surprised they haven't burst at a score of places."

"So am I . . . Well, before we disturb anything else we'd better fix some images. Thilling!"

"Just a moment," the picturist called back. "Awb, can I take a look at that winget?"

He surrendered it gladly. "Do you know if it's a regular local species?" he demanded. "I don't recognize it, but then I've never been so far north before."

"I have, and it's not," Thilling answered grimly. "It's deformed. Its body has tried to—well—double, hasn't it? Byra, I think you should see this right away!"

As she hastened toward the biologist, Phrallet drew close to Awb.

"Do anything to get yourself well in with the folk from Chisp, won't you? Eat any sort of dirt they throw at you! I did my best to be friendly, but I'm leaked if I'm going to bother anymore. I never met such a rude, bossy bunch."

Surprised at his own audacity, Awb said, "Maybe they just reflect your own attitude back at you."

"Why, you—!" Phrallet swelled with renewed anger.

"Awb!" The shout was from Thilling. "Bring those leaves we developed last night, will you?"

"Coming!" Awb responded, mightily flattered.

And Phrallet, luckily, did not dare to follow, but remained seething by herself.

Taking the image-pack, Thilling said, "I was just explaining that I don't expect any images I fix here to be of the usual quality. You haven't seen these yet, nor has anyone else, but . . . Well, look at this one, for example, which was taken right next to the cutinates where there was a leak most probably caused when the top fell off Fangsharp Peak. Notice all those blurs and streaks?"

"It's as though the poison can attack your image-fixer too!" Awb exclaimed.

Passing the picture around, Thilling said dryly, "I shan't argue. I reached the same conclusion. I shall of course try fixing more images here, but like I said I don't expect them to be much good."

"But how—?" Drotninch began, and interrupted herself. "Now I'm going against my own orders, aren't I? We'll wait until we have something to discuss. Lesh, if you'd . . ."

Briskly she issued orders to each of the party, pointedly ignoring Phrallet until, conquering her annoyance, the latter advanced to ask if she could help too. She was sent to fetch samples of the dead plants from the top of the dam, while Byra set up a microscope to examine them with, and Awb followed Thilling to the best points of vantage for general images, before descending to the lake for close-ups of the bare mud and ruined cutinates.

Very shortly after there was a cry from Phrallet, in her usual bad-tempered tone.

"That was a foul trick to play on me! You did it deliberately, didn't you?"

The others stared in astonishment as she fled back from the dam without the samples she had been asked to collect.

"What in the world is wrong?" Drotninch demanded.

"It's hot! The top of the dam is *hot*! Oh, my poor pads! And the water isn't just warm, it's *steaming*! Look!"

"Why, so it is! But I promise I hadn't noticed. By dark I would have, but—Well, you didn't notice either, did you?"

The pressure taken out of her by that awkward fact, Phrallet subsided, grumbling. Regretting his earlier rudeness, for she was bound to seek revenge for it eventually, Awb muttered a word of apology to Thilling and himself hurried to the side of the dam. Cautiously he lowered to minimum height and began to probe the area, reporting in a loud voice.

"There must be water seeping around the end of the dam here—the subsoil is marshy. But it's definitely warm, and I don't understand why. All the roots are dead but they're still meshed together. And the top of the dam . . ."

He moved on, half a padlong at a time. "Yes, it's very warm, and very hard, too. Completely dried out, almost as hard as rock." He rapped it with one claw. "And there's this funny yellow mud; it's building up in layers. And—Ow! That *is* hot!" He recoiled in surprise.

"I think you'd better come away," Thilling shouted, and he was just about to comply when there was an unexpected commotion.

The mount that carried Thilling's equipment, which she had dismissed as an old nag, uttered a noise between a grunt and a scream, lost all her pressure, and measured her length on the ground.

VII

That nightfall none of the party had much maw for food. Byra had carried out a cursory examination of the dead mount, and what her microscope revealed exactly matched the description Eupril had given of the way the poison affected cutinates and precipitators at the quarry. The certainty that at least some of it must be at work in their own bodies took away all appetite.

While Thilling occupied herself developing the day's images, not calling on Awb for help, the rest of them lay up on the branches of the nearest healthy trees, as though being clear of the ground could offer them security in the dark, like their remotest ancestors. Of course, if any of the local animals had been as altered as that mutated winget... But the Freeze, the Thaw, and the greed of the half-starved folk who had exploded across the world during the Age of Multiplication had combined to exterminate almost all large predators, and turned avoidance of animal food among the folk themselves from a moral choice into a necessity. Even fish nowadays was in short supply, more valuable to nourish cities than their citizens.

Awb thought of having to ingest the flesh of the mount whose stench drifted up to him, and shuddered.

As though the trembling of the branch he clung to had been a signal, Byra said suddenly, "What I don't understand is how there can be burns without fire."

"I thought you Jingfired knew all about everything," came the sour riposte from Phrallet.

"I never said I was Jingfired!" Byra snapped. "If I was, do you think I'd be here? They have too much sense!"

In the startled pause that followed, Awb found time to

wonder why she had chosen this of all moments to disclaim the pose she had—according to Thilling—long adopted, and also whether Thilling herself... But there was no time to ponder such matters. Perceptibly desperate to avoid moving the observatory to another site, Lesh was saying, "We've got to isolate this stuff! Once we know precisely what it is—"

"Isolate it?" countered Drotninch. "When it can kill any concentration-culture it comes up against? You heard what Eupril said, and the folk at the quarry have only been dealing with a trace of it, diluted over and over."

"Well, there are filters, aren't there?"

"Filters will trap everything above a certain size. In fact I'm beginning to wonder whether that may account for the dam being so hot."

"Next you show us how to light a fire underwater," muttered Phrallet.

"Any moment now," Byra promised, "I'm going to—"

"Byra!" Drotninch said warningly. But it was too dark and their pressure was too low for combat-stink; the keener note of simple fear predominated, and was compelling them gradually towards cooperation, much as it must have bonded their ancestors into forming tribes and eventually communities.

Awb shuddered again, but this time with awe and not disgust. It was amazing to be participating in so ancient an experience. Of course, something similar happened now and then at sea, when a storm assailed the city, but then wind and spray carried off the pheromones, and the decision to work together was dictated by reason.

How much was left of the primitive in modern folk? He must ask Thilling. If she were truly one of the Jingfired, she would certainly be able to answer such a question.

But the argument was continuing. Sullenly, as though not convinced that the others wanted to hear, Byra was saying, "It was the heat of the water that made me start thinking along these lines. Now I've realized what the tissue-damage in that poor mount reminded me of. I've got a scar where some young fool shone a burning-glass on my mantle when I was a budling. Instead of just comforting me, my budder made me turn even that silly trick to account. She dissected out a tiny scrap of tissue and showed me the way the heat had ruptured the cells. I noticed just the same effect in the mount. Of course, the damage is deep inside, instead of just on the surface."

"But so are the blemishes on Thilling's leaves!" Awb burst out. "They happen right inside a light-tight pack, or inside the fixer!"

Once again there was a pause during which he had time to feel dismayed by his own boldness. Byra ended it by saying, "Phrallet, I can't for the life of me understand why you think your budling is unworthy of you. I'd be proud if one of my young'uns had come up with a point like that."

Set to grow angry again, Phrallet abruptly realized she was being indirectly complimented, and made no answer.

Drotninch, less tactfully, said, "Going back to where we were just now: you can very well have heat without fire, or at least without flame. Using a burning-glass is something else, because we assume the sun to be made of fire fiercer than what we can imitate down here. But if you rub something long and hard enough, it gets warm, and likewise air if you compress it with a bellower. Don't you know about that sort of thing on Voosla, Phrallet?" She sounded genuinely curious.

"You should know better than to ask"—unexpectedly from Lesh. "The People of the Sea did study heat and even flame at one time, using substances that protected their junqs and briqs from feeling the effect. But it was hard to keep a fire alight at sea, and eventually they lost interest because they didn't have any ore to melt, or sand for glass, and they could always trade for what they needed."

"That's right!" Phrallet agreed, and it was plain she was relaxing at long last.

Drotninch rattled her mandibles. "This gives me an idea. Do you think there's enough burnable material around here to start up a—what do they call it?—a furnace?"

"What for?" Byra countered.

"Well, in olden times they used fire to separate metal from ore, didn't they? Even if we can't use a concentration-culture, we might get at this poison using heat."

"Hmm! I'm inclined to doubt it," Byra said. "We don't yet know whether it's a simple substance, for one thing."

"If it weren't, and a very rare one, surely we'd have encountered it before?"

"Maybe we have," Lesh suggested. "Or at any rate its effects. I've never really believed that hot rock—let alone actual volcanoes—can be accounted for by saying that there's a leak from the core of the planet. For one thing the core must be *too* hot; for another, the magma would have to rise for many padlonglaqs, and I can't envisage channels for so much lava remaining open under the enormous pressures we know must exist down there."

"What does this have to do with—?" Drotninch had begun to say, when there was a rustle of foliage and Thilling arrived to join them. Parting the leaves revealed that the new moon was rising, a narrow crescent, just about to disappear again as it crossed the Arc of Heaven.

"I wish we'd had time to force some of those special luminants Voosla brought," said the picturist as she settled in a vacant crotch. "Or that the moon were nearer full, or something. I spend too much of my working life in total darkness to be comfortable by mere starlight. It's not so bad if your maw is full, but... Any of you manage to eat anything tonight?"

They all signed negative.

"Me neither. Never mind that, though. What annoys me most is that I can't examine my images properly before dawn. But I'm sure they're going to be full of smears and blurs again, and it isn't my fault. Any explanations?"

Drotninch summarized the discussion so far.

"Awb hit on that idea, did he?" Thilling said with approval. "I agree: he's a credit to his budder, and I'm glad I decided to take him on as my apprentice. Sorry I didn't ask you to help out this time, by the way, young'un, but you realize I have to be score-per-score certain that any flaws in the images are due to me, or some outside force. All right?"

"Yes, of course," Awb answered, trying not to swell with pride, and realizing this was just the kind of attitude he would have expected one of the true Jingfired to display.

"What I'm going to do tomorrow," Thilling resumed, "is a pure gamble, but if I'm right in my guess, then... But wait a moment. My new apprentice is pretty quick on the uptake, so let's ask him. Awb, in my position, what would you do?"

Awb's pulsations seemed to come to a complete halt. Here in the dark his mind felt sluggish, and with his maw empty the problem was worse yet. Struggling with all his mental forces, fighting to distinguish what he could rationally justify from what was seeping up from wild imagination or even the utterly logic-free level of dreamness, he reviewed everything he had been told at the observatory site, and what he had seen on the way, and what Thilling had had time to teach him...

The silence stretched and stretched. Eventually, reverting to her usual mood, Phrallet said, "Not much use asking him, was it? Now if you'd asked *me*—"

"But I didn't," said the picturist with point. "Well, young'un?"

That insult from his budder had been like dawn breaking inside his mind. Awb said explosively, "Take some of your leaves and just lay them around the dam, see what shows on them without being put in a fixer!"

"Well, well, well!" Thilling said. "You got it! It looks as though that's the only way to detect the effects of the poison short of letting something be killed by it. I like Byra's idea that it's a kind of burning, I like the idea that it may have something to do with hot rocks and volcanoes, and I *don't* like the idea that it's getting to my insides without my being able to sense it. But that's about all we'll be able to do on this trip, isn't it, Drotninch?"

"I'm afraid so," the scholar confirmed. "We'll have to bring safe food not only for ourselves but for the mounts on our next visit, and someone is going to have to travel all the way to the headwaters of the warmest stream, and one way and another I'm not sure we can tackle the job properly before next year. And—Lesh—you know what I'm going to have to say next, don't you?"

"The work we've done at the observatory has gone for nothing," was the bitter answer. "It will have to be sited somewhere else."

She clenched her mantle tight around the branch she lay on, like a mariner preparing for a gale. They left her alone with her thoughts. But it was with deliberate loudness that Drotninch continued, "Still, one all-important purpose has been served. We have found something totally new on our own planet, which we sometimes imagine to have been exhaustively explored. It's well for us to be reminded now and then that the unforeseen can break out under our very pads. If we don't keep that constantly in mind, what's going to become of us when we venture into space?"

Very softly, and for Awb alone, Thilling said, "Spoken like one of the Jingfired . . . ! Think about that, young'un. You still haven't told me what I'm most waiting to hear."

She stretched out and parted the overhanging leaves, and they all gazed up, except for Lesh, at the beautiful and terrifying fires of the Major Cluster, where since time immemorial new stars had, slowly and implacably, crept into view.

VIII

"Might as well use my entire stock of leaves on this," Thilling told Awb as dawn broke. "If anything more important turns up during the trip, I shan't want to know . . . We'll time the job by the sun; every score degrees it moves, we bring in one batch of 'em. Leave the bower set up so I can develop them as they come in."

Still baffled by the implied question the picturist expected him to answer, Awb helped her to lay out unexposed sheets by groups of five along the dam. But he found himself far more fascinated by what was happening in and on the lake. It was impossible to see more than a padlong below the surface, but here and there bubbles rose, and drifts of steam puffed up, and peculiar pale blue water-walkers scuttled hither and thither, avoiding the hottest spots but far more active than their cousins on cool rivers. As soon as Thilling let him go, he gathered up a few and offered them to Byra, who was packing every available container with specimens of flora and fauna.

"Where from exactly?" she demanded. "Near the dam? But how far from it?"

Why, she was a worse precisian than Axwep trying to balance Voosla's food-and-people accounts! But Awb preserved a courteous meekness.

"Between four and five padlongs from the thickest part of the yellow mud, where the bubbles rise most often."

"Hmm! That'll do very well! One thing I must give you, young'un: you have a keen eye on you. Yesterday that mutated winget, now this lot... What I'd really like to find, though, is a thriving root-mass of the spillway plants. We need some clue to resistance against this poison. Without that I don't know what we'll do."

But could any resistance be found to it among the folk? What if the only possible adjustment they could make in this region was the one adopted by the natives, able to feed and breed but nothing more?

However, Awb kept such thoughts to himself. After all, the scientists did have behind them the resources of one of the planet's greatest centers of knowledge.

It was time to take Thilling the first batch of exposed leaves. When he delivered them, she said, "Drotninch wants you to collect samples of the yellow mud. She's going to load one of the mounts with it. I told her to make sure it's the one furthest from my stuff."

"How did yesterday's images come out?" Awb inquired.

"What makes you think they came out at all?" Thilling countered sourly, but fanned a quarter-score of them for his inspection. All were weirdly streaked and smeared.

"What am I looking at?" Awb whispered.

"Something scarcely any eye has seen before," was the muttered answer. "The telescopes they meant to build on Fangsharp Peak were supposed to gather so much light from such faint sources, no one could possibly sit and register it. So they planned to make them deliver their light to sheets like these, using astrotropes whose growth is controllable to a laqth of a clawide to keep the image steady. Oh, the effort they've wasted on breeding those 'tropes!"

"You sound as though the observatory is never going to be built, not here, not anywhere!" Awb cried.

"Maybe it won't. Because the only time I saw patternless faults like these on an unexposed image-leaf..."

She shook her mantle, returning the sheets to their pack. "It makes common-type sense, doesn't it, to grow observatories on mountain-tops? There are four or five such, and I'm an advisor to the one near Chisp. They called me in because even when they're using the finest leaves things go wrong. There are smudges, there are blurs, there are distortions. Often they spoil a whole dark's work, especially when the telescope is aimed at the Major Cluster."

"What causes them?" Awb clenched his claws.

"We think it's tiny particles of matter blasted out from the new stars forming so far away. And they carry with them something of the terrible stellar heat. At any rate, they burn their way into the leaves. But I never imagined that something at the bottom of a valley... *Hmm!*"

As though struck by sudden insight, she turned back to the dark-bower, intent on developing the latest sheets.

"Go get Drotninch's mud-samples," she ordered. "But remember to time the next lot of leaves, too."

Awb hastened to comply. At least, down by the dam, he could be sure of avoiding Phrallet, who still seemed to harbour the suspicion that her heat-sore pads were owed to some sinister plot by Drotninch and the other scientists.

But there was something amiss.

He fought the knowledge for a long while, digging up the yellow mud, collecting the rest of the leaves at proper intervals and bringing them to the dark-bower, making himself as useful as he could to everybody.

Then, tiny as a falling star viewed through the wrong end of a spyglass, a spark crossed his eye.

Puzzled, he looked for more, but found only a red trace across his field of vision, rather as though he had gazed too long at something very bright but very narrow, like—

Like what? There was nothing it was like at all.

Simultaneously he became aware of a sensation akin to an itch, except that it wasn't one. It was just as annoying, but he couldn't work out where it was, other than very vaguely. And whoever heard of an itch in red-level pith, anyway? Determinedly he went on with his work, and shortly was rewarded by spotting another mutated water-walker, not blue this time, but pure white.

He dived after it and trapped it in his mandibles, and bore it to Byra in triumph.

Standing by as she inspected it under the microscope, he heard her say irritably, "Stop fidgeting, young'un! You look as though a mustiq got under your mantle...Oh, this is even more ridiculous than the last one! I don't see how it can survive, let alone reproduce itself!"

He scarcely noticed the last comment. A mustiq under his mantle? Yes, that was a little like it. He'd been twitching without realizing until he had his attention drawn to it. He was pulsating out of rhythm with himself; instead of the normal ratios between mantle-ripple, gut-shift, breath-drawing, ichor-peristalsis and eye-flick which he was accustomed to, in the perfect proportions of bass, third, fifth, seventh and octave, he was shuddering as though about to burst.

Having his maw empty for so long, for the first time in his life, was proving to be a very odd experience indeed.

Yet if hunger were the sole explanation (and surely he hadn't gone without for long enough?)—

Oh, NO!

POISONED???

He peeled apart from himself, much like the brollicans that teachers on Voosla grew excited about when they chanced across a shoal of them so large the city had no time to eat the lot before a few could be salvaged for educational purposes. For scores-of-scores of years they had been providing real-time evidence for symbiosis, the phenomenon that underlay the folk's modern predicament.

Coevolution...said something from the deep red level of his consciousness, but everyone knew that that level didn't deal in speech, only in hunger and breeding-need and the repair of vital organs.

(But who had told him that was true? Maybe someone would come along to tell him different, like Thilling! Maybe the exercises she had promised him, concerning dark-use, didn't refer only to outside-dark but inside-dark as well...)

In the distance, though very close in time, like right now:

"Help!" (It was Byra's voice.) "Drotninch, Thilling, Phrallet, anybody! Awb's gone dreamish!"

Dreamish? Me? Me...?

But he didn't know who he was any longer. There wasn't a "myself" controlling the physical envelope known as Awb. There was a muddle of memory and imagination, a chaotic slew of information and sensory input, and what trace of identity did remain—thanks to his having been budded on a small but wealthy city, where no one in living memory had gone dreamish through simple hunger—was capable of no more than observation: as it were, "So this is what must have happened to our poor ancestors who multiplied themselves without making provision for proper nourishment! I'm amazed they ever clawed their way back out of the mental swamp they fell in, regardless of Gveest's best efforts, or the Jingfired's!"

Then even that last vestige of himself dissolved, and his pith started to react as though he were his own remotest forebear, assailed by predatory gigants and striking out at random in the faint hope that at least his body might block one monster's maw and choke it to death.

It took three of them to subdue his violent flailing.

Late that dark Thilling lay in a tree-crotch well away from the dam, which her images had convinced her was the chief source of danger, while the scientists wrangled among themselves. Awb had been temporarily quieted; Lesh had dispatched two of her assistants to find fruit and funqi from which nourishing juices could be extracted, at a safe distance from the lake, and herself administered a calmative from the first-aid pack she had brought. It was to be hoped that his youth and slightness of build accounted for his extreme vulnerability to—to whatever had afflicted him. At any rate the rest of them seemed to be in fair shape, with the exception, Thilling reflected cynically, of Phrallet, who was on the verge of hysteria. She kept saying over and over, "We must get out of here! We must go back at once! Who knows what damage is being wrought in our very pith? My pads are still hurting, you know!"

And when she found her companions ignoring that line of argument, she tried cajolement: "If only for the sake of my youngest budling, we must go back! Oh, I know

I'm sometimes hard on him, but really I do care for him, and if he dies because of this . . ."

At which the others simply turned their backs in the most insulting fashion possible. So for some while now she had been sulking, which at least allowed the rest of them to debate the core of the problem.

Drotninch was saying, "I'm coming around to the conclusion that we not only have to deal with the poison per se, but also with its effects on living organisms, including disease germs. You know there's a theory that the New Star triggered off the latest round of female mimicry, the one which made so many of us too like males to bud anymore. Given what Thilling has told us about the resemblance between what she finds on her image-sheets and what happens when sheets are exposed at high altitude—"

Lesh cut in. "I've heard that theory, and to me it smacks of the rankest astrological superstition!"

Byra said heavily, "There's only one way of settling the matter. We're going to have to study this poison *in vivo*. Right now, of course, we only have one subject: Awb. But it's beyond a doubt that some at least of the same effect must be working in all of us."

Rousing from her apathy, Phrallet shouted, "What do you want us to do—stay here until we all collapse the way he did? You must be out of your pith! Anyway, I won't let you treat a budling of mine like a laboratory animal!"

Doing her best to disregard the interruption, Byra went on, "We can extrapolate from cutinates to some extent, of course, and I've taken samples from the mount that died, and with luck the rest of them will have been affected—"

"With luck?" Lesh echoed sardonically. "When I need every mount and draftimal I can lay claws on to rescue my expensive equipment from the observatory site? You're not killing any of my beasts for your researches, I'm afraid! In any case, mounts aren't enough like us, are they?"

Sighing, Byra admitted as much. "We'll have to rely on what we can learn by studying Awb, then, and since of course we all hope he'll make a quick recovery, that may not be very much. Still, we can call for volunteers

who've been in the area since the project started, and that
may help."

"You can get all the specimens you need," Phrallet
said. "Why haven't you thought it through? If studying
the poison in a living person means saving our lives—I
mean Awb's life—you could just kidnap a few of the natives. They're worthless for anything else, aren't they?"

Thilling clenched her mantle in horror. Surely this group
of civilized scientists must reject so hideous a notion out
of claw? But no! To her infinite dismay she realized they
were taking it seriously. Byra said after a pause, "It would
certainly be very useful."

And Lesh chimed in: "We have plenty of nets! I'll get
my staff on the job the moment we return!"

In that moment Thilling realized that she despised
Phrallet more completely than anyone she had ever met
or even heard of.

And what would Awb say when he learned that his life
had been spared at such revolting cost?

But perhaps he would care no more than his budder.

IX

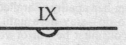

How everything had changed in three-score years! Not
least, of course, thanks to the mutated diseases the workers from the abandoned World Observatory had carried
away with them. Thilling shivered as she reflected on how
vast a mystery those mutations had then seemed, how
simple the explanation had proved to be once it was properly attacked . . .

Why was it that so many people declined to pay attention to such matters? Here in the crowded branchways
of Voosla—a city transformed and twice enlarged since
she last set pad on her—she knew without needing to be
told that anyone she accosted at random would be as
likely as not to dismiss her scientific knowledge out of
claw, as totally irrelevant to their own concerns.

In the distant past, when there had been religions, it must have been similar for a traveler from afar; how had Jing reacted to those who honestly believed that the Arc of Heaven was the Maker's Sling, and shed meteors on the world as a warning of divine retribution? And here she was, under orders to confront a teacher whom his followers regarded as fit to be mentioned alongside Jing himself, even though he encouraged them to despise the greatest discoveries and inventions of his own lifetime.

If only the Jingfired had picked on someone else for this mission... But their old acquaintance had tipped the balance; Thilling was forbidden to disobey.

She had no difficulty in locating the venue of Awb's daily meeting, of course. Scores-of-scores of people were making for it, so she simply let herself be carried along.

It was, she must admit, a considerable achievement for a mere male to have got himself regarded as his city's most outstanding bud, granted the use of the handsome open bower at the very center of Voosla which was normally reserved for public debates on matters of policy. She imagined it was seldom so packed for one of those. It was with relief that she noticed, as she made herself comfortable in an inconspicuous crotch, that she was not the only person present with the traces of old age on her mantle, though the vast majority of the attendance consisted of young'uns chattering away like piemaqs.

But they fell silent the instant Awb appeared: plumper than Thilling remembered, his mantle deeply grooved, his eye—like her own—less keen. Yet his voice was tremendously improved, and at his first utterance she felt she understood at least a little of what drew folk to him.

Persuasive or not, however, what he said was totally repugnant to her. He taught that no "proper" relationship, with one's community, even with one's budder or budlings—let alone the commensality of all living things—could be established without prior comprehension of oneself. Sometimes he urged people to starve in the midst of plenty, like the ancient sacerdotes; sometimes he expounded on ideas drawn from dreamness, as though they warranted equal treatment with rational knowledge; frequently he declared that those who sought means to escape the planet were actually fleeing from true awareness of themselves.

And all this, Thilling thought bitterly, because of the load of guilt he had carried ever since he learned that Phrallet's monstrous scheme to kidnap those mindless northern natives and experiment on their living bodies had saved his life... but not her own.

He spoke freely enough about his illness and recovery; what he never mentioned, according to her briefing—nor did he prove the contrary today—was the self-sacrifice of Drotninch and Eupril and Lesh, who had each in her respective way struggled to make sense of the heat arising in that yellow mud, and in less than a generation revolutionized the folk's understanding of matter. Above all, their legacy offered clues to the processes that lit the stars.

Because of them, and their successors, the chemistry of other elements than woodchar was at long last being studied thoroughly. The ancient use of fire had been resuscitated; brilliant young minds had been brought to bear on the questions posed by metal, glass, rock, plain ordinary water! A whole new universe of knowledge had been opened up. And did Awb care? Not by any clue or sign he gave!

Of course he did still hew to his belief that life among the People of the Sea was inherently superior to life on shore. To this fact he modestly attributed his remarkable success in treating deranged landlivers, whose behavior was sometimes dangerously abnormal even though the most delicate analyses revealed nothing amiss in their nerve-pith or ichor. More cynical, Thilling thought of the cleansing ocean breezes that bore away intrusive pheromones. Sea-travel had been regarded as beneficial long before Awb's reputation converted Voosla into the most sought-after of floating cities, in demand to touch at every continent in the course of every year. And she was sure Awb himself must be aware of that fact.

But if she were to mention it to those around her, would they be interested? Would they believe her? Most likely not. Awb and his disciples seemed to be set on creating a generation of young folk who cared as little for the past as for the future. Neither the study of history nor planning for the salvation of the species could attract them. They were assured that they need only study themselves, and all would be well, for ever and ever...

The meeting had assembled before sundown. Darkness overtook it while Awb was still answering questions. Suddenly Thilling noticed that something was distracting the crowd, and everyone was glancing upward. Copying their example, she realized why. There was a small yellow comet in the sky, but that was commonplace; what had drawn their gaze was a meteor storm, a horde of bright brief streaks coming by scores at a time.

She thought for a moment about challenging Awb to deny that that was a reminder of the doom the planet faced, another promise of the dense gas-cloud the sun was drifting towards. But she lacked the courage. She remained meekly where she was until he was done, and then—equally meekly—made her way towards him, surrounded by a gaggle of his admirers. Most were young she'uns, doubtless hoping for a bud from so famous a teacher.

In old age her own sterility had become a source of gall to Thilling; she strove not to let it prey on her pith.

There was little chance, though, of actually reaching Awb in this small but dense throng, for everyone was respectfully lowering as they clustered about him, leaving no gaps for passage. Hating to make herself conspicuous, but seeing no alternative, she did the opposite and erected to full height...such as it was at her age.

"Awb, it's Thilling! Do you remember me? We used to know each other many years ago!"

There was a startled pause, and all eyes turned on her. A whiff of hostility reached her—how dare this old'un claim acquaintance with the master? But then Awb replied, in a gruffer and lower voice than when addressing the crowd.

"I remember you. Wait until the rest have gone."

And he dismissed them with gentle shooing motions of his mantle. Disappointed but compliant, they wandered off.

When they were alone but for two thick-set individuals who appeared to be his permanent attendants, his age-dimmed eye surveyed her from crest to pad.

"Oh, yes. It is the same Thilling in spite of the time

that's passed. Your voice has changed, but so has mine, I imagine . . . Tell me, are you still subject to your delusion about being able to recruit people to the Jingfired?"

Delusion?

For an instant Thilling, who had devoted her entire life to the cause she regarded as the greatest in history, wished she might hurl herself bodily at him, shred his mantle with claws and mandibles before his companions could prevent her. But she conquered the impulse, as she had overcome so many before, and a gust of wind dispersed her betraying anger-stink.

With careful effort she said, "Why do you call it a delusion?"

He stiffened back, again examining her curiously. "Hmm! Persistent, I gather! Well, if you've come for help, I might perhaps—"

"You haven't answered my question. As once, long ago, you failed to answer another."

Missing the allusion, he countered, "Does it really call for an answer? But for the sake of an old friendship, I'll offer one."

Friendship? Is that what he calls it now? When he begged to be made my apprentice, and ran away as soon as he knew his budder was dead and couldn't plague him anymore?

But Thilling feigned composure in spite of all.

"How life has treated you, I'm unaware, though I suspect unkindly. For myself, I've forced it to treat me well, with the result that I'm now acquainted with the Councils of the Jingfired in every city on every continent and every ocean. They send embassies to me seeking advice and guidance, they anxiously await the appearance of Voosla on the horizon, they take my words and convert them into action—with what advantages to all, you may observe." A large gesture to indicate the globe. "Not one of those people has ever mentioned you. But don't worry. I've kept your affliction secret for the most part, though I confess I may now and then have referred to it during some of my lectures, purely as an illustrative example, you understand."

Everything came clear to Thilling on the instant. Of

course! He had confused her with Byra... Her voice level, she said, "I take it you have studied Jinglore, then?"

"To some extent"—in an offclaw tone. "It does furnish a store of poetic metaphors and images, which may help us the better to understand our experience of dreamness. But that's all."

"I regret to say you're wrong. Just as wrong as you are about my so-called 'delusion.'" She moved so close that, had she been a total stranger, the trespass on his private space would have been an insult, and continued before the bodyguards could intervene.

"How would your followers react to the news that you who preach the need for perfect relationships rejoiced at your budder's death, or to being told how you broke your apprentice's pledge? Or to learning how you, who boast of saving the sanity of others, have become so senile as to confuse me with Byra, may she rest in peace? She too was silly enough to assume that city-bosses who call themselves Jingfired actually are so. But they're not. If your memory isn't totally wrecked, if you have any shred of conscience left, you'll recall my telling you when you pleaded to become my apprentice that it's no use trying to guess who the Jingfired actually are. You have to *know*."

After that she fully expected the bodyguards to close on her and drag her away. But they hesitated; an aura of uncertainty was exuding from their master.

At long last he said, not looking at her, but towards the sky where the rain of meteors had now redoubled, "So it's come to this. A voice has spoken from my past which I can neither challenge nor deny."

Hope leapt up in her pith. For an instant she thought she had already won.

But the hope was dashed when he relaxed with a sigh, and continued: "Such a long-lasting and intractable psychosis is probably beyond even my methods, which normally prove so successful. Still, for old friendship's sake I can at least attempt to show you where you went astray."

He added to the attendants, "Scholar Thilling will be my guest at dinner. Apologize to those who have prior claims on my time, but meeting someone from one's younghood is a rare event. And perhaps good may come of it in the long run."

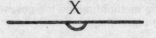

X

If there was one thing Thilling could reluctantly admire about Awb now, it was his skill in keeping up appearances. He closed the gap between them and by embracing her contrived to transfer some of the pheromone-masking perfumes he wore on his torso, leaving the bodyguards confused.

Then he led her along the branchways to a bower where the city's finest foods were lovingly tended by experts who—so he told her—claimed to inherit their knowledge from someone who had studied under Gveest.

But if he expected to impress her by boasting, he was wrong. Nothing could more have firmed her determination than this display of the luxury Awb had attained through corrupting the minds of the younger generation. Had she not needed food to power the argument she foresaw as inescapable, she would have voiced her contempt of his tactics; as it was, she resignedly filled her maw and, confident that even yet he would never have been trained in the Jingfired's techniques of dark-use, waited until he chose to speak again.

Eventually, replete, he let himself slump on his branch and said, "So you thought you could threaten me by raking up my past, did you? That must be because you envy the course my life has taken."

"On the contrary!" she snapped. "Thanks to the images I made on that dam banked with yellow mud, I went on to share in some of the most notable discoveries of this or any age. Have you no faintest notion what marvels lie in the secret pith of matter? Because of my skills, I was close at claw when Eupril first separated the heavy elements which break up of their own accord. I was there when Lesh—"

"It hasn't made amends for being sterile," he cut in.

"Oh, because it was an obsession with Phrallet you

think everything can be reduced to whether or not one
has budded!" retorted Thilling. "Let me remind you—"

He raised a claw. "If you're going to quote Jinglore at
me, be warned that others have tried without effect."

"I have no intention of it. I was about to say that in
your attempts to atone for hating Phrallet, you saw no
alternative but to outdo Jing and Yockerbow and Tenthag
and the other heroes of the past. You're not equipped
to."

Awb had had much practice at appearing resignedly
wise. Adopting the appropriate expression, he said, "If
each age is to surpass its forepadders, then some individual must respond to its unique and particular challenge.
In the present epoch . . . Well, you see the truth all around
you."

"In other words, you think that your success in turning
people inward upon themselves, making them preoccupied with their personal motives and reactions, is the response best fitted to the plight we find ourselves in?"

Awb curled his mantle into a patronizing smile.

"Very interesting," Thilling murmured, resorting to the
ultimate line of attack which the Jingfired had prepared
for her. "This fits superbly with Yegbrot's studies of the
effect of radioactivity on nerve-pith, which demonstrate
how even temporary exposure can derange the system."

She refrained from mentioning how much she hated
Yegbrot's ruthlessness, which stemmed directly from
Phrallet's original proposal. If only Awb had chosen to
attack the fact that nowadays psychologists were using
experimental subjects deliberately rendered mindless by
pithing . . .

In the act of reaching for a fresh and succulent fungus
he checked and twisted towards her, glaring. "How dare
you accuse me of being insane?"

A breakthrough!

"But I didn't. My mission is merely to establish whether
your regrettably successful attempt to distract the best of
our young'uns from the branchway that alone can lead to
the survival of our species is due to perversity or injury.
I now conclude the latter. So you're not to blame."

Recovering, he chuckled. "You're a classic case of the
type I so often invoke in lectures: a sterile she'un determined to project a surrogate immortality on the rest of us

because she can't produce her own buds. Sorry to be so blunt, but there it is. And there are many who would pay handsomely for so accurate a diagnosis from Scholar Awb!"

"Yet you sense my authority, don't you?" she countered. "Despite smearing me with that repulsive muck you wear!"

He clattered his mandibles in amusement. "The more you say, the more you support my theory that people like you at some stage lost the ability to distinguish input due to the real world from what stems out of imagination and hence ultimately dreamness. How I wish I had a way to transcribe this conversation! It would confirm—"

"You'd like a recordimal, you mean."

"Well, out of courtesy I didn't bring one along, but if you'd permit it, certainly I—"

"Do you know who invented the recordimal?"

"No, I don't believe I was ever told," he answered, taking care as usual to protect his ego by not admitting he might have forgotten. "Who?"

"I was at her side during its development. Byra! With whom you won't stop confusing me!"

"That," Awb murmured, "must be because if anyone out of our group at the observatory had devised such a useful tool, I'd have expected it to be you. Sure you aren't being modest?" He settled down with the comfortable air of one who, having turned a neat compliment, was expecting to be paid in kind.

But she reacted otherwise, sure now of her ascendancy.

"Once I hoped you'd find the answer to a question I never put to you. I was hoping you might say of your own accord what I once said, like all the Jingfired—the true Jingfired!—and declare that you wanted to devote your life to ensuring that we can overcome the worst the universe can throw at us. Don't interrupt!"—as he showed signs of doing so. "I know what answer you'd give now, and it's the same you'd have given then, had you been honest enough. In your own words, you're a classic case. Yegbrot could tell me to a fraction of a clawide where particles of stumpium and sluggium have settled in your pith. But the real damage had been done already. Lesh died, Eupril died, Byra died, but to the last they fought to understand why, and to save others from the same fate! Whereas you've given up, for the sake of making over countless scores of young'uns into worshipers of Awb!"

By mustering her resources of contempt-stink, she had finally made an impression on him. He said at length, "But you seem to be claiming that I'm responsible for what Phrallet suggested. At that time, though, I was sick and mindless, remember. And I detest the cost of our recent advances in chemistry and medicine! Of course, I suppose you make out that the benefits outweigh—"

"I do not! What would we have lost if we hadn't kidnapped the natives and experimented on them? Half-a-score years at worst, until we could duplicate isolated cells, create synthetic ichor, grow pith in isolation the way we grow nervograps! But if we'd done that, you'd be dead, wouldn't you? You'd have missed your chance to scorn my friends who've invented intercontinental nervograps and freight-pitchens and recordimals and now are set to outdo floaters by attaining controlled atmospheric flight, a first pad-mark on the road to space! By all *their* work, you're as unimpressed as by a pebble on a pathway!"

Breathing hard, she subsided, wondering whether what she had said had registered, or whether the terrible metal from the accidental stumpium pile at the river-dam had lodged in too many crucial junctions of his nerve-pith.

And also how many of his followers, when they inveighed against fumes and furnaces, were doing so because they had reason on their side rather than because the very metals that experimenters now were working with had deformed their thoughts.

Her own as well...?

The possibility was too fearful to think about. She shut it resolutely away.

Her weather-sense was signaling danger, but she put it down to feedback from the reek of tension she and Awb were generating, about which other clients of the food-bower had started to complain. At their insistence, the roof of leaves was being folded back. Perhaps, Thilling thought, she might exploit the incontrovertible reality of the sky to make Awb see sense...but discovered, even as she glanced upward, that that hope too was vain.

Across the welkin slashed a giant ball of light: vast,

eye-searing, shedding lesser streaks on its way to—where? The Worldround Ocean, with a little luck, rather than dry land. Yet even there—!

Oh, so much like what the astronomers had predicted from the images she had fixed on sheet after sensitive sheet!

Preserving her pride to the last, she rose while Awb— the poor vainglorious victim of a chance mishap, who had been poisoned in his mind before he was poisoned in his pith, yet whom the future would not forgive for contaminating a later generation with his falsehoods—was still struggling to deny the reality of this event.

"The real world has one resource our minds do not," said Thilling loudly and clearly. "It can always chasten us with a discovery we couldn't plan for, like the exploding atoms which spoiled the leaves you brought me from the dam—remember? Well, now it's curing us of arrogance again. This is a tenet of the Jingfired, Awb: not the shabby shams whom you're so proud to know, who usurp the name in cities round the world, but us, the secret ones, who work and slave and hope and always seem to find a fool like you to block our way—"

She got that far, thanks to her greater skill in dark-use, before the noise arrived: a terrible noise such as must last have been heard when the ice-packs broke up after the Great Thaw, worse than the worst growling of a pack of snowbelongs when they crawled into lonely settlements in search of folk to feed their broodmass.

Already the officers of Voosla were issuing orders: cut loose from shore and who cares if we kill our musculators, get into open water at all costs and stay afloat, signal the giqs and hope to pick them up while we're under way . . .

It was all well and correctly done, and Axwep, had she survived, would have been proud, and even Phrallet— so thought Thilling in the grayness of uncalled-for memory—might have relented in her constant criticism.

But it was too late. Like her errand to Awb, it was far too late.

The meteor outmassed a score of Vooslas. It boiled and smashed the ocean all at once, and raised a giant wall of water round its impact point that nearly but not quite outraced the sound of its arrival. Every coast that fringed the ocean shattered under the rock-hard water-hammer;

Voosla herself was carried screaming far inland in a catastrophic shambles of plants and people, which for a crazy instant made Thilling think of what it must be like to fly . . .

"Comet! Comet!" she heard, and moaned, "Fools!" with the last pressure in her body before the blast exploded her.

Speech ended. Thought endured longer, enough for her to think: *Had it not been for Awb . . . No, that's unfair. When we escape to space those like him, poisoned by no fault of their own, must still be a part of us, because who can say what other poisons await us out there . . . ?*

Not Thilling; she dissolved into the dark, while steam and dust and shreds of what had been the folk and all they cherished set off on their stratospheric journey round the globe.

It was to last more than a score of years.

PART SIX

HAMMER AND ANVIL

I

"Your business?" said the house in a tone as frosty as a polar winter. Then followed a dull and reflex hiss as its vocalizing bladders automatically refilled.

At first Chybee was too startled to respond. This magnificent home had overwhelmed her even as she approached: its towering crest, its ramifying branches garlanded with countless luminants, its far-spread webs designed to protect the occupants against wingets and add their minuscule contribution to the pool of organic matter at its roots, cleverly programed to withdraw before a visitor so that they would not be torn—all, all reflected such luxury as far surpassed her youthful experience.

But then her whole trip to and through this incredible city had been a revelation. She had heard about, had seen pictures of, the metropolis of Slah, and met travelers whom business or curiosity had lured hither. Nothing, though, had prepared her for the reality of her first-ever transcontinental flight, or the jobs she had been obliged to undertake to pay her way, constantly terrified that they would make her too late. No description could have matched the sensation of being carried pell-mell amid treetops by the scampering inverted fury of a dolmusq, with its eighteen tentacles snatching at whatever support was offered and its body straining under the weight of twoscore passengers. Nor could anyone have conveyed to her the combined impact of the crowds, the noise, and the universal stench compound of pheromones, smoke from the industrial area to the west, and the reek of all the material that must go to rot in order to support the homes and food-plants of this most gigantic of cities. Never in all of history had there been one to match it, neither by land nor by sea—likely, not even in the age of legend.

From the corner of her eye she detected the house's defenses tensing, gathering pressure to snare her if, by failing to respond, she identified herself as a mindless beast. Hastily she forced out, "My name is Chybee! I've come to hear the lecture! Never say I've missed it!"

Modern and talented as the house was, that exceeded its range of responses; she had to wait for a person to answer. Eventually the thorny barrier blocking the entrance drew aside and revealed an elderly woman wearing a stern expression.

"The professor's lecture began at sundown," she said. "It is now halfway to midnight."

"I know!" Chybee cried, with a glance towards what little of the sky was visible through the overarching branches of this and other nearby homes. By chance the moon was framed by those and by a ring of thin cloud; it was just past the new, and its dark part was outlined by sparkles nearly as bright as those which shot continually through the upper air...a constant reminder, Chybee thought, of the rightness of her decision.

She went on pleadingly, "But I've come from Hulgrapuk to hear her! It's not my fault I've been delayed!"

"Hulgrapuk?" The woman's attitude softened instantly. "Ah! Then you must be one of Professor Wam's students, I suppose. Come in quickly, but be very quiet."

Injunctions to be quiet struck Chybee as rather silly when the hordes of the city made such a terrible droning and buzzing noise, sometimes punctuated by loud clanging and banging from the factories whose fumes made the air so foul, but she counted herself lucky not to have been turned away, and did as she was told.

Wondering who Professor Wam might be.

The woman indicated that she should follow an upward-slanting branchway towards the crest of the house, and there she found at least five-score folk gathered in a roughly globular bower. At its focus, comfortably disposed on large and well-smoothed crotches, were three persons of advancing age whose exudations indicated they were far from happy to be in such proximity. The rest of the attendance consisted of a few males scattered among numerous females, mostly young, who were trying hard not to react to their elders' stench; that was plain from their own emanations.

Recordimals had captured Ugant's voice for her many supporters around the planet. Chybee recognized it the moment she entered, and was so excited to hear her idol in reality that she bumped against a boy not much older than herself as she sought for space to perch.

Instantly: "Chhht!" from half a score of those nearby.

But the boy curled his mantle in a grin as he made room alongside him. Muttering thanks, she settled down and concentrated ... rather to the boy's disappointment, she gathered, but she was here for one purpose and one purpose only: to hear Ugant's views in her own words.

It was clear that the formal lecture must long be over, for she was engaged in debate, either with those flanking her or with some doubter elsewhere in the bower. She was saying:

"... our researches prove conclusively that the fall of the civilization which bequeathed to us most of our modern skills—indeed, which unwittingly gave us this very city, changed though it now is out of recognition by those who created it as a sea-going entity!—was due to the impact of a giant meteorite, whose traces we can only indirectly observe because it fell into deep water. Given this indisputable fact, it can only be a matter of time before another and far larger impact wipes us out too. It's all very well to argue that we must prepare to take the folk themselves into space, with whatever is necessary for their survival. I don't doubt that eventually this could be done; we know how to create life-support systems that will sustain us for long periods on the ocean bed, and they too have to be closed. We know, more or less, how to shield ourselves against the radiation we are sure of meeting out there. But I contest the possibility of achieving so grandiose a goal with the resources available. I believe rather that we, as living creatures, owe it to the principle of life itself to ensure that it survives even if we as a species cannot!"

Suddenly there was uproar. Confused, Chybee saw one of Ugant's companions turn her, or possibly his, back insultingly, as though to imply: "What use in arguing with such an idiot?" Meantime a few clear voices cut through the general turmoil; she heard "True! True!" and "Nonsense!" and then, "But the folk of Swiftyouth and Sunbride will hurl more missiles at us to prevent it!"

That was so reminiscent of what she was fleeing from,

she shivered. Mistaking her response, the boy beside her said, "She does underestimate us, doesn't she?"

"Uh—who?"

"Ugant, of course!"—in a tone of high surprise. "Going on all the time about how we can't possibly succeed, and so we have to abandon the planets to bacteria! You should have been here sooner. Wam made sludge of her!"

"Wam?"

"On the left, of course! From Hulgrapuk, no less! How many scores-of-scores of padlonglaqs did she have to travel to be here this dark? That shows her dedication to the cause of truth and reason!"

I bet she had an easier journey than I did...But Chybee repressed the bitter comment, abruptly aware that she was hungry and that this bower was festooned with some of the finest food-plants she had ever set eye on.

Instead she said humbly, "And whose back is turned?"

"Oh, that's Aglabec. Hasn't dared utter a word since the start, and very right and proper too. But I'm afraid a lot of his supporters are here. I hope you aren't one of them?" He turned, suddenly suspicious.

"I don't think so," Chybee ventured.

"You don't know you aren't? By the arc of heaven, how could anybody not know whether giving up reason in favor of dreamness is right or wrong? Unless they'd already decided in favor of dreamness!"

Aglabec...? The name floated up from memory: it had been cited by her parents. Chybee said firmly, "I'm against dreamness!"

"I'm glad of that!" said the boy caustically. But they were being called on to hush again. Wam was expanding her mantle for a counterblast.

"There is one point on which Professor Ugant and myself are entirely in agreement! I maintain that her scheme to seed the planets with microorganisms is a poor second-best, because what we must and can do is launch ourselves, or our descendants, and our entire culture into space! But we unite in despising those who spout non-sense about the nature of other planets totally at odds with scientific reality, those who claim that they can make mental voyages to Swiftyouth and Sunbride and indeed to the planets of other stars! Such people are—"

What carefully honed insult Wam had prepared, her

listeners were not fated to find out. A group of about a
score of young people, with a leavening of two or three
older, outshouted her and simultaneously began to shake
the branches. Resonance built up swiftly, and those around
cried out as they strove to maintain their grip. The slogans
the agitators were bellowing were like the one Chybee
had caught a snatch of a few moments earlier, warnings
that the folk of other planets were bound to drop more
rocks from heaven if any plan to carry "alien" life thither
were put into effect. But who could respect them if they
were capable of slaughtering fellow beings for their own
selfish ends...?

Chybee caught herself. There was no life on Swiftyouth
and Sunbride; there couldn't be. Modern astronomy had
proved it. Fatigue and hunger were combining to drive
her into dreamness herself... plus the shock of realizing
that she could never go home again. Had she really gambled the whole of her future life on this one trip to Slah,
which her budder had forbidden?

Indeed she had, and the knowledge made her cling as
desperately to rationality as to her swaying branch.

She barely heard a new loud voice roaring from the
center of the bower, barely registered that Aglabec the
leader of the agitators had finally spoken up, and was
shouting:

"You're wasting your efforts! You'll never shake this
lot loose from their grip on the tree of prejudice! Leave
that to the folk of other worlds—they'll act to cure such
foolishness in their own good time!"

Disappointed, his reluctant followers ceased making
the branches thrash about. But at that point Chybee could
hold her peace no longer.

Rising as best she could to full height on her swaying
perch, she shouted back, "There aren't any folk on other
worlds, and there never will be if you get your way! We
can't live there either! Our only sane course is to hope
that the seeds of life can be adapted to germinate and
evolve elsewhere!"

What am I saying? Who am I saying it to?

Mocking laughter mingled with cheers. She slumped
back on the branch, folding her mantle tightly around her
against the storm of noise, and heard at a great distance
how the company dispersed. Several in passing discour-

teously bumped against her, and she thought one must have been the boy from the adjacent perch. It was a shame to have made him dislike her on no acquaintance, but after what Aglabec had said ... after what her parents had tried to force down her maw ... after ...

She had imagined herself young and strong enough to withstand any challenge the world might offer. The toll taken by her journey, her emotional crisis, her lack of food, maybe the subtle poisons some claimed to have identified in the air of Slah, proved otherwise. Her mind slid downward into chaos.

II

Reacting to the reek of hostility that permeated the bower, Wam snapped, "I knew it was a crazy idea inviting Aglabec to take part in a scientific debate!"

She swarmed down from the crotch she had occupied during the meeting and gazed disconsolately at the departing audience.

"You can't have thought it was that stupid if you came so far to join in!" Ugant retorted, stung.

"Oh, one always hopes ..." Wam admitted with a sigh. "Besides, the dreamlost are gathering such strength at Hulgrapuk, even among my own students, and I imagined that things might be better here. Apparently I was wrong. What do we have to tell these folk tø convince them of the doom hanging over us all?"

"Beg pardon, Professor!" a diffident voice murmured, and old Fraij, Ugant's maestradomi, slithered down to join them. "You mentioned your students just now. The one who spoke up at the end hasn't left with everybody else. I think she's been taken ill."

"Hah! As if we didn't have enough problems already ... Well, it's up to you to look after your own." Ugant turned aside with a shrug, scanning the available food-plants in search of anything particularly delicious.

From a pouch she wore on a baldric slung about her, Wam produced a spyglass and leveled it at the other remaining occupant of the bower. After a moment she said, "She could be of a Hulgrapuk strain, I suppose, but clasped around her branch like that I can't be sure. At any rate I don't recognize her."

Fraij said uncertainly, "I'm sorry. She said she'd come specially from Hulgrapuk, so naturally I assumed..."

"I'm afraid your assumption was wrong," Wam murmured, and joined Ugant in her quest for refreshment, adding, "Whatever I may think of your views, by the way, I find no fault with your hospitality. Many thanks."

But Ugant was snuffing the air, now almost cleansed as the roof-leaves flapped automatically to scour away the remanent pheromones.

"I do recognize her... I think. Fraij, do you remember a message from some youngling in that area saying her parents had gone overside into the psychoplanetary fad, and she needed arguments to combat them? About a month ago. Wasn't the trace on that very much like hers?"

Fraij hesitated, and finally shook her mantle. "I'm afraid I can't be sure. You have to remember how much correspondence I deal with that you never get to see because it's a waste of time. However that may be," she added with a touch of defiance, "I'm not inclined to turn her out into the branchways before I know whether she can fend for herself."

"Well, she did sound comparatively sensible..." Ugant crammed her maw with succulent funqi and swarmed over to where the girl was lying. Another sample of her odor, and: "Hmm! I was right! Her name's something like Chylee, Chy... Chybee! I don't know why you haven't met her, Wam. From her message she seemed like just the sort of person you want for your campaign against the— You know, we need a ruder and catchier nickname for the psychoplanetarists. It might help if we persuaded our students to invent one. Ridicule is a powerful weapon, isn't it?"

By now the girl was stirring, and Wam had no chance to reply. Maw full, she too drew close.

"I think she's hungry," she pronounced. "Fraij—?"

But the maestradomi had already signaled one of her aides, a gang of whom had appeared to clear the bower of what litter the audience had left which the house could not dispose of unaided. It was another point of agreement between those who supported Ugant and those who followed Wam that Aglabec and his sympathizers were disgustingly wasteful... to which charge the latter always retorted that what the planet offered it could reabsorb, and in any case the age of psychic escape would dawn long before it was too polluted for life in a physical body to continue. However that might be, some of them had left behind odds and ends of heavy metal and even bonded yellowite, and those could harm the germ-plasm of a house. Had they done it deliberately, or out of laziness? One would wish to believe the latter, but certain rumors now current about their behavior hinted at sabotage....

The girl pried herself loose from the branch, exuding shame from every pore. Fraij gave her a luscious fruit, and she gulped it down greedily; as though it were transfusing energy directly into her tubules—which it should, given that Ugant's home had been designed by some of the finest biologists of modern times—she shifted into a mode of pure embarrassment.

Touched, Ugant settled beside her and uttered words of comfort. And continued as she showed signs of reacting:

"You're not one of Wam's students? No? So why did you come all the way from Hulgrapuk?"

"To hear you! But I had to run away from home to do it."

"Why so?"

"Because my parents are crazy."

"What do you mean by that?"—with a look of alarm aimed at Wam.

"Their names are Whelwet and Yaygomitch. Do you need to know any more?"

On the point of reaching for another clump of funqi, Wam settled back on her branch and uttered a whistle of dismay.

"Even you must have heard of those two, Ugant! Of all the pernicious pith-rotted idiots...!"

"But she didn't identify them in her message," Ugant muttered. "Chybee—you are called Chybee, aren't you?"

Excited, she tried to rise, but lacked pressure. "So you

did get my note! I was afraid it had been lost! You never answered it, did you?"

Fraij said, "Girl, if you knew how many messages the professor gets every bright—!"

"That will do, Fraij," Ugant interrupted. "Chybee, I promise that if I'd only realized who your family are, I'd... Well, I can scarcely say I'd have come running, but I would certainly have told Wam about you."

"But—!" She sank back, at a loss. For the first time it was possible to see how pretty she was, her torso sleek and sturdy, her claws and mandibles as delicate as a flyet's. Her maw still crowded, she went on, "But I always thought you and Professor Wam were enemies! When I heard you were giving a lecture and she had agreed to reply to you, I couldn't really believe it, but I decided I had to be present, because you're both on the other side from my parents. They *are* crazy, aren't they? Please tell me they're crazy! And then explain how you two can be acting like friends right here and now! I mean," she concluded beseechingly, "you don't *smell* like enemies to each other!"

There was a long pause. At last Wam sighed. "How wonderful it is to meet somebody who, for the most naïve of reasons, has arrived at a proper conclusion. I thought the species was extinct. Shall we attempt the real debate we might have had but for your mistake in inviting Aglabec?"

For a moment Ugant seemed on the verge of explosion; then she relaxed and grinned. "I grant I didn't bargain for the presence of his fanatical followers and their trick of trying to shake the audience off the branches. I'm not used to that kind of thing. With respect to your superior experience of it, I'll concur. Who's to speak first?"

All of a sudden the enormous bower became small and intimate. Far above, the roof continued to flutter, though less vigorously because—as Chybee's own weather-sense indicated—rain was on the way, and shortly it might be called on to seal up completely. But, to her amazement and disbelief, here were two globally famous experts in the most crucial of all subjects preparing to rehearse for her alone the arguments she had staked everything to hear.

She wanted to break down, plead to be excused such

a burden of knowledge. But was she to waste all the misery she had endured to get here? Pride forbade it. She took another fruit and hoped against hope that it would be enough to sustain her through her unsought ordeal.

Wam was saying, "We don't disagree that it should shortly be possible to launch a vehicle into orbit."

"It could be done in a couple of years," Ugant confirmed, accepting more food from one of Fraij's aides.

"We don't disagree that, given time, we could launch not just *a* vehicle but enough of them to create a self-contained, maneuverable vessel capable of carrying a representative community of the folk with all that's needed to support them for an indefinite period."

"Ah! Now we come to the nub of the problem. Do we have the time you're asking to be given? Already you're talking about committing the entire effort of the planet for at least scores of years, maybe scores-of-scores!" Ugant made a dismissive gesture. "That's why I claim that our optimal course is to use what's within our grasp to launch not interplanetary landing-craft, but containers of specially modified organisms tailored to the conditions we expect to encounter on at least Swiftyouth and Sunbride, and maybe on Steadyman and Stolidchurl, or their satellites, which if all else failed could be carried to their destinations by light-pressure from the sun. If then, later on, we did succeed in launching larger vehicles, we could at least rely on the atmospheres and biospheres of those planets being changed towards our own norm, so—"

"But you can't guarantee that such a second-best project would enlist enough support to—"

"No more can you guarantee that we have as much time as you need for your version! According to the latest reports, there's a real risk of a major meteorite strike within not more than—"

"Stop! Stop!" Chybee shouted, horrified at her temerity but unable to prevent herself. "You don't know what you're talking about, either of you!"

Fraij tried to silence her, but, oddly enough, both Wam and Ugant looked at her with serious attention.

"Let her explain," the former said at length.

Thus challenged, Chybee strove to fill her mantle for a proper answer, but could not. She merely husked, "You keep assuming that everybody else is going to fall in with your ideas, whichever of you wins the argument. It doesn't work that way! The people I've met at my home—my parents themselves—are too crazy to listen! I *know*! Oh, I'm sure it's wonderful to dream of other planets and other civilizations, but I don't believe they exist! Why not? Because of what you and other scientists have taught me! Of course, it's folk like you that my parents call crazy," she appended in an ironical tone. "One thing I am sure of, though, is what I said before. You don't know what you're talking about... or at any rate you aren't talking about what most other people are prepared to do!"

There was dead silence for a while. Fraij seemed prepared to pitch Chybee bodily out of the house, and she herself cringed at her audacity. But, at long last, Wam and Ugant curved into identical smiles.

"Out of the mantles of young'uns..." Ugant said, invoking a classical quotation. "Wam, I've often felt the same way. Now I have an idea. If she's willing, could we not make good use of someone who has impeccable family connections with a psychoplanetary cult, yet who believes in my views instead of theirs?"

"Whose?"—with a disdainful curl.

"Mine, or yours, or both! You'd rather tolerate my victory than theirs, and I'd rather tolerate yours! Don't argue! For all we know, ours may be the only life-bearing planet in the universe, and it's in danger!"

"I see what you mean," Wam muttered, just as the long-threatened rain began to drum on the roof. "Very well, it's worth a try."

III

For a good while Chybee paid little or no attention to what was being said. The rushing sound of the rain soothed her as it flowed over the tight-folded leaves of the house and found its way through countless internal and external channels not only to the roots of its bravetrees but also to the elegant little reservoirs disposed here and there to supply its luminants and food-plants... and sundry other secondary growths whose purpose she had no inkling of.

Maybe, she thought, if her parents had enjoyed more of this sort of luxury they would not have gone out of their minds. Maybe it was bitterness at the failure of every venture they attempted which had ultimately persuaded them to spurn the real world in favor of vain and empty imaginings. Yet she and her sibs had shared their hardships, and clung nonetheless to the conviction that plans must be made, projects put into effect, to prevent life itself from being wiped out when the sun and its attendant planets entered the vast and threatening Major Cluster.

Then, quite suddenly, normal alertness returned thanks to the food she had eaten, and memory of what Wam and Ugant had proposed came real to her. She could not suppress a faint cry. At once they broke off and glanced at her.

"Of course, if you're unwilling to help..." Wam said in a huffy tone.

"But you're drafting a scheme for my life without consulting me!" Chybee countered.

"A very fair comment!" Ugant chuckled. "Forgive us, please. But you must admit that you haven't vouchsafed much about yourself. So far we know your name and your parents', and the fact that you've run away from them. Having got here, have you changed your mind? Are you planning on returning home?"

"I wouldn't dare!"

"Would your parents want it noised abroad that their budling—? One moment: do they have others?"

"Two, older than I am. But they went away long ago. Until very recently I thought of them as having betrayed the family. Now I've done the same myself. And I can't even pity my budder for losing all her offspring. She didn't lose them. She drove them out!"

"So what plans do you have for yourself now?"

"None," Chybee admitted miserably.

"And your parents would *not* want it published that all their young'uns have rejected them and their ideas?"

"I'm sure they'll do their utmost to conceal it!"

"Then it all fits together," Ugant said comfortably. "I

can help you, and you can help me. Were you studying at Hulgrapuk?"

"I should have been"—with an angry curl. "But Whelwet wouldn't let me choose the subjects I wanted, archeology and astronomy. She kept saying I must learn something useful, like plant improvement. Of course, what she was really afraid of was that I might find out too much about reality for her to argue against."

Wam moved closer. "I've never met any adult dupes of the psychoplanetary movement, only a clawful of fanatical young'uns. How do you think it's possible for grown-ups to become dreamlost, when famine is a thing of the past?"

Conscious of the flattery implicit in having so distinguished a scientist appeal to her, Chybee mustered all her wits. "Well, many people claim, of course, that it's because some poisons can derange the pith. But I think my parents brought it on themselves. They never let their budlings go hungry; I must say that in their defense. Throughout my childhood, though, they were forever denying themselves a proper diet because of some scheme or other that they wanted to invest in, which was going to be a wild success and enable us to move to a grand house like this one, and then somehow everything went wrong, and..." She ended with a shrug of her whole mantle.

"In other words," Wam said soberly, "they were already predisposed to listen when Aglabec started voicing his crazy notions."

"They didn't get them from Aglabec. At least, I don't think they did. Someone called Imblot—"

"She was one of my students!" Ugant exclaimed. "And one of the first to desert me for Aglabec. She—No, I won't bore you with the full story. But I do remember that Aglabec quarreled with her, and she left Slah and... Well, presumably she wound up in Hulgrapuk. Wam, have you padded across her?"

"I seem to recognize the name," the latter grunted. "By now, though, there are so many self-styled teachers and dream-leaders competing as to who can spin the most attractive spuder-web of nonsense...I guess Whelwet and Yaygomitch have disciples of their own by this time, don't they?"

"Yes!" Chybee clenched her claws. "And it's tubule-bursting to see how decent ordinary people with their whole lives ahead of them are being lured into a dead-end path where they are sure to wind up deliberately starving themselves in search of madder and madder visions! They're renouncing everything—all hope of budding, all chance of a secure existence—because of this dreamlost belief that they can enter into psychic contact with other planets!"

"Would I be right in suggesting," Ugant murmured, "that it was as the result of one particular person falling into this trap that you decided to run away?"

Chybee stared at her in disbelief. At last she said gustily, "I could almost believe that you have psychic powers yourself, Professor. The answer's yes. And I was so shocked by what was happening to him, I just couldn't stand it anymore. So here I am."

"You yourself accept," Ugant mused aloud, almost as though Chybee had not made her last confession, "that the planets are uninhabitable by any form of life as we know it." Raising a claw, she forestalled an interruption from Wam. "Granting that we don't yet know enough about life to say it cannot evolve under any circumstances but our own, at least the chance of other intelligent species existing close at claw is very slim. Correct?"

Wam subsided, and Chybee said uncertainly, "Well, we have discovered that Sunbride must be much too hot, let alone the asteroids that orbit closer to the sun, which are in any case too small to hold an atmosphere. And even Swiftyouth is probably already too cold. Some people think they've detected seasonal changes there, but they might as easily be due to melting icecaps moistening deserts during the summer as to any form of life. And what we know of the larger planets, further out, suggests that they are terribly cold and there are gigantic storms in their immensely deep gas-mantles. Just possibly their satellites might provide a home for life, but the lack of solar radiation makes it so unlikely . . . Oh, Professor! This is absurd! I'm talking as though I were trying to persuade some of my parents' dupes not to commit themselves to dreamness, whereas you know all this much better than I!"

"You have no idea how reassuring it is to find a person

like you," Ugant sighed. "If you'd followed formal courses in astronomy, you might just be parroting what your instructors had told you. But you said you haven't. Yet you take the result of our studies seriously. Someone is listening, at least."

"And sometimes I can't help wondering why," muttered Wam. "Dreams of colorful and exotic alien civilizations are obviously more attractive than dull and boring facts. The giant planets which you, like us, believe to be vast balls of chilly gas—are not they among the favorite playgrounds of the psychoplanetarists?"

"Indeed yes!" Chybee shuddered. "They like them particularly because they are so huge. Thus, when two—well—teachers, or dream-leaders, make contrary claims about the nature of their inhabitants, Imblot can reconcile them with one another on the grounds that on such a vast globe there's room for scores, scores-of-scores, of different species and different cultures."

"That may be relatively harmless," Ugant opined. "What frightens me above all is this new yarn that's spreading so rapidly, most likely thanks to a pithstorm on the part of Aglabec himself."

"You mean the idea that our ancestors were on the verge of spaceflight, so alien creatures hurled the Greatest Meteorite at them?" Wam twisted her mantle in pure disgust. "Yes, I'm worried too at the way it's catching on here. Chybee, had you heard of it in Hulgrapuk?"

"It's very popular there," the girl muttered. "Just the sort of notion my parents love to claw hold of!"

"Not only your parents," Ugant said. She turned back to Wam. "I'll tell you what worries me most. I'm starting to suspect that sooner or later projects like yours and mine will be attacked—physically attacked—by people who've completely swallowed this kind of loathsome nonsense and now feel genuinely afraid that if either of us achieves success we can look forward to another hammer-blow from on high."

"But we have to anyway!" Chybee cried.

"Yes indeed!" Wam said. "That's why it's at once so subtle and so dangerous, and also why Ugant proposes to enlist your help. Will you do as she suggests?"

Chybee searched her memory for details of Ugant's plan, and failed to find them. She had been too distracted during the earlier part of the discussion. At length she said, "Perhaps if you could explain a bit more . . . ?"

"It's very simple." Ugant hunched forward. "What we don't understand, what we desperately need to understand, is how to prevent the spread of this—this mental disorder. As you mentioned just now, some folk suspect that modern air-pollution has already rendered a counterattack hopeless. Even our ancestors, according to the few records we've managed to excavate or recover from under the sea, realized that tampering with metals can be dangerous to our sanity—not just radioactive metals, either, like stumpium and sluggium, but any which don't occur naturally in chemically reactive form. If I start using too many technical terms, warn me."

"I understand you fine so far!"

"Oh, I wish there were laqs more like you in Slah, then! But we're trapped by this fundamental paradox: no substance of organic origin can withstand the kind of energy we need to deploy if we're to launch even the most basic vehicle into space. Correct, Wam?"

"I wish I didn't have to agree, but I must," the other scientist grumbled. "Though I won't accept the view that we've been poisoned into insanity. If that's the case, then our opponents can just as well argue that we too have lost our wits. Hmm?"

"Not so long as we benefit from the best available advice concerning our homes and our diet. But few people share our good fortune—Yes, Chybee?"

"I was thinking only a moment ago that if my parents had been as well off as you, then maybe . . ." She broke off in embarrassment, but she had given no offense. Ugant was nodding approval.

"One reason why I feel that trying to go the whole way at once is over-risky! We might harm the very people we're most eager to protect from the consequences of their own folly . . . All right, Wam! I'm not trying to reopen the whole argument! I'm just asking Chybee whether she's willing to act as a spy for us, pretend she's still a dedicated follower of Aglabec and infiltrate the psychoplanetarist movement on our behalf. I won't insist on an immediate

answer. Before you return home, I want you to look over
my experimental setup. We'll take her along, and leave
it to her to judge whether what we're doing justifies our
making such a demand."

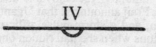

IV

In fact, by first bright Chybee had already made up
her mind. What alternative lay before her? Even at Hulgrapuk, far smaller than Slah, she had seen too many
young people struggling for survival because they had quit
the fertile countryside, or life at sea, to seek a more glam-
orous existence in the urban branchways, ignorant of the
fact that in a city every fruit, every funqus, every crotch
where one might hope to rest, belonged to somebody else,
perhaps with a claim stretching back scores-of-scores of
years. Consequently they often fell into the clutches of
the psychoplanetarists, who offered them a meager diet
(spiked, some claimed, with pith-confusing drugs) in order
to recruit yet more worshipful admirers for their fantastic
visions. If she could do something to save even a clawful
of potential victims—

No: she was too honest to believe the yarn she was
spinning herself. There was nothing impersonal or public-
spirited about the decision she had reached. It stemmed
partly from the fact that she was terrified she might otherwise creep home in a year or two's time, dreamlost
from hunger and misery, reduced to just another of what
Wam had termed "dupes," and partly from . . . She hesitated to confront her knowledge, but at last she managed
it.

She wanted revenge, precisely as Ugant had guessed.
She wanted a revenge against all those who had stolen
his future from a boy called Isarg.

* * *

Before dawn the rain drifted westward. As soon as the sun broached the horizon, creatures she recognized only by descriptions she had heard appeared to groom and cleanse the occupants of the bower: expensive variants of the cleanlickers used in medicine since ancient times. At first she was reluctant, but they exuded such alluring perfumes that she was soon won over, and readily submitted to their mindless yet enjoyable attentions.

A little later Fraij announced that Ugant's scudder was ready for them, and a storm-pulse afflicted Chybee. On the rare occasions when she had ridden one before, it had been in the wild forest around Hulgrapuk; the idea of traversing Slah in competition with so many dolmusqs, haulimals and—come to that—people, alarmed her.

But Ugant was being unbelievably generous and helpful, and it was such a privilege to be in her and Wam's company. As best she might, she controlled her reaction.

She could not, of course, conceal it entirely; her exudates betrayed her. Ugant, however, was affability itself as the beast swung into the interlocking tree-crowns and headed east, adroitly dodging other traffic without further orders, and her small talk was calmative, at least.

"Is this the first time you've been to Slah? Yes? But perhaps you know the story of how it came about?"

"I'm not sure," Chybee muttered, thinking how many padlongs they were from the ground. Once beyond the city boundary, things might not be so bad; here, though, everything happened so fast!

"As nearly as we can establish, Slah was once a city of the People of the Sea," Ugant expounded in a perfectly relaxed tone. "That may sound ridiculous, given how far it now lies above sea-level, but our researches have confirmed what for countless generations was only a folktale. When the Greatest Meteorite hit, the city Voosla was borne many padlonglaqs from the nearest ocean. Naturally the over-pressure killed its inhabitants.

"But by chance enough salt water was carried up with it to fill that valley you see to our left—yes? All the creatures originally composing the city died off too, but their secondary growths flourished thanks not only to the nutriment offered by the carcasses of the barqs and junqs and whatever that it was assembled from, but also to the availability of the same kind of dissolved salts they had been used to before. By the time the temporary lake drained away or was diluted by rainfall, the plants had adapted themselves and spread to occupy much of the area we're now looking down on. Naturally, when the folk started to recover from the effects of the meteorite, this was one of the places they made for first, to see whether anything useful could be found hereabouts. There must have been several brilliant biologists in the community, because some of the food-plants in particular were unique. You've probably been enjoying them all your life without realizing they were rediscovered right here."

"The changes weren't just brought about by the plants' new environment," Wam put in. "The radiation flux as the meteorite hit may account for some of them, and sunshine must have been cut off for scores of years by the dust and vapor it threw up. Besides, it's unlikely that there was a single meteorite. The one which moved Slah to its present position was probably the biggest among a full-scale storm. By boiling off part of their mass in the upper air, the others spread metallic poisons clear around the globe. And that could happen again at any time!"

"Ah, we're clearing the edge of the city at last," Ugant exclaimed. "Stop fretting, Chybee! The air will be a lot fresher from here on, space-budded poisons or not!"

And, still apparently convinced that chitchat was all the girl needed to help her relax, she continued pointing out sights of interest as the scudder hurtled onward, no longer having to make do with the random grip afforded by bravetree branches within Slah itself, where the wear and tear of traffic might lead to accidents if a single over-loaded vehicle added too great a strain, but racing along a specially planted line of toughtrees that slanted around a range of gentle hills. Below, morning sun gleamed on a stream diverted and partly canalized to make a route for freight-pitchens, mindlessly plodding from loq to loq with their massive burdens. Now and then flashes showed how they were being overtaken by courier-pitchens, but of course most urgent messages were conveyed these days by nervograp or by air. Above, looming as vast and brilliant as the sparse white clouds, passenger-floaters were gathering for a landfall at Slah: some, Chybee knew, must have crossed three oceans since the beginning of their voyage. And how much air had been gulped into their ever-flexing bellowers to drive them over such colossal distances? If mere interference by the folk could bring about such incredible modifications, then . . . !

"Is something wrong?" Ugant said suddenly.

"No—But I mean yes!" she exclaimed. "If plants were changed, and . . . Well, don't they also think that some kinds of animal were exterminated too?"

"It's generally accepted that that's what happened," Ugant confirmed gravely. "Many fossils have been found that scarcely resemble the species we're familiar with."

"So what about ourselves?"

The scudder, relieved at having reached open country, was swinging along with a pulsating rhythm; now and then it had to overtake another vehicle, so the rhythm quickened, and occasionally it had to slow because traffic grew too dense for speed. For a while Wam and Ugant seemed to be absorbed by it. If they were exuding pheromones, the wind of their rapid passage carried them away.

Finally, though, Ugant sighed loudly.

"To quote my colleague and rival: I wish I could disagree, but I can't. We *were* altered by the Greatest Meteorite. We had the most amazing luck, to be candid. Or, putting it another way, our ancestors planned better than they imagined. Would you believe that some of the records we've recovered suggest we were in a fair way to extinction *before* the meteorite?"

"Ugant!"—in a warning tone from Wam. "Galdu hasn't published her findings yet, and they may be adrift."

Chybee was feeling light-pithed by now. Never before had she imagined that her idols, the scientists, could argue as fiercely as any psychoplanetarist maintaining that her, or his, version of life on the moons of Stolidchurl must be more accurate than anybody else's.

She said, "Oh, spin your webs for me! You said I was coming along today to make up my own mind!"

But they both took the remark seriously. Ugant said, "If we can't convince her, who can we hope to convince?"

Wam shrank back, abashed. "You're right. And Galdu's primary evidence, at least, does seem convincing."

"She's a pastudier, remember, working in a field you and I know little about . . . What it comes to, Chybee, is this." Adapting herself to the swaying of the scudder as it rose to pass over the lowest point along the line of hills that up to now they had been paralleling, Ugant drew closer. "None of our biologists can see how we could have escaped dying out ourselves unless some genius of the far past foresaw the need to protect us against just such an event as the fall of the Greatest Meteorite. Almost all the large animals on the planet disappeared because they were—like us—symbiotes. The regular adaptive resource of the 'female' sex among them was to become more male. In the end, naturally, this resulted in a zero bud-rate. But because we'd been somehow altered, the process came to a dead stop in the folk. In you and me, that means."

"Not a complete dead stop," Wam objected. "Another such calamity, and . . . !"

"Now you're arguing for Galdu's most extreme ideas!" crowed Ugant. "A moment ago—Still, that's of no significance right now. What is important is that once again young Chybee here has clawed hold of something most people overlook even when they have access to the evidence. I'm impressed by this girl, you know!"

"Save the compliments," Wam grunted. "Stick to the point she originally set out to make. Yes, Chybee, there was a change in us too, and the only reason we can conceive for it is that some of our ancestors must have arranged it. Compared with that gigantic achievement, what use are our petty undertakings unless they result in the exportation to space of our entire culture?"

"I thought we were going to sink our differences for the time being!" Ugant began.

But Chybee had already burst out, "How? How was it done?"

"We think most of the food-plants we rely on had been modified," came Ugant's sober answer. "We think they had been so far modified that merely by eating them we arrested part of what until then had been our normal evolutionary adaptation. We think—some people think, in deference to Wam's reservations, but I'm an admirer of Galdu—that had it not been for this most important of all inventions, we would have long ago become extinct. If you and I met one of our male ancestors right now, for instance, we couldn't bud together. We'd been used for generations to believing that evolution took place over countless score-score years. Suddenly it turns out that someone, long ago, must have ensured a change in us such that next time a crisis of habitability occurred on this planet—"

"Stop! Stop!" Chybee cried, and a moment later added in an apologetic tone, "You did tell me that if you started to use too many technical terms . . ."

Ugant relaxed with a mantle-wide grin.

"Point well taken," she murmured. "Well, a crisis of habitability is what follows, for instance, a meteorite fall or an ice-age. What, with deference and respect to our forepadders, we are trying to avoid by creating such research projects as the one you can now see yonder."

She gestured with one claw, and Chybee turned her eye as the scudder relaxed into a crotch at journey's end. What met it dismayed and baffled her. Across a broad and level plain flanked by low hills, not familiar plants but objects unlike anything she had encountered before extended nearly to the skyline.

"All this has been created," Ugant said, "because what saved us last time may all too easily not save us twice."

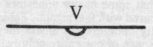

V

"How much do you know about the dual principles of flight?" Ugant inquired of Chybee as they padded between countless huge and glistening globes, each larger than any unmodified bladder she had ever seen. Because pumplekins were forcing them full of pure wetgas, and there was inevitable leakage—though it was not poisonous—their surroundings were making the girl's weather-sense queasy. Sensing her distress, the professor went on to spell out information most of which in fact she knew.

"The first clues must have come from cloudcrawlers so long ago we have no record of it. Archeological records indicate that we also owe to the study of natural floaters the discovery that air is a mixture of several elements. Of course, it was a long time before the lightest could be separated out by more efficient means than occur in nature. And floaters drift at the mercy of the wind, so it again took a considerable while before we invented bellowers like those over there"—with a jab of one claw towards a bank of tubular creatures slumped in resting posture on a wooden rack. "How did you travel from Hulgrapuk to Slah?"

"I flew," Chybee told her, wide-eyed with wonder.

"So you've seen them in operation, gulping air and tightening so as to compress it to the highest temperature they can endure, and then expelling it rearward. We got to that principle by studying the seeds emitted by certain rock-plants. But of course it's also how we swim, isn't it? And there's even a possibility that our remotest ancestors may have exploited the same technique by squirting air from under their hind mantles. You know we evolved from carnivores that haunted the overgrowth of the primeval forest?"

"My parents don't believe in evolution," Chybee said.

"Ridiculous!" Wam exclaimed. "How can anybody not?"

"According to them, intelligence came into existence everywhere at the same time as the whole universe. On every world but ours, mind-power controls matter directly. That's how Swiftyouth and Sunbride hurled the Greatest Meteorite at us. Our world alone is imperfect. They even try to make out that other planets' satellites don't sparkle or show phases, but are always at the full."

Wam threw up her claws in despair. "Then they *are* insane! Surely even making a model, with a clump of luminants in the middle to represent the sun, would suffice to—"

"Oh, I tried it once!" Chybee interrupted bitterly. "I was punished by being forbidden to set pad outside our home for a whole moonlong!"

"What were you supposed to learn from that?"

"I suppose: not to contradict my budder..." Chybee gathered her forces with an effort. "Please go on, Professor Ugant. I'm most interested."

With a doubtful glance at her, as though suspecting sarcasm, Ugant complied.

"What, though, you might well say, does our ability to fly through the air have to do with flying into vacant space? After all, we know that even the largest and lightest floaters we can construct, with the most powerful bellowers we can breed to drive them, can never exceed a certain altitude. So we must resort to something totally new. And there it is."

Again following her gesture, Ugant saw a long straight row of unfamiliar trees, boughs carefully warped so as to create a continuous series of rings from which hung worn but shiny metal plates and scores of nervograp tendrils.

"Ah!" Wam said. "I've seen pictures of that. Isn't it where you test your drivers?"

"Correct. And the storage bladders beyond are the ones we had to devise specially to contain their fuel. What can you show to match them?"

Wam shrugged. "As yet, we've concentrated less on this aspect of the task than on what we regard as all-important: eventual survival of the folk in space."

"But what's the good of solving that problem," Ugant snapped, "if you don't possess a means to send them there?"

"With you working on one half of the job, and me on the other..." Wam countered disprongingly, and Ugant had to smile as they moved on towards the curiously distorted trees. Hereabouts there was a stench of burning, not like ordinary fire, but as though something Chybee had never encountered had given off heat worse than focused sunlight. Under the warped trees there was no mosh such as had cushioned their pads since leaving the scudder; indeed, the very texture of the soil changed, becoming hard—becoming *crisp*.

"You're in luck," Ugant said suddenly, gazing along the tree-line to its further end and pointing out a signal made by someone waving a cluster of leaves. "There's a test due very shortly. Come on, and I'll introduce you to Hyge, our technical director."

Excitedly Chybee hastened after her companions. They led her past a house laced about with nervograps, which challenged them in a far harsher tone than Ugant's home, but the professor calmed it with a single word. Some distance beyond, a score of young people were at work under the direction of a tall woman who proved to be Hyge herself, putting finishing touches to a gleaming cylinder in a branch-sprung cradle. It contained more mass of metal than Chybee had ever seen; she touched it timidly to convince herself that it was real.

In a few brief words Ugant summed up the purpose of their visit, and Hyge dipped respectfully to Wam.

"This is an honor, Professor! I've followed your research for years. Ugant and I don't always see eye to eye, but we do share a great admiration for your pioneering experiments in spatial life-support. How are you getting on with your attempt to create a vacuum?"

"Fine!" was Wam's prompt answer. "But unless and until we resolve our other differences, I don't foresee that we shall work together. Suppose you continue with your test? It may impress me so much that... Well, you never know."

Smiling, Hyge called her assistants back to the house, while Ugant whispered explanations to Chybee.

"To drive a vehicle those last score padlonglaqs out of the atmosphere, there's only one available technique. If there isn't any air to gulp and squirt out, then you have to take along your own gas. We borrowed the idea from certain sea-creatures which come up to the surface, fill their bladders with air, and then rely on diving to compress it to the point where it's useful. When they let it go, it enables them to pounce on their prey almost as our forebudders must have done."

"I don't like to be reminded that our ancestors ate other animals," Chybee confessed.

"How interesting! I wonder whether that may account for some of the reaction people like your parents display when confronted by the brutal necessity of recycling during a spaceflight... But we can discuss that later. Right now you need to understand that what Hyge has set up for testing is a driver full of two of the most reactive chemicals we've ever discovered. When they're mixed, they combust and force out a mass of hot gas. This propels the cylinder forward at enormous speed. Our idea is to lift such a cylinder—with a payload of adapted spores and seeds—to the greatest altitude a floater can achieve. Then, by using the special star-seekers we've developed, we can orient it along the desired flight-path, and from there it will easily reach orbital height and velocity."

"But scaling it up to carry what we'll need for actual survival out there is—" Wam began.

"Out of the question!" Ugant conceded in a triumphant tone. "Now will you agree that our best course is to—?"

Hyge cut in. "Scaling up is just a matter of resources. Save your disputes until after we find out whether our new budling works! Don't look at the jet! Slack down to tornado status! Keep your mandibles and vents wide open! The overpressure from this one will be *fierce*!"

And, after checking that the cylinder's course was clear of obstructions and that all the stations from which reports were to be made were functional, she slid back a plank of stiffbark in the control house's floor and imposed her full weight on something Chybee could not clearly see but which she guessed to be a modified form of mishle, one of the rare secondary growths known as flashplants which, after the passage of a thunderstorm, could kill animal prey by discharging a violent spark, and would then let down tendrils to digest the carcass.

Instantly there was a terrible roaring noise. The cylinder uttered a prong of dazzling flame—"Look that way!" Ugant shouted, and when Chybee proved too fascinated to respond, swung her bodily around and made her gaze along the tree-row—and sped forward on a course that carried it exactly through the center of the wooden rings, clearing the metal plates by less than a clawide.

Almost as soon as it had begun, the test was over bar the echoes it evoked from the hills, and a rousing cheer rang out. But it was barely loud enough to overcome the deafness they were all suffering. Chybee, who had not prepared herself for pressure as great as Hyge had warned of, felt as though she had been beaten from crest to pads.

"Oh, I'm glad we were here to witness that," said Ugant softly. "Wam, aren't you impressed?"

"She should be," Hyge put in caustically, checking the recordimals connected to the incoming nervograps. "That's the first time our guidimals have kept the cylinder level through every last one of the rings. And if we can repeat that, we'll have no problem aiming straight up!"

"Are you all right, Chybee?" Ugant demanded as she recovered from her fit of euphoria.

"I—uh . . ." But pretense was useless. "I wasn't ready for such a shock. I was still full of questions. Like: what are the metal plates for?"

"Oh, those," Hyge murmured. "Well, you see, not even

the most sensitive of our detectors can respond to signals emitted by the cylinder as it rushes past faster than sound. If you were standing right near the arrival point, you'd be hit by a sonic blast, a wave of air compressed until it's practically solid. Even this far away it can be painful, can't it? So we had to find a method of translating the impact into something our normal instruments can read. What we do is compress metal plates against shielded nervograp inputs, compensating for the natural elasticity of the trees, which we developed from a species known to be highly gale-resistant—"

She broke off. Chybee had slumped against Ugant.

"Does she need help?" Hyge demanded. "I can send an aide to fetch—"

At the same time making it clear by her exudates that this would be an unwarrantable interference with her immediate preoccupations.

"No need to worry," Ugant said softly, comforting the girl with touch after gentle touch of her claws. "She's a bit distraught, that's all. Wam and I are at fault; on the way here we should have explained more clearly what we were going to show her."

"Yes, I'm all right," Chybee whispered, forcing herself back to an upright posture, though lower than normal. "I just decided that all your efforts mustn't go to waste. So I'm willing and eager to do what Ugant wants."

"What's that?" Hyge inquired with a twist of curiosity as her assistants started to arrive with the first of the non-remote readings.

"You'll find out," Ugant promised. "And with luck it may make the future safe for sanity. If it does, of course—well, then, the name of Chybee will be famous!"

VI

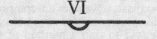

Here, houses and food-plants alike were neglected and ill-doing, surviving as best they could on what garbage was thrown to rot at their roots. Many rain-channels were blocked and nobody had bothered to clear them, allowing precious growths to die off. Even a heavy storm might not suffice to wash away all the stoppages; several were sprouting weeds whose interlocking tendrils would hold against any but the most violent onslaught of water. There were scores of people in sight, most of them young, but with few exceptions they were thin and slack, and their mantles were patched with old or the scars of disease.

Chybee almost cried out in dismay. She had thought things bad enough at Hulgrapuk, but in that far smaller city there was no district which had been so completely taken over by the psychoplanetarists. How could anybody bear to live here, let alone come sight-seeing as that well-fed couple yonder were obviously doing?

She caught a snatch of their conversation. "It's a different life-style," the woman was saying. "Simpler, nearer to nature, independent of things like nervograps and scudders and luxury imports. You have to admire the underlying principle."

Preening a little as he noticed Chybee looking at him, the man retorted, "If living the simple life means you have to put up with all sorts of loathsome diseases, I'd rather settle for the modern way."

"Come now, you must admit that it's a devastatingly attractive notion..."

Still arguing, they drifted on along the branchways.

But the woman was right. There was something subtly alluring about this run-down quarter of Slah, and the reason for it was all around them. The air was permeated with the pheromones of people experiencing utter certainty. A single breath was enough to convey the message.

Here, the aroma indicated, one might find refuge from constant warnings about how any dark or bright might bring just such another meteorite as had carried an ocean-going city far inland to create the foundations of modern Slah. (How deep underpad were those foundations now? Some of the oldest houses' roots were alleged to stretch for padlonglaqs, though of course not directly downward...)

And, inevitably, the path to that sense of security lay through hunger. Why should anyone worry about tending food-plants, then? Why should anyone care if the rain-channels got stopped up? Why should anyone object if a patch of mold started growing on her or his mantle? It all liberated precious dreams which could be recounted to innumerably eager listeners. It all helped to reduce the intolerable burden of reality.

Moreover, there was an extra benefit to be gained from moving to this squalid district. It was the lowest-lying part of Slah, sheltered by thickly vegetated hills, and the prevailing wind rarely did more than stir the pool of air it trapped. Little by little, the pheromone density was building up to the point where feedback could set in. Some time soon now its inhabitants might conceivably cease to argue about the content of their visions. No longer would there be endless disputes about the shape and language of the folk in Stumpalong. Gradually the chemical signals they were receiving would unify their mental patterns. And then: mass collective insanity...

It had never happened in living memory, but it was theoretically possible. Archeological records indicated that certain now-vanished epidemic diseases had had a similar effect in the far past, possibly accounting for the collapse of once-great cities. All this and more had been explained to Chybee by Ugant and her friends after Wam's return to Hulgrapuk: Glig the biologist, Galdu the pastudier, Airm the city councillor... the last, the most pitiable, because she was worn out from trying to persuade her colleagues that the psychoplanetarist quarter represented a real danger to the rest of the citizens.

What a topsy-turvy universe Chybee's prong-of-the-moment decision had brought her into, where she could pity a major public figure in the world's greatest metropolis! Yet how could she not react so when she listened to what Airm had to complain about?

"They always think it's other people's budlings who wind up in that slum!" she had explained over and over. "Well, I grant that's been the case up till now. Young'uns from prosperous and comfortable homes are relatively immune. What are they going to do, though, if this threatened mass hysteria actually sets in? The likeliest effect will be to make all the victims decide they have to drive the rest of us around to their way of thinking, correct? And how could they achieve that goal? By spoiling other people's food! By cutting off nutrients and water from their homes, by fouling cargoes at the docks, even by spreading drugs which suppress normal appetite! Worse yet, they could poison our haulimals, and how could we feed everybody without them? If Slah attempted to support its citizens off its internal resources, we'd all be dreamlost within a moonlong! What are we going to *do*?"

Hearing that, the full magnitude of what she was committed to came home to Chybee. A few brights ago, all she had thought of was escape from her crazy parents. Now, because of who her parents were, she was embarquing on a course that might mean the difference between collapse and survival for the planet's most populous city. She could scarcely credit how completely, as a result of Ugant's unpremeditated suggestion, people were coming to rely on her.

Was she equal to the task? She greatly feared she was not; nothing had prepared her for such immense responsibility. True, she had chided her budder again and again for continuing to treat her like a budling when she believed she was grown-up enough to think for herself. What a world of difference there was, though, between the ambition and the reality!

But the reality was the buried ruin of Voosla, deep beneath the branchways scudders swarmed along. The reality was the corpses of its inhabitants that had rotted to fertilize evolving plants. The reality was that modern Slah could be overrun by scores-of-scores of madfolk. The reality was that unless Ugant and Hyge and Wam saw their efforts crested with success life itself might be abolished by the mindless workings of celestial chance.

She had not so far found words to explain what had

overcome her while watching Hyge's driver being demonstrated. In her most secret pith, though, she had already started to compare it with what her parents, and their psychoplanetarist friends, called "stardazzle"—a moment of total conviction after which one could never be the same.

At its simplest, she had abruptly decided that so much effort and ingenuity, dedicated to so worthwhile a goal, must not be allowed to go to waste because of a bunch of dreamlost fools.

Hidden under her mantle was a bunch of leaves which, so Glig had assured her, would protect her against the insidious effect of the local pheromones. She slipped one into her mandibles as she reviewed her immediate task. They wanted her to ingratiate herself with the psychoplanetarists; she was to establish what food they ate and what if any drugs they used, and bring away samples not just of those but, if possible, mantle-scrapings or other cells from their very bodies.

Ugant had been blunt. She had said, "If necessary accept a bud from one of them! Embryonic cells are among the most sensitive of all. Glig can rid you of it later without even a scar, if that worries you"—glancing down at the two bud-marks on her own torso. "But that would help us beyond measure in determining how close we are to disaster."

Chybee hoped against hope it wouldn't come to that . . .

Well, she had stood here gazing about long enough. Now she must act. Presumably she ought to start by getting into conversation with somebody. But who? Most of those nearby were clearly lost in worlds of their own. Over there, for example: a girl about her own age, very slowly stripping the twigs off a dying branch and putting them one by one into her mandibles. She looked as though, once having settled to her task, she might never rise again.

And to her left: a boy trying to twist his eye around far enough to inspect his mantle which, as Chybee could see—but he couldn't—was patched with slimy green and must be hurting dreadfully.

She knew, though, what kind of answer she would get were she to offer help. She had seen similar cases at home. Her parents even admired young'uns like that, claiming

that they were making progress along the path that led to
mind being freed from matter, so that it could exert total
power instead of merely moving a perishable carcass. She
had often angered them by asking why, if that were so,
they themselves didn't go out and rub up against the foulest and most disease-blotched folk they could find.

She tried not to remember that by now Isarg might all
too easily have wound up in a similar plight.

So she left the boy to his endless futile attempts to
view his own back, and moved along the branchway. The
pheromones grew stronger with every padlong.

Abruptly she grew aware that people were staring at
her. It wasn't surprising. At Ugant's she had enjoyed the
best diet of her life, and she was tall and plump—too much
so, in fact, to suit the role she was supposed to adopt.
Who could believe she was a dedicated psychoplanetarist
when she was in this condition?

She clung desperately to her recollection of how well
favored Aglabec had appeared at Ugant's house. More
than once, thinking back over his appearance, she had
wondered whether he was sharing his followers' priva-
tions. If not, did that imply that he was crazy for some
other reason? Was he spreading his lies for personal power
and gain? If only one of the scientists she had met at
Ugant's had broached the subject . . . But none had, and
she was too timid to suggest the idea herself.

Suddenly she wanted to flee. It was too late. Three
young'uns—two girls and a boy—detached themselves
from the group who had been looking at her with vast
curiosity and approached in such a way as to cut off her
retreat. She summoned all her self-control.

"Hello! My name's Chybee and I'm from Hulgrapuk.
Maybe you heard tell of my parents Whelwet and Yaygomitch? They sent me here to dig into a report they
picked up off the wind, about how it was the folk of
Swiftyouth and Sunbride that threw the Greatest Meteorite at us. I can trade information about life on Sluggard's
moons for fuller details."

She curled her mantle into an ingratiating posture and
waited for their response.

It came in the form of excitement. One of the girls said,
"I didn't know Sluggard had any moons!"

"Sure it does!" the boy countered. "Much too small to see, but there they are! Five, right?"—to Chybee.

Ugant and her friends had briefed Chybee carefully. "Only four. What they thought was a fifth turned out to be last year's red comet on its way to us."

"I made contact with the folk on that comet!" the other girl declared.

How can anyone be so crazy as to believe that comets are inhabited? But Chybee kept such thoughts to herself as far as her exudants allowed; at least the all-pervading pheromones masked most of them.

"Well, if your budder is Whelwet," the first girl said, "I know who'll want to talk to you. Come with us. We're on our way to a meet with Aglabec himself!"

Oh, NO!

But there was no gainsaying them; they fell in on either side like an escort and swept her along.

VII

At least the leaves Glig had provided were working. Chybee had no idea what they were, but the scientists of Slah had many secrets. Not only did they protect against the terrifying pheromones surrounding her; they seemed also to mask her own exudations. And that too was terrifying, in a way. It was a popular pastime for younglings at Hulgrapuk and elsewhere to reenact stories from the legendary past, but only the very young could so far submerge themselves in a false identity as to make each other and their audience believe in the rôles they were playing. As soon as they started to secrete adult odors, the illusion waned.

But suppose adults too could fake such a transformation. Suppose, for instance, Aglabec had figured out a way ... ?

She wanted not to think about him, for fear of betraying her imposture, but her companions kept chattering on with mad enthusiasm, saying how he must be the greatest male teacher since Awb. Privately, Chybee did not believe Awb had ever existed. She had often been punished by her parents for saying so. If she were to voice a similar opinion right now, though, she could surely look forward to something worse than the penalties meted out to a budling. What if Aglabec were to recognize her from the meeting at Ugant's? She could only reassure herself that there had been too many people present for anybody to single out one person's trace, and try and believe that he would have refused on principle to register what she said.

Struggling to divert the conversation along another path, she demanded what the trio's names were. The replies added to her dismay.

"I'm Witnessunbride," stated the first girl.

"And I, Cometaster!" declared the other.

While the boy said, as though it were the most natural thing in the world, "Startoucher!" He added with curiosity, "Do Chybee and Whelwet and Yaygomitch have arcane meanings? At Slah we discard our old names after entering the knowledge state."

But before Chybee could reply, Witnessunbride rounded on him. "And your new one is ridiculous! I could cite five-score of us who know more about what goes on under other stars than you do! Don't take him seriously, Chybee! But how and why did you choose your new name?"

Chybee was briefly at a loss. Then inspiration struck. She said with contempt she did not need to feign, "Some of us, including me and my parents, felt no call to change our names, because they turned out to have significance in the speech of other worlds."

Impressed, Cometaster said, "And yours means . . . ?"

With stiff dignity, Chybee answered, "Those who attain enlightenment will recognize its purport in due time."

The other three exchanged glances.

"Aglabec is going to be very interested in you," said Witnessunbride. "He's the only other person I ever heard say anything like that. *And* the only other person so advanced he can contact other planets without needing to fast. That is, assuming you got your knowledge about Sluggard direct. Did you? Or were you just told it by your budder or someone?"

Chybee was so taken aback by the audacity of Aglabec's excuse for being in better fettle than his disciples, she could not think of a suitable answer. Luckily they mistook her silence for wounded pride.

"Hurry up!" Startoucher said. "It's nearly sunset!"

And, hastening towards the fringe of this decrepit quarter, he explained how it was that he and his friends were going to meet Aglabec in person.

"Every full moon, unless he's traveling to spread his knowledge, he returns to us, going from home to home to visit his oldest and most loyal followers. Sometimes, when he's due to leave for a long trip, sick people choose to liberate their minds in his presence, for fear of never seeing him again. Isn't that marvelous?"

To liberate—? Oh. Chybee hoped against hope that Glig's leaves would mask the signs of her nausea. Hastily she said, "How did you earn your name?"

"Witnessunbride is jealous of it," Startoucher said with a pout of his mantle. "But I'm fully entitled! Aglabec told me so—he said there are going to be a lot more cases like mine, people who start getting knowledge from other stars instead of just our local planets. Well, I mean I must have done! None of what I see and hear matches with what other people get from Sunbride, or Swiftyouth, or Stolidchurl, or *anywhere*! Unless, of course—"

He broke off, while Chybee wondered how anyone could be deluded by so transparently silly an explanation. But it was politic to seem interested. She said, "Unless what?"

"I was going to say: unless it comes from somewhere like the moons of Sluggard. But if that were so, then Aglabec would have told me, wouldn't he?"

Much relieved, he hurried on in advance of the group, announcing that they were almost at their destination and it looked as though Aglabec must already have arrived, since nobody was outside watching out for him.

Oh, why could these people not have been on their way to a meeting where she could melt into the crowd? Inside a house, how could she disguise her true detestation of Aglabec? How could she keep up the pretense that she and her parents were still on good terms?

She would simply have to try.

The house was a little better cared for than most in the

area. In its main bower Aglabec rested in a curved crotch, surrounded by fervent admirers. He acknowledged the late arrivals with a courteous dip; if his gaze rested longer on Chybee than the others, that could be ascribed to her being a stranger and much better nourished than the rest...except himself.

"As I was about to say before you came in," he stated in resonant tones, "it always does my pith good to learn how many more people are coming around to the view that we must not and *dare* not allow scientists to persist in their crazy attempts to launch artificial moons and even space-going cities. They are, of course, impervious to reason; it's futile to warn them that they risk forcing our planetary neighbors to act against us in self-defense. I know! I've tried, and I haven't yet given up, but it's a weary task...Scientists they call themselves!"—with vast contempt. "Yet they don't appear to realize how dangerous it would be to convey life from one planet to another. Some of them are actually plotting to do precisely that: to export bacteria and other organisms to Swiftyouth and Sunbride, to *infect* them, to *contaminate* them! How would they like it if the prong were in the other claw? Luckily for us, all the planetfolk we've contacted so far seem to be cognizant of the risks. They would never dream of doing such a thing, would they?"

Able to relax a little now that it was plain that Aglabec did not after all remember her, Chybee joined in the murmur of agreement which greeted his declaration. Witnessunbride, to her surprise, did not, and Aglabec inquired why.

"You did once say," the girl ventured, "that next time we try to fly into space we can look forward to being stopped not by another gigantic meteorite but perhaps something subtler, like a plague."

"Ah, I'm glad that registered. My compliments on your excellent recollection. Yes, I did say that. Moreover a number of our comrades have reinforced me, have they not? There is, however, a great moral difference between seeding organisms into space merely to conduct a blind and futile experiment, and doing so with infinite reluctance in order to prevent invasion from another world. What point is there, anyhow, in traveling through space? It would be absurdly dangerous; it would be terribly slow, and living in such confinement—even assuming we can survive in the absence of gravity, which has not been proved—would be a strain on anybody's sanity. What purpose would it serve to deliver a briqload of lunatics to another world? In any case, those of us who have discovered how to make mental voyages have chosen the path that avoids all such perils. If not instantaneously, then at speeds which exceed that of light itself, we can find ourselves on virtually any planet, any moon, we choose, to be greeted by the inhabitants as honored guests, because we understand and accept the reasons why we must not make a physical journey. If the discipline we have to endure in order to achieve our goal is harsh, so be it. Once we have been stardazzled, the need for it dies away, and we can enjoy the best not of 'both' worlds but of as many as we like! I emphasize that because I notice among us a stranger who seems unwilling to enter upon the pathway of privation."

All eyes turned on Chybee, who mustered maximum self-control. She was saved from immediate speech, though, by Startoucher.

"She's already been 'dazzled! She can tell us about life on Sluggard's moons! I never met anyone who's been in contact with those folk before—except you, of course," he added deferentially. "And she came all the way from Hulgrapuk specially to find out about how it was Sunbride and Swiftyouth that hurled the Greatest Meteorite at us."

"Hulgrapuk," Aglabec repeated, his voice and attitude abruptly chill. "Now, that is a city I have little truck with. To my vast regret, the traitor Imblot, whom some of you may remember, who rebelled against me on the grounds that I was a 'mere male,' has established a certain following there. It would not in the least surprise me if by now she had persuaded a clawful of ignorant dupes that there is no need to fast, or cultivate the welcome assistance of a moldy mantle, in order to attain the knowledge state. But, as you know very well, it is granted only to a dedicated few to learn that mind is all and matter is nothing. It is dependence on the material world which blinds us to this central truth. Our luxury homes, our modern transport and communications, our telescopes and our recordimals and everything we prize in the ordinary way—those are the very obstacles that stand between us and enlightenment. If they did not, why, then there would be enough mental force in this very bower to put a stop to what the so-called scientists are doing!"

He hunched forward. "Who are you, girl? By what right do you claim to have been stardazzled?"

Terrified, Chybee could do nothing but concentrate on masking her reactions. With a puzzled glance at her, Cometaster said, "Her name is Chybee and her parents are Whelwet and Yaygomitch. At least that's what she told us."

"You're a long way from enlightenment, then, you three, despite having dared to take new names!" Aglabec quit the crotch he had been resting in and erupted to full height. "I hereby decree you shall renounce them! Revert to what you were called before! It will be a fit punishment for your indescribable stupidity!"

Cringing in dismay, the trio huddled together as though their dream-leader's wrath were a physical storm.

"But—but what have we done that's so bad?" whimpered Startoucher-that-was.

"You brought among us, right here into *my* presence, a follower and a budling of followers of Imblot! You took her story at mantle value, didn't you? You forgot that I have many enemies, who will stop at nothing to ruin my work!" Aglabec checked suddenly, leaning towards the petrified Chybee.

"I thought so," he said at last. "I've seen you before, haven't I? You were at Ugant's, at the pointless so-called debate she organized. Very well! Since you've chosen to come here, we shall find out why before we let you go. It may take some time, but we'll pry the truth out of you whether you like it or not!"

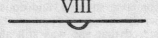

VIII

Being in so much better health, Chybee might have fought free of any two, or even three, of Aglabec's adorers. But, as he himself watched with a cynical air, everyone else in the bower either seized hold of her or moved to block the only way of escape. A tight grasp muffled her intended cry for help...though, in this quarter of Slah, who would have paid attention, let alone come to her rescue?

Half-stifled, wholly terrified, she felt herself being enclosed in some kind of lightproof bag that shut the world away. Still she resisted, but within moments she discovered that it was also airtight, and she must breathe her own exudations. Just enough power of reason remained to warn her that if she went on struggling she would lose consciousness at once, and the sole service she could do herself was to try and work out what her captors intended. She let her body go limp, hoarding the sourgas in her tubules.

"What shall we do with her?" demanded a voice much like ex-Startoucher's; perhaps it was his, and he was eager to curry new favor with his dream-leader.

"There's a place I know," replied Aglabec curtly. "Just follow me."

And Chybee was hoisted up unkindly by three or four bearers and carried bodily away.

If only odors as well as sounds could have penetrated the bag! Then she might have stood some chance of working out where she was being taken. As it was, she had to rely on fragmentary clues: there, the moan of an overloaded draftimal; there, the chant of someone selling rhygote spice; there again, the boastful chatter of a gang of young'uns...

But so much might have identified any part of any large city, and the strain of concentration was too great. Despairing, at the last possible moment she surrendered her grip on awareness, wondering whether she would die.

"Water!" someone shouted, and doused her with it. She opened her maw, but not soon enough. By the time she had registered that she was still alive, reflex had dropped her to the floor, gasping for any drop that might remain. But she lay on an irregular mesh of tree-roots with wide gaps between them; it drained away. There was a stench of ancient rot. What light reached her came from phosphorescent molds, not decent luminants.

Moaning, she tried to raise her eye quickly enough to identify the person who had soaked her. She failed. A barrier of tightly woven branches was being knotted into place above her. A harsh laugh was followed by slithering as her tormentor departed.

But at least she wasn't dead.

Summoning all her remaining energy, Chybee felt for any spongy-soft areas that might have absorbed a little of the water. She found two or three, and though the taint nauseated her, she contrived to squeeze out enough to relieve the dryness of her maw.

By degrees she recovered enough to take stock of her predicament. The roots she was trapped among were so tough there was no hope of clawing or gnawing through them. The sole opening was blocked. Her weather-sense informed her that she was far below the bower where she had encountered Aglabec. There was one and only one explanation which fitted. He had ordered her brought to the deep foundations of Slah, where nobody had lived for scores-of-scores of years. Above her there must be layer upon layer of dead and living houses, totaling such a mass that it amazed her to find this gap had survived without collapsing.

With bitter amusement she realized how fitting his choice had been. Did he not wish to lure everyone into the pit of the dead past, instead of letting the folk expand towards the future?

And those he could not dupe, he would imprison...

Was she close to the outcrop of rock which must account for the existence of this tiny open volume, little wider than she herself was long? She hunted about her for a probe—a twig, anything—and met only slimy decay and tough unbreakable stems.

At that point she realized she was wasting energy. What she needed more than all else was something to eat. Because otherwise...

Oh, it was clear as sunlight. They were going to starve her. When she was as dreamlost as Isarg, they would lay siege to her mind with fawning talk. In the end she would accept passively whatever Aglabec chose to say, until she betrayed Ugant and Hyge and Wam, until—

No! It must not happen! Feverishly she scoured her prison, tasting the foulest patches of rot in the hope that some trace of nourishment might inhere in them...and at last slumped into the least uncomfortable corner, having found not a whit of anything less than utterly disgusting. Somehow she had lost even Glig's protective leaves. She could only hope they hadn't been noticed and identified.

Well, if all else failed, she could gulp down some poisonous mess and cheat Aglabec that way. But she was determined not to let him overcome her hatred of him and all he stood for. She would fight back as long as she could.

And surely, long before she was driven to such straits, Ugant would have started to worry and sent out searchers!

Compacting her body to conserve warmth, for there was a dank chill draught here, redolent of loathsome decay, she set about giving herself instructions for resistance, even though already a hint of anger colored her thoughts when she remembered Ugant so prosperous in her fine home, so ready to enlist a stranger in her cause...

The only way she had to measure time was by the changing air-pressure of successive dawns and sunsets, for as it turned out the person who had been assigned to pour water over her—the absolute minimum needed to keep her alive—was also instructed to do so at random intervals. Sometimes the chilly shower occurred four times in a single day; then a whole one might pass without it, and she was almost reduced to begging as she watched, in the wan glow of the molds, how her mantle was shrinking from thirst. Enough of her pride remained thus far to protect her against that humiliation. But she could discern how hunger was taking its toll. At first she had kept careful count of darks and brights; then after a while she was alarmed to realize she no longer knew precisely how long she had been shut up. Her trust in Ugant gave way first to doubt, then to sullen resentment. The pangs of anger multiplied, until it came to seem that the scientist, not Aglabec, was her true captor, because as yet she had not succeeded in locating this secret prison.

Then voices began to whisper to her.

At first she was aware that what she heard formed part of Aglabec's plot. Out of sight behind the mesh of roots must be two or three of his disciples, under orders to confuse her by telling fantastic tales about life in Swift-youth and Sunbride, Steadyman and Stolidchurl and Sluggard and their multiple moons unknown before the telescope. She called to them, demanding food, and they refused to answer, but kept on with their whispering.

For a while she argued, reciting what astronomers had worked out from the planets' spectra concerning conditions there, inquiring why anyone should believe Aglabec rather than Ugant and her colleagues. At last, when she was so weak she could scarcely raise herself to half normal height, she received an answer.

Someone said, and it could have been Startoucher: "You and all those like you want to deny life. But we affirm it. We share the fiery joy of existence near the sun. We enjoy the frozen beauty of the giant worlds. We know what it means to be weighed down by gravity a score-score-fold, and not to care, because we borrow bodies suited to it. From searing heat to bitter cold, we transcend the dull plain world of every day, and eventually we shall perceive the universe. When our task is done, no one will care if this petty planet is destroyed."

"The destiny of bodies is to rot," said another voice. "The destiny of mind is glorious!"

"I'm losing mine!" whimpered Chybee against her will. The confession was greeted with a chuckle, then with silence.

But it didn't last. After she had made one last futile search for something she might eat, new whispering began. This time she could not convince herself there was anybody talking to her. There was only one voice, and it was inside her very pith, and it was her own, so how could she deny what it said? It told her that life must exist everywhere, in an infinite range of guises, and that only a fool could imagine that this was its sole and unique haven. It told her she was guilty of despair, when she needed only to look within her and seek the truth. It echoed and repeated what her parents told their followers, what they had learned from Imblot... but she was a traitor, wasn't she? She'd dismissed Aglabec as a "mere male" although Aglabec was powerful, *all*-powerful, exercised the right of life and death over this person Chybee...

Occasionally she stirred as though touched by a sharp prong. Then the suspicion did cross her mind that some of her thoughts were being imposed from outside. But she lacked the energy to claw hold of the idea. Likewise, she sometimes experienced the shock of realizing that she was beginning to digest her own tissue, and that her mantle was patched with molds like those afflicting her cage of roots, as though the tiny organisms had decided she too was fit to putrefy. But she shut such notions out of thinking, obsessed with yearning for the beautiful visions of life on other worlds which she had been promised. Where were they? Why could she only perceive this horrible, this revolting dungeon?

Because... Ah, but bliss, but miracle! Something sweet and delicious had been poured into her mandibles, restoring her strength. She strove to thank whoever had aided her at last, and could only whimper, but at least the sound was recognizable.

"Ugant... ?"

"Ah, so it was Ugant who reduced you to this plight!"

A booming voice, a waft of pheromones redolent of well-being and authority. Timidly she agreed.

"She sent you to spy on us, was that it?"

"Yes, yes! More food, more food!"

"Of course you shall have more! I'm appalled to find you in such a state because of what Ugant did! Help her out, quickly!"

Suddenly she was surrounded by familiar figures: Aglabec, ex-Cometaster, ex-Startoucher. She curled her limp mantle into a sketch for gratitude as they half led, half carried her upward, pausing now and then to offer more of the delicious liquor which had so revived her.

At last they reached the open air, under a clear sky

sown with stars. Weakly she raised a claw to indicate Stumpalong.

"I see the folk up yonder!" she declared. She did not, but she knew it was what her saviors expected.

There was a puff of excitement from the young people. Aglabec canceled it with a quick gesture.

"You believe at last?" he challenged Chybee.

"How could I not, after all the visions that have come to me?"

"Are you obliged to Ugant for them?"—in a stern commanding tone.

"Ugant? What I've been through, all my suffering, was due to her! You saved me, though! You saved me!"

"Then," said Aglabec with enormous satisfaction, "you must tell us what Ugant is planning, and all the ways in which we can forestall her frightful plot."

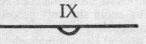

IX

But Aglabec did not begin his interrogation at once, as though afraid that Chybee's obedience might still be colored by excessive eagerness to please. He had her taken to the home of one of his followers, a certain Olgo. It was neither large nor well kept, but in comparison with the place where she had been incarcerated it was paradise. There she babbled of indebtedness while her sore mantle was tended and food and drink were meted out to her, enough to restore part of her lost bulk, but far from all.

This, though, was only half the treatment he had decided on. Much more important was the fact that by dark and by bright other of his disciples came to visit, and greeted her as one saved for the cause of truth, and sat by her telling wondrous stories about their mental voyages to the planets. Dimly she remembered there was a reason not to believe such yarns, but she was afraid to claw hold of it; she knew, though nobody had said so, that if she expressed the slightest doubt she would be returned to captivity.

Besides, the pheromones inciting to credulity were denser than ever, not only within the house but throughout the psychoplanetarist quarter. Docile under the impact of them, she listened passively as she heard about the vigorous inhabitants of Sunbride, reveling in the brilliance of the solar glare, absorbing and transmuting it until by willpower alone they could sculpture mountain ranges to amuse themselves . . . or hurl a giant rock on any reckless race that tried to bridge the spatial void.

Others told her of the ancient culture on Swiftyouth, so far advanced that bodies were scarcely necessary to them anymore. There, she learned, budding and death had long been obsolete; perfected minds could don and doff a physical envelope at whim.

Yet more marvels were recounted to her, concerning the giant planets each of which was itself a conscious being, the end-product of craws of years of evolution, so perfectly and so precariously adapted that a single seed from any other world might destroy them, and thus waste the fruit of an age-long study of the universe. (Dimly Chybee realized that this contradicted what she had been told at Hulgrapuk, but that of course was due to Imblot's heresy.) To such colossal beings even the inhabitants of their own moons were dangerous; therefore the latter had been taught, by channels of mental communication, to rest content with their own little spheres. Awed, yet determined to fulfill their several destinies, they had set about contacting intelligences more like themselves, using techniques the giant worlds had pioneered, with success in every case bar one: this world whose moon was dead.

"Our world!" Chybee whispered, and they praised her for her flawless understanding.

"Perhaps, in the very long ago," someone said, "our moon too was an abode of life. But arrogant fools down here must have sent a vessel thither. What else can account for it being barren, when none other of the solar family is so except the asteroids, which orbit too close to the sun?"

"Not even they, in one sense," someone else objected. "We know of life existing in hot gas-glouds, don't we? I think some of them make use of the asteroids, for purposes we dare not dream of!"

All the listeners murmured, "Very likely!"

And one of them added with a sigh, "What miracles must be taking place in the Major Cluster! What would I not give to eavesdrop on the feelings of a new-budded star!"

"Oh, yes!" whispered Chybee. "Oh, *yes!*"

They turned to her, their exudations sympathetic and inviting. Thus encouraged, she went on, "And to think that what Ugant and Hyge are planning could despoil it all!"

"Would you not work with us to stop them?" demanded her hostess, Olgo.

"Of course! I want to! It's my duty!"

A wave of satisfaction-odor rose from the company, and one who was near the entrance slipped away, shortly to return with Aglabec in high excitement.

"At last!" he said as he accepted the place of honor at the center of the bower. "I've been making inquiries about the situation at Hulgrapuk. It seems that the traitor Imblot has ensnared many folk there who should be wiser than a youngling like yourself. Yet you came hither, did you not, in search of truth?"

"I did!" Chybee confirmed excitedly.

"Well, you were guided to where I was, even though you failed to understand the reason. Now you've been shown the error of your ways, are you resolved to make amends?"

"With all my pith! I never dreamed what harm would stem from what Ugant and Hyge are doing!"

"And what exactly does that amount to?"

So she described what she had seen at the test site— the metal tube with its prong of fire, the huge floaters designed to lift it to the limits of the atmosphere, the instruments which reported on its behavior even when it was traveling faster than sound. At each new revelation the company uttered fresh gusts of horror, until by the end Chybee was dreadfully ashamed of her own words.

"You said they're close to success?" Aglabec demanded at last.

"Very close indeed!"

"That breeds with what I've been hearing recently."

The dream-leader pleated his mantle into a frown. "We must move against them before it's too late. Chybee, have you been in contact with Ugant or any of her associates since—well, since our meeting before last?"

There was a reason for his awkward turn of phrase; she was aware of the fact, but the reason itself eluded her. She uttered a vehement denial, and Olgo confirmed that at no time had she been away from the supervision of someone utterly trustworthy.

"Very well, then," Aglabec decided. "We must rely on you for a delicate mission. Presumably Ugant will be expecting you to make a report. You are to go back to the test site, but this time on our behalf, to lull the suspicions of those who work there. To make assurance doubly sure, I'll send you with a companion, supposedly someone you've converted to the scientists' views. Creez, I offer you a chance to redeem yourself!"

And Creez was he who had braggartly been known as Startoucher . . . and who voiced a question Chybee meant to.

"But how can we possibly conceal our true opinions?"

"I will give you a—a medicine," Aglabec said after a fractional hesitation. "It will suffice for a short time."

That too should have been significant, Chybee thought. Once again, though, the notion was elusive.

"Now pass the news," said Aglabec, rising. "At dawn tomorrow we shall strike a blow against the scientists such as it will take them a laq of years to recover from! By then, I trust, no one will any longer pay attention to their foolishness! You, Creez and Chybee, come with me, and receive your full instructions."

All the next dark the word spread among the psychoplanetarists, and the pool of pheromones in their quarter of Slah became tinged with violent excitement. Around dawn they started to emerge from their homes and move towards the test site, not in a concerted mass but in small groups, so as not to alert the authorities. The morning breeze today was very light, and few outsiders caught wind of what was happening.

Aglabec was not with them. He had declared that he was too well known and too easily recognizable.

Chybee and Creez, fortified with the "medicine" which

disguised pheromones, went in advance of the others. They were to announce an urgent report for Ugant or Hyge, which would require everyone working at the site to be called together. For so long the psychoplanetarists had merely talked instead of acting, Aglabec was convinced this simple stratagem would suffice to postpone any warning of the actual attack. And the nature of the latter was the plainest possible. The huge bladders being filled to raise the rocket contained fiercely inflammable gas; let but one firebrand fall among them, and the site would be a desert.

"Though of course," Aglabec had declared, "we only want them to yield to our threats, and—like you, Chybee—acknowledge that the popular will is against them."

With a nervous chuckle Creez had said, "I'm glad of that!"

And now he and Chybee were cresting the range of hills separating the city from the site, formerly a bank of the salt lake where Voosla had taken root. On the way she had repeatedly described for him what he must expect to see. But the moment she had a clear view from the top of the rise she stopped dead, trembling.

"What's wrong?" Creez demanded.

"It's changed," she quavered, looking hither and yon in search of something familiar. Where was the row of distorted trees along which Hyge's pride and joy had become a shining streak to the accompaniment of sudden thunder? Where was the monstrous cylinder itself, built of such a deal of costly metal, with its clever means of guidance warranted to thrive in outer space? Where was the control-house, which surely should have been visible from here?

Nothing of what she remembered was to be seen, save a mass of gigantic bladders swelling like live things in the day's new warmth, rising at the midpoint of the valley into a slowly writhing column tethered by ropes and nets.

"It looks as though they're actually going to try a shot into space!" Chybee whispered, striving to concentrate on her errand. The clean morning air was stirring buried memories, and they were discomforting.

"Then we have to hurry!"

"Yes—yes, of course! But where is everybody?"

"We must go and look," Creez declared, and urged her down the slope.

A moment later they were in the weirdest environment she had ever imagined, under a roof of colossal swollen globes that looked massive enough to crush them, yet swayed at every slightest touch of the breeze, straining at their leashes and lending the light an eerie, fearful quality, now brighter, now darker, according to the way it was reflected from each bladder to its neighbor.

"It's like being underwater!" Creez muttered.

"My weather-sense disagrees," Chybee answered curtly, fighting to maintain her self-control. "Listen! Don't I sense somebody?"

"Over there! Something's agitating the bladders!"

And, moments later, they came upon a work-team wielding nets and choppers, harvesting more and ever more full bladders to be added to the soaring column. One of them had incautiously collected so many, she risked being hoisted off her pads by a puff of wind.

Keeping up her pretense with all her might, Chybee hailed them.

"Is Ugant here, or Hyge? We have an urgent message!"

Resigning half her anti-burden to a colleague, the one who had so nearly soared into the sky looked her over.

"I remember you!" she said suddenly. "Weren't you here with Ugant a moonlong past?"

All that time ago? Chybee struggled more valiantly than ever to remember her promise to Aglabec.

"Is she here now? I have to talk to her!"

"Well, of course! Didn't you know? Today's the day for the trial launch—that is, if we turn out to have enough floaters for a really high lift, which is what we're working out right now. We got our first consignment of modified spores of the kind which ought to reproduce on Swift-youth, and the line-up of the planets is ideal for them to be carried there by light-pressure! Of course, we can't be certain things will all go off okay, but we're doing our utmost. Only there have been some nasty rumors going around, about crazy psychoplanetarists who'd like to wreck the shot."

"That's exactly what I've come to warn you about!" Chybee exclaimed, seizing her opening. "I've been among them for—well, ever since I last saw Ugant! Call everybody together, please, right away! I have important news!"

"Say, I recall Ugant mentioning that you'd agreed to go undercover for us," said another of the work-team. "But what about him?"—gesturing at Creez.

"It's thanks to him that I know what I do!" Chybee improvised frantically. Something was wrong. Something was changing her mind against her will. She was still thinner and lower than when she set off on Ugant's mission, but with regained well-being those buried memories were growing stronger . . . particularly now that she was clear of psychoplanetarist pheromones.

"Hurry!" she moaned. "Hurry, *please!*"

But they wouldn't. They didn't. With maddening slowness they debated what to do, and at last agreed to guide her and Creez to the control-house, whence messages could be sent faster by nervograp.

She was going to be too late after all, Chybee thought despairingly as she plodded after them under the canopy of translucent globes. Oh, to think that so much effort, so many hopes and ambitions must go to waste because—

Because Aglabec knows how to disguise the pheromones which otherwise would betray his true convictions.

Enlightenment overcame her. Suddenly she realized what was meant by being stardazzled.

She looked about her with a clear eye. They had reached the entrance platform of the control-house, whence Ugant was emerging with cries of excitement. Chybee ignored her. From here she could plainly see the way the bladders were humped, netful by netful, in a carefully planned spiral. Without being told she deduced that the first batch due for release must be that over there; then those; then those—and lastly those through which could now and then be glimpsed the shining metal of Hyge's cylinder.

And on the hills which she and Creez had lately crossed: Aglabec's disciples, surging this way like a sullen flood. They were passing flame from each to the next under a smear of smoke, igniting firebrands turn and turn about, seeking a vantage point from which to hurl them.

"But Aglabec promised—!" Creez exclaimed. Chybee cut him short.

"He lied! He's always lied to all his followers! He has a means to hide his lying, and he gave some to us for this mission! Ugant, forgive me, but they starved and tortured me until I couldn't help myself!"

Taken aback, the scientist said, "Starved? Tortured? Oh, it can't be true! I knew they were crazy, but surely even they—"

"No time!" Chybee shouted as Hyge too emerged from the control-house. "Everybody slack down to tornado status! *I mean now!*"

This drill was known to all the personnel from their test-firings. A single glance at the threat posed by the psychoplanetarists and their multiplying firebrands caused them to respond as though by mindless reflex, dragging Creez inside with them.

But, seizing one of the work-team's choppers, Chybee flung herself over the side of the platform and rushed back the way she had come.

Without realizing until she had an overview of the complete spiral, she had noticed how the bladders were lashed to pumplekins by clusters, each connected by only a single bond for the sake of lightness, and if she could sever just one of those ropes, one that was all-important, there was a thin, faint, tenuous chance that when Aglabec's crazed disciples began to fling their torches, then . . .

But which one? Where? She had imagined she fully understood the layout, yet she came to an abrupt halt, baffled and terrified. Had she wandered off course in her panic? All these groups of bladders looked alike, and all the ropes that tethered them—

A chance gust parted the dense globes and showed her the horde of attackers moving down the slope with grim determination, poising to toss their firebrands, heedless of any hurt that might come to them. Well, she had long craved vengeance on behalf of her friend Isarg; how could she do less than match their foolhardiness?

With sudden frantic energy she began to slash at every restraining rope in reach, and cluster after cluster of the bladders hurtled upward as though desperate to join the clouds.

To the psychoplanetarists perhaps it seemed that their prey was about to escape. At any rate, instead of padding purposefully onward they broke into a rush, and some of those at the rear, craving futile glory, threw their brands so that they landed among the others in the front ranks.

A reek of fury greeted the burns they inflicted, and many of the foremost spun around, yelling with pain. Later, Chybee found herself able to believe that that fortunate accident must have saved her life. At the moment, however, she had no time to reason, but frenziedly went on cutting rope after rope after rope...

Abruptly she realized the sky above was clear, but the attackers had recovered from their setback, and were once more advancing on the remaining floaters.

Flinging aside her chopper, she fled towards the control-house, her mind failing again as she exhausted her ultimate resources. Suddenly there was a dull roaring noise, and a brilliant flare, and heat ravaged her mantle and dreadful overpressure strained her tubules.

She slumped forward to seek what shelter was offered by a dip in the ground, welcoming her agony.

For one who had been a double traitor, it felt like just and proper punishment.

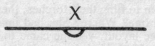

X

Piece by painful piece Chybee reconstructed her knowledge of the world. While being carried to a healing-house she heard a voice say, "She cut loose just enough of the bladders to create a fire-break. Naturally it's a setback, but it'll only mean a couple of moonlongs' extra work."

Later, while her burns were being tended: "A lot of the poor fools inhaled flame, or leaked to death because their tubules ruptured, or ulcerations on their mantles burst. But of course the updraft swept away the mutual reinforcement of their pheromones. Once they realized what a state they'd been reduced to, the survivors scattered, begging for help. Apparently they're ashamed of what they tried to do. It doesn't square with the perfect morality of these imaginary other worlds of theirs. So there's hope for them yet—or a good proportion, at any rate."

Chybee wanted to ask about their dream-leader, but for a long time she lacked the necessary energy to squeeze air past the edge of her mantle. By the time she could talk again, she found she was in the presence of distinguished well-wishers: Ugant, Wam, Glig, Airm, Hyge...

"What about Aglabec?" she husked. As one, they exuded anger and disappointment. At length Ugant replied.

"He's found a score of witnesses to certify that you came to him pleading for enlightenment, and that what he subjected you to was no more than the normal course of instruction all his disciples willingly undergo."

"It's a lie!" Chybee burst out, struggling to raise herself from the mosh-padded crotch she rested in.

"Sure it is," Glig the biologist said soothingly. "So are all the fables he's spun to entrap his dupes. But he defeated himself after a fashion. The 'medicine' he provided to disguise your exudates when you returned to the test site has been known to us for scores of years; it's based on the juice of the plant whose leaves I gave you. His version, though, doesn't only suppress one's own pheromones and protect against the effect of others'. It eventually breaks down the barrier between imagination and direct perception. No one can survive long after that stage sets in, and he's been using the stuff for years. Very probably he was already insane when he called out his followers to attack the test site—"

"He must have been," Airm put in. "Even though the shot was almost ready, his disciples weren't. If he'd waited a little longer, their madness might have been contagious!"

She ended with a shrug of relief.

"Insane or not, he mustn't be allowed to get away with what he did!" Chybee cried.

"Somehow I don't believe he will," said Wam with a mysterious air. "And I've come back specially from Hulgrapuk to witness the event that ought to prove his downfall."

"It's expected to occur not next dark, but the dark after that," Ugant said, rising. "By then you should be well enough to leave here. I'll send my scudder to collect you at sundown and bring you to my place. I rather think you're going to enjoy the show we have for you."

Turning to leave, she added, "By the way, you do know how grateful we all are, don't you?"

"And not just us," Airm confirmed. "The whole of Slah is in your debt, for giving us an excuse to clear out the pestilential lair of the psychoplanetarists. We've been flushing it with clean air for days now, and by the time we're done there won't be a trace of that alluring stench."

"But if Aglabec is still free—" Chybee said, confused.

"It isn't going to make the slightest difference."

At the crest of Ugant's home was an open bower where a good-quality telescope was mounted. Thither, on a balmy night under a sky clear but for stars and the normal complement of meteors, they conveyed Chybee, weak, perhaps scarred for life, but in possession of her wits again.

Not until they had plied her with the finest food and liquor that the house could boast did they consent to turn to the subject preying on her pith: the promised doom of Aglabec.

With infuriating leisureliness, after consulting a time-pulser hung beside the telescope, Ugant finally invited her to take her place at its ocular and stare at Swiftyouth.

"That's where we're going to send our spores," she said. "Before the end of summer, certainly, we shall have grown enough floaters, we shall have retested our star-seeker, we shall have enlarged and improved our driver. Once beyond the atmosphere, at a precisely calculated moment, the raw heat of the sun will expand and eventually explode a carefully aligned container, so that it will broadcast spores into the path Swiftyouth will follow as it reaches perihelion . . . Why, you're shaking! What in the world for?"

"I don't know!" came the helpless answer. "But . . . Well, just suppose we're wrong after all. Just suppose not all of what Aglabec teaches is complete invention! Do we have the right to put at risk creatures on another world?"

There was a pause. At length Ugant said grayly, "If there are any life-forms on Swiftyouth—and I admit that, without voyaging there, we can never be certain—then they are due for suffering worse than any we have been through. Be patient. Watch."

Not knowing precisely why, Chybee obeyed, and waited. And then, just as she was about to abandon the telescope with a cry of annoyance...

That tiny reddish disc changed to white, and shone out more brilliantly than half the stars.

"Congratulate your colleagues at the Hulgrapuk Observatory, Wam," said Ugant dryly. "They were most precise in their calculations."

"But what are you showing me?" demanded Chybee.

"The kind of proof we needed to destroy Aglabec," the scientist replied composedly. "We maintain a constant watch for massive bodies drifting into the system. Recently we spotted one larger than any on record, or more precisely a whole cluster of them, perhaps the nucleus of a giant comet which was stripped of its gas when passing by a hot white star, then whipped into the void again. At first we were afraid they might collide with us, but luckily... Well, you're seeing what saved us: the attraction of an outer planet. So how exactly is Aglabec going to account for the collision of Swiftyouth with not one meteorite but maybe half a score of them, each greater than the one that washed Voosla and half an ocean high into the hills?"

At that very moment the whitened disc of Swiftyouth redoubled in brilliance. Chybee drew back from the ocular and tried to laugh at the prospect of Aglabec's discomfiture.

But she could not, any more than she could explain why to her concerned companions. She only knew she was in mourning of a sudden, for all the marvelous and lovely beings on—or in—the other planets, whom she had known so briefly and who now, even to imagination, were lost for evermore.

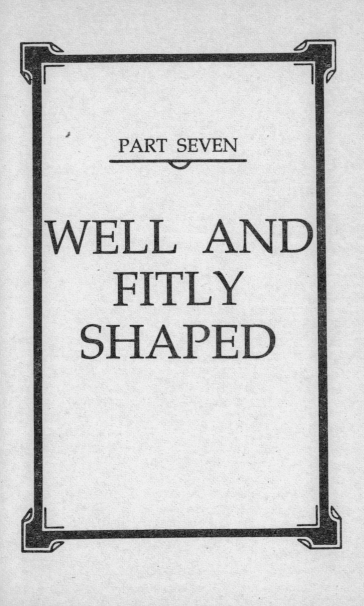

PART SEVEN

WELL AND FITLY SHAPED

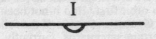

I

Even before the sun had broached the dawn horizon, warm breezes wafted over the launching site and made the laqs of gas-globes swell. The mission controllers revised their estimates of available lift to record levels, and congratulated one another on the accuracy of their weather-sense. All was set fair for the first piloted flight beyond the atmosphere, the first attempt to link a group of orbiting ecosystems into what might become a colony, a settlement, and finally a vehicle, a junq to sail the interstellar sea. Compared to this climactic venture, all that had gone before was trivial. The seeding of the moon, the fact that the spectra of Swiftyouth and Sunbride kept changing in amazing fashion since those planets had been sprayed with spores intended to assure the continuance of life after its home world met disaster—those were experiments whose results might well not become known until after the race responsible was extinct. Here, on the other claw, was an undertaking designed to ensure that its extermination was postponed.

Now, just so long as their chosen pilot didn't let them down...

Karg was elated. He felt the eyes of history upon him. Soon his name would join the roster of the famous; it would be coupled with those of Gveest, Yockerbow, even Jing—

Stop! Danger! He was over the safe limit of euphoria, and took action to correct it. He had been adjusting to his life-supports since sundown. Years of experience underwater had accustomed him to similar systems; moon-longs of practice had prepared him for this particular version. Nonetheless it had taken a fair while before he persuaded it to eliminate from the cylinder's sealed atmosphere all trace of the pheromones that beset the launch site, redolent of doubt about himself, and he must have overcompensated.

Yet there were excellent reasons for choosing a male to venture into orbit first. Had it not been long accepted that legendary Gveest's revision of the folk's genetic heritage lacked certain safeguards, currently being supplied with all possible expedition? Was it not past a doubt that radiation or even minor stress might trigger the masculinizing effect again? Which of the mission controllers would risk such a doom falling on their own buds—?

Unfair! Unfair! They were the latest in line of those who for generations had dedicated themselves to ensuring that the folk of Slah should benefit to the full from the bequest of that astonishing pioneer of genetic control. Without such experience there could have been no hauqs, no life-supports in space or underwater . . . and Karg's epoch-making flight today would have been impossible.

Even so, there were many who resented it!

He struggled to dismiss such thoughts, and failed. What was one to make of people who knew their world might be destroyed without warning, yet scoffed at any attempt to seek refuge in space, called it foolish to obey the dictates of evolution, held that the only moral good consisted in multiplying the folk as much as possible? Oh, they were glad that the astronomers kept constant watch, for the whole world knew they had been right about the comethead that crashed on Swiftyouth, and nobody in Karg's lifetime had tried to revive the sick and crazy teaching about "planet people" which their forebudders had swallowed—and been poisoned by. On the other claw, if Swiftyouth's gravity had been inadequate, or if it had been elsewhere in its orbit, then the folk of today might be struggling back from the swamps again.

But the past was dead, regardless of how vividly it might survive in one's imagination, and he was due for a ground check. He tensed his right foremantle, his left side being reserved for on-hauq maintenance. The hauq herself was a very refined version, maybe excessively so; she now and then responded to casual pheromones and did her mindless best to please her pilot without asking permission . . .

Well, so did scudders sometimes. Nobody could expect a trailblazing flight like this to be a simple task.

His pressure on the farspeaker stimulated its pith and woke it to signal mode on the correct wavelength. Its response was prompt. Would it perform as well in space? No good saying others like it had done so; never before had a living person been carried into orbit...

"Karg? You register?"

"Clearly! How long until lift-off?"

"Full gas-globe expansion predicted imminently. Final confirmation of system status! Body cushioning?"

Karg reviewed every point at which his mantle and torso were braced by the conformable shape of the far tougher hauq, and announced, "Fine!"

"Propulsion mass and musculator pumps?"

There were no complaints from the docile creatures responsible for his maneuvers in orbit. He said so.

"Respiration?"

"Sourgas level normal."

"Pheromone absorption?"

Traces of his own exudations were still, he feared, leaking back to him before the purifiers could cancel them. But he had endured worse underwater, and it seemed like a trifling matter to complain about.

"Seems satisfactory so far."

The distant voice—he assumed it must belong to Yull, second-in-command at the launch site, but there was a degree of unreality about any communication by audio alone—took on a doubtful note. "Only 'so far'?"

He turned it with a joke. "How far have I got?"

However, there was no amusement in the response. "You realize we can't abort after you leave the ground?"

"Of course I do! Next is remote readings, correct?"

"Ah...Yes: we report normal signals. Mutual?"

"Confirm."

"Any unusual textures or odors that might indicate potential navigation or orientation errors?"

"None."

"Unusual coloration of any life-supports?"

"None." Though it was hard to judge under these luminants, selected not so much because they were known to perform well in low pressure and zero gravity as because they tolerated their own wastes in a closed environment.

"We copy automatic reports confirming subjective assessment. All set for release. Clasp your branch!"

There was of course no branch. Yull was trying to sound sociable. Karg couched his answer in equally light tones.

"The next signal you receive will be from our outside broadcast unit. A very long way outside!"

"It's a big universe," came the dry response. "Very well; as of the mark, you're on your own. Ready?"—to someone else. "Confirm! And *mark*!"

"Now I'm just a passenger," said Karg, and waited for the sky to let him through.

To make this voyage possible scores-of-scores-of-scores of folk at Slah and in its hinterland had gone without for generations ... though never without food, for the effects of starvation, voluntary or not, were much too horrible. Rather, they had resigned themselves and their budlings to less than their share of the wonders of the modern world: houses that thought, scudders and floaters, falqon-mail that flew from continent to continent where pitchens had only skimmed, communications that no longer called for nervograps, recordimals offering faithful transcriptions of the greatest thinkers and entertainers, newsimals and scentimals and haulimals, and the rest.

It was the tradition of their ancestors, and they were proud to keep it up.

Elsewhere the pattern had been otherwise. But that was the greatest source of conflict in the world today.

Nothing at all, however, could have prevented the citizens from gathering to marvel at the outcome of their self-denial. As a result of their efforts, gas-globes sprawled not just across the valley whence the launch took place, but over hill and dale and out to artificial islands in the nearest bay, wherever pumplekins might root to fill them with wetgas so light it bore up them, and their tethers, and a burden eloquent of eventual salvation.

Thanks to their hard work, too, Karg was promised survival and return. It had been their forebudders who devised means to break out into the vacuum of space; then they had found themselves short of essential raw materials. Ashamed to cheat their ignorant cousins on Glewm, the southern continent, out of what they did not so far know the worth of, they had resorted to their ancestors' domain, reinventing means to keep mind and pith together in mid-ocean, to locate themselves beneath dense cloud a season's trip from home, and ultimately to visit the sea-bed and supervise the work their creatures were undertaking there on their behalf. All the live tools they had bred to aid them in this venture had been exploited by the scientists who now were offering up Karg as a challenge to the stars.

The moon sparkled whether full or new. Comets were common; one had devastated Swiftyouth. Other rocks from out of nowhere had struck Stolidchurl and Steadyman, their impact sometimes bright enough to see without a telescope. Pure chance so far had saved the folk from another such disaster as created Slah.

All this they fervently believed. Whereas the inhabitants of other lands, not beneficiaries of what had been learned by digging Slah's foundations, reserved the right to doubt, and—almost as though they still accepted crazy Aglabec's ideas—acted as if their planet could endure forever.

That, though, the universe did not permit. The folk of Slah bore the fact in mind as they waited for Karg to take leave of this petty orb.

First on the smooth mirror of the water they cut loose the initial score of bladders. Up they went! A five-score bunch came next, and hoisted far into the clear blue autumn morning. Each batch was larger than the one before, and as the mass of them gathered it seemed that land and sea were uttering messages of hope about the future. Across the beach, across the nearer hills, then across the valley of the launch site, the sequence flowed without a flaw. This was the hugest skein of gas-globes ever lofted, almost a padlonglaq in total height.

At last they stirred the metal cylinder that held not only Karg but the drivers which would blast him beyond the atmosphere, along with creatures designed to keep him alive and in touch, navigate him to his rendezvous, assist his work and bring him back a moonlong hence.

But most of his voyage the watchers would not witness. No one was sure as yet what continent the vessel would be over when its drivers fired. As for its time and place of landing . . .

Oh, but it was a privilege to be present at the launch and see the countless bladders soaring up! (Countless? But they were counted, and farspeakers reported on the state of every single one of them during their brief lives. At a certain height they must explode, and leave the cylinder to fall, and orient, and rise again on jets of vivid fire.)

Through transparent ports Karg watched the world descend, much too busy to be frightened, never omitting to react to what his fellow creatures told him as they drifted towards the moon. It was changing color almost by the day as the life-forms sown there adapted to naked space and fearful radiation. *And what they have done*, he thought, *the folk will do . . . Albeit we may change, we shall endure!*

In a while he was looking down at clouds over Prutaj, that other continent he had never set pad on, where it was held that the hard work of Slah was misconceived, where present gratification was prized more than the future survival of the species.

And then the meteor struck.

II

Before the impact of the Greatest Meteorite, when folk debated concerning centers of learning and research, one was acknowledged to stand eye and mandibles above the rest. But Chisp was gone, save for what pastudiers could retrieve from the mud-slides which had buried it.

Now there was argument. Some held for Slah, as hewing truest to the principles of the past. Some still named Hulgrapuk, and certainly that city, though in decline, did not lack for dedicated scholars. When it came to innovation, though, there was no contest. Out of Fregwil on

Prutaj flowed invention following insight following theory, and almost every theory was audacious, so that students from around the globe came begging for a chance to sit by the pads of those who had made its name world-famous.

And once each lustrum it was not just students who converged on it, but sightseers, merchants, news-collectors . . . for that was when the newest and latest was published to the admiring world. The tradition dated back five-score years. Much interest had then been aroused by the identification of solium in the atmosphere: so rare an element, it had previously been detected only in the spectrum of the sun. An intercontinental meeting of astronomers and chemists being convoked, it was overwhelmed by eager layfolk anxious to find out what benefit such a discovery might bring.

Yet most pronounced themselves disappointed. This news was of small significance to them in their daily lives. What the public mainly liked was something they could marvel at. What the scientists wanted was to attract the best and brightest of the next generation into research. Accordingly, every quarter-score of years since then the staid professors—and some not so staid—had mobilized to mount a spectacle for strangers. Indulgently they said, "We are all as budlings when we confront the mysteries of the universe, and a touch of juvenile wonderment can do no harm!"

Those who made a handsome living out of converting their experiments into practical devices agreed without reserve. And those who were obliged by their knowledge to accept that this touchy, fractious, immature species was unlikely to attain adulthood because the whole planetary system was orbiting into the fires of the Major Cluster—they resigned themselves to compliance on the grounds that there was nothing better to be done.

This time the Fregwil Festival of Science was nicknamed "The Sparkshow," because it was devoted to sparkforce, that amazing fluid known to permeate stormclouds and nerve-pith alike, which held out promise of an infinity of new advances over and above the miracles it had already performed. And the name on everybody's mantle-rim was Quelf.

* * *

Sometimes when voyaging abroad citizens of Prutaj were tactless enough to boast about their superior way of life at home. On being challenged to offer evidence, as often as not they invoked Fregwil as a perfect symbol of the ideals to which Prutaj was dedicated. Its university, along with the healing-house from which it had originally sprung, dominated the city from its only high peak, and looked down on the local administrative complex, thereby exemplifying the preference Prutaj gave to knowledge over power; besides, it was surrounded by huge public parks where the folk might bring their young to enjoy the sight, the smell, the sound, even the touch and taste, of plants and animals that otherwise might long ago have disappeared from this continent at once so wealthy and so well controlled. (Which met, as often as not, with the retort: "So what? We have that stuff underpad anyhow!" And it was hard to tell whether they were jealous of Prutaj's progress, or despiteful of it.)

Sometimes, though, foreigners came to see for themselves, and departed duly abashed...

Exactly that was happening today. The parks were crammed with sparkforce exhibits which had attracted visitors from half the world, including a delegation from Slah: new ways of carrying messages, new means to control the growth of perfect primary and secondary plants, new and better styles in housing, feeding, moving, curing... Some objected, saying all they found was change for the sake of change. More stood awestricken, particularly those making a first visit to Fregwil. Now and then mongers of overseas news tried to distract the crowds with reports about Karg's spaceflight, but they were generally ignored. Almost everybody took it for granted that the most important and successful research in the world was happening right here at Fregwil. If ever it did become necessary to quit the planet, then it would be Fregwil scientists who found the way.

And the most amazing demonstration was to come by dark.

There was a little ceremony first. Quelf took station on an artificial mound to be invested with the baldric of the Jingfired, a simple garland of phosphorescent leaves such as anyone might gather in a private garden. This provoked hilarity among the onlookers, shaming to her and her nominee Albumarak, and quickly reproved by Doyenne Greetch, who reminded those in range of the loudeners of the antiquity of this custom. But who in this generation, without visiting Glewm, or maybe the hinterland of Slah, could understand how differently their ancestors had lived? Albumarak, for one, enjoyed the symbolism of the ritual, devoid though it might be of historical authenticity.

At any rate she strove to. It was the least she could offer in return for Quelf's generosity in nominating her at so early an age as a candidate in her eventual turn for the status of becoming Jingfired. Whole families had gambled their possessions, and even the future of their offspring, on the chance of "being nominated."

And it had overtaken her although her parents scorned her. She was rebellious, so they called her stupid . . .

Quelf disagreed. This prestigious neurophysicist had chanced across one of a quarter-score of recordimals which Albumarak had turned loose (she could not afford more, but she had modified them to ensure that they went about stinking good and loud!) to publicize a disagreement with her teachers. Quelf cared little for the argument—she said later it was clever but trivial—but she admired the neatness of the programing, and decided to enroll Albumarak among her students.

So here she was, doing her best not to seem bored even though the ceremony was going on for an awfully long time.

Eventually her attention was distracted by the shrill cry of yet another newsmonger announcing the launch of a piloted spaceship, and she found herself shuddering. At Fregwil the received opinion about such undertakings was the converse of the view the late Professor Wam had imposed at Hulgrapuk. Here it was dogmatically asserted that all preparations to meet a future catastrophe were pointless. No means existed to turn aside such another celestial missile as the Greatest Meteorite. However, if the next one were no larger, then at least some people would survive, conscious of the fact that there was nothing they could have done to fend off the disaster. If it were far bigger, nobody would be left to recriminate. As for lesser meteorites, thousands were falling every day, and patently no precautions could be taken against those because they were far too numerous. The folk of Prutaj were smugly proud of their acceptance of such arguments, and flattered themselves that they were being realistic.

As for escaping into space, out there either radiation or the lack of gravity was sure to kill any creature more advanced than a lowly plant, while dreams of substituting for the latter by spinning a huge hollow globe were countered with calculations showing how much it would cost in time, effort and materials to construct even the smallest suitable vessel. The figures were daunting; most layfolk accepted them without question. Besides, there was one additional consideration which weighed more with Albumarak than all the rest: how, demanded the psychologists at Fregwil, could anybody contemplate fleeing into space and abandoning the rest of the species to their fate? Recollection of their callousness would drive the survivors insane...or, if it did not, then they would have forfeited their right to be called civilized.

Albumarak concurred entirely. She could not imagine anyone being so cold-ichored. And yet—and yet, at the very least, this pilot must be brave...

Abruptly she realized that the ceremony was over, and it was time for the demonstration which everybody was awaiting. Hastily, for she had a minor part to play in it, she made her way to Quelf's side. By now it was full dark, and a layer of low cloud hid the moon and stars and the ceaseless sparkling of meteors. Moreover the nearby luminants were being masked, to render the spectacle yet more impressive. The crowd, which had been chattering and moving restlessly, quieted as Doyenne Greetch introduced Quelf over booming loudeners.

After a few formalities, the neurophysicist launched into the burden of her brief address.

"All of us must be familiar with nervograps, whose origin predated the Greatest Meteorite. Many of us now benefit, too, from sparkforce links, which carry that all-pervading fluid from pullstone generators like the ones you can see yonder"—her left claw extended, and the crowd's eyes turned as one—"or the more familiar flash-plants, which many people now have in their homes. And we've learned that there is a certain loss of sparkforce in transmission. In some cases we can turn that loss to our advantage; anyone who has raised tropical fruit in mid-winter thanks to sparkforce heaters knows what I mean by that! But in most cases this has been a serious draw-back. And the same holds for communications; over a long circuit, messages can be garbled by system noise, and to ensure accuracy we have to install repeaters, not invariably reliable.

"That age is over, thanks to the hard work and inge-nuity of our research team! We can now transmit both simple sparkforce, and messages as well, with negligible loss!"

Some of the onlookers had heard rumors of this break-through; others, though, to whom it was a complete sur-prise, uttered shouts of gleeful admiration. Quelf preened a little before continuing.

"On the slope behind me there's a tower. Perhaps some of you have been wondering what it is. Well, it's a device for generating artificial lightning. It's safely shielded, of course. But we now propose to activate it, using a spark-force flow that will traverse a circuit more than five score-of-scores of padlonglaqs in length, using only those few generators you can see right over there. Are we ready?"

"Just a moment!" someone shouted back. "We're not quite up to working pressure."

"Well, then, that gives me time to emphasize what's most remarkable about the circuit we've constructed," Quelf went on. "Not only is it the longest ever laid; part of it runs underwater, part through desert, part through ice and snow within the polar circle! Nonetheless, it func-tions just as though it were entirely in country like this park. We all look forward to the benefits this discovery must entail!"

"I could name some people who aren't exactly over-joyed," muttered Presthin, who stood close enough to Albumarak for her to hear. She was the goadster of the giant snowrither that had laid the arctic portion of the circuit. Many of her ancestors had been members of the Guild of Couriers in the days before nervograps and farspeakers, and she regarded modern vehicles, even sno-writhers, as a poor substitute for the porps her forebud-ders had pithed and ridden. She was blunt and crotchety, but Albumarak had taken a great liking to her.

Right now, however, she had no time to reply, for the

ready signal had been given, and Quelf was saying, "It gives me much pleasure to invite the youngest participant in our researches to close the circuit! Come on, Albumarak!"

To a ripple of applause she advanced shyly up the mound. Quelf ceded her place at the loudeners, and she managed to say, "This is indeed a great honor. Thank you, Quelf and all my colleagues . . . oh, yes, and if you look directly at the flash you may be dazzled. You have been warned!"

She stepped forward on to the flashplant tendril through which this end of the circuit was completed. At once the park was lit as bright as day. A clap of local thunder rolled, and a puff of sparkforce stink—due to a triple molecule of sourgas—assailed the watchers.

After an awed pause, there came a storm of cheers. Quelf let it continue a few moments, then called for quiet.

"But that's only part of the demonstration we have for you!" she declared. "In addition to the power circuit, we also have a message link, and in a moment you'll get the chance to inspect it for yourselves, and even to send a signal over it, if you have someone at its far end you'd like to get in touch with. The far end, in fact, is half this continent away, at Drupit! And from Drupit, on receipt of a go signal, one of the people who worked on the northernmost stretch of the message link will tell us the very latest news, without repeaters! Watch for it on the display behind me. Are we ready? Yes? Albumarak!"

Again she closed the circuit, this time using a smaller and finer linkup. There was a pause. It lasted so long, a few people voiced the fear that something had gone wrong.

Something had, but not at Fregwil nor at Drupit.

At long last the display began to show the expected symbols, and some of the onlookers recited them aloud:

"METEORITE BRINGS DOWN PILOTED SPACECRAFT—BELIEVED CRASHED IN CENTRAL UPLANDS—RESCUE SEARCH UNDER WAY!"

Before the last word had come clear, someone giggled, and within moments the crowd was caught up in gusts of mocking merriment. Even Quelf surrendered her dignity for long enough to utter a few sympathetic chuckles.

"You're not laughing," Presthin murmured to Albumarak.

"Nor are you," she answered just as softly.

"No. I've been in the uplands at this season. It's bad for the health. And if nothing else, that flier must be brave. Foolhardy and misguided, maybe. Nonetheless—!"

"I know exactly what you mean. But I don't suppose there's anything that we can do."

"No. Not until he's spotted, anyway. At least they've stopped laughing; now they're cheering again. Quelf's beckoning. You'd better go and pretend you're as pleased as she is, hadn't you?"

III

The meteorite might well not have massed more than one of Karg's own pads or claws, but the fury of its passage smashed air into blazing plasma. Its shock-wave ripped half the gas-globes asunder, twisted and buffeted the cylinder worse than a storm at sea, punished Karg even through its tough protective walls with a hammer-slam of ultrasonic boom. Gasping, he wished indeed he had a branch to cling to, for the conviction that overcame his mind was primitive and brutal: *I'm going to die!*

Spinning, he grew dizzy, and it was a long while before an all-important fact began to register. He was *only* spinning. The cylinder was not tumbling end over end. So a good many of the gas-globes must be intact, though he had no way of telling how many; the monitors which should have been automatically issuing reports to him, as well as to mission control and its outstations scattered across one continent and three oceans, were uttering nonsense.

Was he too low to activate the musculator pumps intended for maneuvering in space? They incorporated a reflex designed to correct just such an axial rotation, but if the external pressure were too high...Giddiness was making it hard to think. He decided to try, and trust to luck.

And the system answered: reluctantly, yet as designed.

The cylinder steadied. But beneath the hauq on which he lay were bladders containing many score times his body-mass of reactive chemicals. If they sprang a leak, his fate would be written on the sky in patterns vaster and brighter than any meteor-streak. After establishing that all fuel-pressures were in the normal range, he relaxed a fraction, then almost relapsed into panic as he realized he could not tell whether he was floating or falling. Sealed in the cylinder, he was deprived of normal weather-sense, and the viewports were blinded by dense cloud. Suppose he was entering a storm! He could envisage much too clearly what a lightning-strike might do to the remaining gas-globes.

If only there were some way of jettisoning his explosive fuel . . . ! The giant storage bladders were programed to empty themselves, more or less according to the density of air in which the driver fired, and then when safe in vacuum expel whatever of their contents might remain. After that, they were to fold tight along the axis of the cylinder, so as not to unbalance it, and await the high temperature of reentry, whereupon they would convert into vast scoops and planes capable of resisting heat that could melt rock, and bring the cylinder to a gentle touch-down.

But this was not the sort of reentry foreseen by the mission controllers.

Karg's air had begun to stink of his own terror. Frantically he forced the purifiers into emergency mode, squandering capacity supposed to last a moonlong in the interests of preserving his sanity. Then the clouds parted, and he saw what lay below.

He hung about two padlonglaqs above a valley full of early snow, patched here and there with rocky crags but not a hint of vegetation. It was his first view of such a landscape, for he had spent all his life in coastal regions where winter was short and mild, but he knew he must be coming down in the desolate highlands of Prutaj.

Was there any hope that the wind might bear him clear of this continent where the achievements of Slah were regarded with contempt? Noting how rapidly the bitter frost of fall cut his lift, he concluded not, and chill struck his pith, as cruel as though he were not insulated from the outer air.

Striving to reassure himself, he said aloud, "The folk of Prutaj aren't savages! Even in their remotest towns people must have heard about my flight, officials may be willing to help me get back home—"

A horrifying lurch. More of the bladders had burst, or maybe a securing rope had given way. A vast blank snow-slope filled the groundward port. He could not help but close his eye.

The cylinder had been swinging pendulum-fashion beneath the remaining gas-globes. Loss of the topmost batch dropped it swiftly towards a blade-keen ridge of still-bare rock, against whose lee a deep soft drift had piled. A chance gust caught it; swerving, it missed the ridge, but touched the snow. Drag sufficed to outdo the wind, and it crunched through the overlying glaze of ice. Absorbed, accepted, it sank in, and the last gas-globes burst with soft reports.

But the driver-fuel did not explode.

In a little while Karg was able to believe that it was too cold to be a threat any longer. That, though, was not the end of the danger he was in. His hauq, and the other creatures which shared the cylinder, had been as carefully adapted to outer space as its actual structure. They were supposed to absorb heat—not too much, but precisely enough—from the naked sun, store it, and survive on it while orbiting through the planet's shadow. As soon as the mandibles of the ice closed on them they began to fail. That portion of the hauq's bulk which kept the exit sealed shrank away, and the sheer cold that entered made him cringe.

Also, but for the sighing of the wind and creaks from the chilling cylinder, there was total silence.

He sought in vain for any hint of folk-smell. Even a waft of smoke would have been welcome, for he knew that in lands like these some people managed to survive by using fire—another wasteful Prutaj habit. He detected none. Moreover, now that the pressure inside and out had equalized, he had normal weather-sense again, and it warned of storms.

He wanted to flee—flee anywhere—but he was aware

how foolish it would be to venture across unknown territory rendered trackless by the snow. No, he must stay here. If all else failed, he could eat not only his intended rations but some of the on-hauq secondary plants. He might well last two moonlongs before being rescued...at least, so he was able to pretend for a while.

By dawn the overcast had blown away, and the next bright was clear and sunny. But though he searched the sky avidly for a floater or soarer that might catch sight of his crashed spacecraft, he saw none, and the air remained intensely cold. Shortly before sunset the clouds returned, and this time they heralded another fall of snow.

As Karg retreated for shelter inside the cylinder, he found he could no longer avoid thinking about the risk of freezing to death before he starved.

Next bright he was already too stiff to venture out. Little by little he began to curse himself, and the mission controllers, and his empty dreams of being one day remembered alongside Gveest and Jing.

Then dreams of another kind claimed him, and he let go his clawgrip on reality.

For the latest of too many times Albumarak muttered, "Why couldn't he have crashed where a floater could get to him?"

Perched forward of her in the snowrither's haodah, empty but for the two of them, some hastily grafted warm-plants, and a stack of emergency supplies, Presthin retorted, "We don't even know he's where we're heading for! Slah could be wrong about the point where the meteor hit—our wind-speed estimates might be off—someone may have calculated the resultant position wrongly anyhow...Not *that* way, you misconceived misbudded miscegenate!"

She was navigating through a blizzard by dead reckoning, and had to ply her goad with vigor to keep their steed on course. Like all the folk's transport, snowrithers had been forcibly evolved, from a strain naturally adapted to polar climate and terrain, but the original species had only spread into its ecological niche during the comparatively recent Northern Freeze, and despite expert pithing this beast, like its ancestors, would have preferred to follow a spoor promising food at the end of its journey.

"Now I've got a question," Presthin went on, peering through the forward window, on which snow was settling faster than the warmplants could melt it. "And it's a bit more sensible than yours. I want to hear why you volunteered to come with me! No guff about your 'moral duty,' please! *I* think you're here for the same reason I am. You want to see one of these famous space-cylinders, and there aren't apt to be any of them grown on our side of the world!"

"That has nothing to do with it! Anyway, they aren't grown! They're—well—cast, or forged, or something," Albumarak concluded lamely.

"Hah! Well, it's not because you're so fond of my company, that's for sure. Then it must be because you want to get out of Quelf's claw-clutch for a while."

"That's part of it"—reluctantly.

"Only part? Then what can the rest be?"

Albumarak remained silent, controlling her exudations. How could she explain, even to unconventional Presthin, the impulse that had overcome her after she heard the crowd at Fregwil greet the failure of Karg's mission with scornful jeers? Suddenly she had realized: she didn't believe that a person willing to risk his or her own life in hope of ensuring the survival of the species could truly be as nasty as her teachers claimed. So she wanted to meet one, well away from Quelf and all her colleagues.

Of course, if she admitted as much, and they didn't find him, or if when they did he were already dead, as was all too likely, Presthin's coarse sense of humor might induce her to treat the matter as a joke. Albumarak had never liked being laughed at; mockery had been one of her parents' chief weapons against their budlings.

Nonetheless she was bracing herself to disclose her real motive, when Presthin almost unperched her by jerking the snowrither to a convulsive halt.

Why? The blizzard had not grown fiercer; on the contrary, they had topped a rise and suddenly emerged under a clear evening sky.

"Look!" the goadster shouted. "They steered us to the right place after all!"

Across the next valley, on a hillside whose highest and steepest slope, still snow-free bar a thin white powdering, caught the last faint gleam of daylight: the multicolored rags and tatters of burst gas-globes.

"Just in time," Presthin muttered. "By dark we could have missed it!"

Inside the cylinder the luminants were frosted and everything was foul with drying ichor. At first they thought their mission had been futile anyway, for they could find no sign of Karg. Presthin cursed him for being such a fool as to wander away from his craft. And then they realized he had only grown crazy enough to slash open the body of his hauq and burrow into it for warmth. It was long dead, and so within at best another day would he have been.

IV

Ever since Karg's arrival at Fregwil the university's healing-house had been besieged by sensation-seekers. Over and over it had been explained that the pilot would for long be too weak to leave his bower, and even when he recovered only scientists and high officials might apply to meet him. The crowds swelled and dwindled; nonetheless, as though merely looking at the place where he lay gave them some obscure satisfaction, their number never fell below ten score. Some of those who stood vainly waiting were local; most, however, were visitors to the Festival of Science, which lasted a moonlong and was not yet over.

Now and then Quelf graciously consented to be interviewed by foreign news-collectors, and took station in the nearby park behind a bank of efficient loudeners. The questions were almost always the same, but the neurophysicist's answers were delivered with no less enthusiasm each time. She was positively basking in this welter of publicity, though of course she maintained that her sole

ambition was to promote the fame and well-being of Prutaj
in general and Fregwil in particular.

Certainly she missed no opportunity of boasting about
her city and its skills. For example, to someone making
the obvious inquiry about Karg's physical health, she
would describe how frost had ruptured many of his tubules and he might lose his right pad, and then continue:
"Luckily, as you know, we now have a loss-free sparkforce lead all the way to Drupit, so when one of our
ultramodern snowrithers brought him there, a local physician was able to apply penetrative heating to the affected
tissues. Now we're attempting to regenerate his damaged
nerve-pith, too."

Whereupon someone would invariably ask, "Has he
regained full normal consciousness?"

"No, I'm afraid he's still dreamlost, though there are
signs of lucidity. When he does recover, by the way, the
first thing we shall want to know is whether he still feels
the way he used to about the respective merits of what
they do at Slah with their resources, and what we do with
ours this side of the ocean. I think his views may well
have changed since his unreliable toy fell out of the sky!"

Cue for sycophantic laughter...

As Quelf's nominee for Jingfired status, Albumarak
was bound to dance permanent attendance on her, but
the duty was becoming less and less bearable. Today,
listening to the latest repetition of her stale gibes, feeling
the change in air-pressure which harbingered bad weather,
she wished the storm would break at once and put an end
to the interview.

If only Presthin had not gone home... The goadster
had been persuaded to accompany her and Karg to Fregwil, and spent a couple of grumpy days being introduced
to city officials and other notables. Suddenly, however,
she announced she'd had her mawful of this, and returned
to her usual work with the snowrither, surveying the trade-
routes which kept the highland towns supplied in winter
and making sure that they were passable.

In the pleasant warmth of Fregwil, Albumarak found
it almost impossible to recapture in memory the bitter
chill of the valley where Karg had crashed. How could
anybody want to be there, rather than here? There was,
she realized glumly, an awful lot she didn't yet understand

about people. Worst of all, she had not yet had a chance to fulfill the purpose which had induced her to join Presthin's rescue mission. All the time she had been in company with Karg, he had been unconscious or dreamlost, and since he had been brought here she had not been allowed to see him. Nobody was, apart from Quelf, a few of her associates, and the regular medical staff.

Wind rustled the nearby trees; the air-pressure shifted again, very rapidly, and people on the fringe of the crowd began to move away in search of shelter. With a few hollow-sounding apologies Quelf brought her public appearance to an end just as the first heavy drops pounded down.

"Do you need me any more right now?" Albumarak ventured.

"Hm? Oh—no, not until first bright tomorrow. Come to think of it, you could do with some time off. You don't seem to have recovered properly from the strain of bringing Karg back. Actually meeting someone who's prepared to abandon the rest of us to our fate is a considerable shock, isn't it?"

Albumarak recognized another of Quelf's stock insults, which the curtailment of today's interview had prevented her from using. But she judged it safest to say nothing.

"Yes, get along with you! Go have some fun with young'uns of your own age. Enjoy your dark!"

And the famous neurophysicist was gone, trailing a retinue of colleagues and admirers.

Dully Albumarak turned downslope, making for a branchway that would take her into the lower city, but with no special destination in mind. She had few friends. Some of her fellow students cultivated her acquaintance, but she knew it was because of her association with Quelf, not for her own sake, so she avoided them as much as possible. Now and then, and particularly since her return from the highlands, she found herself wishing for the old days when she could afford to do outrageous things in order to annoy her family. But she had not yet decided to risk trying that again, for Quelf would never be so tolerant... How strange to think of her parents as tolerant, when a year ago she would have sworn they were cruel and repressive!

She was aware of a sort of revolution going on within her. Attitudes she had taken for granted since budling-hood were changing without her willing it. It was like having to endure a private earthquake. She had been daz-zled by the idea that one day she too could be Jingfired; she was growing into the habit of behaving herself ap-propriately. But now she was constantly wondering: do I really want it after all?

"Excuse me!"

A voice addressed her in an unfamiliar accent. She turned to see a she'un not much older than herself.

"Yes?"—more curtly than she intended.

"Aren't you Albumarak, who helped to rescue Karg?"

It was pointless to deny the fact. Any number of strangers recognized her nowadays.

"My name is Omber. I'm from the space-site at Slah."

Albumarak's interest quickened. She knew that a del-egation of scientists had arrived a few days ago, to take their pilot home and negotiate for recovery of his cylinder. But this was the first time she had met one of them.

"Ah! I suppose you've been to visit Karg, then."

"They won't let us!" was the astonishing response.

"What?"

"Literally! Not even Yull—she's my chief, second-in-command of the entire project and the senior member of our group—not even she has been allowed to see him yet. Do you have any idea why?"

"This is the first I've heard about it!" Albumarak de-clared.

"Really?" Omber was taken aback. "Oh...Oh, well, then I won't trouble you any further. But I did rather assume—"

With rising excitement Albumarak interrupted. "No, I assure you! I'm horrified! What possible reason can they have to stop Karg's friends from visiting him, even if he isn't well enough to talk yet?"

"I'm not exactly a friend of his," Omber said. "I only met him once or twice during his training. If it were just a matter of myself, I wouldn't be surprised. But Yull...! How is he, really? I suppose you've seen him recently?"

"They won't let me see him either," Albumarak an-swered grimly. "They didn't let Presthin, come to that."

"Presthin—? Oh, yes: the goadster! You mean not even

she . . . ? This is ridiculous! Excuse me; one doesn't mean
to be impolite to one's host city, but it is, isn't it?"

"It's incredible!"

"You don't suppose . . . No, I oughtn't even to say it."

"Go ahead," Albumarak urged.

Omber filled her mantle. "You don't suppose he's being
submitted to some sort of experimental treatment, and
it's going wrong? We can't find out! Not many people
here care to talk to us, and the people from our permanent
trade mission say it's always the same for them, too."

"You make me ashamed for my own city!"

"That's very kind and very reassuring." Abruptly Omber sagged, revealing that she was dreadfully tired. "Excuse me, but I haven't had a proper rest since we boarded
the floater. Yull sent me up here to have one more go at
persuading the staff to admit us, while she went to see
some official or other about recovering the cylinder. Not
that there's much hope of our getting it back before the
spring, apparently. They're making excuses about the
danger from its unexpended fuel, and nobody understands
that the colder it is, the safer. I mean, I work with it every
day of my life, back home, and we haven't had any accidents with it, not ever, not even once. By the spring,
though, venting it could really be hazardous. Still, with
a bit of luck Yull will manage to make them listen."

There was a pause. Except for the hardiest, most of
the crowd surrounding the healing-house had dispersed
or sought shelter. Abruptly Albumarak realized that she
had kept Omber standing in the pouring rain, and hastily
urged her to the nearest bower.

"Do you think your colleagues will believe that even
I haven't been allowed to see Karg?" she demanded.

Omber gave a curl of faint amusement. "I believe you
entirely. And nothing in this weird city is likely to surprise
me after that. Yes, I think they will."

"But just in case they don't . . ." Albumarak's mind was
racing. "Would you like me to tell them personally?"

"Why—why, that's too much to ask! But it would be
wonderful! That is, if you can spare the time?"

"I have nothing much to do," Albumarak muttered,
thinking how accurate that was not only of the present
moment but of her entire life. Quelf's idea of encouraging
her students' research was to let them watch what she

herself was doing and then take over the repetitive drudgery involved . . . and blame them for anything that afterwards went wrong. "Where is your delegation lodged?"

"In a spare house near our trade mission, which they had to wake up specially for us. It's a bit primitive, since it hasn't been occupied for several moonlongs, but if you're sure you wouldn't mind . . . ?"

"It will be a pleasure," Albumarak declared. "Let's go!"

Nobody paid attention to the creature which Yull, Omber and Albumarak turned loose as they entered the healing-house at first bright next day. It looked like a commonplace scrapsaq—on the large side, perhaps, but one expected that in a public institution. Its kind were conditioned to go about disposing of spent luminants, spuder-webs full of dead wingets and the like, attracted to one or several kinds of rubbish by their respective odors. Having gathered as much as they could cope with, they then carried their loads to the rotting pits, and were rewarded with food before setting off again.

This one, however, was a trifle out of the ordinary.

Having seen it safely on its way, Albumarak turned to her companions.

"Follow me!" she urged. "Quelf is always in the neurophysics lab at this time of the morning."

With Yull exuding the pheromones appropriate to a high official, and Omber playing the role of her nominee as Albumarak had taught her, they arrived at the laboratory unchallenged, along a high branchway either side of which the boughs were festooned with labeled experimental circuitry. Pithed ichormals lay sluggish with up to a score of tendrils grafted on their fat bodies; paired piqs and doqs stirred uneasily as each tried to accept signals from the other; long strands of isolated nerve-pith, some healthy and glistening, some dry and peeling, were attached to plants in an attempt to find better repeaters for nervograp links, for despite Quelf's optimism it would be long before loss-free communication circuits became universal.

"I don't like this place," Omber muttered.

"That's because you're more used to working with raw chemicals than living things," Yull returned, equally softly. "But we exploit them too, remember."

"Yes. Yes, of course. I'm sorry."

Nonetheless she kept glancing unhappily from side to side.

One of Albumarak's fellow students, engaged in the usual drudgery of recording data from the various experiments, caught sight of her and called out. "Hey! You're late! Quelf is fuming like a volcano!"

"I'm on my way to make her erupt," was the composed reply.

And Albumarak led her companions into the laboratory itself, where the neurophysicist was holding forth to a group of distinguished visitors, probably foreign merchants anxious to acquire and exploit some of Fregwil's newest inventions. That was an unexpected bonus!

Albumarak padded boldly towards her, not lowering as she normally would in her professor's presence. Abruptly registering this departure from ordinary practice, Quelf broke off with an apology to her guests and glared at her.

"Where've you been? When I wished you a good dark I—"

"I want to see Karg," Albumarak interrupted.

"What? You know perfectly well that's out of the question! Have you spent your dark taking drugs?"

"Not only I," said Albumarak as though she had not spoken, "but my companions. Allow me to present Scholar Yull, head of the Slah delegation, and her assistant Omber."

"Who are both," murmured Yull in a quiet tone, "*extremely* anxious to see our old friend."

She was a tall and commanding person in her late middle years. Albumarak clenched her claws, trying to conceal her glee. The moment she had set eye on Yull, last evening, she had suspected that she could dominate

Quelf—and here was proof. She had an air of calm authority that made the other's arrogance look like mere bluster.

Taken totally aback, and hideously embarrassed that it should have happened in the presence of strangers, rather than only her students whom she could always overawe, Quelf reinforced her previous statement.

"Out of the question! He's still far too ill! Now show these people out and resume your duties!"

"If Karg is still so ill after being so long in your care," Yull said silkily, "that indicates there must be something wrong with your medical techniques."

"They are the best in the world! He was half-frozen! It was a miracle he didn't lose both pads instead of one!"

"I see. How is regrowth progressing?"

"What?"

"I said how is regrowth progressing?"—in the same soft tone but taking a step towards Quelf. "In such a case we would grow him a replacement, which would lack sensation but restore normal motor function. Has this not been done?"

"We—uh, that is, it's not customary..."

"Well, it's not important; it will be better for him to have the job done at home anyway, since your methods appear to be suspect." Yull was ostensibly unaware of the grievous insult she was offering, but Quelf's exudations ascended rapidly towards the anger-stink level. She went on, "At least, however, we must insist on verifying that he is not at risk from secondary infection."

"He's in our finest bower, guarded by a score of winget-killers, with filter-webs at every opening!"

"In that case, judging by his medical record, he should have recovered from a slight attack of frostbite long ago. Did the crash cause worse injuries than you've admitted?"

Albumarak was trying not to dance up and down with joy.

But Quelf gathered her forces for an equally crushing rebuttal.

"What you regard as good health may perhaps not correspond with what we of Prutaj take for granted," she said, having recovered most of her poise. "Indeed, perhaps we have made a mistake in trying to bring him up to that level. But you must not prevent it happening, if it can be done."

Yull turned her eye slowly on all those present, while drawing herself up to full height. She overtopped Quelf by eye and mandibles; moreover her mantle was sleek and beautifully patterned for her age. Only the youngest students' could match it. The distinguished visitors, and Quelf too, betrayed the puffiness due to overindulgence, and here and there a fat-sac peeked out under a mantle's edge, yellowish and sickly.

"I like your boss!" Albumarak whispered to Omber.

"She's a terror when you cross her," came the answer. "But this kind of thing she's *very* good at."

There was no need for Yull to spell out the implication of her scornful survey; many of the visitors fidgeted and tried to pull themselves into better shape. Only Quelf attempted to counter it.

"Well, if you prefer to go about half-starved, forever on the verge of becoming dreamlost, that's your lookout!"

"You're implying that I'm in that condition now?" Yull's manner suddenly turned dangerous.

"You? I wouldn't know about you for certain, but it seems pretty obvious that only people who were good and dreamlost would think of trying to send someone out into space!"

Yull turned away. "There seems little point in pursuing this conversation," she said to Omber. "Show them what you're carrying and let's find out the truth."

"Ah! The truth is that your costly toy fell out of the sky!" Quelf declared in triumph, using a phrase she had grown fond of. "You can't deny that, so you refuse to—"

But nobody was paying attention to her. All eyes were on Omber, who had produced from a bag she was carrying something which all present recognized by its unique odor: a farspeaker, smaller, yet patently more powerful, than they had ever seen before.

"This," said Yull didactically, "is one of the miniature farspeakers we developed to communicate with our spaceship when in orbit. We brought a few of them with us so as to keep in touch with the authorities at Slah."

She pinched the creature with a gentle claw. Its colors altered slightly and it gave off an aroma of contentment.

"Albumarak programed a scrapsaq carrying another of these to seek out Karg. By now it should have reached the place where you're imprisoning him. When I—"

"Imprisoning? You have no right to say that!" Quelf shrieked.

"Let's find out whether I do or not," said Yull imperturbably, and activated the farspeaker to maximum volume. At once a voice rang out, impersonal, repetitive: the sound of a recordimal.

"—is better than life at Slah. Having seen for myself, I honestly think life at Fregwil is better than life at Slah. Having seen for myself, I honestly think—"

"They're trying to condition him!" Albumarak burst out.

Silencing the farspeaker, Yull nodded gravely. "I can come to no other conclusion. Having had this gift from the sky drop into their claws, seeing the chance of a propaganda victory over us whom they regard as their rivals, Quelf and her colleagues set out to force poor Karg into such a state of permanent dreamness that when they eventually decided to let him appear in public again he would renounce his former allegiance. Luckily, as is evidenced by the fact that after so long they are still having to force one simple sentence into his memory, this is so transparent an untruth that even in his weakened state he continues to reject their dishonest overtures."

"Untruth?" bellowed Quelf. "What's untrue is what you are saying!"

"Really?" Yull turned an icy gaze on her. "How, then, about the statement 'having seen for myself'? What of Fregwil have you permitted Karg to see? The inside of a healing-house bower, correct?"

"That's exactly what I was thinking!" One of the visitors thrust forward. "I'm Yaxon, merchant from Heybrol! I came here to buy nervograp specifications—never mind that—and I know a conditioning program when I hear one! But I thought they'd been made illegal!"

She was echoed by an angry mumble from the others.

"In *civilized* cities," Yull murmured, "yes, they have!"

Having closed on Quelf, the company now drew back, as though from something emitting a noxious stench. The professor uttered a faint whimper, looking about her for support. None was forthcoming; even her students regarded her with sudden loathing.

"Albumarak," Yull said, returning the farspeaker to Omber's bag, "show us the way to Karg's bower."

They all went, exuding such a reek of fury that no one dared gainsay them. There they found him, comfortable enough to be sure in a luxurious crotch padded with the best of mosh, with a nursh in attendance to change the cleanlickers on his frostbitten pad, and with plenty to eat and drink . . . but dazed, and totally unable to escape the message repeated and repeated by recordimals either side of him. When one grew fatigued the other took over automatically; the programing was impeccable, and—as Albumarak abruptly realized with a renewed access of horror—that meant it had almost certainly been prepared by Quelf in person.

She rushed forward, snatched up both of them, and hurled them out of the bower, careless of the fact that their passage slashed great gaps in the protective spuder-webs which filtered incoming air of not only wingets but microorganisms.

"And now," said Yull with satisfaction, after checking Karg and finding him in good physical condition, at least, "we can arrange for this poor fellow to regain his normal senses. I understand that Quelf is only a research professor here. Who is the actual director? I require to speak with her *at once!*"

Her voice rang out like thunder, and one might have sworn that it altered the air-pressure like an actual storm.

The frightened nursh quavered, "I'll go find her!"

"Does she know about this?" Yull demanded.

"N-no! I'm sure she doesn't! We have at least eight-score folk in here at any given time, so she—"

"Then she's unfit to occupy her post, and I shall tell her so the moment she arrives! Fetch her, and fetch her *now!*"

VI

"What's going to happen to Quelf?" Omber asked.

Recriminations had continued all day, and would doubtless resume next bright, but by nightfall everyone was tired of arguing and moreover hungry. The city officials had agreed to arrange for immediate recovery of the space-cylinder, and promised to announce in the morning what other compensation they would offer for Karg's mistreatment. The Slah delegation regarded that as acceptable.

As to Quelf, she had fled the healing-house in unbearable humiliation. Her last message as she mounted her scudder and made for home had been relayed to Albumarak: "Tell that misbudded traitor not to expect any more help from me!"

So there went her future, wiped away by a single well-intentioned decision... but how could she possibly have acted otherwise and lived with herself afterwards? Wearily she summoned the energy to answer Omber as they and Yull left the university precincts under a blustery autumn sky.

"Oh—nothing much, probably. She's just been made one of the Jingfired, you know, and they're virtually untouchable. Also she's far too brilliant a researcher for the authorities to risk her moving elsewhere, to Hulgrapuk, for example. On top of that, her sentiments are shared by just about all the teachers here. They really do regard people from other continents as basically inferior to themselves."

"Is the incidence of metal poisoning exceptionally high at Fregwil, then?" Yull murmured, provoking her companions to a cynical chuckle.

And she continued, "I feel a celebration is in order, now that Karg is being properly cared for at last." They had been assured he would be well enough to leave his bower within two or three days. "Let's dine at the best restaurant we can find, and afterwards make a tour of this Festival of Science; I gather it finishes tonight. Albumarak, you'll be my guest, of course. And perhaps you can advise us what we might ask by way of compensation if the proposals made to us tomorrow are inadequate. That is, unless you have a prior engagement?"

"No—no, I don't! I accept with pleasure!" Albumarak had difficulty concealing her delight. Already she had been favorably impressed by the unaffected way these people treated her: naturally, casually, as though she were one of themselves. Rather than seeking a reward for her assistance, she felt she ought to be performing further services for them, if only to salve the good reputation of her city, so disgracefully mildewed by Quelf.

"Then where shall we eat? For choice, suggest an establishment patronized by members of the Jingfired. I feel an unworthy desire to snub their mandibles."

Quelf had invited Albumarak to dine with her the day she decided to cite her as her nominee. The idea of taking her new friends to the same place appealed greatly.

"I know just the one!" she declared. "And there's a dolmusq bound in the right direction over there!"

After the meal—which was excellent—they swarmed the short distance to the park where the Sparkshow was coming to its end. Though the weather was turning wintry, a number of special events had been mounted to mark its final night, and throngs of folk were vastly amused at being charged with so much sparkforce that they shed miniature aurorae from claw-tips and mandibles, yet felt no ill effects.

But Yull and Omber dismissed such shows as trivial, and paid far more attention to experiments with a practical application: gradient separation of similar organic molecules, for instance, and the use of rotating pullstones to prove that the fields they generated were intimately related to sparkforce, though as yet nobody had satisfactorily explained how. Someone had even bred back what was held to be a counterpart of the long-extinct northfinder, and claimed that its ability always to turn towards the pole must have been due to metallic particles in its pith—a challenge to those who believed that reactive metal in a living nervous system invariably led to its breakdown.

At last they came to what had proved the most popular and impressive item in the Festival: the creation of artificial lightning by means of a charge sent along a loss-free circuit. Despite having been fired a score of times every dark for a moonlong, it was still operating perfectly, as was the message-link over which news of Karg's crash had come to Fregwil, although the display on which the information appeared had had to be replaced twice.

Here Yull and Omber lingered longer than at all the other demonstrations put together, insisting on watching two of the artificial lightning-flashes and sending an unimportant message—"Greetings to Drupit from citizens of Slah!"—over the communication link. For the first time Albumarak felt excluded from their company as they discussed what they had seen in low and private tones.

But eventually they turned back to her, curling their mantles in broad grins.

"Did you work on this remarkable discovery?" Yull asked.

"Ah . . . Well, yes, as a matter of fact I did. Quelf has the habit of delegating the details to her students, and—"

"You understand the principle?"

"I'm not sure anybody does, really, but I certainly know how the circuits are grown. Why?"

Yull began to pad meditatively downslope, and the others fell in alongside her.

"Quelf was right in one thing she said to us today," she went on after a lengthy pause. "Our 'costly toy' did fall out of the sky. What served us well when we were only launching spores and spawn and automatic systems designed to fend for themselves in orbit has turned out to be much too risky when it comes to a piloted mission. For a long time we've been seeking an alternative to wet-gas-bladders as a means of lofting spacecraft. We even went so far as to consider using giant drivers directly from ground level, or rather from a mountain-top. But the life-support and guidance systems would burst under the requisite acceleration. As for what would happen to the crew—!

"Have you, though, padded across standing-spark-force repulsion?"

"Of course," Albumarak replied, staring. "But it's a mere laboratory curiosity, with about the power of one of those seeds young'uns put under a burning-glass to watch them leap as their internal gas heats up."

"You do that here too?" Yull countered with a smile. "I guess budlings are pretty much the same everywhere, aren't they? But, as I was just saying to Omber, if one could grow sufficient of these new loss-free circuits . . . Do you see what I'm getting at?"

Albumarak was momentarily aghast. She said, "But if you mean you want to use that method to launch spacecraft, you'd need laqs and craws of them!"

"I think we're less daunted by projects on such a scale than you are; the skein of gas-globes that lofted Karg was already more than a padlonglaq in height. And we don't waste our resources on private luxury the way you do on Prutaj. Excuse me, but it is the case, you know."

"It's often seemed to me," said Albumarak meditatively, "that most of what we produce is designed to keep us from thinking about the ultimate threat that hangs over us all."

"You're very different from most of your own folk, aren't you?" Omber ventured. Albumarak turned to her.

"If Quelf is to be taken as typical—and I'm afraid she is—then I'm proud of the fact!"

"You'd be quite at home in Slah, then," Yull said lightly. "But before we wander off down that particular branchway: do you think we might reasonably, in compensation for what's been done to Karg, ask how to grow a loss-free sparkforce circuit?"

Albumarak pondered for a long moment. Eventually, clenching her claws, she said with barely suppressed glee, "Yes! Yes, that's exactly what you should ask for!"

And if they refuse to part with it—well, then, I'll go to Slah with you and bring the knowledge in my memory!

She did not speak it aloud, but the moment she reached her decision, she felt somehow that it was far more right than waiting for her turn to be made Jingfired.

On the morrow Yull and the rest of the Slah delegation were bidden to attend a Full Court of Council, held in a huge and handsome bower in the most ancient quarter of the city. Albumarak tagged along, though on arrival she was quite ignored. It pleased her to see her "superiors" in such a plight; the atmosphere was stiff with the reek of embarrassment, and the welcome offered to the visitors, though correct, was a hollow one.

Sullen, Quelf had been obliged to put in an appearance, and perched with a few of her closest colleagues on one side of the bower. At the center was Ingolfine, old, excessively fat, but the senior of the living Jingfired, to whom all others must defer when matters of high policy were debated.

"Were there not once Jingfired at Slah?" Albumarak asked Omber in a whisper.

"Oh yes! Indeed, they still exist. But ours are mostly scientists who do not make their rank the excuse for show and pomp. They regard it as the greatest possible honor to be elected, and they are charged never to boast about it. Yull may be one; I'd rather lose a claw than ask her."

The more she learned about the way of life at Slah, the more Albumarak approved of it.

And then Ingolfine wheezed a command for silence, and they composed themselves to listen to what she had to say.

"It has been concluded by the members of our Council that a grave—ah—*error of judgment* has occurred in the case of the foreigner Karg, inasmuch as although—and let me emphasize this—he has been afforded the best of medical care, excessive enthusiasm for the merits of life at Fregwil led respected Quelf to overpad the boundary of normal courtesy towards one who was sick and far from home."

Quelf looked as though she would like to disappear.

"Honor obliges us therefore to make restitution. We propose to endow a studentship tenable by a young person from Slah for up to a quarter-score of years, to be devoted to any subject taught at our university."

And she waited for Yull's response to what she clearly regarded as a generous offer.

It followed promptly. "We would be dreamlost and foolish to commit any of our young people to the claws and mandibles of so-called teachers who regard us as an inferior folk!"

The insult provoked a furious outcry. When Ingolfine quelled it, she demanded, "Then what do you ask for?"

"The secret of loss-free circuitry, so we can put it to better use than what you're sure to waste it on!"

This time the hubbub was reinforced by combat-stink. "Out of the question!" Ingolfine declared after consulting her advisers.

"Very well, then," Yull said composedly. "We have an alternative demand. Regardless of the medical care given him, which we have certain reservations about, it is an undeniable fact that Karg was maltreated here. We will settle for taking one of your citizens home with us, not against her or his will, in order to demonstrate to the world how much better we at Slah can make a foreigner welcome."

Ingolfine and the other officials relaxed. If the Slah delegation were content to achieve a mere propaganda coup... More private discussion followed, and finally Ingolfine announced, "To that we see no objection."

"You state that publicly, as a matter of principle?"

Again, hurried consultation. Then, defiantly, "Yes!"

"Very well. We choose Albumarak."

There was a horrified hush. Quelf broke it, rising to full height and shrieking, "But she's my best student!"

"Was!" shouted Albumarak, marveling at how clearly Yull had read her secret intentions. "After what you did to Karg, nobody will respect you again so long as you live!"

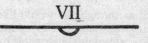

VII

During the dark that preceded her departure, Albumarak perched alone in one of the shabby neglected bowers of the house where the Slah delegation had been obliged to take up lodging. Her mind was reeling under the impact of the hatred she was having to endure. Even in her fits of bitterest loathing for the "high-pressure citizens" of her

bud-place she had never imagined that they, in full awareness of what had been done to Karg, would regard her
as the traitor and not Quelf. It showed that they too would
have wanted the foreigner to be cheated into turning his
mantle, heedless of how much he suffered in the process,
in order to delude those who were striving to escape the
truth.

Soft slithering at the entrance aroused her. The bower's luminants were withering and dim, and the night was
cloudy; neither moonshine nor the glimmer of stars and
comets lent their light. Not waiting to sense the newcom-
er's aroma, she said in a dull tone, "Who's there?"

"It's Karg. Do you mind if I join you?"

"Why—why, certainly you may!" She had met him
earlier; he was still weak, but had insisted on remaining
at Fregwil until arrangements for recovering his cylinder
were complete. Thinking he might need assistance, she
moved towards him, but he waved her aside with one
claw.

"I may not be able to walk properly right now, but I
can swarm along a branch all right . . . There." He settled
in the crotch next to hers, where they could look out at
the city through gaps between the bravetree trunks.

"I suspect I owe you my sanity as well as my life," he
said after a while.

Embarrassed, she shifted on her perch. "It was Presthin who actually rescued you. I just went along for the
ride. And it was Yull who suggested how we could eavesdrop on what Quelf was doing to you."

"But you programed the scrapsaq, didn't you? She told
me it was an amazing job, given the time available."

"Well, we had to keep the snowrither's haodah sealed
all the way to Drupit, so I had plenty of time to get to
know your aroma. Mimicking it well enough to condition
a scrapsaq wasn't hard."

She found herself feeling a little uncomfortable in the
presence of this person who had risked and suffered so
much in a cause which, a moonlong ago, she had been
accustomed to dismissing as worthless.

Sensing her mood, Karg inquired, "Are you having
second thoughts about going to Slah?"

"No, quite the reverse!"—with a harsh laugh. "I'm

looking forward to it. I never thought my folk could be so brutal!"

After a pause, Karg said, "I've been talking to Yull about your people. She said . . . I don't know if I ought to repeat this. It's indecent to talk that way about another folk."

"Say anything you like and I'll say worse!"

"Very well. But there isn't really another folk, is there? We are all one. We're budded, and we die, and in between we make the most of what's offered to us, and afterwards whatever it was that made us *us* returns to whence it came. Maybe next time it will animate creatures under another sun, so different from ourselves that when what used to make up you and me comes back we won't recognize each other. But of course there can't be any way of knowing."

Albumarak was not in the habit of debating the mystery of awareness; the academics of Fregwil had long ago decreed that certain problems were inherently insoluble and should be left to take care of themselves. She said hastily, "You were about to quote Yull, weren't you?"

"All right, since you insist. She holds that your folk must be less than civilized because you take no thought for the future, and won't invest effort to promote the survival of our species but only for your own immediate enjoyment. She says this is proved by the way you waste so much of your resources on entertainment and distraction. You don't have enough left over to make sure either that your food-plants are healthy or that the air you breathe has been purged of poisonous metals. If you did, you'd be working to ensure that even though we as individuals can't escape into space our budlings or their budlings may. She's so convinced of this, she's going to insist on all of us being purified from crest to pad when we get home. And she swears that's why the people of Fregwil went crazy enough to want the futile victory of conditioning me by force!"

He ended on a defiant note, as though expecting Albumarak to contradict.

And only a short while ago she would have done so. But her journey with Presthin, brief though it was, had given her the shadow of an insight into what Karg must have braced himself for when he volunteered to fly into space. To her the snowbound wastes of the highlands were alien enough; how much more, then, the boundless desert between the stars!

Hesitantly she asked, "Did it do any lasting harm? The conditioning, I mean?"

He gave a dry chuckle. "Probably not very much, vulnerable though I was. I had to learn to cling hard to reality a long time ago. I used to supervise an underwater quarry, you know, in an environment nearly as harsh and lonely as outer space."

"I didn't know! In fact, I know almost nothing about you, do I? This is the first time we've met properly."

He stretched himself; his injuries were tightening as they healed, causing discomfort. "Well, that was why they picked me—that, and the fact that I was much smaller than the other candidates, so they could loft a bit of extra reaction mass for free-fall maneuvering. Do you understand how my craft works, or rather, was supposed to work?"

"I think so. The gas-globes were to carry it above most of the atmosphere, and then the drivers were to blast you into orbit, and then you'd fire them again to—"

"Not quite. Out in space I was to use regular musculator pumps to expel a heavy inert liquid that we've developed. The fuel used for the drivers becomes unstable under free-space radiation. We lost two or three of our early cylinders that way, before we figured out what the problem was. Or rather, I should say 'they,' not 'we,' because that happened long before I joined the team."

Karg heaved a deep sigh. "I was looking forward to it, I really was! And now I've lost my chance forever."

"Surely not! After your pad has grown back"—Albumarak could still not mention that promise without a hint of awe in her voice, for it bespoke medical techniques far surpassing those boasted of at Fregwil—"they won't want to waste someone with your special talents and training."

"Oh, I gather Yull impressed everybody mightily with her reference to regrowth, but the process is actually still in the experimental stage, and in any case you don't get the feeling back. And every square clawide of my body was pressed into service to control the hauq, and the purifiers, and the maneuvering pumps, and the farspeakers and the rest. No, I had my chance, and a meteorite stole it once for all."

"So what will you do now—go back to underwater work?"

"I could, I suppose; it isn't so demanding...But I'd rather not. I think I'll stay on at the space-site. I gather Yull told you that we're going to have to abandon our existing plans and try another course."

"Yes, but..." Albumarak clacked her mandibles dolefully. "You said your regrowth techniques are still at the experimental stage. The same is true of our loss-free circuits. They still take ages to grow—we'd been working on the one which we demonstrated at the Sparkshow ever since the last Festival of Science—and they haven't yet been proved under field conditions. For all we can tell, they may be vulnerable to disease, funqi, wild beasts, parasitic plants..."

"Yes, it seems more than a padlong from demonstration of a pilot version to what Yull is talking about. Even so, a fresh eye cast on the principle...What *is* it?"

"The principle? Well...Well, how much do you know about sparkforce?"

Karg shrugged; she felt the branches stir. "Take it for granted that I know a little about a lot of things."

"Yes, you'd have to, wouldn't you?" Embarrassed again, Albumarak went on hastily. "What she seems to have in mind isn't even at the experimental level yet. It's a mere oddment, a curiosity. It depends on using sparkforce charges to repel each other."

"I thought that must be it, but if you did put such a huge charge on one of our cylinders, then...Hmm! Wait a moment; I think I see how it might be done. If there were some way to alternate the kinds of repulsion—Ach! I'm taking an infusion to control my pain, and my mind is still too foggy for constructive reasoning. But I'll remember to mention my idea to Yull in the morning."

He shifted in the crotch, turning his eye on her. "Did you get enough to eat this sundown?"

"As much as I wanted."

"If you didn't eat properly, you may find your mind is as sluggish as mine when you arrive in Slah. It can take quite a long time to adjust to local dark and bright after traveling to a different continent at today's speeds—Oh,

hark at me! I hadn't set pad on a foreign continent myself
before my crash. I'm not the person to lecture you. But
I thought it was worth mentioning."

"How would you have coped in space, then? There
isn't a dark-bright cycle up there!"

"In the orbit I was supposed to follow, there would
have been, but six or seven times as fast as a regular day.
I didn't expect any trouble, though. Deep underwater you
have no dark-bright cycle at all, and I lived through that."

"What exactly were you to do out there?"

Karg stretched again, and a hint of agony discolored
his pheromones, but it lasted only a moment.

"Bring together two of our automatic orbital cylinders
and connect their ecosystems, then work inside them for
a while, making sure everything was going as well as the
farspeakers indicate. We do seem to have beaten one
major problem: we've developed plants that purge themselves of deleterious mutations due to radiation. Some of
them have been through four or five score generations
without losing their identity, and should still be fit to eat.
But of course there may be changes too tiny for our monitors to locate and report on. How I wish we could get to
the moon and back! We need samples of the vegetation
up there in the worst way!"

Listening to him in the gloom of the ill-tended bower,
Albumarak found herself wondering what Presthin had
been like when she was younger and less cynical; much
like Karg, she suspected . . . She decided once for all that
she had been right to throw in her lot with these people.
If they succeeded with their plan to survive in space, they
would not be driven mad by the fate of their fellow creatures, any more than Karg by Quelf's mistreatment. But
they were no less civilized for that. Yull's contempt for
the folk of Prutaj was justified. Worse than primitive, they
were insane . . . if sanity consisted in doing the most the
universe allowed, and she knew no better definition.

In a tremulous tone she said, "I admire you very much,
Karg. I'd invite you to pair with me, but I shouldn't be
in bud during my first few moonlongs at Slah, should I?"

"Quite right," was the answer. "And in any case I'm
still too weak, though I look forward to the time when it
will be possible. And—ah—you say you admire me. But
all my life I've been trained under the finest tutors to do

unusual and extraordinary work. You've had a truly awful teacher, and yet for me at least you've performed not just one miracle, but two. Thank you again."

And he swarmed away, leaving her delighted with the world.

VIII

For the first few days, what fascinated Albumarak about her new home was less its modern aspect—its space-site, its laboratories which in many ways were more impressive than those at Fregwil, perhaps because the staff were under less pressure to be forever producing novelties— than its sheer antiquity. She had been vaguely aware that Slah enshrined the last remaining traces of the only ocean-going city to have outlasted the heyday of the People of the Sea, but it was very different to hold in her own claws the mandible of a long-extinct fish, found among the roots of its most ancient trees, or nibble a fragment of funqus and know the species had last been modified by Gveest in person.

As she had expected, the pace of life here was calmer, yet she detected few signs of discontent or boredom. More people were occupied with old-fashioned tasks—such as disposing of dead luminants—which at Fregwil were deputed to creatures programed for them, but there was a greater sense of being in touch with the natural world, which Albumarak found refreshing, and the citizens, most of whom had naturally heard about her, seemed never to lack time to offer advice or assistance.

By stages she began to grasp the full sweep of the plan these people had conceived for the salvation of their afterbuds, and its grandeur overawed her. They referred casually to the astronomers' estimate that it might take ten thousand years for the sun to orbit through the Major Cluster; they accepted without question that its dense gas—from which stars could be observed condensing—

would raise the solar temperature to the point where the planet became uninhabitable; they were resigned to the high probability that there would be a stellar collision, and if that did not eventuate, then so much random matter was bound to fall from the sky that it would come to the same thing in the end; and all this was equally well known at Fregwil.

But instead of closing their minds to the catastrophe, these people were prepared to plan against it. They spoke confidently of vehicles carrying scores-of-scores of folk, along with everything needed to support them, which could be moved away from the sun as it heated up, maneuvering as necessary to remain within its biosphere, while adapted plants freed raw materials from the outer planets and their moons. Then, later, they envisaged breaking up the smaller orbs and converting them into cylinders which could be spun on their long axis to provide a substitute for gravity. These, they predicted, would permit at least some isolated units of the folk to navigate between the nascent stars, using reaction mass or the pressure of light itself.

All this, of course, was still theoretical. But Albumarak was astonished to learn in what detail the history of the future had been worked out here. She wondered whether she was worthy to contribute to it.

Inevitably, the bright arrived when she was summoned to the neurophysical laboratory attached to the space-site, well beyond the city limits. Omber appeared to guide her. There she was welcomed by a tubby, somewhat irascible personage called Scholar Theng, who lost no time in getting down to business.

"Well, young'un," she boomed, "it seems we have to reconsider our ideas. Yull tells me loss-free circuits are the answer. She brought me a sample—Don't look so surprised! Turned out a good many of your citizens didn't care for what Quelf did to Karg, and gifted her with a piece of one, enough to culture a few cells from."

"You didn't tell me!" Albumarak cried. "I'd have been here long ago if I'd realized you weren't going to have to start from scratch! I've wasted time trying to reconstruct from memory everything I know about designing the things!"

"So that's what you've been doing, is it?" Theng

growled. "I had the impression you were just sight-seeing... Well, come and look at what we've got so far."

If it was true that she had started with "a few cells" she had made remarkable progress. Already a web of thin brownish tendrils stretched back and forth over a patch of heavily fertilized ground under a transparent membrane that gathered winter sunwarmth and protected them from storms.

"But this is wonderful!" Albumarak declared.

"Oh, we can grow them all right, and they seem to perform as advertised. Question is, can we make them do what Yull wants? You're an expert on sparkforce, they tell me. What do you think?"

The likelihood of putting Yull's proposal into effect seemed suddenly much greater. Albumarak filled her mantle.

"Omber, it is the case, isn't it, that one would still have to loft drivers and their fuel, even if one did build a—a launcher capable of replacing gas-globes?"

They had occasionally discussed the matter; she knew the answer would be yes before it came. And went on, "So the next step must be to grow a miniature test version of your cylinders and see whether"—*thank you, Karg!*— "we can put sufficient charge on it."

"We can't," Theng retorted briskly. "We already went over that with our chief chemist Ewblet. It would de-stabilize the fuel. Want to see the simulation records?"

Albumarak was minded to clack her mandibles in dismay, but controlled herself and, so far as she could, her exudations. She said in a tone as sharp as Theng's, "Then let Ewblet find a way of preventing it! My business is loss-free sparkforce circuitry, and I'd like to get on with it!"

Theng looked at her for a long moment. At last she said, "Well spoken. What do you expect to need?"

It was like being on a different planet. Colleagues much older than herself consulted her without being patronizing; others of her own age reported to her the problems they had encountered, described their proposed solutions, and asked for her opinion; in turn, when she swam into a snag they were prompt to offer information and advice. She had already grasped the overall pattern of what the folk here were committed to, but now she was given insight into its minutiae...and the multiplicity of details was frightening. So too, in a sense, was the dedication she discovered. She almost came to believe that there was no one in the whole of Slah, bar a clawful of budlings, who lacked a part to play in converting their vision into reality.

Space-launches using gas-globes were continuing despite the winter storms, along with work on every other aspect of the scheme. The orbits of some of the space-cylinders were decaying; it was essential to send up more reaction mass, using automatic control systems, so they could be forced further out. Everybody, not just Karg, wanted to learn what was happening to the vegetation on the moon; one of the younger scientists proposed crashing a cylinder there which would survive sufficiently intact to gather samples and then emit two or three others much smaller than itself, propelled by a simple explosion on to a course that would bring them to rendezvous with a collector in local orbit, and then recovering the collector in the way designed for Karg. Simulations showed it might well succeed, and the job was promptly put in claw.

Eventually Albumarak said despairingly to her new friends, "I don't know how you stand the pressure!"

But they answered confidently, "We enjoy it! After all, is there a better cause we could be working for?"

And then, to their amazement, they realized she had never learned the means to make the most of dark-time, devised long before the Greatest Meteorite, which depended on freeing consciousness from attending to the process of digestion. With only the mildest of reproaches concerning Fregwil's standards of education, they instructed her in the technique, and after that she no longer wondered how they crammed so much into a single day.

As Karg had predicted, casting a fresh eye on the loss-free circuits led to rapid improvement. Winter was milder here than at Fregwil, but that alone did not account for the speed with which the tendrils grew, nor for the flawless way each and every one checked out. Quelf's team had been resigned to losing two or three in every score; here, when one slacked in its growth, the cause was sought and found and in a few days' time it was back to schedule.

Albumarak detected something of the same phenomenon in herself. She was eating an unfamiliar diet, but her mind had never been so active. She mentioned as much to Theng once, when the latter was in a particularly good mood, and was told: "A few generations ago, the air at Slah was always filthy thanks to the metal-working sites nearby. That was at the time of Aglabec and his disciples—heard of them? I thought you would have! Rival cities like Hulgrapuk and Fregwil made the most of it, to disparage us! But we retained our wits well enough to realize it was no use sending crazy people into space, so we put that right, and now there's not a city on the planet where you breathe purer air or drink cleaner water or eat a more nourishing diet. We're allegedly possessed of intelligence; we judged it right to apply our conclusions to ourselves as well as our environment. And it's paid off, hasn't it?"

Indeed it had...

At one stage Albumarak came near despair, when a simulation proved that nothing like enough sparkforce could be generated to drive even the smallest of the Slah cylinders to the heights achieved by gas-globes. There were no pullstones worth mentioning on this continent; the world's only large deposit was on Prutaj. Suddenly someone she had never heard of reported that by adding this and this to the diet of a flashplant, and modifying it in such a way, its output could be multiplied until it matched the best pullstone generator. Someone else suggested means of deriving current from the wind; another, from compression using the beating of ocean waves; another, from conversion of sunshine...

Yull was in the habit of visiting the laboratory now and then, sometimes with Karg or Omber, more often alone. One day in spring she arrived with a grave expression, and asked Theng, in Albumarak's hearing, what progress had been made.

"Good!" Theng declared gruffly. "Ewblet has stabilized the fuel at last, we have enough sparkforce and nearly enough loss-free circuitry to loft a driver to where it can be fired into orbit, and the eastern side of Spikemount slopes at pretty well an ideal angle to build the launcher. We expect to be at status go by fall."

"You're going to have to do better than that," Yull told her soberly.

Sensing disaster, Albumarak drew close.

"Take a look at these," Yull invited, proffering a pack of images. They were regular astronomical pictures of the kind produced at any major observatory, and they showed a patch of night sky in the vicinity of the Major Cluster. Theng glanced at them and passed them to Albumarak.

"You'll have to explain what's so special about them!"

"This is!" Yull tapped one tiny dot with a delicate claw. "Look again. They were taken on successive nights."

"It's not on this one," Albumarak muttered. "But it's on this one, only fainter, and—no, not on this one, but on this one as well, and brighter if anything...Oh, no!"

"I think," Yull murmured, "you've caught on. For nearly a moonlong past, something has been appearing and vanishing in that area of the sky. We have here a score of images that show it and a quarter-score that don't. What is it?"

Albumarak's mind raced. "Something spinning! It's rough on one side and smooth on the other, so it only catches the sun at certain angles!"

"Exactly what our most eminent astronomers suspect," Yull said, reclaiming the pictures. "In addition, though, they can show that it's very far out, beyond Sluggard."

"Then it must be huge!"

"Yes. As big as the moon. And what little of its orbit has been analyzed suggests it may be going to intersect with ours in at most a score of years. Even if it misses us, it will certainly crash into the sun."

IX

Albumarak felt unbelievably old as she strove to judge the relative merits of a score of rival projects competing for time on the world's only full-scale sparkforce launcher.

Yull's inspiration had been justified over and over. Cylinders had been flung skyward first to where half the mass of the air was below, then four-fifths, then nine-tenths, the magic altitude from which the drivers could reach escape velocity. Now it glowed vivid blue ten times every moonlong, summer and winter alike, and the air for padlonglaqs reeked of sparkforce stink, and the night sky was crowded with artificial stars, one of which loomed brighter than the moon at full: an orbital colony-to-be.

But should she recommend to Theng that their precious future charges be expended on yet more automatic linkup systems, in the hope of making that "moon" habitable by more people than the schedule called for, or should priority be given to this new scheme to win time by crashing on the wild planetoid a load of rockeater spawn modified to digest it into dust? Now it was crossing the orbit of Stolidchurl, so even if all went perfectly the encounter could not occur earlier than when it reached the distance of Steadyman...

Life at Slah had grown hard over the past five years.

But there were others it had treated worse. She didn't look up at the visitor who entered her bower in the control-house. A familiar aroma preceded him, tinged with mingled rage and weariness. As soon as she could, she uttered a greeting, and was horrified to see, as he slumped into a crotch, how limp Karg's posture had become.

"I heard how you were received at Hulgrapuk," she said.

"No worse than last time," he sighed. "Same old story! 'There's no means of avoiding the impact of this greater-than-greatest meteorite, so . . . !' But I do have some good news. I bet you won't guess where it's from."

"Fregwil," she offered, intending a joke.

"Correct. Quelf's coming here."

Reflexively she rose to full height. "Incredible! Why?"

"Officially they're talking about a fact-finding mission. Our local informants say different. There's likely to be a revolution at Fregwil if the city officials don't start actively helping our project."

Albumarak slowly subsided. "There are some kinds of aid we'd be better off without," she muttered.

"Don't I know it!" Karg winced, flexing his regrown pad; it continued to give pain, especially when he was under stress. "As we came in to land, I had a fine view of the campfuls of 'volunteers' outside the city. I gather they're proving more of a nuisance than a blessing."

"Our propaganda has been too successful. They expect to be lofted into orbit right away. When they find out their role only involves making sure there are enough raw materials, enough food, enough of everything that has to be at a given place at a given time, they turn nasty on us."

"Figures. But they're leaving Hulgrapuk in droves, you know. And the exodus from Fregwil is scaring Quelf and the rest of her coterie. Their young people are simply moving out, flying here if they can, or taking passage on any old barq or junq that might carry them to Slah. I saw the port at Fregwil. I think a lot of them may get drowned."

After a pause Albumarak said, "I've been asked if I'd like to go to orbit one of these days."

"Grab the chance! I still dream of how wonderful it would have been if I—"

"But everything is still theory! We're investing this colossal effort, and we still haven't sent anybody into space, let alone proved that folk can survive up there!"

Rigid as a rock but for the flexing of his mantle as he spoke, Karg said, "I'd have proved it. I didn't insist on waiting until your huge new complex had been spun up to a rate that will mimic gravity. My chance was stolen from me!"

"Everybody knows that!"

"Everyone except you seems to have forgotten!"

And he erected and stormed out.

For a moment Albumarak thought of rushing after him,

to offer consolation. She abandoned the idea. She had come to know him intimately since arriving at Slah, and when a mood like this overcame him there was small point in arguing. Besides, she had more urgent matters on her mind.

Calmly she activated the nervograp that connected her with Theng's bower, and dictated to a recordimal: "Data at claw indicate that we cannot modify rockeater spores in sufficient quantities to demolish the wild planetoid prior to estimated encounter time." She hesitated, then went on, "It is my opinion that far more effort should be directed towards ensuring that the conditions we are establishing for survival in orbit *are actually survivable up to and including reproduction of the species*! Because otherwise we're done for . . . aren't we?"

But the prospect of making an alliance with Fregwil was too good to miss. If the resources of Prutaj were put at Slah's disposal, within a decade most of what the space-planners hoped for could be brought about. Fevered discussions ensued, in which Albumarak resolutely declined to take part, ostensibly on the grounds that she had been away from home too long, in fact because she still hated Quelf's pith.

Obviously, a special demonstration had to be laid on to coincide with Quelf's visit, and in a fit of the same kind of exasperation which had plagued her youth Albumarak suggested they might as well loft her into orbit. Both Theng and Yull vetoed that at once; they maintained she had too many useful skills to let her risk her life. Yet she garnered the impression that someone, at least, had taken her seriously.

She forced herself to continue her normal daily duties, wondering constantly whether she had been wrong to advise against the rockeater project, whether someone had miscalculated the wild planetoid's orbital velocity, whether . . .

Her mind remained incessantly in turmoil. Talking to Omber, talking to Karg now that he was back from the latest of his trips around the world to recruit support—nothing helped, until the dark when Karg said acutely, "You would flee into space, wouldn't you, if it meant escaping Quelf and the memory of shame you brought here?"

That made her laugh at herself, and she said as she embraced him fondly, "Had it not been for the wild planetoid, we would have paired by now. I'd like your bud!"

"I know!" A shadow fell across his words. "You were correct to say we don't know whether we can survive as well as our creatures do in space. I wouldn't curse a budling with deformity—yet evolution must compel it, no?"

"Our distant ancestors..."

"Exactly. They were very different from ourselves." She pondered that.

The floater from Prutaj that brought in Quelf and her party was larger and clawsomer than any other at Slah's touchdown-ground. Albumarak had begged to be excused from the official welcome party, but she was unable to resist joining the crowd which gathered to witness this unprecedented visit. Polite applause greeted Quelf's appearance—from those who had somehow missed hearing about what she had done to Karg, she thought sourly. But when she recognized the second person who descended from the floater, she could control herself no longer.

"Presthin!" she shouted, and rushed towards her.

"That same," came the dry response. "I felt it was high time I said hello to Karg. We never met properly, remember?"

"I must introduce you at once! If he's here, that is. I haven't seen him, but then he has small reason to love Quelf." Albumarak glanced around, but was abruptly reminded that there were formalities to get through; Quelf was fixing her with the same withering glare she had learned to know so well when she was still a lowly student at Fregwil.

"Later!" she whispered as Yull and Theng led Quelf towards the waiting loudeners... exactly at the moment when a chorus of execration thundered forth from half the crowd.

Of course! Who more likely to turn up today than those who had quit Fregwil in fury at its rulers' indolence?

Suddenly there was chaos. Albumarak clenched her

claws as the speeches of welcome were drowned out. But Presthin only said, "Sometimes I wonder whether this species we belong to can be worth preserving..."

Eventually order was restored, and Yull and Theng were able to utter a few generalizations about the value of cooperation between Slah and Fregwil. Then Quelf launched into a carefully planned address, praising the astronomers who had located the wild planetoid and the efforts of those who for so long had been reaching out towards the stars.

"Hypocrite!" Albumarak muttered.

"Oh, no. She means precisely what she says," countered Presthin. "It's finally penetrated her pith that if there is another giant meteorite strike in a few years' time, she won't be more immune than anybody else. Just listen to the conclusion of her speech. She's been rehearsing it on the way here."

Albumarak composed herself. Quelf was saying, "—and if you prove you can actually keep the folk alive in space, as you have for so long been promising, then you may rely on our supplying both matériel...and personnel!"

"She's as bad as the volunteers in the camps!" Albumarak cried. "She expects us to send *her* into orbit!"

"It might be a good way of getting rid of her," said Presthin caustically.

The crowd erupted again, and this time individual shouts were discernible: "About time! What were you saying five years ago? Couldn't you have led instead of following? What were you made Jingfired for?"

Reeking with anger, Quelf bent towards Yull. Albumarak barely caught what she said; it sounded like, "This rowdy reception is no advertisement for your city!"

Turning ever so slightly, just enough for the loudeners to pick up her words, Yull countered, "Normally, at Slah, we don't waste time on this sort of ceremonial. We have urgent work to do. Apparently you've not acquired that habit."

Quelf towered, exuding combat-stink. But Yull's point had registered with the crowd and delighted everyone else within hearing, not just the Fregwil expatriates. A burst of hilarity allowed Theng to claim the loudeners.

"I'm sure you're all anxious," she stated with heavy

irony, "to hear more of what our guest has to say. Regrettably"—a well-timed pause—"we've arranged a demonstration of precisely the kind she wishes to see, and it's overdue, so... A scudder is waiting, Scholar Quelf. Do come this way!"

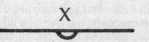

X

Albumarak was unable to avoid being caught up in the exodus towards the space-site, though she and Presthin did at least manage to mount the scudder behind Quelf's.

"Still no sign of Karg?" the goadster inquired.

"No, but... Well, I haven't seen him around much lately, anyhow. Not since the news of Quelf's visit broke."

"Can't say I blame him," Presthin grunted. Surveying the scenery, she went on, "So this is the city you prefer to your own. What's life like here, that it attracts you so?"

"I used to wonder what attracted you to the highlands. I found my own equivalent at Slah. Life is much harder and we enjoy many fewer luxuries. But there's a sense of purpose in the air, a feeling that we're all working towards the best possible goal. Also our leaders aren't so... I don't quite know how to define it. Maybe I should just say that nobody like Quelf could wield such influence at Slah."

"All by itself that explains why you like the place," Presthin said dryly. Craning for a better view, she added, "And that must be your space-launcher, right?"

In a dead straight line at the circle/2^3 angle, the giant tube sloped sunsetward up the mountain they were passing. At its base a cylinder was being readied for launch. Presthin gazed at it long and hard.

"I've seen images," she said at last, "but the reality is something else. How long is it now?"

"Ten padlonglaqs. We just extended it. But it's been

launching cylinders successfully since it was only half that length."

"And you're going to dispatch another specially for us. What sort?"

"I don't know," Albumarak muttered.

"I thought you were among the top scientists here now!"

"Yes, but—well, frankly, Presthin, I didn't want anything to do with making Quelf welcome. I said as much, and they respected my wishes."

Their scudder checked and dropped off the branchway just behind the one carrying Quelf. Yull, compelling herself to be polite, ushered the Fregwil delegation towards the control-house. Contriving to fall back a little, Theng muttered to Albumarak, "No wonder you dislike your old teacher so much! She must be the vainest and most self-important person on the planet! Do you know what she was saying on the way here? Because it was her team that developed the loss-free circuit, we ought to have invited somebody from Fregwil to supervise the construction of the launcher and dictate what missions were flown with it!"

"We're not all like Quelf," Presthin countered.

"Ah . . . No, of course." Theng exuded embarrassment. "I spoke out of turn. I'm sorry. Well, we'd better go inside, or we shall miss the launch-gap."

"Is Karg around? Presthin would like to say hello."

Theng's expression changed to one of utter surprise. She started to say something, but it was drowned out by the racket of a klaxonplant, warning everybody on the site to prepare for launch. The acceleration imparted to a space-cylinder was relatively gentle now, and created less overpressure than a driver test, but there was still a sonic boom to brace oneself against.

"Inside!" Theng directed, and they hastened to obey.

By now so many launches had occurred, they were reduced to a matter of routine, but this one was made different by Quelf and her companions, who were wandering around demanding the function of this, that and the other device, and on being told declaring that they would have organized things otherwise. Yull withstood the temptation as long as possible, but at last erupted in ill-disguised annoyance.

"Permit me to remind our *distinguished* visitors that

from this site we have achieved four-score successful orbital missions employing gas-globes, and twice that number using the sparkforce launcher! I submit this as evidence for the correctness of our approach!"

Albumarak could guess the nature of Quelf's retort before it was uttered. She was right.

"And you still haven't proved that the folk can survive in space. Have you?"

Her tone was harsh, yet unmistakably her exudations contradicted it. She wanted to be told there was an escape from this endangered planet; she simply didn't want anybody but herself to be the one who gained the credit for making it possible.

Her posture eloquent of disdain, Yull snapped her claw against a farspeaker hanging from a nearby branch. At once a voice rang out.

"On-hauq status is *go*! I've been ready for ages—how much longer do you plan to keep me waiting?"

Karg!

Albumarak padded half a step towards Yull, but Theng caught her by the mantle's edge.

"Did you really not know?" she demanded.

"I haven't seen him for nearly a moonlong!"

But there was no time to say anything else. Yull was turning to the visitors again.

"I am about to give the launch command. You will oblige us by remaining still and saying nothing as from— *now*!"

First the long straight tube began to hum. Apart from its size, in appearance this launcher was not so different from the ranks of rings which once had served to guide under test the primitive drivers known to Chybee, three generations ago. But it operated on a very different principle. Both the amount of sparkforce it could withstand and the subtlety of its controls bore witness to the unstinting effort of its creators, who had condensed five-score years' worth of development into less than five.

After the humming came the glow. No matter how perfect the insulation of the circuits, there was always a trace of energy that leaked out as light, because matter was matter and would be so until the universe's end. Ideally it should have been enclosed by vacuum, but the best that could be done was to create a low-pressure zone within the tube. The necessary pumping made a low and grumbling noise.

The cylinder, at this point, began to stir. The charge upon it was enough to counteract its weight.

Inevitably, all communication ceased.

"Why did you let him?" Albumarak whispered to Yull.

"It was a promise," she replied elliptically.

"But he's a cripple!"

"Yes..." Yull was scanning the remotes; they were as normal as for any launch. "You never paired, did you?"

"We've always wanted to, but after hearing about the wild planetoid we both agreed it was too risky to start budding. But what does that have to do with—? Oh! *No*!"

"I think you worked it out. He'd never have told you, or anyone, but of course he couldn't keep it from the doctors who treated him after his return. He thinks the reason he can't pair anymore wasn't due to frostbite, but to something done to him at Fregwil, maybe under Quelf's instructions. Those who regard other folk as their inferiors—No time for more! Slack down! You visitors, copy us! There's going to be a very loud noise!"

Those with experience set a prompt example, dropping to the ground as though prong-stabbed. From the corner of her eye Albumarak saw how reluctantly Quelf complied, and hoped she would fail to relax completely. If so, she would be taught a lesson by pain.

A lesson that she clearly well deserved.

The air was full of a familiar grinding noise, like the sound of pebbles on a headland fidgeting under the impact of the tide. This was always the most fearful moment. The launcher, if it failed, would do so now, when the charge on both the cylinder and the tube was at its peak.

No one was watching. No one could watch. All must be reported through sensors and monitors, at which Albumarak stared achingly. All normal—all normal—GO!

She struggled to remember that Karg had lived underwater, that he had survived frostbite, that he had resisted conditioning, that he had retained enough self-control not to become embittered at losing his chance of pairing, and indeed had lived half his life in the hope of just this opportunity. But then the sonic boom made the control-house rock, and he was gone.

When the echoes died away there was another noise: Quelf moaning. It was, as Albumarak had half expected, beneath her dignity to slump on the ground like everybody else. She had no doubt ruptured some unimportant tubule, which would heal. The rest of the company seemed to have reached the same conclusion, for no one was paying attention to her.

"How long do we have to wait before we hear from him?" Presthin asked.

"Oh, quite a while." Yull curled her mantle in a cryptic grin. "But then it won't just be us; it will be everyone who hears from him. Let's go outside. There's very little cloud. We should be able to see his drivers fire."

Leaving Quelf to worry about herself, they quit the control-house. A number of portable telescopes had been provided; Presthin appropriated one at once.

She said what she had said before: "On Prutaj, you know, we aren't all as bad as Quelf!"

"Working with Albumarak has taught me that much," Yull replied. "And you'd agree, wouldn't you, Theng?"

"Of course!" was the bluff and prompt reply. "Our only problem is apt to be with the ones who ran away from Fregwil—because they've never learned the meaning of an honest day's work, and we have to support them until they do!"

"Things are going to change back home," said Presthin, her eye to the ocular. "Of course, as you know, I'm not from Fregwil myself, but I can state that for too long the self-indulgence of that city has offended the ordinary folk on Prutaj. It's been fun having the goodies they produced, but how many of them are directed at ensuring the survival of the folk? Since news of the wild planetoid broke there's been a radical shift of attitudes. I like the young'uns at Fregwil now, and I used to loathe them! By the way, tell me something, Scholar Yull."

"If I can."

"Do you honestly believe we can survive in space?"

"There it goes!"

A unison cry greeted fire blooming at the zenith. Karg's cylinder had reached altitude and was spearing into space.

For a while no one could think of anything else but that slowly fading gleam.

When it had been masked by drifting cloud, Yull said, "Yes."

"What?" By then Presthin had forgotten her question.

"I said yes! We're very sure we can survive! It's as though evolution designed us for precisely the role we hope to play out there. Do you know much about biology?"

Unconsciously Presthin echoed what Karg had said to Albumarak: "I know a little about a lot of things!"

"Well, then, you doubtless know that there were once creatures on this planet that had rigid bodies. They supported their weight by using substances so stiff that they became brittle, like a dead tree, and had constantly to be renewed. Imagine what would happen to a species like that if they tried to survive without gravity! They'd become amorphous—they'd wither like spent luminants! But we..."

She spoke with swelling pride.

"*We* depend for our survival on nothing more than the tone of our musculature and our tubules! We can live underwater, where effectively one has no weight, and sometimes folk have returned after years without noticeable damage to their health. Karg was chosen for precisely that reason! In the imagery of the Mysteries of the Jingfired, which always have to do with forging metal, we are 'well and fitly shaped'!"

Karg's voice echoed from the control-house. Yull signaled for it to be relayed by loudeners, and instantly they knew he was exultant.

"Listen to me, you down there—listen to me! My name is Karg, and I'm in space, and I feel wonderful! I'm free at last! I'm not trapped on a lump of mud that may be smashed at any moment by gods playing at target-practice! I'm *free*!"

Suddenly grave, Yull was about to suggest that the level of euphoria be reduced, when Karg calmed of his own accord.

"But I'm not out here purely for the pleasure of it. I have a mission to perform. I'm to be the first inhabitant of another planet—a world we devised at Slah, which is just coming over my horizon, so I'm activating the maneuvering pumps—just a moment...Done. If you're watching with telescopes, you'll be able to see my cylinder match orbits with the artificial world. And from there, using its farspeakers, I'm going to tell everybody the good news. You and I won't survive our system's passage through the Major Cluster. But we'd be long dead anyhow, remember! What I'm here to prove is that the species can!"

His voice rose in a jubilant crescendo as Albumarak and Presthin clutched each other, not knowing whether to laugh or sob.

"We can escape! We can survive! *We shall!*"

nervously, turning away to something.' Done. It won't
working with telescopes, you'll be able to see my ray
under normal orbits, with the Stretch? works. And from
there, being its inspector, I'm going to tell every body
life with power, you and I won't appear in our starship
phase as through the space cluster. But we'd be surprised
anyhow, remember? What I'm here to prove is that the
sparks, too?

His voice rose in a jubilant cross, and as Alminius
and Pavlinn clutched each other, not knowing whether
to be in dread.

"We can escape! We can survive! Immortal!"

EPILOGUE

"And, of course, we did," said the preceptor.

Afterwards there was a long pause. Inevitably one of the youngest budlings broke it by demanding, loudly enough to be heard: "What became of the wild planetoid, then?"

"Wait!"

The center of the globe, where the marvels of modern technology had recreated Jing and Chybee, Yockerbow and Aglabec, all the characters famous and infamous from the long story of their species, swirled and blurred and resumed its original configuration.

Now, though, everything was in closer focus. The bud-world was emphasized, the sun and planets far away. Then, from the threshold of infinity, the wild planetoid rushed in. For one pith-freezing moment, which even those who had witnessed the spectacle a score of times found fearful, it seemed as though they were about to crash!

A shift of perspective: they were back on the budworld. Its oceans were rising to the wild planet's tug, beating the shores and swamping the cities. The air wrought havoc with fantastic gales. Closeups revealed the naked panic of those who were caught up and burst to death.

The youngest of the budlings screamed in terror.

"Our species could have been destroyed," said the preceptor as the view shifted again. This time it could be seen how the wild planetoid swung past, disturbing the orbit of the moon, but sweeping by towards the belt of asteroids that ringed the sun.

"We think, but because it was hidden from our fore-budders we'll never know, that it collided with an asteroid behind the sun. At all events, it did not reappear. But it had done harm enough. Had not the joint resources of both Slah and Fregwil been applied to launching vessels into space, it is beyond a doubt that by this time we'd be extinct. *The show is over. Ponder the lessons that it teaches—all your lives!"*

And suddenly the feigned imagery that had filled the center of the globe was replaced by the reality of what surrounded their fragile home. Beautiful, yet terrible, there loomed the Major Cluster, from which they were being borne away by the pressure of light from its exploding stars; there too was the Arc of Heaven which their fore-budders had imagined to be the weapon of a god; there was the sun that had shone on the budworld, fading to the petty status of just another star . . .

And far beyond lay the safe dark deeps that they were steering for, where they were certain of energy, and the means to feed themselves and grow more drifting globes, choosing what they wanted from the resources of the galaxy.

"Yes?" said the preceptor to another young'un, knowing what question was invariably put.

"Scholar, do you think there's anybody else out there?"

"There's bound to be!"—with total confidence. "And when we meet them, we shall be able to stand proud on what we've done!"

ABOUT THE AUTHOR

John Brunner was born in England in 1934 and educated at Cheltenham College. He sold his first novel in 1951 and has been publishing sf steadily since then. His books have won him international acclaim from both mainstream and genre audiences. His most famous novel, the classic *Stand on Zanzibar*, won the Hugo Award for Best Novel in 1969, the British Science Fiction Award, and the Prix Apollo in France. Mr. Brunner lives in Somerset, England.

Winner of the Hugo Award and international acclaim...

JOHN BRUNNER